GIANT EDITIONS

MODERN
SOUTH AFRICAN
STORIES

Revised and expanded edition of
On the Edge of the World
Edited by Stephen Gray

AD. DONKER/PUBLISHER

AD. DONKER (PTY) LTD
A subsidiary of Book Marketing & Distribution (Pty) Ltd
P.O. Box 2105
Parklands
2121

Originally published as *On the Edge of the World* in 1974
This expanded and revised edition, 1980
Reprinted 1981, 1983, 1987, 1990

ISBN 0 949937 76 2

Typeset, printed and bound by National Book Printers, Goodwood, Cape

Contents

Acknowledgements

The publisher is grateful to the following for permission to reproduce copyright material:

Lionel Abrahams for *The Messiah;* Jillian Becker for *The Stench;* Yvonne Burgess for *If You Swallow You're Dead;* Cherry Clayton for *In Time's Corridor;* Jack Cope for *Harry's Kid;* Leon de Kock for *Something Great;* C. J. Driver for *The Cry;* Ahmed Essop for *Gerty's Brother;* Sheila Fugard for *The Angel of Death;* Nadine Gordimer and A. P. Watt & Son, Ltd., London, for *You Name It,* © Nadine Gordimer; Stephen Gray for *The Largest Dam in the World;* Bessie Head for *The Prisoner who Wore Glasses;* Christopher Hope for *The Problem with Staff;* Bob Leshoai for *Masilo's Adventures;* James Matthews for *11.41 to Simonstown;* Es'kia Mphahlele for *A Ballad of Oyo;* Mothobi Mutloatse for *Don't Lock up our Sweethearts;* Mbulelo Mzamane for *My Cousin and the Law;* Alan Paton and David Philip, Publisher, Cape Town, for *The Hero of Currie Road;* Richard Rive for *Riva;* Sheila Roberts for *Coming In;* Sipho Sepamla for *MaPuleng;* Mongane Serote for *Let's Wander Together;* Barney Simon for *Our War;* Adam Small for *Klaas;* Pieter-Dirk Uys for *God Will See You Now;* Christopher van Wyk for *Twenty Years' Experience;* and Peter Wilhelm for *Lion;*

and to the editors of the following magazines and newspapers, in which the following material first appeared:

The Argus (Harry's Kid); Bolt (The Problem with Staff, The Hero of Currie Road); The Classic (Let's Wander Together); Contrast (If You Swallow You're Dead, In Time's Corridor, The Largest Dam in the World, Lion); Donga-Inspan (Something Great); Drum (11.41 to Simonstown); Heresy

(Twenty Years' Experience); IZWI (The Messiah, Don't Lock up Our Sweethearts, My Cousin and the Law, Coming In); The London Magazine (The Cry, You Name It, The Prisoner who Wore Glasses); New Classic (Masilo's Adventures); Purple Renoster (Gerty's Brother); Staffrider (Riva); and *The Sunday Express (God will See You Now).*

Introduction

The twenty-eight short stories in this collection have all been written by writers resident in, or intimately connected with, modern southern Africa. All, without exception, are also currently in production. Their relationships with the subcontinent are a deep and on-going business, as evidenced by their other stories, novels, plays, collections of poetry, and by the magazines which reflect this literary engagement, from which the stories here are selected.

Those magazines are one of the gauges of a society's literary health: they include in southern Africa *The Purple Renoster* and *Contrast, The Classic* and its successor, *New Classic;* the mortality rate is exceptionally high – *Bolt, IZWI, Donga-Inspan;* recently we've gained *Staffrider* and *Heresy;* others are planned, launched, maintained for a correct moment of time and talent, often proscribed in part or even in whole, die. Out of this editorial activity, this fugitive drive to publish as testimony, as example, as entertainment, as prediction even, emerges the contents of this collection.

It has a precise origin – in 1974 Ad. Donker published a paperback selection of 'Southern African Stories of the Seventies', *On the Edge of the World,* which endured, even though it was drawn from a minute segment of the history of story-making here: the period 1969-1973. Those were good years; new writers were gaining footholds individually, and in groups, turning in fiction which led one to feel the excitement and force of a rising new generation – a diverse, multicoloured, multilingual one at that, too. The arrival of that generation made the seventies not only a promising but, it turns out, an accomplished decade. Eighteen of the original stories re-appear here, some of which were by writers barely known in 1974; they have established themselves today and their stories remain worthwhile and valid.

9

To give this revised edition greater range and scope – and to celebrate our emergence into the 80s – it was decided to push the 1969 starting date back to the turn of the 60s, and to extend the collection up to the present time. The new title, *Modern South African Stories*, implies this greater period.

Hence work by some well-known names has now been included: from those who came into prominence or maintained their stances in the 60s we have Jillian Becker, Jack Cope, C. J. Driver, Bob Leshoai, Es'kia (Ezekiel) Mphahlele, Richard Rive. Others who have moved into the forefront since 1974 include Pieter-Dirk Uys and Christopher van Wyk.

All the writers whose work is represented here not only write about, but were born in, South Africa. Some are in exile across the border (Bessie Head, Mbulelo Mzamane and Mongane Serote in Botswana, for example) or in a less compulsory exile further afield (Jillian Becker, C. J. Driver, Christopher Hope). But there are others born in South Africa whose work is not included in this collection, for the reason that they or their books are banned in South Africa (Alex la Guma, for example, or – internally – Mtutuzeli Matshoba, Don Mattera – the list is a lengthy one). It would be tempting to believe that for every writer whose work is suppressed, another one takes his or her place – writing here is an expanding, not a dying, art. But the gaps are nevertheless there, extensive, unbreachable; one chooses perforce from where one may.

This collection comes about, in a profound sense, thanks to the contributions of the 'maturer' writers: Jack Cope, Nadine Gordimer, Bessie Head, Es'kia Mphahlele, Alan Paton; for the younger need the older not only in matters of the influence of style, theme and technique. A larger statement of faith is made by the very continuity, the endurance of such writers' output, and they signify that turning their times into fiction is a process that, given our mutual embattled circumstances, has more meaning to those who follow than is contained in the printed word alone. Staying power, authority – those are the virtues that exacerbate further literary production.

Amongst the younger writers many are active in other fields: as poets (James Matthews, Sipho Sepamla, Mongane Serote, Christopher van Wyk), in theatre (Bob Leshoai, Barney Simon, Adam Small, Pieter Dirk Uys), as journalists (Mothobi Mutloatse, Peter Wilhelm), as scholars of literature (Mbulelo Mzamane, Richard Rive), as educationalists (Cherry Clayton, Sheila Roberts). Very few are uniquely prose-writers (Yvonne Burgess, Ahmed Essop, Sheila Fugard). The norm is a varied career, for no writer in southern Africa has yet lived by the short story alone; markets are small, unreliable, even hazardous, and the short story as a form is on its way out as a literary genre here as well.

On its way out – but leaving an immense and complex range of human experiences of southern Africa behind, encoded, stored, accessible. The happening of Hitler's war is the threshold *(MaPuleng, Our War)*. Sharpeville, Langa are reflected *(The Cry, The Hero of Currie Road)*. The arrival of, ramifications of, abutments of apartheid are its main focus *(The Stench, Don't Lock up our Sweethearts)*. Decolonization outside in Africa *(You Name It, Coming In)* is matched by segregation at home *(Gerty's Brother, Klaas)*. For all, the experience of the urban nexus is paramount *(If You Swallow You're Dead, My Cousin and the Law, Let's Wander Together, Twenty Years' Experience)*. Some respond personally from within *(The Messiah, In Time's Corridor, Something Great, Riva)*, others in terms of myth, community and a new African personality *(The Angel of Death, Masilo's Adventures, A Ballad of Oyo)* or in terms of satire *(The Problem with Staff)*; and there are those who ride the apocalypse of Soweto 76 too *(God will See You Now, Lion)*, projecting the moderns into their future.

All cross-refer and inter-relate. Best of all, for the reader, all expand in one another's company.

Stephen Gray

Johannesburg, 1980

Lionel Abrahams

The Messiah

On Sunday mornings and Wednesday evenings there was Service, run by a member of the committee or a real priest, in the Big Playroom. Being Jewish did not stop Felix from attending. He learnt that only faith was needed to save one's soul – faith in Jesus, who was so good and had such powers, and who was a Jew on top of everything else. The parts about him suffering and being crucified – by Jews – made Felix less comfortable. He wished those parts could be left out. Then Service would just be interesting and enjoyable to go to.

But those parts wouldn't be left out. They came into the thing every day, in a way, even when it wasn't prayers at school or grace at table or anything that was supposed to do with God. He was 'Jewboy' and had to hear about Jews having long noses and being stingy and cheats, all because Jesus got crucified by those old Jews – even though it was the Romans who really did it.

The old carpenter boy, Moses, who had a wonderful workshop opposite the kitchens near the end of the drive where he would do anything from fixing a crutch or the wheel of a wheelchair to sharpening a pencil, old Moses who walked with a limp because one of his thick muscly legs was shorter than the other, who was so clever with his hands and so kind that everybody loved him and he seemed like someone out of the Bible even though he was black – he said one day, while Felix could hear him: 'No, I don't like Jews. They killed Jesus.' The boys were always saying that and Felix felt half cross and half ashamed. But when Moses said it, it was much worse: it seemed to be true, and Christians and Jews had to hate each other.

All the same, Felix went on going to Service. He learnt there about the lamb that had been lost being more precious to the shepherd than the ninety-nine that were never lost and somewhere he heard about converted

Jews. He decided to be a converted Jew and to believe in Jesus and love him. He said prayers in bed every night, and he knew that good Christians, apart from forgiving everyone who hurt them, had to try to save other souls by converting them too. So when he was home on holiday, one night he told his mother the parable about the one lost lamb and begged her to be converted also. But she wouldn't be. She seemed uncomfortable about what he was saying, but she only laughed a little and went on not even believing in God. All the same, Felix hoped that he would be able to convert her one day. He knew that his father did believe in God because he sometimes said Jewish prayers; he did not try to convert him.

Once Felix heard something wonderful. It was about the Messiah. The Jews believed that one day the Messiah would come to the world from heaven to save everyone. The Christians believed that the Messiah had already come and was Jesus. But they also believed that one day, any day, he would come again. When that happened, surely Christians and Jews would all believe the same thing and wouldn't need to hate each other any more.

The Messiah, when he came, must be Jewish, a Jewish Christian. So any Jewish boy, any day now, could be Him. Felix, loving Jesus and believing in him with all his heart – as the ministers always begged everyone to (Felix's favourite was the committee member, Mr Cooper, who told wonderful stories and made him feel it would be lovely to go to exciting places with him) – believing so much in Jesus and always managing not to do any of the things that the naughty ones among the children did, and caring so much about Moses and all the other Christians hating the Jews, began to think that it might, it could, it must be him. The Messiah. Although nobody knew it yet, and he wasn't ready to tell anyone – he would know when it would be the right time to let the secret out – he, Felix, was that special Jewish boy who was Jesus back in the world for the second time to make the different people love each other, and to cure all the cripples and blind people and do all sorts of miracles that would make everybody believe in God.

He loved it on Sundays and Wednesdays when the ministers told about the miracles Jesus had done and the stories he had told, or about people who had got converted in wonderful ways or been helped by God when they were in trouble or had been very brave about doing what they knew God wanted them to do or about going on having faith when something was making it very hard. He wished he had a chance to show his faith like those strong believers, and he longed for the time when he would be able to do miracles that would be better than any of the tricks that he had seen

14

magicians do at concerts and parties. Waiting for the day when he would show everyone that he was the Messiah, he didn't mind so much any more what the other boys said about Jews, or when they said things like: 'Don't try to Jew me' when someone wanted to make a bargain that wasn't fair. They were only the chaps at the home, and they didn't know his secret yet. Anyway, one of the things Christians had to do was to forgive those who trespassed against them, so it proved that he had faith because he was always forgiving the other boys for all their insults.

Mr MacDavid was the Chairman of the committee and he came up to the home much more often than any of the other members. Sometimes he came to show special visitors around, and sometimes to inspect with Matron if anything had to be done to the building. Once or twice when some of the biggest boys had done something extra naughty, Mr Mac-David came and shouted at them in his big voice in a terribly angry way. He also came very often to be the minister at Sunday morning Service.

He was a big, oldish man with grey hair who spoke and sang in a strong Scotch accent. He always seemed to wear the same greyish-brown suit and, just like Moses, the old carpenter boy, he walked quickly but with a deep limp. He did not make his preaching as friendly and interesting as Mr Cooper, who came quite seldom and always looked as if everything he wore was brand new. But Felix could tell by the loudness of his voice when he preached ('Oh, yes, boys and girrls, I can tell you that ourr Lorrd Jesus today . . .') and sang the hymns and prayed that he had very strong faith.

Felix also sang the hymns and choruses ('Build on the Rock' was the one he liked best, because of the bang they had to make for 'earthquake *shock*'), as loudly as he could so Mr MacDavid knew that he was there at Service. Mr MacDavid also knew – because Felix had been at the home for years already – that he was Jewish: there were hardly ever any other Jewish children.

One Sunday morning Mr MacDavid preached the Bible story of Joseph and his brothers. He was at the part where the jealous elder brothers had put Joseph into the pit and were getting ready to kill him when the traders from Egypt came by. 'When the eldest brother, Reuben, saw the traders,' said Mr MacDavid, 'he said to the others, "Why should we kill Joseph, when we can sell him as a slave to these traders?" Well, Jews, you know, are always ready to sell anything, even their brother – so they agrreed to do as Rrreuben said . . .'

Felix gave a little jump. The boy on the bench next to him nudged him and he saw two other boys turn to look at him with quick grins on their faces. He heard nothing more of the preaching or prayers and did not join in the singing of the last hymn.

On Wednesdays Service was after supper, so all the children had to go because there was nowhere else to be. It was always the same minister, Mr Harty, who was not a committee member but a real priest who wore a black shirt with a stiff white ring collar that none of the children could guess how he put on or took off. Mr Harty was telling them a long story like a serial, about the adventures of a man named Christian and his friend Faithful. Even after what had happened that Sunday morning, Felix didn't have to miss the rest of the story.

But on the next Sunday morning at Service time, instead of being in the Big Playroom with all the others, Felix was sitting outside on the lawn looking at *Pip, Squeak and Wilfred's Annual*, and hearing the hymns and the preaching without being able to make out the words. It was Mr Cooper today, but that didn't matter.

No one else was outside until Nurse Verster came past on her way to the dormitories. When she saw him she said, 'Hello, Felix. Why aren't you at Service?'

Felix tried to look up at her, but the sun shone into his eyes. 'Because I'm Jewish,' he said.

Jillian Becker

The Stench

They were boiling a horse.

That, the schoolmaster was to discover eventually, was the cause of the stink which rose from the mud-hut village half-way up an adjacent hill to his own house on the top of the higher rockier one; and also sank into the valley where the road wound, forcing the rare passing drover or rider to narrow his eyes, pinch his nostrils closed, twist his head this way and that but without escape, while his oxen plodded and swung on imperturbably, their noses too close to dust and perhaps too full of it to be irritated by anything else; but the ponies and hinnies snorted, nodded, and stamped harder in the warm powdery margins of the stony track. The occupants of the car which bumped along in the late afternoon of the second day since the stink had begun were less exposed, but could not have missed it.

The schoolmaster Schwallendorf – a bald, stout, heavy-jowled Saxon – did not make the discovery himself. He had hesitated to venture down among the huts – the presumable source of the stink – into its density and to its very nidorous epicentre. But then a directive came, tactful, amiable, but unmistakable; in the form of a request but nonetheless compulsory; from District Commissioner Bertel Maria Pik, a small Afrikaner in black serge forever troubled by facial impetigo and hay-fever, who, with respect to his hay-fever, shirked the task which should have been his immoveably. He climbed to Schwallendorf's house – four rondavels united by a central square kitchen roofed with pleated tin – by a steep, circuitous path, in an effort to get round the nastiness he had had to drive through: leaving his official blue Chevrolet in the charge of his Xhosa driver, who parked it in the bedraggled shade of eucalyptus, within sight of the store where the tribeswomen came and went.

Schwallendorf was sitting in creased white clothes on the stone step outside his back door, the cooler but hardly less smelly side of the house, and rose to greet his visitor as Pik reached the level pressing a white handkerchief to his wet, erupting face, and poking it down under the high collar of his shirt.

'Good evening, Meneer. How goes it?'

Meneer Pik had no breath to answer. He slumped into a bamboo chair on one side of the small table on which a whisky bottle stood and two glasses as though he had been expected, or been seen approaching.

'If you please,' he panted as Schwallendorf raised the bottle, and he stuffed the crumpled handkerchief into a trouser pocket, took a fresh one from his jacket, unfolded it, wound a corner over the tip of a forefinger and dabbed gingerly at his nose.

'Fiff! But what a stink, hey? You'll do me a favour Schwallendorf. If you please. I cannot go and see myself. This nose of mine. You would oblige me. Or do you know what it is?' He bubbled as he breathed. His nostrils red and damp, his eyes brimming over.

'I've asked the washgirl and the houseboy,' Schwallendorf assured him. 'But they pretend not to know. So I'll go and see what I can find. Of course. Certainly.' – As if to oblige and not obey. And they toasted each other with a raising of their glasses.

Pik fastidiously refolded his handkerchief to dry his lip with its sore spot or two. 'It's this nose of mine, you must see. It's an allergy, you must understand. A lot of people are allergic to something. But I am allergic to everything. Alles.' He swung his infected head to indicate all; and closed his eyes on the long-suffering of all; enflamed western clouds, abrasive gravel, pungent leaves of eucalyptus, a black mote of a bird in the exposure of blue.

'Shall we move into the house?' Schwallendorf suggested. 'It's not so bad with the windows shut.' And he puffed out his lips and cheeks as he waited for the answer.

'No! I cannot stay here any longer under these circumstances.'

'Oh!' The schoolmaster's lips remained open and round on the syllable, his eyes wide, but his cheeks falling flaccid again; a foolish expression, not as if he were disappointed but as though he had been rebuked.

Pik drained his glass and rose. 'I must go. I should never have come up.' He plied his handkerchief again. 'I should have gone on home and telephoned you. Even with the windows up it filled the car like a poisonous gas. I've borne as much as I can. But we'll get to the bottom of this thing. Find out what those kaffirs are up to.' (For men as much as nature plotted

against Pik.) 'I can't bear it much longer,' he warned, standing there and
dabbing.

It was as if Pik were waiting for Schwallendorf to confess – that he had
had a hand in starting the smell, or had carelessly allowed it to erupt, or
had tolerated it when he might have stopped it. Schwallendorf felt guilty
for having postponed investigation – but the smell had been even more
intense then than it was now.

But Pik reassured him. 'I regard,' he said, narrowing his eyes as though
what he regarded might sting, 'your co-operation. I must go, I must go.'
He hurried off. 'Ring me up in the morning, ja?' He started down.
'Obliged,' he called. And again after a moment, 'Obliged!'

Schwallendorf felt the ambiguity of it, and looked unhappily after Pik
as he sidled away down the rocky path, handkerchief over nose; and
plodded along a dry stream-bed past yellow-blossoming thorntrees which
could only torment him with their sweetness.

Now the screendoor of the kitchen groaned as it was opened behind him,
creaked as its tendency to bang shut was curbed, so that it rejoined its
jamb without violence; from which Schwallendorf knew without turning
round which of the several possible persons who might be coming out of
the house this was.

He said, 'That was the D.C. He wants me to find out what's causing
the stench. I can't blame him for shirking it. I'm not sure I can stomach
it myself.'

'I'll go!' The peremptory announcement was made. *'Ich werde gehen!'*

As the man who said this with such finality came to stand beside him,
Schwallendorf turned to him with the look if not the words for 'Are you
sure you want to?' The words had been forbidden by that tone. But the
younger man was deliberately looking away, and the schoolmaster could
not see much of his face, only the firm-set line of the jaw, at the end of
which a ball of muscle was thrust out by the clench of determination, and
was throbbing and quivering a denial that this man was made of anything
harder, less vulnerable, than other men are – and so also a plea that his
resolution go unquestioned.

The schoolmaster grunted.

He believed that he understood: nasty as the stink was, it was not such
a challenge, and the grit with which it was being met was less a response
to the occasion than a habit of resolution and self-discipline.

'So – if you will,' the easy-going schoolmaster accepted. 'But there
is no hurry. Tomorrow will do. By the morning it may have cleared a
little.'

That was most probable. Which could have been the reason why the other man said, 'No, I'll go now.'

The large surface of Schwallendorf's face was flattered by the softening light.

And the other's face was also flushed. Its skin was of that sensitive thinness which quickly reddens on exposure to the sun. It was a face in which the bones showed, not gauntly but distinctly enough. Unlike Schwallendorf's, this face – and body – had no redundancy of flesh. Because of its physical hardness it was not a face which changed much with the shift of thoughts or feelings in the man. It might have been unexpressive, set to the point of impassivity, had not conflict – of the will against weaknesses – revealed itself through that quiver in the muscle. No – the hardness was itself an expression, conscious and consciously maintained; so much so – and so plainly to anyone who observed or talked to the man for more than a moment – that even the narrow nose, the cheekbones, would seem to have been wilfully achieved rather than naturally endowed: and further evidence could have been found in the hair, for although Konrad Reitzger was not yet twenty-six, his black, thick, short-cut hair was turning an iron-grey at its edges. His eyes were pale as steel, deep under black eyebrows, but there was no animosity in them. They were clear, questioning, open. Not, they would seem, the eyes of a self-obsessed introvert, but of a man who would probably look well before he judged: a man more interested in seeing a thing clearly than in expressing a quick reaction to it.

'As you prefer, Reitzger,' the older man consented – or gave formal permission to the volunteer. He added, 'Danke!'

Schwallendorf watched the rather strange young man, in conventional white shirt and grey trousers, go off round the house to make his discovery.

Schwallendorf's oldest friend, Max Feuchthaber, had sent young Reitzger to him. The letter had arrived a month ago. Barry Theobald had brought it over from the store as soon as he got back from meeting the train at Butterworth. It looked important, he said, coming all that way, and could he have the stamps for his step-son who was at the T.B. hospital in the Transvaal, yes improving thanks, but very slowly. Theobald knew that Schwallendorf had been waiting some months now to hear whether he'd be granted a pension if he went 'home' to the Bundesrepublik where in fact he had never set foot except to sail from Bremerhaven.

'Dear August –'

Disappointed, and simultaneously pleased, Schwallendorf read the letter from his friend.

'We were at school together,' he told Theobald. In Leipzig, the Gymnasium, and then the University; where he had studied Theology, and Feuchthaber had studied Physics and laughed at God, so their intimacy had begun to lessen. Then Schwallendorf had come to Africa, and they might have lost touch altogether, but their mothers too were friends: and during the war – when August himself was in the internment camp – his mother had moved to the south to live near her sister in Augsburg, and old Frau Feuchthaber had also moved to some small town near Munich where she had relations. Both were widows, both lonely, and they visited each other from time to time. So from his mother, after the war, August heard news of Max. He heard he had become Professor at Heidelberg. He wondered if Max was less lonely than he. Ten years ago his mother had died, and he had heard no more of his friend, until now.

'If you receive this, write at once so that I can give your address to a former student of mine who is coming to "investigate" Africa . . .'

Feuchthaber had used the English word, perhaps because *untersuchen* or *erforschen* could equally well mean 'explore', which is what anyone might do who was coming to Africa. Schwallendorf had wondered about this, and now he thought that Feuchthaber had cleverly caught, with that one word, something of the character of young Reitzger. He could see exactly what Feuchthaber – whose affection for Reitzger had also, *nichtsdestoweniger*, been suggested – had meant to imply when he said 'investigate'. Or was it perhaps a word that Reitzger himself had used, when telling Feuchthaber his plans? Reitzger spoke excellent English, at least as good as Schwallendorf himself.

'Investigate.' Yes. In three days this Reitzger had asked more questions about the country, its climate, its people, its past and present, its birds, beasts and plants than Schwallendorf had learnt the answers to or even thought to ask in thirty years.

Well, this appetite for information might be useful now. Reitzger was not the man to miss whatever was happening down there, and if the reasons were not obvious he'd do his dogged best to find them out. And yet, even if he persuaded some of the villagers to use their English, they were unlikely to tell him much. Not enough to satisfy Pik. He should have thought of that. He'd have to go himself, after all.

But then again, Schwallendorf had to admit, they were not likely to tell any white man more than they had to – certainly not Pik. Only last week Pik had taken away one of the men – Johnjohn, whom everyone knew was the headman's son and who'd come back from the mines a year ago to his home village. But Pik had maintained that he had no right to be here, and had 'endorsed' him out of the territory, no one knew where. The headman had asked him, Schwallendorf, to intercede – and he'd gone at once to Butterworth, but who on earth could make Pik change his mind? 'I'm sorry, Meneer Schwallendorf, the law is clear and I do my duty.' Then the headman had ridden off to Butterworth himself, as if he could succeed where a white man failed. Perhaps he hadn't even believed that Schwallendorf had done his best. For the sad thing was, they didn't trust him either. This was the tragic *Ausfall* of his whole life. Though most of them had been or were still his pupils, they no longer trusted him with their secrets. In the last five years he seemed to have lost what he'd gained so patiently and conscientiously in the twenty-five years before. Now there was an atmosphere of disgruntlement, if not rebellion: or building up of storm clouds in the minds of men – that's what they were achieving, Pik and his kind! And though it wasn't through any fault of his own – he was sure of that – it amounted to a personal failure all the same. There was no reclaiming the lost ground now. He had wanted to stay in this job for their sakes, but what good was a man to those who didn't trust him? 'Co-operation' with Pik might keep him his job for a while yet, though most of the other white Protestant teachers – and all the Roman Catholic missionaries – had been sent away. But if that co-operation meant his losing the trust of the very people he wanted the continued chance to serve, what was the use of his staying on anyway?

He sighed. A stout old man getting fuller of doubts and shorter of the spirit to deal with them. Feuchthaber had laughed at God, and yet became Professor at Heidelberg, and had many friends. While he – Hadn't he wanted to be a father to them, no matter his colour and theirs?

He was feeling particularly dejected this evening, as though something were missing that he depended on: yes, it was like nostalgia, but not for anything he could name; not for lost friends, or youth, or Germany; but for something the past had always contained until recently. Hope for something perhaps. But for what exactly, he could not grasp; though it wavered about him, inapprehensible but pervasive, like the stench – which was probably, he concluded, itself the actual cause of the unpleasant mood.

He went into his house, seeking some refuge from the pervading rotten smell.

As Reitzger descended into the stronger zones of the smell, he reminded himself that squeamishness was easy to overcome. He had wanted to make this investigation since he had woken up to the foul stench on the second morning after his arrival, but Schwallendorf had insisted no, they would wait, he would ask, there was no need. Reitzger liked answers. He wanted all the phenomena of this country to be identified and explained. The impact of Africa was strongly physical; it appealed immediately to the senses. It could hardly be expected to stimulate the imagination as old cities and man-worked landscapes did. Rather, it assailed a man: these primitives of heat, wilderness, mountain and valley and plain, of intense colours in a generally unrelenting sunlight under a ceiling of hard even blue, harsh sounds of birds shrieking and chattering and purring but not singing, the tastes of things distinctive but not subtle, and now this penetrating smell, roused mood, distracted the mind with irritation and offence, if one didn't keep hold. It could distort one's view – in the atmosphere of sunset and stench the whole landscape might seem warmed to the point of decay: gangrene of the bush; the sulphur-yellow of fever-trees. But his eyesight was extraordinarily good. He saw, as red rocks crumpled in the deepening – at last relenting – light, each ridge defined; and grasses burning out individually.

He reached the valley, where the stink seemed less intense: but as he climbed up again towards the village it thickened. And when the path brought him to a level where he turned off to walk among the huts he was enveloped and filled with it, he could have choked on it, but refused to of course.

Women long skirted and bare breasted continued to pound with pestles into deep wooden mortars – but they watched him pass, and the babies on their rocking backs gazed at him. Men dressed in togas of blue cotton with matching turbans, and girls in little more than beads, appeared from all sides, and as they passed they turned their eyes towards him, but none of them stopped or spoke to him. They surely knew why he had come. There was curiosity and perhaps amusement in their glances, but not fear. The pounding went on, the walkers passed him, this one with a tin of water on her head, that one with a bundle of sticks across his shoulders. And Reitzger said nothing to them. He did not even nod at them. His nose directed him.

He came out beyond the last of the huts into a stony space. There was a fire in a square shallow pit; and over it, balanced on logs, a huge tank with a scaffolding erected on one side providing a ladder and a platform. One man was pushing branches down into the pit. Another stood on the platform and was using a branch to stir the contents of the tank. A woollen scarf was wound round his nose and mouth. He was smoked and steamed, but persisted. The job must be very important to keep a man at it in such discomfort. Women approached him, one hand pressed to mouth and nostrils, and he would let go of his huge spatula to lift the tins from their heads and empty the water into the tank. The smoke came round and billowed over Reitzger. He did not move away but waited for it to be shifted again by an otherwise undetectable current of air. His eyes watered and stung. The slow procession of water-bearers continued to advance towards the platform, and the attendant up there to empty the tins and stir. His presence did not apparently perturb them. Whatever it was they were doing was calmly proceeded with, as with any normal occupation. He could look on to his heart's content, no one minded in the least. But the smell was abnormal, terrible. And in the red light, in the stench, in the smoke, the silent business seemed lurid and sinister.

Reitzger stood watching, and prepared himself for what he might see when he climbed the ladder. Prepared himself, that is, for the worst, that experience, which had exceeded imagination, could warn him of: a scene which came back to him vividly from his first day at the University of Heidelberg. In a large hall of the Medical Faculty, a rectangular pool, wide and long enough to be a swimming-pool, but full of mustard yellow water. He had gone to the edge and peered down into it, expecting what? – fish? – lilies and reeds? – and found it was full of floating human corpses; with swollen green-white flesh, streaming hair, bulging eyelids. He had felt his gorge rise, but stood still and ordered it down, closed his eyes, drooped his shoulders; and though sweat had broken out on his forehead he had been able to walk steadily down a busy passage among bustling white coats, and vomited when he reached the lavatory. So his shame had not been public, but in any case severe. He was aspiring – had intended since childhood – to become a surgeon! Before the war he had dissected animals without a qualm. What had reduced him to this then? The cold eye of the dissector, the detached mind of the science-student had surely not been changed by hunger or fear. Fear had been overcome, by grit, which was the product of willpower and intelligence. So why should not an augmented courage, which had helped him face the near possibility of his own death and the actual deaths of others who if not exactly friends were by then in any case familiar, help him to look calmly at a tankful of cadavers? What was this – was it pity, or was it revulsion? Neither was called for. And as for why – though a question one did ask – a man cannot take a scalpel to himself!

One had not changed one's course then, or at least not for some time, and not for that cause; and one would not now, when one was quite prepared.

He climbed the ladder of rough split eucalyptus logs, tatty with peeling bark, to stand beside the cook who paused in his stirring but did not look at him. The reeking steam made his eyes sting, and at first he could see nothing through the billows of vapour and the scum and the bulges of heaving water at the boil. Then it swam up, the horse. Stiff legs, enormous hooves, open bulging eyes, streaming mane and tail, split skin, the bowels floating out. A scene by Hieronymus Bosch, he thought. And he stood steady, and steadily looked down, breathing in the sickening stench without nausea or even disgust.

He climbed down unhurriedly, and went back among the huts. 'Pardon,' he said to one of the busy villagers, and stepped in front of him to make him stand still.

'Boss?'

'Is Walter here? Walter? Is he still here? I want to speak to him.'

The man stared at him stupidly.

'Walter,' Reitzger repeated, louder but not impatiently.

The man tipped back his head as he understood, and then he pointed. Round there and straight on, his hand told the stranger.

Reitzger went the way he was shown, and soon saw the person he was seeking, standing in front of a hut. It was as if he had been standing there waiting for Reitzger to appear, for he promptly raised one hand and smiled in greeting.

'Mr Reitzger!' he called, pleasantly, familiarly. 'Welcome, my friend!'

Reitzger had found Walter for the first time three days earlier.

Two cranes, huge awkward birds with gold crowns; grey, white bellied, with tails of butter and mauve, soared up and slumped upon the top of a tree in full blossom of scarlet, but with no leaves. The tree grew beside a river – of water, not a dry bed. Still water, in a valley at noon. On the other side a cornfield, wrecked by its harvest; pale bent sticks in stony furrows of the red earth. And in the middle of the field, in the sun, on a high chestnut horse, a hefty black man in a yellow shirt, smooth polished riding-boots with silver buckles, a crop in his hand.

Reitzger had crossed a bridge made of heaped stones. Then over the hard red earth through the devastation of the sticks. And called out, 'Good morning!'

The man raised a hand in salute, then lowered it to the pommel of his saddle and leaned forward graciously to enquire.

'Yes sir. Can I be of some assistance to you?'

Reitzger asked for directions.

'It happens,' the equestrian replied, 'that I am proceeding there myself immediately. It is unfortunate that I cannot procure another horse for you to accompany me.'

How far was it? Could one not walk?

'It is not too far. In nine - ten hours you could be at your destination. But you would conclude your journey in a state of exhaustion, even if you did not lose your way.'

They considered the problem, which both placed at a distance from themselves where the valley flowed away into the sky. One of the cranes rose, circled widely, returned to its mate. It took time.

Reitzger turned back to look up at the man again.

'My name,' he said, 'is – Konrad.'

'Conradie?'

'Not Conradie. Just Konrad. It is my first name. The other is hard to pronounce.'

Reitzger had been told by two or three women – one of them his mother – that he lacked not only 'charm', but, more seriously, 'tact'. He was intending to achieve tact now, but as he spoke became uneasily aware that he was falling short of it again.

The man said, in the same clear, strong but quiet tone as before, and without straightening again with any bridling movement, 'I have been through High School, and I have matriculated. I was in the war as a medical assistant. I can read and write three languages. In particular my spelling of English is exemplary.'

Exemplary. Reitzger gave in.

'Reitzger,' he said. 'Konrad Reitzger.'

'Mr Reitzger.' The man pronounced it impeccably. And went on, 'You are German then. Which means that once you were officially my enemy.' This time the two men in the middle of the red and plundered field made their considerations while looking at each other's eyes: the one straightened now on his height, looking down; the other on stiff legs planted apart in the red dust, looking up. Waiting. The valley held the heat in stillness. But then the horseman smiled, widely, showing his white teeth. 'But not necessarily my enemy now. What would your opinion be on that question?'

'Not necessarily,' Reitzger agreed, who was however in no hurry to reassure or befriend, and saved his emphasis for what he must insist on – his own determination. He would not plead. He would not make strenuous efforts to convince. He was the last man to smile foolish smiles and stutter in efforts to create goodwill.

'So,' the other went on, content enough with this answer, 'you can call me Walter. Yes. That is my English name. My Xhosa name clicks, and white men have difficulty with clicks. You, Mr Reitzger – ' again he repeated it just as he had heard it, with the guttural German 'r' – 'would not be able to pronounce it.'

Touché!

Reitzger moved his eyes from the dark ones of the mounted man to the tail of the horse which was flicking at horse-flies on its haunches. The same idea was growing in both of them. But neither was in a hurry to tell it. They looked away to the birds, one of which raised its wings in a restless half-rise, then flopping and wing-rowing scrambled again for a claw-clutch.

Reitzger's awkwardness, his shyness, was concealed – or divulged – by stiffness. 'Walter,' he said, looking at the cranes, 'could let me ride on his horse –'

Walter did not move or speak.

'– behind him, on the haunches.' He put a hand on the wide flanks of the animal. Another man might have slapped it.

'You mean,' Walter corrected him, 'if it would not make me uncomfortable, would I consider such an arrangement?'

'I could pay –'

But Walter raised his voice to stop him. 'With pleasure. And if you were to offer me recompense, Mr Reitzger, I should definitely refuse.'

And he smartly removed foot from stirrup on Reitzger's side, and held the leg forward and one arm rigidly down, so that Reitzger could use stirrup and arm to swing himself up, to sit astride the horse close to the broad yellow back of its master.

'Forward Ukuthula!' Walter commanded, and tapped the hefty shoulder with his crop. Ukuthula curved his neck and paced through the field, stamping down the sticks, the bent and the straight, and some still with papery leaves, which stood in his way, crackling and faintly rustling, and starting up small spurts of the soft red dust. Over the bridge, past the tree with its reflection, scarlet and scarlet, and the four cranes, two high in the heat and two low in the cool brown water.

Konrad Reitzger did not like to entrust himself to another person. Equally he would not like others to entrust themselves to him. Not because he shirked responsibility but because, on the contrary, he believed that everyone should accept full responsibility for his own actions. Men should meet on terms of equality. Respect yourself and respect others – unless they should prove themselves unworthy.

As, in his opinion, his father had. Who had demanded the respect of his children as a duty, denying their right to judge what he was or what he did. 'A weak man, a moral coward, afraid of authority, inclined to be servile, kowtowing to his bosses,' was the conviction he had confided to Professor Feuchthaber, one of those rare people whom Reitzger found it possible not only to respect but even to like. 'I know the type well,' Feuchthaber had said. And yet, while Konrad had no doubt that these qualities belonged to his father, he was not convinced that having said that he had said all there was to say about the old man. As a boy he had been puzzled by him – why was he so grand and grave with the family at dinner, and so different, loud and laughing, winking and whispering, when there were visitors? What was it about him that made the younger children hang their heads and answer in whispers when he spoke to them, and made Konrad, though he would stand straight, and look into his father's eyes, and speak up, feel his face grow hot as if he had something to be ashamed of, or was lying when he wasn't?

Kurt Reitzger was a thick man, not fat but solid, who sat and stood and walked in a rigid manner, with the straight back of an old Prussian officer – though he came of a Bavarian burgher family none of whom had ever been in any regular army. He had worked for a chemical company, one of the biggest in the world. His position was secure but not eminent. When he found out that Bernhard Kuhn, the son of his chief and classmate of his own eldest son, often invited Konrad to the palatial Kuhn house on the other side of the river near the Schloss, he summoned Konrad into his study ('in that pompous way he had,' Konrad recalled), to inform him of his approval of such a 'respectable association' and hoped it would 'blossom' into a 'close and lasting friendship'.

For years Konrad had squirmed for his father's sentimentality and vulgarity; though he only put the names to these things when he was quite grown-up. In the evenings after dinner they all had to sit together for an hour 'to show that we are a proper loving family'. If there were guests, his father would tell his Joke. It didn't matter to him if he'd told it to the same guests a dozen times before, it must be told again because it proved him an amusing fellow. It was about a stutterer walking inadvertently into a cow-pat, and exclaiming *Sch- sch- schon reingetreten!* When this joke stopped being one of the great adult mysteries because he came to understand it, Konrad wondered why his father bothered to tell it, and why the visitors pretended to find it funny.

On Sundays they had all to go to Mass together. When he was fifteen he had asked his father, 'How can you be a scientist and believe in God?' To which he received a long, solemn and unconvincing reply. The expression of disbelief or even contempt on his son's face roused his father eventually to red-faced anger. And it may have been out of a desire for revenge that a few days later he refused Konrad's request for a set of scalpels of his own. Konrad had been staying late after school in the laboratory to investigate the quadrate bone of the snipe, and write a paper on it under the supervision and encouragement of his new but very old biology teacher, who had been called back from retirement now that the war was absorbing the young men. Konrad wanted to carry on at home after the school had to be locked up. He wanted to finish his paper in time to enter it for a national competition, and now his father was too mean to help him. '*Scheiss!*' he hissed, as he left his father's study. He was called back at once. 'What did you say?' the old man demanded, his eyes bulging. 'I said, *schon reingetreten*,' Konrad said, stiff with defiance. The old man stared helplessly, his mouth opening and shutting silently, and Konrad marched out of the room.

Perhaps old Reitzger was afraid of losing his son's respect. He took him once to Ludwigshafen, to the laboratories of the Company. There was a fat woman there, some kind of secretary. His father called her Lili and patted her bottom. She had metallic yellow hair wound up in plaits, and wore a dirndl. She giggled when the old man whispered to her. He looked stupidly pleased with himself, but became serious, pompous as ever, as he showed Konrad how to filter chemicals and how to mix them by shaking them in a test-tube. Still the boy looked unimpressed. 'Ask me anything you want explained,' he said. But it was obvious that he didn't really know the answers to the boy's questions. He filtered some more chemicals, and shook them in the test-tube. Konrad's face remained wooden, and they drove home in silence.

Konrad won a prize for his paper – an ornate certificate which he soon lost, and more importantly an exemption from service as an anti-aircraft gunner which would otherwise have been compulsory when he turned sixteen. He was allowed to stay at school until he was seventeen. In that year he began to investigate genetics, breeding generations of *Drosophila melanogaster*. Then, in the last year of the war, he had to go into the army.

'Now be careful you don't catch syphilis,' was all his father could think of to say in his jocund bar-room manner the day Konrad left for his training.

The regiment was sent by train into the Battle of the Bulge. 'I may die soon,' Konrad thought, 'and I hardly know anything.' What was there, he wondered, that he could learn at this late hour? Perhaps he could learn to drive a locomotive. He went to ask the driver to give him lessons, and drove himself into battle.

He was wounded, not severely, but hospitalised at Mannheim. His father came to see him.

'You just get better, my boy, and when all this is over you won't have to worry. With the contacts I've got you'll get a good start up the right ladder. That I can promise you. You know you can rely on me,' he said. 'When peace comes –,' he kept saying. '*Kommt der Friede. Hab' keine Angst* – don't worry!'

And very soon after Konrad was sent back to the front, the peace did come. He was captured in a town called – he appreciated – Misery.

The prison camp was an open field enclosed with barbed wire, without shelter of any kind. A perpetual drizzle and the piss of thousands of men turned it to slush. The prisoners, wet and hungry and itching, sat or lay in the mud and scraped at it with their hands in the hope of reaching firmer ground. The young pink Americans watched suspiciously from the wooden towers at the corners of the field from behind their machine guns. Sometimes a prisoner, soaked and mind-wandering, would get up and try to run through the mud towards the fence, and the fingers of a frightened Pinkface would fly to his trigger, the gun would rattle and bullets spray the running, the digging, the sleeping, a whole line of be-wildered men. Once one of the guards shot his counterpart in the diagonal-ly opposite tower. But despite wild and frequent rumours few of the prisoners believed that their extermination was intended. Each was given a bar of chocolate – his only rations – per day. Konrad Reitzger wondered if his bowels had lost their capacity to function, but after three weeks, an hour's labour, and a contribution of blood to the communal bog, he shat a rock.

In the fourth week – it was early March – some officer conceived the idea that it would be better to intercept and reason with those men who lost their nerve and squelched towards the fences than to shoot them down, especially as this method of dealing with them had proved so hazardous for the guards themselves. They needed an interpreter, and enquiry soon brought them to Reitzger, who thereafter spent his days sitting high on the back of a jeep, being driven round and round the mudfield, spotting, shouting at, explaining how things stood to those who'd had enough of mud and chocolate and lice and rain and thought they might prefer bullets. His padded uniform was so torn that all over it the padding hung out in little clotted mudballs, reminding him of a costume hung with bells that he had seen on Papageno when his mother had taken him to the opera in Salzburg on his tenth birthday.

The jeep was an improvement on the mud – to which however he returned to sleep. And it wasn't long before his English took him to the green pastures of a bed, regular meals, clean clothes, water and soap at the American base, for he was handed over to a priest who needed an interpreter who was also Catholic and educated. Reitzger hid his atheism and his contempt. 'The Mess was worth a Mass,' he was to explain to those who would agree, like Feuchthaber.

His usefulness delayed his return to civilian life, but one did not starve as long as one stayed with the American army. Home in Heidelberg that winter of forty-five to forty-six he found out how scarce everything was. Or would have been, even for him, had not the American High Command set up its headquarters there. And of course the intelligent man would survive if survival was possible. And not only survive, but survive well. And the real test of intelligence (Konrad Reitzger said) was life itself.

He became a waiter at the American Club. One took one's tips and commission in cigarettes. A 'bar' of them was a bar of gold. Clumsy money, but it bought food, clothes and even books.

The Americans themselves organised a lending library for civilians. As 'Now the war for the minds begins,' the padre had been fond of saying who had been Reitzger's patron, and to whom he had therefore restrained himself from answering with his own opinion – 'Nazism – Catholicism – one irrational faith or another – is a poor choice if any at all.' And when he searched the library he found nothing there either – mostly the conqueror's naive and misplaced faith in Steinbeck and O'Neill. The first time he went in there a woman kept trying to catch his eye and smirk at him. On a later visit she said, 'Don't you remember me? I remember *you*. My name's Lili – I used to work at – ah, now you remember! And tell me, how is your father these days? He used to be very amusing your father, very good company!' Lili's hair was shorter and darker, and no longer plaited and wound. She was thinner and usually dressed in a red suit; and her lips and nails were red. She told him she was engaged to an American called Al. When he told her that he was working as a waiter at the Club she became cooler. Yet she couldn't have earned as much in a month as he did in a single night.

The Club was smoky and noisy with a piano and singing and frivolity, and full of women with square beaded shoulders and hair in sausages on top of their heads. At four in the morning Konrad would go home to sleep. At eight he would go to the apartment of two stout old ladies, the central exchange and chief agents of the Black Market.

Little pearl earrings pressed into their lobes. One wore a tangled wig like beige coir; the other's white hair was pinned in a tight knot with big black hairpins. The skin of their necks looked like grey used chamois. They smelt as musty as their apartment. The wigged one had been married, and the broad gold ring pressed into her flesh. The other had a big watch chained to her belt. Their feet were squeezed into schoolgirl shoes, on each a cushion of flesh between the curve of leather and the strap. Their many high dark rooms were crowded with enormous articles of polished furniture, and silent motionless clocks, antimacassars, a multitude of ornaments – bucolic china children with faces like buttocks, orange dogs with blunt muzzles and blank round eyes. Rugs worn to the jute. Canvases of cracked oil paint in pompous frames. Crowds of portrait-photos on an upright piano. The Goethe, the Schiller, the aspidistra. Torn velvet curtains with fringed valances. The windows nailed shut. The chandeliers in calico bags, grey and lumpy and bulbous as wasp-nests. One waited and waited, so often and so long, in the dining-room or a drawing-room or a music-room or a bedroom or even in the kitchen, that one became familiar with the objects and the atmosphere. In each room someone waited. And the two old ladies came and went between them, arranging the deals. Buyers and sellers never saw each other. No doubt the old ladies took the biggest profit, but nobody did badly who had patience.

Socks, twelve pairs of, whisky, pens, watches, wool-tweed a bale of, one overcoat. How many bars for the overcoat? Wait. A cut-glass vase on a painted cloth in the middle of the oval table had grey dust in the bottom. Things taken no notice of, no longer admired or used. As though the ladies were only tenanting lives which their former selves had built and owned.

Sixty bars for the overcoat? Very well, I'll take it.

The cold air of the street was welcome then. A thick white light. Agitated grey river, grey light-stained river. Harsh rattle and sparks of the trams. Hungry intent faces, mufflers across mouths as if people were deliberately gagging themselves. Once, a man standing on a bridge, his bare red-raw hands held out in front of him like a sleep-walker: a cap so low over his eyes he could surely not see, and its flaps tied down over his ears, and a muffler across his mouth – I have seen no evil, heard no evil, spoken no evil, but what have I *done?* A cloud on others' spirits as on the mountains compressing the town. Pigeons, grey flocks of. Sorrows, other people's. For oneself there was a new warm overcoat, and one knew where one could go and buy Russell on Einstein in the original English.

And then there was still one bar of cigarettes left over.

'Ach, Konrad! Is that you?' the old man would call from his study, putting on surprise, when he'd been watching from the window, craving what he would not ask for – 'You've brought cigarettes for me? That is very lucky!'

Konrad would reach round the door, drop the bar of ten packets on the desk without glancing at his father and retreat without a word.

'I must pay you back!' – the old man hurrying out into the hall and following him to the foot of the stairs, brandishing a few useless Reichs-marks, pretending that these cigarettes were some sort of extra ration that his son was somehow regularly awarded by the new authorities. As if he were deaf, the son would go on up, to his room at the top of the house, with his new book.

There had always been English books at home, belonging to his mother, who had gone to school for a time in Sussex. He and his sister and two brothers had been brought up to speak English by a nursery-governess named Miss Baldwin, who claimed relationship with the Prime Minister of Great Britain. She had never learned to speak German well, but had gone home in nineteen thirty-nine very reluctantly, having become so fond of the children and their mother.

Konrad's mother was stern and practical, but witty and intelligent. She was much younger than his father and, the adult Konrad realised, scornful of him. At this time she used her cleverness at cards which she played twice a week, with ladies who came in from the country. Their debts were paid in eggs, chickens, ducks, potatoes, which stocked the otherwise empty larder of the Reitzger house in Handschuhsheim, though occasionally Frau Reitzger had to part with pieces of her family silver. Her books were mostly novels, some poetry. Her son had no use for them any more. Nobody had. And they were less likely to recover value one day than the silver was.

The old man, home all day now with nothing to do but complain, had always enjoyed food and wine. He had kept a good cellar before the war, and had tried to teach Konrad about wines. And the boy had been interest-ed enough, but found that his father could make any subject boring. Now he was boring them all with his complaints. His children not only refused to sit and listen in the hour after dinner, but Konrad, always the most recalcitrant of them, wouldn't even come to the dinner table. When he was in the house at all he kept to his own room. And 'the Lord knew where he got to the rest of the time,' old Reitzger groused to any of his other children who might be provoked into answering.

But he did know where Konrad got to.

Visitors, of whom there were few enough, but at least the farmers' wives – 'not unrespectable women' he would have it known – who came to play skat with his wife, would be told: 'My son is working for the Americans, you know. Yes, I arranged – that is to say, I encouraged him to offer his assistance to the officers –'

To his son he said: 'A waiter! With your education. With that science prize you won. Surely you can get yourself a better job than that. Have you spoken to the right person at the right level?'

The son would mount the stairs away from the voice, shut the door on it. His room contained nothing but a bed, a table, a chair and a bookcase. There had been a wardrobe which he'd moved out on to the landing. Bare floor. No heater: though he would leave his door open at night to let in the warmer air rising from the rooms below. Konrad thought of himself as an ascetic scholar, cleanly occupied with science, the opposite of his father who was weak, soft, ineffectual, a sensualist. He could imagine how his father would behave in the Club with all those women: the coarse jokes, the bottom-slapping. Of course his mother must despise such a man.

– About whom, however, there was something elusive. What had he now to be so proud about? He still strutted, he still tried to dictate – the useless, snobbish ignorant old ninny! Konrad dismissed him from his thoughts to concentrate on algebra.

The time for real study came at last. – But on the very first day, the shock of the bodies in the tank. Of course he had not allowed that to deflect him from his intention of studying Medicine. Not, at least, until he was sure, and reassured by all his teachers, that his talent was really for Mathematics and theoretical Physics after all.

'Mathematics!' old Reitzger had protested, peevish because he had not been consulted, and barely informed. 'What is the use of Mathematics? It never earned a living at the best of times!'

But he wasted his breath, and he knew it.

The two men on the horse swayed through the valley.

'What do you call those big birds?'

'That bird? In my language? We call him i-Hem. It is the noise he makes. It is good that he is here – he brings the rain.'

Soon Reitzger wanted to change the position of his dangling legs, shift the weight of his shoulder-hung bag from left hip to right, but instead sought distraction. He asked, 'Are you a chief?'

'No sir. But I am a chief's son.'

'Will you be Chief when your father dies?'

'My father has many sons. My personally becoming Chief is a matter only of possibility.'

'Do you want to be Chief?'

'I would be glad to have the opportunity to govern my people. Or rather, let me say, to help them in the government of themselves. You understand, that is a different thing from being Chief of a people under the government of foreigners?'

The foreigner asked, in his direct way, 'For the sake of power? Or because you wish the good of your people?'

'That,' Walter granted, 'is an important question. It is a necessary question that a man must ask himself. And I can answer it. I say, because I wish the good of my people.'

'I've heard that the Government talks of letting this land of yours become self-governing.'

' "Self-governing"? Now please, I ask you for your opinion sir, as a man of the world. What sort of freedom will we get? All the big country – it will be their Republic. They say that soon – five years, ten – it will be their Republic. No more English Kings and Queens over the water. They will divide it. Yes sir. We must live in the parts they call our "homelands". But they will be our guardians, because they say we are like children and not yet civilized enough to look after ourselves. Paternalism, Mr Reitzger. I have just been to see a white father. He told me he knows better than I do what is good for my son. He does not mean good for my son, of course. My son Johnjohn is a big man already among my people, although he is only young like you, Mr Reitzger. The white fathers fear Johnjohn because my people listen to him and believe what he says. So they send him far from his land of the Transkei, far away among strangers.'

'What does Johnjohn say?'

'He says, this division of the land of which the white fathers speak, it will not at all be equal. They are very few and have very much land. Very good land, where the rain falls. We are very many and will have little. Look, Mr Reitzger. Look all about. Look down there, at those big holes in the earth.'

They had come out between the narrowing hills, on to a winding road along a ridge. The land dropped away on either side, dry rocky hill after hill to both horizons, where the red of earth met the blue of sky. An ox as thin as if constructed of sticks grazed the margin of the road. There seemed to be no other grass in the land, in all the billowing dark plush of dust.

Walter pointed with his crop, a wide-armed gesture.

'Dongas, that is all we are rich in, sir. Look at our cattle. Are your cattle in Europe like that, sir? They say it is our bad farming which makes the dongas. Look there on that hill – that is where the government agricultural expert showed us how to plough. Last September month. Where did the seed go? What will be the harvest? You can see the furrows but you cannot see the crop. The man said, do it this way and when the rain comes your crop will not be washed away. The soil will not be washed away. But where was the rain, sir? Where was the rain?'

'Yes, I see.'

They proceeded for a while in silence, through the barren but beautiful land. Only the deepening light enriching the red hills.

'Not even,' Reitzger enquired, 'the hope of freedom then?'

'No hope? How can you say that? How can a people live without hope of freedom?'

'How then?'

'Men can live without hope for themselves if they can have hope for their children. We hope for good land, and we hope for freedom. Perhaps we must have freedom before we have good land.'

'How will you get it?'

'Ah Mr Reitzger sir, we have much to learn. Now we will rest for a short time.'

They dismounted in the shade. The African stood looking over his plains. The European sat against a thin tree trunk, his knees bent, an ache in his thighs.

'If your friend Mr Schwallendorf,' Walter said, 'had been my teacher when I was a boy, I would have asked him to teach me German. Do you know why? Because if any man has anything to teach you that you do not know you should try to learn it from him. Europeans have very much they can teach us Africans. What they know makes them very strong. Very powerful. So we must learn from them.'

'I think so too, that one must learn whatever one can,' the European said.

A pair of small black birds dipped and went. What were they called? Beans dangled on the trees. What sort of tree was it? Pink-spotted seeds lay scattered in the shade. Were they edible? The sun bloomed as a poppy. The earth-holes brimmed with shadows. They mounted again and proceeded. Reitzger dozed and woke, to find that his head was pillowed on the warm wet yellow back of the big African. He felt too sleepy to lift his head. He had dozed like this on the back of his grandfather, who had carried the infant Konrad up and down in the shade of his garden when the boy had had his terrible headaches, which the doctors had said he might grow out of, and which he had in fact seldom suffered from in the last ten years or so. Again he shut his eyes, and again he woke. Red of earth and red of sky were infusing each other until their meeting-line could no longer be distinguished. Slept again, woke again. The sun was on a level with his own bent head. An orange disc sunk into, and cutting, as the horse jerked up and down, like a round saw, through the red earth. And slept again.

'Mr Reitzger, we are here.' The man's voice resonated through his back. The horse had stopped.

Dark hills. Big bulging stars and splinters of stars, the alien configurations. Orange window-lights from a house on a hill, the shapes of huts dancing in firelight on one another.

He climbed stiffly down.

From among the stars Walter bent down and held out his hand.

'It was my pleasure, Mr Reitzger,' he said.

'It is good you have come to visit me.'

They were sitting facing each other, on flat-topped stones.

'I came,' Reitzger corrected, 'to find out what is causing the smell.'

'I hope you are well sir.'

'I am well. I have been living further from the smell than you. I am surprised it has not made you sick.'

'I found it very bad at first, but now I am used to it. And it is diminishing, I think?'

'I came to find out.'

'Ah,' Walter said, not 'why', but perhaps Reitzger thought he had, or meant to. So he answered, 'It is always interesting to know what is the cause of something.'

'And you have completed your investigations? You know what is the cause?'

'Yes. I know that the cause is the boiling of a horse.'

'The curiosity is satisfied sir?'

'It would be interesting also to know *why* the horse is being boiled.'

'Ah.'

Walter's eyes were bloodshot. So were the others, of the men and women and children who came and went near the stranger, looking at him but not stopping. It seemed that everybody's business took him along this route past Walter's hut.

'You will drink some beer with me, Mr Reitzger?'

Reitzger bent his face to the stuff in the tin; tipped it until it showed yellowish white, and smelt it. Not too bad. Nothing like the smell from the horse-cauldron. He glanced at Walter, who was watching him, and as he looked up Walter said, 'I drink to the coming of the rains.'

'The rains,' Reitzger agreed, and tasted the stuff. Gritty, flaky, sour.

'Do you like the taste of our beer, Mr Reitzger? It is different from yours, is it not?'

'It is completely different!'

'Do you like it?'

'No.'

Walter laughed. Perhaps he enjoyed the man's candour. Or perhaps he intended to tease him. 'Some white men are afraid to drink it. They are afraid that we brew it with harmful or disgusting ingredients.'

'And do you?'

'No sir!'

'Where is your horse?'

'My horse? *Ukuthula?* Mr Reitzger!'

'Where is he?'

'My horse? You think I would kill my horse? I will tell you how much I have paid for my horse. Six cows, Mr Reitzger. It is more than some men give for their wives. *U-ku-thu-la*. It means Peace, Mr Reitzger. What is that in your language?'

'*Der Friede*. But why are you boiling the horse?'

'*Derfriede*. That horse,' Walter said, 'died. One, two weeks ago, he died.'

'Two weeks ago? Where was he found?'

'He died here, near here, on the grass beside the road, where he was eating.'

'Why?'

Walter shrugged. 'He was old.'

'He died a natural death?'

'Yes, sir.'

'And then?'

'And then what, Mr Reitzger? What is "and then" for a horse after he has died?'

'What did they do with him? They weren't boiling him the day you brought me here. It started up the next night, the smell. Had he just been left lying about?'

'No sir, Mr Reitzger. He was du-ly *buried*.'

'Buried.'

'Yes sir. Buried in the earth. And now I am going to ask you a question if you will permit.'

'Go ahead.'

'You say it is only out of interest that you have come to see what is the cause of the smell?'

'That is so.'

'I see.'

'You and your friend received a visitor this afternoon, I believe.'

'A man came. I did not meet him.'

'You did not have the pleasure of meeting the Commissioner of the District? The Grootbaas? Meneer B. M. Pik, *E*squire?'

'No.'

'But your friend has told you what an important gentleman is this Grootbaas?'

'No.'

'Ah. So you are making these enquiries entirely on your own behalf.'

'Yes. I have come only because I wanted to come. But Mr Schwallendorf has also been disturbed by the smell. He would also like to know about it.'

'We have no wish to disturb Meneer Schwallendorf. On the contrary sir. He has been our friend for many years. We have much respect for Meneer Schwallendorf. And poor Meneer Pik – he has such a weak nose! He would like to know about us here in the village. He asks us questions, questions, questions, all the time. But he does not believe what we tell him. He believes only what he can understand. And what does Meneer Pik understand? He understands that kaffirs are liars. He knows we are dumb kaffirs and liars. He knows. But you are a visitor, Mr Reitzger.' (Was there a slight mockery now in the way he said the name?) 'You may come, you may ask. I will tell you about the horse. And please – you will inform Meneer the Teacher. He will be very pleased to know why we are boiling the horse. We say to each other, we must listen to what the Teacher tells us. He is a white man who knows many things we do not. He knows how we must plough our fields. He tells us and we do not listen, and when the rain comes it will wash away our crops. We are dumb kaffirs, so we must listen. He tells us about hygiene. He tells us how we must boil to kill the goggas that jump a sickness from one to another. So maybe this horse did not die from just being old. Maybe he had a bad sickness. We must dig up this horse and boil him. That is what we say to each other. I am giving you this information, Mr Reitzger, and if you will tell Meneer the Teacher he will be very pleased.'

And the 'dumb kaffir' reached for his beer. The matriculant whose spelling of English was exemplary, and who believed one must learn from the white man, learn from any man whatever he could teach! He drank deep, but kept his eyes on his confused visitor, and when he lowered the pot, he laughed. The laughter spread. Reitzger looked about at the villagers, who had stopped at last and were all showing their teeth. As Walter laughed his eyes narrowed and almost disappeared, but now and then as he opened his mouth for a loud guffaw, his eyes opened too, very wide, to take in the sight of his serious visitor, and then shut deep in their folds again as his shoulders shook and his hands thumped his knees. He stopped at last. The others too.

Reitzger did not mind the mockery as much as the disappointment – in the explanation, but also more importantly in Walter himself.

'It's sheer nonsense,' Schwallendorf spluttered. 'They can't have gathered from me that they must dig up dead animals and boil them for reasons of hygiene! If it's some dreadful medicine they're brewing, I only hope they pour it on the lands and not down their own throats. Well, Pik will have to make what he can of it. He's suspicious enough to invent some fantastic reason for anything.'

All the windows had been shut against the smell. But the house was unbearably stuffy. So Schwallendorf opened the two leaves of the dining-room door, leaving the screen closed against the insects which flashed out of the darkness into the light and left bits of their wings and bodies stuck to the wire. A glow on the hill opposite and below marked the village, the source of the air's sepsis, and the persistent doubt.

'They and I,' Schwallendorf mourned. 'We built the first school-house together, with our own hands. I worked with them, I didn't just give the orders. We made it out of galvanised iron. Just a great shed, yes?

You should have heard it when the rain came down. Like being inside a drum! We used to try and sing above the noise.'

Schwallendorf swallowed his whisky and looked down glumly upon the red glow on the other hill, his cheeks hanging heavy as if from the habit of disappointment.

Reitzger wanted to ask him about Walter. But he did not want to be questioned about him. So he did not even mention his name.

'But there must be a reason,' he insisted. It bothered him more than it did Schwallendorf, who was soon asking him, as he had on the previous nights, about what it was like 'at home' nowadays. But he seldom listened to what Reitzger told him. Instead he would interrupt to explain how it used to be, as though it had not only been better then, but right. He didn't ask about the war, not Reitzger's war, though he did mention that his father had been killed, as Feuchthaber's had too, in France in nineteen-seventeen.

But tonight, as he drank more, he began to describe the past differently. A childhood cold, obscure, in a greyness of weather and closed houses, snow and rain; shame of body, guilt of sin; autocratic, devout parents; joylessness. And then he had come here – to a four-roomed house on a hill and a piece of ground in the valley where his school was yet to be built: but to a country which seemed new from the Creator's hand, sounding out, scented, shot-from-the-dye! And tall people, in bright blue cloth, riding over the hills. He had succeeded in making friends with them. Why had they become his enemies? Why had his achievements rotted away?

'From Ezekiel – do you know – ?' His hand shook as he poured more whisky. ' "Wearing clothes of blue, captains and rulers, all of them desirable young men, horsemen riding upon horses." '

'Goodnight, Herr Schwallendorf!' Konrad said.

'Goodnight, Max!'

Another sentimental old fool, the young man thought. Feuchthaber had certainly sent him to this man only because of where he was, not what he was. Feuchthaber could not have remembered, perhaps, just what his friend was really like. Or had he lost respect for him – Reitzger – since he'd had to leave the University after the currency reform, and take up journalism? No! Feuchthaber knew that he had every intention of going back and taking up the struggle again, with relativity, and the quantum. It was hard to be young, and to know what potential you had in you, while no one else knew it and you had to be patient, and prove it.

And yet he could not think of a reason for the boiling of the horse.

He left Schwallendorf, who was still drinking; and as he lay in the dark in his rondavel he could hear the old boy bumping about, still muttering to himself. '. . . *alle junge, liebliche Gesellen, Reisige, so auf Rossen ritten.*'

Reitzger felt the sort of throbbing which used to come before a headache, but he fell asleep, and dreamt of his father.

Kurt Reitzger had had some of his wealth restored to him when his shares in the company, which had been wound up after the war, became valuable again as new companies were made from remnants of the old. But the gloom which had settled on him did not leave him. It had started when his chief, Friedrich Kuhn, had been tried for war-crimes at Nürnberg. Old Reitzger seemed to have been disturbed both by the fear that he too might be called to answer for having worked in the department that first made and patented the Zyklon-B crystals for the gassings in the extermination camps, and a strange humiliation that he was not considered important enough. Or so his son had interpreted him.

The old man died one night in his sleep. In the morning, in the darkened room, by candlelight, the son reviewed the father, whose skin was beige now and blobbed with blue. Konrad had waited to feel what emotions would come to be instantly quenched – remorse, regret, guilt, or painful realisation of his own mortality: but all that came was a thought, in English (a language the old man had never spoken well): 'Old Gorgonzola – there he lies!'

Now, in his dream not his memory, his father was being lifted out of the bed by his mother and Feuchthaber. They heaved him off and away in his crumpled white nightshirt. Then Konrad himself, against his own will, protesting but compelled, climbed into the bed, laid his head on the pillows and was covered with the eiderdown. The stench filled his nose, his whole head, which swelled as if to split; and it went down his throat into his lungs to choke him.

He woke suddenly, fully and perfectly understanding what the boiling of the horse was for.

Exactly what it had achieved – that was what it was for. It made a stench, and the stench kept Pik away, because Pik suffered from an oversensitive nose. So someone or something was there which Pik must not find. Something which, however, Schwallendorf might come looking for on Pik's orders. So the secret must be of a kind which Schwallendorf would probably not betray to Pik. And the secret of who or what this was which Pik must not discover in the village was clear to Reitzger beyond all doubt.

In the morning, before Schwallendorf was up or the table laid for breakfast in the largest rondavel, Reitzger went out through the front door, not letting the screen-door bang behind him. It was past six o'clock, but as he went down into the valley he could hear the cocks of the village still crowing as lustily as if it were dawn. The cool air was spoilt by the smell, which had not lessened much if at all. And as on the evening before, it was worse in the village itself.

The bare-breasted women were stirring pots over fires. Again they watched him pass. There were a few men about, dressed only in loin-cloths and blankets worn as shawls. Some of them followed him at a distance as he made for Walter's hut. In front of it there was a young woman feeding a fire with sticks.

'Is Walter awake yet?' he asked her.

The girl looked up at him and then returned her attention to the fire. The men who had followed him drew nearer.

'You want me, Mr Reitzger?' Walter came out, dressed in trousers only.

'Yes.'

'You have something you want to ask me, or tell me?'

'Both to ask and to tell.'

'You still wish to know why the horse is being boiled?'

'No. I know why. That is what I have to tell you.'

Walter said nothing. Everyone was still.

'At least,' Reitzger went on, 'that is part of what I have to tell you. I must also say that I shall not tell anyone else, not even Meneer Schwallendorf.'

Still Walter said nothing. The girl watched the fire. But the other men, young and old, edged forward, and more appeared between the huts on either side.

Reitzger raised his voice so that all might hear him. 'Now I shall ask my question. Walter, which of these young men is your son, Johnjohn, who has been endorsed out of the Transkei?'

Nobody laughed at him this time.

'I believe,' Walter said, 'that your curiosity may be satisfied without the answer to that question, Mr Reitzger.'

His curiosity, yes. And his need to solve this problem. But the great problem which the solution revealed, Walter's problem, Johnjohn's problem, the problem of all these people and millions more, that was not within his power to solve even in theory. Men like Pik made such problems, out of beliefs which Reitzger scorned: beliefs he was all too familiar with: beliefs which stank much worse than a dead beast.

'In the end,' he said loudly but sadly, looking round at the men, 'you'll have to fight.'

'We know that, Mr Reitzger,' Walter said. 'When we met, you and I, sir, I told you we had been enemies once. The truth is, sir, that we were enemies still, we are enemies now, and we will be enemies for a long time. Sir.'

'You and I? Why? I am not your enemy. I am the enemy of Pik and what you call the white fathers.'

'You are white. I am black. That is enough reason, Mr Reitzger.'

'What nonsense!' Reitzger said, the way Miss Baldwin used to say it. But that way was not strong enough. '*Stinking* nonsense,' he shouted. 'The sort of nonsense Pik believes.' He turned round, glaring at the faces round him. 'You'll rot your noses with stinking ideas like that. You – you'll be another Pik, Walter, another Pik, that's all.'

He walked away. The men parted to let him through. He walked on to the edge of the village, then he tried to run, stumbling among rocks and tufts, slipping on stones, down and up again, to reach the other survivor of the spreading, rising, inescapable stench, in the ark on the top of the hill.

Yvonne Burgess

If You Swallow You're Dead

Seven days after Mr Labuschagne's visit the hearse, adorned with four wreaths and followed by two cars, wound its way slowly past the Mercedes Benz showroom.

At Berry's Corner, where the traffic is always heavy, it went through against the red light, and on, past the neat grass verges of the factories, past the General Dealer's, Gent's Tailors and Star of the East Fruit, painted in dry, scratchy, childish strokes on boards nailed to the communal dirty-brown verandas, past the shanties huddled incongruously under the bright new Gold Dollar sign, and on to the cemetery where the prickly pears and headstones are a uniform sooty-grey from the smoke of the shunting trains, where the khaki-coloured trees lean crookedly, their naked boles turned like camels' backs to the wind, where a bedraggled brown donkey, having wandered in through a hole in the fence, was snuffling at the sour scrub for food.

There Alida Slabbert was, as the dominee put it, 'laid to rest'.

And afterwards when her husband Kobus, her children Chrissie, Ivy and Susie, her brothers Chrisjan and Pieter, her sisters-in-law Hester and Marie and her lodger Luigi Sersoni had returned to the house in Uitenhage Road, they sat solemnly, still in a state of shock, around the kitchen table where Alida had so often sat peeling potatoes on *Die Vaderland* and reading as she peeled those bits and pieces of news she had missed the evening before.

The Slabberts had moved into the house in Uitenhage Road shortly after Alida's father, Oom Chrisjan Koen, had died leaving the farm near Graaff-Reinet to her and her two brothers. They had bought her share between them and the money had come just at the right time when the room in the boarding-house in Myrtle Avenue had become oppressively

small, when the children were beginning to play in the street, and Alida
and Kobus to bicker and snap.

On the very first evening Alida shivered and rubbed at her thick fore-
arms because the hairs on them, she said, were 'standing straightup'.
She looked around into all the shadowy corners and up at the mottled
ceiling. She walked from room to room with the children holding hands in
their excitement and apprehension following her, and Kobus wondering
what it signified, this search, when houses were not so easy to come by
and they had already put the deposit down.

From half-way up the stairs that led to the attic Alida called out urgently: 'I can feel it now.'

'Oh Alida . . . ' Kobus said, stroking his bald patch in exasperation.

'A ghost. Up there,' Chrissie whispered down to Ivy who passed it on
to Susie.

The front part of the attic which had been converted into a bedroom
with ceiling and floorboards was empty, but in the part that had been
partitioned off Alida found tied securely to a strong beam a rope with its
edges hacked off and frayed just above the place where the knot of a
noose may have been.

She came down then, her bluish lips puckered into a thin line of satis-
faction. In the kitchen the children crouched down in front of the stove.

'Is it up there?' Chrissie asked loudly, seeking not so much confirmation
as reassurance in the brash sound of his own voice.

Alida took a handful of rice out of the tin on the kitchen dresser, poked
vigorously at the coals in the grate and sat down grinding a few of the
grains between her false teeth. At last when she was ready she nodded.

'What is it?' Ivy quavered.

'A ghost, man,' Chrissie said.

'How do *you* know?'

Gently Susie touched her mother's knee. 'Did Mammie see it?'

'Shhhhh . . . ' Ivy said.

Alida loosened her top plate with her tongue to retrieve a grain of rice
which had stuck underneath.

'A ghost!' Chrissie said, raising his arms menacingly. 'Up there! A big
ghost with long yellow teeth and eyes like turnips – *boooooooh!*'

The girls jumped.

'Ag no man,' Ivy said.

Unperturbed, her jaws moving sideways like those of a ruminating
cow, Alida chewed.

'Is it a bad one?' Ivy, filled with ghost-lore, knew there were good ones and bad ones; that the good ones had a white light shining around them and the bad ones a red light like the glow from a fire.

'A bad one,' Alida said. 'I won't see it. Not this one. But I can feel it in the ringing of my ears. And the tickling in the soles of my feet.'

They waited for her to go on but she sat stolidly staring at the fire and chewing her rice, her rough hands kept warm under her unconfined spreading bosom.

'But *why* does Mammie feel it?' Ivy asked. 'Why are *all* the houses haunted?'

'I was born with the caul,' Alida said contentedly. 'I told you. And my mother, your late ouma, before me. *She* was the eldest daughter just like I was the eldest daughter. Just like *you* are the eldest daughter.'

Chrissie and Susie looked at Ivy with some envy.

'It's funny, but I also feel funny,' Ivy said.

'You weren't born with it,' Alida said regretfully.

'And what sort of a thing is a cau-au-l supposed to be?' Chrissie asked, irritated as he always was to discover something he did not know.

'It's a skin over your face that you are born with,' Alida said.

'Where is it then?' he scoffed.

'The doctor pulls it off,' Alida said. 'And when he does that a person's eyes are opened onto the other world. That person has got second sight for the rest of her life.' She leaned back yawning and tugging at the spiky black hairs that sprouted from the mole on the side of her nose. '*That's* why. *They* know when a person can see them and feel them. Ghosts. And premonitions too. I know when someone is going to die. Sometimes I *see* them, sometimes I just know. I look at them and I can feel it, I can *smell* it, like the flowers at the funeral . . . a sick sweet smell just like the flowers at a funeral . . . '

'Like Tannie Louisa,' Susie reminded her.

Alida sighed. 'Poor Tannie Louisa. Before your poor late Tannie Louisa was taken away . . . I still remember as if it was yesterday . . . ' Alida closed her eyes and putting the last few grains of rice into her mouth wiped her slightly floury hands off on her apron.

'Yeeees . . . ' Chrissie encouraged.

'Tell us,' Ivy begged.

'But haven't I told you already?' Alida asked, knowing that she had, several times.

'No,' the children cried, 'no, but we've forgotten.'

'Well then. It was still on the farm. I was sick, lying in bed. It was a Sunday morning. I was sick with . . . '

'Mumps!' they prompted. 'Mumps!'

'Was it mumps? I don't know any more . . . but I must have been feverish it was so hot in that feather-bed although it was winter and your late Tannie Louisa came in and said to me: "Sister," she said, "can I borrow your hymn-book, sister?" She always called me sister because I was older than her, and she was dressed for church. I remember that dress as if it was yesterday. Your late ouma made it for me but she made the sleeves too tight so your Tannie Louisa got it. And later when your ouma came in I said to her: "Mammie," I said, "why is Louisa still here then? She will be late for church." And your ouma looked at me and her face went as white as this apron and she said: "But Louisa went to church hours ago," she said. "What are you talking about?" But she knew. And it was only three weeks after that. And your Tannie Louisa had three flowers on her hat that Sunday morning.'

The children were silent for a while, savouring the unimpeachable precision of the premonition. Then they began to coax. 'Tell us about the dog, the big black dog!'

'The ball of fire!'

'No, the stones that fell . . . '

'The thing that said "shh, shh, shh" behind you and Tannie Louisa like chasing chickens!'

Alida tugged absent-mindedly at the hairs on her mole, her blue eyes vague, fixed upon that time eons ago when she was a child . . .

'The piccanins around the fire,' the children pleaded.

Alida got up. 'Go wash your feet,' she said. 'It's school tomorrow.'

When Mieta came into the kitchen, as she did at eight every morning, having wiped her fawn felt slippers on the folded sack at the back door and hung her shopping bag made of coloured patches of leather on the hook behind the door, she went at once to the sink where Alida had stacked the breakfast dishes in a basin because the 'old Miesies' had always used a basin and Mieta had, like Alida, a respect for tradition.

While Mieta washed the dishes Alida made the beds, folded the night-clothes and emptied the chamber pots just as her mother had done, and if she had thought to question it she would have discovered as the reason that white man's pride – so deeply instilled in her – which precluded the leaving of any tasks as intimate as these to a servant.

By the time Mieta was ready to go into the house to sweep and dust, Alida had begun to tidy her lodger's room.

This matter of taking in a lodger had occasioned one of the few really bitter quarrels in the Slabberts' married life, and it was, moreover, one of the very few Kobus had won.

They were still stuggling to furnish the house when he suggested that they offer a room to Luigi Sersoni who worked at the factory with him and was looking for a place to stay.

Alida had set her thin lips tightly and refused. He was a bachelor, she had said, and worse, a middle-aged bachelor. Bachelors were the same the world over, especially middle-aged bachelors. She had two young daughters and her heaven-invested duty lay in protecting them from the crudities of life and, she gave Kobus to understand, there was nothing on earth more crude, if only potentially, than a middle-aged bachelor. He would have women there at night and he would drink.

Nevertheless it was true that the extra money would come in handy. School-books, blazers and shirts cost the earth; and then, as Kobus had argued, what difference would there be in making meals for one more as long as the payments on the house remained the same?

Sersoni therefore came and he was given the best room in the house, the front room with its white fireplace and large window looking out across the street at the wood-and-iron fence of the Showgrounds, the room which would have been the living-room, kept locked with its curtains drawn to be used only for special visitors like the dominee and the members of the Mothers' Union who came once a year with their lists to inquire what Alida would be willing to contribute to the bazaar in the way of jellies and puddings.

To Alida's consternation Sersoni appeared to be a model lodger. He took all his meals in his room and hardly ever ventured out except to go to work and sometimes to issue a formal invitation to Kobus to come in and play draughts with him.

He did not have women as far as Alida could tell, and she had risen in the middle of the night for several weeks to listen at his door for suspicious sounds. He did not drink either; or if he did she had yet to discover evidence of it.

A less determined woman would have given up but as far as Alida was concerned there were simply too many factors pointing towards secret vice: Sersoni was a middle-aged bachelor – that anomaly on God's earth worse only than a middle-aged spinster and twice as unnatural – he was a foreigner and a Catholic and the foreigner who was a Catholic as well could not exist, in her opinion, without being guilty of some profligacy or other. She had even considered the possibility of indecent pictures and had rifled through every book in his room without finding anything but holy pictures; Papish pictures, that is, of doll-like Virgins and chubby Infants but these, even if the Infants were rather too obviously naked, could hardly be called indecent.

Convinced as she was that she would one day unearth proof of Sersoni's secret vice, Alida not only made his bed and folded his pyjamas (he was not in the least bit nervous about going to the bathroom of that haunted house at night and so would not have a chamber pot) but swept and dusted there as well, for worse than that he should have some secret vice would be Mieta's discovery of it. Alida never forgot that although a bachelor, a Catholic and a foreigner, Sersoni was a white man still and that her duty therefore lay in hiding whatever weakness he might have from the eyes of a native servant.

Never knowing what she might find, Alida experienced a little flutter of excitement whenever she went into Sersoni's room and it was while she stood there one morning with her slightly startled curious blue eyes surveying it, the strange man's room, that she heard the click of the bottom gate. She rushed to the window and saw the visitor, a man and certainly not the dominee, just before he opened the second gate at the top of the steps and disappeared behind the wall of the stoep.

Alida whipped her apron off and ran to her room to dust her face with the musty powder which she kept in a plastic bowl. Quickly she twisted a turban around her head, but as she daubed at her thin blue lips with the drying tube of Pond's Natural, her old affliction, *hartkloppings* – the shivering and shaking instead of a regular beating of her heart – brought on no doubt by the presence of a strange man on her stoep, caught at her breath and forced her to go to the triangular wall-cabinet where she kept among other remedies, the *groenamare* for her cramps, the *versterk-druppels* for her nerves, and the *rooi laventel* for her heart.

By the time she opened the front door just a crack and holding on to it firmly because one never knew with strange men, Alida's heart had quietened down sufficiently for her to say impassively as though strange men called every day: 'Good morning?'

The man raised his hat to reveal a scalp shaved clean to the tuft of greying hair right on top.

'Listen Mrs,' he said, 'I'm looking for a Mrs Slabbert.'

'Yes,' Alida admitted cautiously. 'That's me.'

'Oh,' he said. 'Well look. I come from Graaff-Reinet. Labuschagne's the name.'

'Graaff-Reinet!' Alida's heart began to thump.

'No,' Mr Labuschagne said. 'It's nothing. I'm just bringing greetings from Chrisjan and Pieter.'

'Chrisjan and Pieter.'

'And a chicken. A rooster. From Chrisjan and Pieter.' He gestured towards the old black Dodge parked in front of the house. 'I was coming to the Bay.'

Her fears allayed with Mr Labuschagne's credentials thus satisfactorily established, Alida invited him in.

'But don't look at the house,' she said.

'I'm early,' Mr Labuschagne apologised, and he followed her in, looking, out of politeness, neither left nor right. In the kitchen Alida asked him to sit down and distantly instructed Mieta to pour coffee.

'Have sugar,' she said. 'You come from Chrisjan and Pieter?'

'Yes.' Mr Labuschagne, sitting stiffly in his black town suit and hard collar, took small polite sips, carefully keeping his elbows off the table.

'From Chrisjan and Pieter.'

'And how are they all then?'

'I must say all right,' Mr Labuschagne said.

'You can tell Chrisjan and Pieter that we are also all all right.'

There was an awkward silence, broken only by the sound of Mr Labuschagne sipping his coffee through politely pursed lips.

'And you brought a chicken, you say?'

'In the car outside. Yes.'

'Well,' Alida said, pushing her cup aside, 'you can tell Chrisjan and Pieter and Hester and Marie that we are also all still well.'

Mr Labuschagne tilted his cup to catch the last grains of partially melted sugar and wiped his mouth on the back of his hand. 'Yes,' he said. 'Yes, yes, I will surely tell them that.'

After he had put the small crate containing the rooster next to the shed in the backyard Alida took him down the narrow lane at the side of the house to the front gate where he gripped her hand hard, scratched the back of his head, put his hat on firmly and said: 'Thank you for the coffee. It was a pleasure to meet you and I will tell Chrisjan and Pieter that you are all still well.'

'And thank them for the chicken,' Alida said.

'Not at all,' Mr Labuschagne answered for them.

That afternoon Alida went to lie down as she usually did, tucking her feet in under the old moth-eaten kaross which had come down to her from her grandmother. It was then that she heard, quite distinctively, five loud knocks on the floor next to the bed.

She knew at once what they portended. Poor Mrs Labuschagne, she expressed silently and in advance her sympathy for the soon-to-be-bereaved. Poor man. Poor widow and how many orphans? And how long? Five months, five weeks, five days, even, heaven forbid! five hours – on the road back, perhaps, to Graaff-Reinet?

'We've got a chicken,' Alida told the girls when they came in. 'From your uncles Chrisjan and Pieter. I want you to put some bread out for it and some water.'

'Alive?' Susie asked. 'A live chicken?'

'Dead chickens don't eat bread.' Alida swung her legs down and felt for her slippers under the bed. 'I better come,' she said. 'You'll only take the fresh bread.'

The girls ran out to stare at the little rooster. He stared back at them pertly through the netting which covered the top of the crate.

'Oh the lovely thing,' Ivy said. 'Oh, what a lovely thing.'

'Look,' Susie cried rapturously. 'The tail so dark blue like purple.'

'*Koo-koo-koo*,' Alida crooned as she crumbled a crust of stale bread over the rooster. '*Kooo-koooo-koooo* . . . Get some water.'

'Oh our lovely chicken,' Susie said, clapping her hands with joy.

Ivy lifted a corner of the netting wire and put a tin of water into the box. The rooster looked at it suspiciously.

'It's clean,' she assured him. 'It had some polish in but I washed it clean.'

'Why don't you drink then, little chicken?' Susie asked plaintively.

The rooster scratched at the breadcrumbs and the girls laughed in delight at the way his bright comb flopped from side to side.

'What's his name?' Ivy cried. 'What will we call him?'

'*Cooked-chicken-and-gravy!*' Chrissie shouted close behind them.

'No man,' they chorused indignantly. 'You'll frighten our chicken.'

'*Your* chicken?' Chrissie poked his finger through the netting. '*Your* chicken? Where do you come from then?'

'Give us a name for him,' the girls begged.

'I told you. Cooked-chicken-and-gravy.'

'We don't want to call him *that*.'

'*You* don't want to call him . . . ' Chrissie laughed. '*You* don't want to . . .

oh help me, before I die. I'm just telling you. He will be Cooked-chicken-and-gravy, never mind what *you* want to call him.'

Ivy's eyes turned dark with anguish. 'It isn't true,' she said. 'Mammie, say it isn't true.'

'True?' Chrissie screeched. 'It's true as true as true! And you want to know how?'

'That's enough now,' Alida said. 'You're making my head sore.'

Chrissie skipped away beyond her reach. 'Mieta will take him *here* and she'll throw him down *there* and she'll take the axe and *bam!*'

'Chris*jan!*' Alida warned.

'And the stupid body doesn't even know it's dead and it . . . '

Alida lunged suddenly and Chrissie fell over backwards in trying to evade her, his small eyes wide with surprise.

Within a moment, her anger forgotten, and despite the girls' wailing, Alida began to laugh, holding her hand up to her mouth although she had got her false teeth six months before.

'Do you still remember your first chicken?' Alida asked Mieta as they plucked, squatting in the backyard with the fowl between them on a sack.

'Ag, Miesies,' Mieta said, 'I've cleaned so many already.'

'My first chicken,' Alida shook her head. 'Really you won't believe it.' She worked quickly and the beautiful speckled feathers came out in handfuls, to be dropped carelessly onto the sack. 'The old Miesies was away, I can't remember where but they were all away, for a funeral, I think, and only coming back on the Sunday and I wanted to surprise them – how old was I then, eight or ten, I don't know any more – but it was my first chicken. We had an old brown girl called Sannie and she was sick, she was always sick when the old Miesies was away, you know how these people are, but the chicken was already killed for the Sunday and Chrijan, Baas Chrisjan and me, we were going to pluck it. We were in the kitchen I remember because it was late and dark outside so we lit the lantern and did it in the kitchen just like this on a sack. We didn't even know about the hot water, we just plucked and the skin was coming off with the feathers, but the funniest part, when the feathers were all off Baas Chrisjan took a blade to cut it open with, a blade! No, really! I don't know why. He was playing doctor again, I think, he was always playing doctor, so he cut a little V here and took the gut, not all together, just one end and he pulled and the whole lot came out, like crinkle paper at

Christmas, spraying stinking water all over me, my dress, my hair, everything . . . ' Alida laughed briefly, nostalgically.

'Oh Lord, Miesies,' Mieta giggled.

'On the farm . . . ' Alida tugged fretfully at the feathers.

'On the farm . . . ' Mieta echoed. 'We had our own old jersey cow . . . '

'Not only that,' Alida sighed. 'Not only that. But what if a person dies
here in the Bay? You must lie in that graveyard there next to the shunting
trains, in the middle of rows and rows of people that you don't even
know . . . '

'Ag, Miesies mustn't talk like that,' Mieta said.

'No, old soul, but really, they must take me back! They must take me
back where I can lie with my own flesh and blood. These others they can
lie where they like but they must take me back so that I can lie with my
own people on the koppie behind the windbreak. I don't want the wind
to howl over my grave . . . '

The fowl lay between them, its pocked blue-white skin flecked with
blood and its legs stretched out stiff and cold. On the sack the dark-blue
tail feathers had already lost their lustre.

Alida heaved herself up. 'I'm not saying anything,' she said. 'But Baas
Chrisjan must just understand that I want to lie behind the windbreak . . . '

Alida stroked the old kaross and allowed the all-but-forgotten sights
and sounds and smells to overwhelm her: the coffee in the afternoons, the
Mazawattee tin filled with the slightly sour *soetkoekies*, the veranda sagging
under the weight of the vine; the path down to the quince hedges which
wound past the dam where the ground was always muddy and trampled
and smelt of manure, the orchard, the fruit, and before the fruit, the
flowers; the bedroom she had shared with Louisa, smelling of polish and
methylated spirits, and always dim and cool, right through the hottest
summer day; the big bed and cupboard which even at noon were little
more than darker masses so that at night, when the lamps were lit, one
looked at everything with interest, seeing them properly for the first
time that day.

Alida remembered lovingly, longingly, even the inconveniences: the
nervous trips to the outhouse at night with a candle and matches, the
struggle to keep the candle burning in the draught and the stomach-
squirming fear that one would be left sitting there, helpless and alone in
the dark.

And the games, oh, the games they had played, she and Chrisjan,
Pieter and Louisa, when the grapes were ripe and Chrisjan was the doctor

and he squashed them, collecting the purple rivulets of 'medicine' which he squirted into their mouths so that it trickled and tickled down into their throats. And they weren't allowed to swallow. Not one. For if they swallowed they were 'dead' . . .

Alida pulled at the hairs of her mole until her eyelids turned red and her eyes filled with tears.

Was the vine still there? she wondered. Were the grapes ripe? But no, it was the wrong time of the year for grapes. It was the wrong time of the year for everything . . .

Aching all over with a sense of irreparable loss, Alida brought out the gramophone and the records she had bought long before she met Kobus. Her favourite, badly scratched and buckled as it was, wobbled round and round before the balladeer began, dolefully drawing out the vowels: 'Oooooo ek *Diiiiink* weer va*naaaaaand* aan my *blouuu* oë . . . '

Alida sang with him in a high, reedy voice; and as she sang she thought not of Kobus but of Chrisjan, Pieter and Louisa and of the boys she had known as a young girl: of Joop Vermeulen, Marius van der Linde, and Attie Vermaak who had a motor-bike and looked like a film star.

'Didn't I say so?' Chrissie smirked as he ate his chicken. 'Isn't that your name, old Cooked-chicken-and-gravy?'

Ivy and Susie ate only their vegetables.

'What is it?' Kobus asked mildly. 'Are you sick?'

'They were stupid about this chicken,' Alida said. 'What do you think? Do you think a rooster can lay eggs?'

'It was so nice and *live*,' Susie said.

'And now it's *nothing!*' Ivy added, and at that both of them burst into tears.

'What do you mean nothing?' Chrissie asked. 'It's damn nice chicken and gravy! *Nothing!*' he snorted.

'You can *shut up!*' Ivy screamed.

'Well now dammit!' Alida said, losing her temper. 'Mustn't I give them something to cry about now? If I was so stupid about a chicken your oupa would have knocked me off my chair! It's too easy for you. That's the trouble. I didn't have it so easy.' She looked reproachfully at Kobus. 'I said their oupa would have knocked me off my chair!'

'Your chair?' Kobus stroked his bald patch.

'You're the *father* aren't you?' Alida shouted. 'You're supposed to be the *head!*'

But before Kobus could do anything to prove that he was the head, Alida clapped her hand to her heart, leaned back heavily, turned quite blue, and would have fallen if he had not caught hold of her in time.

'Louie!' he called in panic. 'Chrissie! Get your Uncle Louie!'

Sersoni hurried in, still chewing, and between them they half-carried, half-supported Alida to her bed.

There they stood around her, astounded by the suddenness of the collapse, Sersoni so embarrassed in the presence of the whole family and at such a distressing moment that he could only beam in an effort to hide his discomfiture and pat the kaross they had put over Alida, as much to keep his hands busy as to soothe her.

'A doctor,' Kobus suggested helplessly. 'Musn't we get a doctor now?'

'The *laventel*. . . ' Alida begged weakly.

Weeping with fear, the rooster forgotten, Ivy knocked over the bottles labelled *Duiwelsdrek* and *Wonderlijksens* (which were, fortunately, empty, Alida having been unable to procure those remedies in Port Elizabeth) before she found the *rooi laventel*.

'Alida,' Kobus persisted half-heartedly. 'What about a doctor?'

But she, her face as stoically expressionless in pain as it was in pleasure, had already recovered sufficiently to ask: 'Now what can a doctor do?'

'Is there still some chicken left for my lunch?' Chrissie asked on Monday morning.

Alida gave him a pile of old newspapers to make the fire in the copper geyser for the weekly wash and said: 'No. Thank heaven. That chicken made enough trouble. That chicken had a hex on it.'

'A hex!' Chrissie whooped. 'Then the hex went into my stomach! I've got a hex in my stomach!'

'Don't joke about hexes,' Alida warned him sternly. 'A hex is nothing to joke about. Lettie Potgieter joked about hexes and look what happened to her.'

'What happened to her again?' Ivy asked.

'Her bladder swelled up like a balloon,' Alida said.

'Oh yeeeeees,' Chrissie said. 'She went to pee in the veld and that Slaams followed her and buried a live bullfrog there and then she couldn't pee any more.'

'That's not nice,' Alida said. 'You mustn't say that. Say . . . '

'She wanted to be excused,' Ivy said.

'That's what *we* must say,' Susie said.

'Yes,' Alida said. 'That's nicer. It's nicer to say it like that . . . '

To save water (although in the city there was no need) Alida always bathed on Monday mornings, afterwards putting the washing in to soak ready for Mieta when she came in.

By the time she had stripped the beds and gathered up the soiled clothing the old geyser was rumbling and leaking boiling water. Alida drew her bath and lowered herself carefully into the scalding water. She scrubbed herself hard all over and lay back, only to find that she could not move, could not get up again, could hardly hold her head up, for the pain in her chest.

'Mieta,' she whimpered. 'Kobus.'

She struggled to keep her head above water. Her children were young. She had told no one but Mieta where she wanted to be buried, and she had yet to discover Sersoni's secret vice.

'The *laventel*,' she groaned; but even as she called for it Alida lost faith in the efficacy of the brew. Pneumonia and tuberculosis could be cured if the warm skin of a newly-slaughtered cat were applied to the chest of the sufferer; *uittrekpleisters* could draw out boils and even a cancer if it were not too deeply rooted; there was nothing like *rooi laventel* for *hartkloppings*. But what must be, must be. Five days had passed since she had heard the knocks on the floor, and there had been no bad news of Mr Labuschagne.

The water lapped against her jaw, washed over her blue lips and finally covered the mole with its stiff black hairs.

Alida let the water trickle and tickle down into her throat. The big black grapes, she saw through the steam and the grey-green water, were ripe. It was the right time of the year after all. Chrisjan, Pieter and Louisa were watching her. If she swallowed she was dead.

Cherry Clayton

In Time's Corridor

Alice stood on the gravel driveway at the side of the house, watering a few wilted flowers that straggled in a single indefinite line down the length of the flowerbed. The bed was very stony, perhaps because it lay under the roof drainpipe. She had made a few half-hearted attempts to remove the small, smooth stones, but there were always more, in new heaps and formations, as if shaped by a brisk mountain stream. Now she watered them with the flowers, enjoying the way the dry sandy surfaces became wet and glistening.

Since she had been pregnant she had begun to enjoy watering the garden, feeling a new concern that the plants should not shrivel and die under the relentless summer sun. The phrase 'transferred anxiety' presented itself to her. She was as irritated by it as if a smug stranger had whispered it in her ear. Jargon like that was quite useless. In any case, surely it was the same anxiety, not transferred at all? She remembered how her mother, in the week of her grandmother's death, had gone about the house, plucking dead blooms from the vases, her fingers nervously efficient, the flesh about her mouth soft and bland with grief. Women effaced the signs of decay because they lived at its heart. Surely that was very simple?

Alice moved a step down the driveway, her reflections at a temporary point of clarity. She could sense a new anger in herself. She could no longer bear evasions or half-truths; they were as offensive as lies. Intimations of birth, small lacings of pain, were thrusting her into this hard anger, developing it as precisely as a twin embryo.

Moving down the path, her awareness lifted upward and outward to the surface of her body. It was pleasant to stand there, the late afternoon sun warming her neck, the dusty hose slithering and uncoiling behind her like a live thing as she tugged it round the corners of the house. When she had turned on the tap there had been a rush of surprisingly hot water, followed by the cool underground stream that she had to regulate with her finger, spreading the single, heavy outpour into a fierce, wide spray until her finger ached from the pressure.

It was typical of their garden that there should be no nozzle on the hose. She had never before felt much interest in gardening, so she found she was ill-equipped and ignorant about basic things. She knew all the more obvious names – roses, geraniums, violets and daisies – and discovered other names stored in her memory from childhood, but many of them she could not attach to particular flowers. Every now and again she bought little plants from a shop she had noticed near the supermarket. She liked the ceremony of choosing them. They came in plastic, earth-filled containers, growing densely like a small forest with a proportionate wooden signpost. After a while, with very little care, they would sprout lovely, anonymous blooms.

Their garden was a fairly large one, about two-thirds of an acre, though, like the house itself, it was in the state of semi-neglect in which a series of temporary residents leave a place. It had the usual Johannesburg features, but only in an inferior, parodic version of the lush gardens that throve on either side of them, where cool sprinklers turned and black gardeners trimmed the hedges, their voices, in desultory conversation with the maid or passers-by, floating over the sleepy silence of the afternoons.

Alice and Brian had a grape-vine arbour, bearing small, inedible green grapes that grew no larger than beads, and were thoroughly infested by all the fungi and pests that the gardening columns, which she had now begun to read, grew scientific and murderous about. There were fruit trees in varying conditions of health, three good apple trees, a few peach and plum trees whose fruit was rotten before it was ripe, a fig tree and one bushy quince. Alice did not quite know what to do with the quinces – hard, furry, lime-coloured things that seemed intractable among the softer summer fruits.

Apart from the flowerbeds and fruit trees, and a spreading, uncontrollable compost heap, there was kikuyu grass, a name she remembered from her childhood. The wiry, leaping African word described the grass very well. Each piece was like a K turned over onto its legs and, once rooted the legs took off in the rapid tentacular way of a cartoon plant, soon covering great stretches of muddy earth. She could remember her father lecturing her on the difference between kikuyu and Kentucky blue grass. Kentucky blue, its name trailing the ideal vision of the American ranch-type house and white picket fence of their Cape suburb in the 1950s, was real lawn grass. It was a true green, and came shyly out of the soil in tender, separate blades, merging into a thicker green around the edges of their small luridly blue swimming pool. Kikuyu had been known to destroy fences, an un-South African and un-neighbourly habit that had banished it from most middle-class property. She found that she preferred kikuyu, its springiness and its stupid, bulldozing vigour, much as she had come to like the cool shabbiness of their house. Good taste – even the casually disarrayed good taste of their friends – had come to seem an empty thing.

Recalling her father's enthusiastic voice, the grass and the pool, Alice found that patches of her childhood fell into place. Her pregnancy and the gardening put her in touch with forgotten' areas of the past. Sometimes, on days like today, there was a small current of cool air under the heat, carrying the very flavour and smell of earlier days. It would softly bump into her as she went about the house or garden, surprising her with its sweetness.

She bent over the tap, removing her wedding-ring to rinse the dry, caked earth off her hands. Bending rather heavily, she looked down at the damp, reddened palms. So much of her life had slipped away unnoticed. She could no longer remember how she had arrived here, in this place, at this point in time. Choices and decisions had vanished into a tangled network behind her.

She stood briefly at the back door. Their lawn was really only a lawn in this patch just behind the house, where it had been properly mown and cultivated. For the rest it was rough, yellow and interrupted by stony patches. In the wilder parts of the garden were the stone outlines of what had once been terraces and rockeries, now blurred and defunct, like a suburban Stonehenge overgrown by the grass of a newer era.

The garden was too large to care for properly. And there was never enough rain. She had found it difficult to adjust to the dryness of the Transvaal, not simply the lack of the ocean, but the immense aridity that hung like a pressure behind the small storm showers, waiting to reassert itself as the spattered drops dried up in defeat. As a child she had known little about the Transvaal, but in the colouring of her imagination it was a distant region of disaster, chiefly because of the sinkhole or mining accidents that would claim the Cape headlines for days at a time. One of these had been particularly vivid. A child had fallen down a disused mine shaft and had lain there a long time before the body could be brought to the surface. The report had been accompanied by a crude sketch, a line with bristle for grass indicating the surface of the earth, and then a thicker line twisting interminably downward until the artist's thick white cross marked the spot where the body was assumed to lie. The proportions of the drawing had stunned her mind, awakening a vast, cold adult sorrow that had momentarily invaded the secure boundaries of childhood. It had occupied her dreams for some time.

She went inside. She and Brian had been in the house for a year. The previous tenants, called Marais, were a mining engineer and his wife. Their first child had been born just before they moved out, and when Alice called to look over the house, Mrs Marais was uncomfortably pregnant. She had given Alice that sense of being a hard-hipped girl that a pregnant woman infallibly conveys to a childless one. They were a nice, competent couple. When they moved out, the house was impeccably clean, the shelves newly lined with red and white waxed paper. Alice was daunted by the woman's efficiency. She herself always left places with objects spilling out of plastic bags and an uneasy sense of rubble in corners, unexplained cardboard boxes and curtain-rods scattered over the lawn.

Now it was her turn to be pregnant, and stand watering the garden in suitable young mother's frocks, dresses she had adopted to reassure herself that the new role was possible. Her pregnancy, after five years of marriage, had taken them by surprise. They were so inwardly resigned to a childless marriage that her pregnancy was well on its way before they accepted it. As the weeks passed, Alice was filled with a panic-stricken excitement.

The sensations of early pregnancy were at first as she had been led to believe by books and folklore. Outwardly she was often passive and somnolent, but inwardly the upheaval was more vigorous than she had thought possible. It was as though a small tree had taken root in her, gripping the floor of the womb with its roots and sending its branches shooting out of her breasts. Its simple assertiveness was comic. She was reminded of the bean plants they had cultivated as children as part of school biology lessons in elementary growth patterns. They covered a speckled bean with soggy cotton wool and charted its progress up the sunny kitchen window: root-threads, a thrusting stem. Sometimes she could almost hear the sour buzz of fermentation within her.

The pregnancy brought a kind of peace to her relationship with Brian. The first years of marriage had been uneven, difficult. There were times

61

of closeness and moments when she could hardly distinguish the border between her consciousness and his. One night, watching him lean over to switch off a lamp, his head tilted and feminine in outline, she felt a small shock of mingled perception, as if she had caught sight of herself in a mirror she had forgotten was there. Yet each seemed to be awaiting in the other some central reassurance that neither had the confidence to give. So there was often a distance between them, a dead area that sat heavily at the centre of their marriage. The coming child simplified things, gave them a pattern they did not have to forge themselves, day after day. They turned with relief to the world of expectant parents: a cot to buy, booking a bed at the nursing-home, visits to the doctor. Their lovemaking, too, was different. It was no longer so fierce or selfish, but gentle, languorous, circular, as if drawn in under the half-comic dominance of her swelling abdomen.

As her pregnancy advanced the lazy peace of the first few months began to slip away. Her stomach grew uncomfortably heavy; she was uglier. She was becoming a pale host-body, a receptacle for another life. This denial of her self caused her a curious kind of suffering. The explosion within her was cruelly forcing her onto the outskirts of her own life.

One afternoon she was with her mother-in-law, watching her as she demonstrated how to bottle fruit. The older woman's grey hair was newly-set, curling crisply to her neck, which was still slightly reddened from the hairdryer. She moved about her kitchen, every gesture that of a woman at home in her territory. Alice was amazed at the elaborate procedures involved in bottling fruit, the slow heating of the jars, the process of turning them upside down to ensure an airtight fit. She could see her mother-in-law enjoyed the ritual, that she liked the handing on of traditional wisdom. Alice watched the deliberate movements of her hands over the jars, the skin on the back of the hands slightly mottled with browner spots. What were they called? Grave spots. Or death spots. As if death casually drummed on your hand in warning, before reaching out with a fuller grasp. What a melodramatic figure death was, like the old lady in *Hansel and Gretel*, poking at the children through the bars as she fattened them up.

Her mother-in-law's voice broke into her reflections. She glanced at Alice as she scooped soft fruit into a jar.

'Do you know what they call pregnancy in Afrikaans?'

'No.' Her tone was expectant, interested.

'*Die ander tyd.*'

'Good heavens – but that's very accurate.'

'Yes.' Her mother-in-law smiled, nodding, amused at her vehemence. She said no more. She was not a woman for personal exchanges.

Later, Alice pondered the phrase. It was accurate. She did feel as if she was living in a subtly altered perspective, passing down one of those time corridors that science-fiction stories always seemed to explore. But if, she thought with persistent, chilling logic, you passed into a time tunnel, who was to say you would ever make it back to the sunny realities of the garden you left behind? What if it was the dream that increasingly claimed you? The questions could not be anwered. Still, the words comforted her. She liked the way the phrase was passed on, like a secret baton in an endless relay race, thrust into the hand of the new runner, offering to the palm its small warmth and consolation.

In late pregnancy the frustration she felt sometimes rose to a frenzy that would not let her sit still. One morning she slept later than usual and woke with a stale headache. As she woke she heard the gardener, Solomon, outside, singing his usual joyless hymns below her window. Sometimes she liked to hear him, starting softly, the music rising to great reverberant phrases as he got into the swing of the work. He was an itinerant gardener, appearing at intervals to help with heavier tasks. Today his singing irritated her. She sat up. She poked her head out of the window. She was even more annoyed to see that he was watering the garden.

'Solomon, why are you watering the flowers? I have told you that I will water the flowers. You must dig up the front flowerbeds. They are full of weeds.'

'But the madam she does not water the flowers. The flowers they die, madam.'

It was true. She would not allow the truth.

'But Solomon, I need you to do the heavy work. Don't worry about the flowers. Leave them alone.'

'But madam . . .'

She cut in. His words came out of his mouth so slowly. He was preparing for the old argument to be enjoyably rehearsed. On another day she would have played along. Today his slowness infuriated her. Why did he never obey her?

'Please just do as I say, Solomon.' She flung on her dressing gown and went outside. She pulled the hose away from him.

'Come, Solomon, I will show you.'

She spoke grimly. He followed, still smiling. He did not realize that she was in earnest.

'This is what I want you to do. See.'

She dug the spade into the flowerbed, throwing up chunks of earth. He put back his head. She noticed big flat drops of sweat near his hairline. He laughed. He found it really funny to see a white woman digging. He scratched his head.

'And the flowers, madam?'

'I will look after them, Solomon. This is your job. You must finish this by twelve o'clock. This would be a very nice garden if you worked properly.'

As she spoke she believed it. His laziness really thwarted her. He was always taking breaks. She would come outside and find him cleaning his shoes, or ironing his trousers in the sun. Or he would have disappeared completely to fetch his drycleaning. He had an amazing amount of drycleaning.

He looked at her in real surprise. Then his eyes slid away from hers. He was becoming sullen.

'I am not a machine, madam.'

'I know you are not a machine, Solomon, but you waste my time when you do things that I can do myself. Why do you waste my time? Do you think I pay you to waste my time here?' She walked away. She was shaking with anger, and close to tears, as though everything would be different and better if only Solomon would work more efficiently.

Later, she flushed as she recalled her tone, a parody of the capricious white madam. How could she do it? She had ruined a pleasant relationship. It was inexplicable, a fit of some kind, a form of possession.

At other times she came close to losing all control. One hot afternoon she was lying on her bed, reading, when an electric saw started up next door. The sound curved up into the air like a model aeroplane, dying away and then beginning again. It set up an unendurable pressure in her head. She flung down her book and ran outside. She scarcely knew what she meant to do.

She ran across the garden to the fence, tearing the skin of her legs on the thorny undergrowth. There was a hedge on the other side of the fence, so she knelt, finding a thin patch to peer through. On the other side, surprisingly close to her face, she could make out the cool, quiet outline of a swimming pool. Beyond it, near a big wrought-iron gate, stood a cluster of pine trees. The branches were being lopped off; logs with naked white ends were piling up on the ground. She could see the splinters flying upward. The calm of the scene, like a woodland engraving, merely fanned her rage. She could not believe that there was nobody there. She needed someone to call to account for the outrage she felt. Seething emotions prodded her on, as sharply as if needles were being plunged into her flesh. She knew she was glaring through the fence like a mad-woman, kneeling in a ridiculous position, sweating profusely.

She ran out at their rickety front gate and around the corner to the big iron gate she had just seen. It was locked. She stood there, her body as rigid as the bars, unable to attract attention above the noise of the saw. There were two workmen, but they were too far away, preoccupied with the task. Nobody had seen her.

Suddenly the rage left her. Her body went slack, and she felt damp and sleepy. She yawned. She relaxed against the gate, letting her forehead rest on the cool metal. It was as pleasant as a pillow. As she walked home, weak tears slid down her cheeks. She felt bored and cheated. Nobody had told her the truth.

After these losses of control, she felt some shame, though the incidents passed from her memory unusually quickly, like a dream that slides whole out of the mind just before dawn. In retrospect, she could not laugh at her behaviour, absurd though it was. Her actions seemed to spring from some deep protest within herself. Too much of her life was being sub-dued and ignored.

One evening, after another outburst, she tried to tell her husband what it was like. She lay on her elbow, sipping the cup of tea he had just brought her. He sat close to her, knowing she was troubled. He stroked her hair.

'Is there anything I can do?' he said.

She spoke with difficulty. 'I do such . . . silly, irrational things . . .' Her voice sounded high in her head. Words were useless. She could feel the real dimensions of the thing slipping away as she spoke.

Later that night she lay within the circle of her husband's arm, drifting on the edges of sleep. She saw herself walking into the garden and picking up the hose. Lifting the raw, open end to her eye, she looked down a dark tunnel. In it were women of all ages, her mother, her aunt, her cousins, women in the pain of labour, women bent over the dead bodies of their children, women tugging small bodies out of darkness, women in all the final postures of grief, woe and abandonment. Their tenderness was obscene. She would have liked to put her foot out, to turn aside her face, to brake the slippery speed at which she was sliding along to join them. She feared the harsh, puzzling truth she had seen at the end of that journey.

Jack Cope

Harry's Kid

The duty nurse pulled back the sheet and he looked, under the flat neutral light of the theatre, at the lithe little figure, now slackened and death-like. Jet black unruly hair in a mass of close curls made the girl's face seem small; a pale brown face, the head held slightly to one side, the lips open and eyes half closed. Beautiful but changing, fading, as if some expression of joy had been there the moment before she was hit and still faintly lingered. The shock had been sudden, swift, unseen, like a bullet through the brain. The body was uninjured, not a scratch or a bruise, the skin slightly clammy and cool. She was about twelve or thirteen and under-sized, the stomach flat, the rising muscles of the thighs, an hour ago full of agile force, now unsprung. Every nerve and sinew inert, and she lay breathing shallow and her pulse a thready flutter.

He examined her carefully but rapidly, and all the while above his trained clinical reserve there came back to him a curious inner sense of singleness and beauty. So many races, currents, destinies met in this little street arab in a sudden harmony; and she lay there stretched on the theatre table, perhaps dying.

Returning to her head he drove the thoughts out of his mind. When he opened the eyes they stared black and unseeing into his. The pupils were dilated, though he noted they were of even size. There was a wide open wound in the scalp above the right ear but no sign of local bone fracture. Internal contusions and possibly a fracture at the base of the skull – he was guessing. The scalp wound needed a suture and he could do that anyway, if there was nothing else by which he might stave off the feeling of powerlessness in the face of overwhelming damage.

'There's lice in her hair,' the nurse said.

'Have it all off, and back with her quickly for stitching. Then X-ray. And I want Dr Welburn called, please.'

'Dr Welburn! Do you mean . . .'

'Yes, I mean it.'

The nurse, taller than Dr Harry Engers even in her flat shoes, glanced across doubtfully and with a start met his full dark eyes.

'Very well,' she said.

'Hurry please. And by the way, what's her name?'

She looked at the card – 'Baatjes. Dina Baatjes.'

The patient was wheeled out and the next brought in, a youth with three stab wounds in the back. Engers patched up the warped and degraded body, working swiftly with delicate and exact movements. It was a Friday night in early December, hot and still with a full moon over the drowsing city. Every ambulance poured in more casualties and blood ran on the floor of the hospital reception bay. When the doors opened he could hear the noises and the hurrying feet, somebody crying, the moans of an injured man.

The girl was brought back and he did the suture cleanly so the gash was hardly visible. Her face, without its frame of black curls, had a new pity, waxlike and immobile. There was a fleck of blood on one of the even pearly teeth that he had not noticed. He felt over the jaws and again examined the mouth and throat interior and the ears but found no injury. Then the child was turned on her side and he did a lumbar puncture. Watching the slow drip into the test tube, he was struck again with a sense of his futility. The cerebrospinal fluid was clouded and discoloured pink.

'Brain damage, of course,' he said aloud to himself. The nurse sealed the tube for an urgent lab test. They added nothing more but were thinking – what chance has this spark of a life, and still more, what hope of recovery without permanent disability? He endorsed the card CRITICAL in heavy blue and recommended intensive care. The theatre sister signed the patient out and he saw Dina Baatjes wheeled off to the X-ray department.

'Nurse Farman, will you be able to special that patient?' he asked the duty nurse.

'What, tonight!'

'Yes, tonight. Look, she might have a fighting chance. And, well, there's this staff shortage in the wards. I wouldn't ask you otherwise.'

'Really, doctor, I . . .'

'You can say no.'

'I'll do it, of course. Only I was thinking of a good night's sleep.' She laughed merrily, flushing up, and then was suddenly serious. It was not for the staff shortage, bad as it was. He asked her because he had an instinctive faith in her, in her naturalness and vitality and also in the current of tenderness that ran deeply in her, or so at least he imagined.

She was an Afrikaner girl from some dorp in the endless wastes of sand and thorn scrub south of the Kalahari, nearly six feet tall with green eyes, high cheekbones and vivid colouring. More than common humanity, she was a phenomenon, a life force. In his year at the hospital he had not once seen her daunted or unwilling; what suffering she hid in her heart he did not know. A few times, under stress, he had seen tears flood her eyes that she tried to hide. Soon she would laugh again and continue her work; and the patients, waiting for her, smiled as she came to their bed-sides.

An hour later Welburn, visiting brain specialist, arrived to examine the girl and Harry Engers attended, together with a senior surgeon of the hospital staff and a radiologist. With the shock and exhaustion, Dina's blood-pressure had fallen dangerously low and her pulse and respiration fluttered weakly on. Her face, smooth against the pillows and bandages, had settled to a painless calm; the eyes were closed and on the lips there seemed to hover the phantom of a smile. The X-ray plates showed a fracture of the skull base and the tests confirmed haemorrhage, probably from severe brain injury.

'The condition is inoperable, I'm afraid,' Dr Welburn said. 'I'll see her again tomorrow night. Let me know how she is.'

Engers understood what he meant – Let me know if she's still alive. He listened to the specialist's instructions and asked a few questions. The extent of the damage might be assessed later by electroencephalograph, depending on the degree of initial recovery.

'What happened to her?' Welburn asked.

'Playing in the street, I believe. She was hit by a car, a fast sports car. And, oh yes, the man did not stop.'

'Ah, so! – Uncommon face,' he said, looking down at the girl. 'She might stand a chance if she were better nourished.'

They shook hands at the door and Welburn glanced into the dark eyes of the young intern. 'Maybe something can be done, we'll see. You'll keep me in the picture?'

'Yes.'

'And take things a bit easier. Spare yourself, Engers, you've got a long way to go.'

Engers turned back to see the instructions were put into effect.

Dina was moved to an intensive care unit in the children's section and the apparatus at once set up for intravenous feeding and a stomach tube. In the next few hours the small body rallied slightly and the breathing and heart action slowly improved. At midnight Nurse Farman came into the small ward on relief duty, looking rosy and dark-eyed from an early sleep. She joked with the doctor while she took in the situation and studied the pulse chart. Softly she felt over the cheeks of the unconscious child.

'Poor thing,' she said. Everything she did, her expressions and gestures, radiated a kind of reliance that caused eyes to follow her, even those of terminal patients, the dying – hopes flaming up against their own certainties; a little frightening too.

Engers felt with a momentary lift of mood like some isolated commander dug in and calling up every resource he knew in a fight with death – science, skill, humanity, perseverance.

Then later, as he left the buildings and crossed a wide courtyard under the faint stars, his thoughts turned with a sudden revulsion. Bafflement, hopelessness swept over him. How easy it was, so ingrained, so compulsive to hurt and kill and destroy, to scatter the whole earth by violence or neglect with uncountable victims, with sorrow and death. What could he do against this, a single individual, a mere speck, a member of the most ill-used race in all time? Why not answer blow for blow, an eye for an eye? 'Spare yourself!' He knew what was meant, and he could not do it; for there was some inseverable bond – perhaps some weakness in his blood – that drove him always on and caused him to feel each hurt himself. He walked on gloomily as if he carried the night on his back. Near dawn . . . the moon low above the shoulder of the mountain and turning already a pale yellow.

Dina lay for day after day, for weeks, in total oblivion. She had not once been left alone, and all the facilities of a great hospital had been concentrated, like sun rays through a burning-glass, to preserve the glimmer of her life. The slow drip of an enriched milk by tube into her stomach, a saline solution fed through the veins of a helpless arm, kept her nourished. A tube sucked away saliva and another inserted by tracheotomy in her throat kept her lungs from filling. A blueing in her skin was a signal to the watching nurse to give her long gulps of oxygen. The treatment was changed, drugs administered cautiously and the reaction monitored.

The struggle was becoming an agony to Harry Engers. Against the general overwork and the staff shortfall at the time he had to make his own provision for a special nurse continually at the bedside – he, one of the most junior interns. He had this small authority, and they left him to it, but it meant placating the matrons and leaning on the goodwill of the sisters and nursing staff. Criticism seeped down to him and he began to be personally associated with the case as if he also was ill. They called Dina 'Harry's Kid' and behind the nickname was a hint of resentment.

Dina's hair was now an inch or two long, a nest of short glossy curls. The wound had healed and X-rays showed the bone fracture uniting. Physically she was slowly mending and a slight tinge of health stole into the pale face. The tubes could be taken for periods from her mouth and then she lay, composed and tranquil, as if asleep and on the point of waking.

Engers sat at the bedside and stared at the face which had become so intimately woven into his thoughts that he began to realise uneasily what importance it had assumed for him. The face rose in his dreams. Harry's Kid. Partly he could put it down to an insistent and inescapable feeling of pity (call it sentimentality?) and plain stubbornness, the ordinary desire to succeed with a difficult case. He knew, though, that the dream image was a reflex of his own myth. But objectively there was the final disturbing thing for him, the mysterious beauty of the face, all human, that he had seen at the first glance. Would he have become so engrossed had she been a plain little imp, or disfigured and maimed like some of the patients in the children's wards?

He opened her eyes and tried to connect her vision with his moving hand, with bright objects, a hand mirror, a pencil light. He repeated her name. 'Dina, Dina, do you hear me? You are getting better, you are going to get well. Jy sal weer lewe – you will come alive again.' Her body was purely spastic, decerebrate. She lay like a thing, alive and no more. Somehow the brain had become disconnected and under the crisp new curls was not a thinking mind but a polyp, a mass of unconscious plasm.

He found out where Dina's parents lived, in a tenement off Canterbury Street, and he himself brought her mother, Sophie, to the hospital in his car. Sophie was a decrepit and wrinkled little laundry-woman of not much more than forty, and humble. She made him feel her greatest happiness was to be walked over and trampled.

'Is it Dina?' she cried shrilly, laughing. 'Dina, wat maak djy da?' Dina's wide eyes stared away into a corner of the ceiling. To Sophie, the white, grey and pink ward, the magnificent young woman in a white cap and uniform (Nurse Farman was on duty), the great corridors and glass doors, were so stupendous that she could not imagine why anyone had allowed her in. She did not seem to grasp that here lay her body's child, ill almost to death. They had told her at the inquiry counter when she first called that Dina, who was her sixth, was being looked after but could not yet be visited. She had two smaller children as well, and no time for the long trek to the hospital.

The girl's father, Arend Baatjes, was a painter and handyman, tall and silent, with thick black hair and an old fashioned country manner. He came later and stood at the bedside, trembling and twisting his paint-splashed cap into a knob. Again there was no recognition.

'Dinatjie,' he pleaded, 'Dina, my kind.' He wiped away his tears and turned, questioning, to the slim young man who had brought him.

'She's going to get well, Mr Baatjes,' Engers said, 'I hope.'

'Dankie, my seur.'

In the common room on a Saturday morning they discussed the case of Harry's Kid. Since he could not avoid it altogether, Engers tried to keep the talk on a flat medical level. And all the while he felt they were getting at him. They suspected what they sometimes called his mono-mania, the intensity he put into the most everyday work and the pace he set. And here was a case on which old points could be hung.

'What do you do next with the kid, anyway?' The questioner was Magor, a young Canadian on transfer from a Toronto hospital, big and powerful as any lumberjack.

'Wait,' Engers lit a cigarette.

'You know what, Harry, you can't put so much . . . I mean, a case shouldn't eat you up.' He paused, and getting no response he went on. 'I guess there isn't any of us with the talent you have, Harry. Only set yourself limits. Look at all the thousands we get through here, the hun-dreds who can't even be given beds, waiting outside. How can you take each patient on your soul? Hell man, you're going to crack up. It's not asked of you, it's not asked of the profession.'

'Well, who can speak for the medical profession?' Engers smiled, holding himself in and his narrow, sensitive face showing nothing. He liked Magor, perhaps envied him his physique.

'Time's coming when you'll just crack up,' the Canadian repeated. 'Or if you don't, the staff will. You can drive them nuts.'

'Who for instance, Paul?'

'Well, take Farman for one.'

'Farman never said anything.'

'Look Harry, some things you may not notice. Take this kid – cerebral laceration, it must be three months and there's been no real improvement. But you don't let up, no, not at all. It's just one example. A man can't get personally involved, he can't spend all this – this passion. You're not a priest or a god, Harry. I guess you've got to settle for being just a doctor.'

'All right, I'm a doctor, and then I'm a man, and beyond that I'm a Jew, and beyond that I'm a son of decent hard-working parents. And one day I may be a father myself. It never ends, and I am personally involved. I am, now and always. Don't ask me to let up, Paul. That's something you have no right to say to me.' He spoke softly but his face was white and tense.

Afterwards he was bitter with himself. An ordinary conversation and he had to go on to drag in his parents and his race, and his hands had actually shaken when he prided himself on iron nerves and the steadiest hand in the hospital. He was not angry with Paul Magor. Paul had given him the other side, that was all, the side of plain horse-sense as he called it. Referring to the case, he had meant that Dina's chances were about exhausted. If she lived it might be as a helpless imbecile or at best a cripple. And in that light to prolong her life could prove a cruel trick, inhuman and absurd. This he tried to put out of his thoughts, to convince himself that the scales were held evenly and that life came first. Life, life . . . what sort of a life had she had till now, and what of the future?

On the way to see Dina, he stepped in at the general children's ward. One of the beds was empty and rumpled. He glanced about for the occupant, then he saw a little creature wriggling across the open floor of the ward. With quick deft jerks the child dragged himself by his free arms. Engers approached quietly and squatted down. 'Hello.' A small bright face turned up to him in surprise; blue eyes, and suddenly a dimpled, mischievous smile. 'Hello oldtimer.'

Engers laughed outright at this irrepressible sauciness. 'And who are you, Big-boy?'

'I'm Spinal Ataxy.'

The strange shock of this answer passed swiftly over the young surgeon. 'Oh, so that's who you are. And where are you off to?'

'I'm going to visit him.' He nodded at a nearby cot.

'Who's he?'

'Oh, he's a Muscular Atrophy.'

'Is that so!' Engers picked up the small sad bundle, feeling under the gown the limp legs that would never function. 'And what's your other name?'

'Jonathan.'

'I'll come and see you again, Jonathan; would you like that?' An eager nod. 'And what shall I bring you?'

'Bring me a grasshopper – a live one!' The little boy burbled with laughter. Engers put him in the cot with his helpless friend and promised to do something about the grasshopper. In a corner bed a small girl with long yellow hair lay with her face to the wall, quietly sobbing. He left the ward and crossed the corridor to Dina's door. Nurse Farman was there with a probationer, and the younger woman went out. 'Any change?'

'No, doctor.'

'Is this case getting on your nerves?'

'Not at all, why?'

'Driving you nuts?' He stood with his back turned, studying the charts, but he was aware of her sudden embarrassment.

'Has Dr Magor been talking to you?'

'Yes, he's worried. He thinks I'm sending you up the wall.'

'I never said that and I'm telling the truth. I want Dina to live – I do, I would breathe my own life into her if I could. I pray for her to God. But, doctor . . .'

'But why have you stopped believing it possible?'

'It's not that, only what if her mind never comes right and she's just – a thing?'

'Do you believe God would allow that?'

She shot him a single glance, hurt and a little panic-stricken, and busied herself with the patient. After a while she said flatly: 'I think something may be happening to Dina. She's getting weaker and . . . and I don't know what it is but I just feel it.'

'Who's on tonight?'

'Nurse Joubert.'

'I'm going to a party, but I'll phone her.'

The house looked over a stretch of white sand and beyond it across the immense space of the ocean with a low moon and a path of light on the water. He was relaxed and listened to the music and the light-hearted talk. Some of the guests sat on the parapet and watched the moon setting.

'The year is about finished in February,' a woman's voice said, 'and it only starts again next December. For the rest of the time one might as well be asleep.'

'Are you like a cicada, coming to life for the three hot months?'

The woman laughed. 'Do they do that? Yes, sometimes I just want to stop the clocks and sleep.'

Dr Engers put down his drink and went in to call the hospital. Nurse Joubert hesitated, and then she told him the patient was in difficulties and that Dr Magor was with her. He could sense something in the tone of the remote voice and he said at once, 'Okay, I'm coming in. I'll be there in half an hour.'

He found Dina in extreme distress and the frail thread of her life at its thinnest. Her breath had almost failed and she had developed pneumonia. For thirty-six hours the struggle – and the vigil – lasted, and Dr Engers was seldom out of the ward for more than a few hours. Antibiotics and intensive physiotherapy of the chest fought off the disease.

He had a long while in which to think round the case and he began to see in himself a kind of inflated egoism, an ignoble craving for justification if not success. In a world stunned with needless suffering, what was a little personal triumph? 'Dina,' he said aloud when he was alone with her. 'Dina, you've got to pull through. Do you hear me? For your sake and my own.' My own . . . my own – that was it. He thought the staff looked at him in a peculiar way, all except Nurse Farman. He had come to terms with her and she stood by him without being asked; she arrived in her own time, fresh and blooming, and grasped everything in the net of her strong, tender spirit.

Dina survived. Shell-like and almost unreal, the small head lay on the pillow and the flame in her seemed to kindle. Her coughing reflex improved and new strength crept back into her heartbeat. Engers threw his full intensity into the general hospital work and he tried to keep away from the special ward. Then he would come quietly in for a few minutes to see his 'Kid'. There was a change in her, or maybe it was an illusion like sun alternating with shadow over the veld. The nurses said nothing beyond routine remarks.

On a calm windless morning some weeks later Nurse Farman came into the ward early. She drew the curtains and opened the windows to the sun. Turning to the bed, she thought, with a faint start, that the girl's large dark eyes were fixed on her, following her movements. When she looked again a moment later, she was still held in that deep, eerie gaze. Now she moved slowly to the bedside and her heart quickened. Dina's eyes still followed her. Then the pale lips parted in a smile and very softly she said 'Hello.'

'Hello, my treasure,' the nurse said, and for no reason her eyes brimmed with tears. 'You've made it, little one. Lord, Lord!' She pressed the bell urgently and a probationer ran in. 'Call Harry, quickly.'

'Harry?'

'Dr Engers. Oh, don't just stand there.'

'Is it serious?'

'Yes it's serious – I mean it's wonderful. She's come round. Look.' They bent over the bed and the child blinked at them, half smiling and confused.

They did not find Dr Engers for some time, and when he came in later in the morning trying to look detached and unmoved in a professional manner there was a disappointment waiting for him. Dina was asleep, and save for a new warmth in her skin her condition might be no different from the weeks and months of unconsciousness which had passed. He felt her pulse – steady. 'Are you quite sure?'

'Of course I'm sure. How could I be mistaken?'

'She said hello?'

'Yes, so quietly. Oh I could have fallen over backwards.'

He sat gazing at the face, so familiar and yet subtly altered. What had happened? What benign force of nature had been at work beyond human grasp, reknitting the tattered threads of the brain? And if the healing had gone so far, why should it not become complete, and revive and revitalize the whole mind and body? He waited a long time at the bedside, but the child slept on.

The next month and a half were times of bewildering change and experience for the injured girl. Hours of special therapy slowly unlocked the springs of her limbs. She cried easily and talked incessantly, sometimes pouring out a mere babble of words. Only one thing held up the speed of her recovery – with the return of consciousness had come pain. Pain, torturing pain, sometimes racked her whole frame and blinded her with agony. And then the pain would go as if it had never been.

Engers was there in the general children's ward when Dina made her first trial at walking. She had thrown on him the full violence of her childish love and she clung round his neck, laughing and crying, while she tried to manage her weak and ungainly legs. The children in the surrounding beds joined in a shrill chorus of laughter and shouts.

Nurse Farman brought Dina a red dotted dress with a flared skirt over its crisp petticoat and she helped her dress and arranged her shining curls;

and she had new white socks and shoes and a red hair-ribbon to match her frock when Harry took her home. She seemed to have grown older and was nervous and reserved, clinging tightly to a miniature handbag. As the car pulled up at the arch which gave entrance to the tenement yard the children recognised Dina and they looked at her and at the young white man with unaccustomed awe. Sophie came meekly out and every minute the crowd gathered.

In the small cobbled square surrounded by the grim peeling faces of the buildings there was hardly room to move among the children and the Saturday afternoon loafers, the dogs and flapping pigeons. Sophie held her handkerchief to her eyes but she had time to take in the strange lost look of her girl, the pretty dress and the shoes. Dina had grown, she came up to the shoulder of the doctor, the beautiful clever man with his white teeth and serious eyes.

Arend Baatjes, Dina's father, was moderately drunk and he tried to make a speech. He kept on starting: 'Doctor, my seur, you know a . . . you know a man's heart, I mean . . .'

'Thank you Mr Baatjes,' Engers shook him by the hand. 'I know your heart and it's a solid gold-lined model . . .' the people roared with laughter and clapped, '. . . and I'm not your seur, Arend. I'm really your servant. And I've done a little job for you on Dina, that's all.'

The crowd took this for another prime piece of humour. Arend kept his dignity. 'Excuse me, Doctor is not my servant,' he said. 'He is a king . . .' He struggled on but the words got rolled up in his teeth like cotton wool and stuck there.

Dina raised one hand timidly and waved her fingers as the doctor backed out towards the car. She was too overcome to speak or to cry. As Engers dived under the arch the noise and shouting and clatter of the poor streets closed over the girl again.

Leon de Kock

Something Great

I used to love the quiet of the night when I was young. I would lie in bed and listen to the stillness, disturbed by so many things: the insistent cricket right outside my window, the car passing at high speed, the train screeching to a halt, and the noise of neighbours laughing, neighbours fighting, neighbours' dogs barking, neighbours' cats making love, the neighbours' girl and her husband, both drunk, fighting in the neighbours' backyard, the neighbour threatening to shoot the girl's husband if he doesn't waai gou-gou, the sound of a gunshot terrifyingly close and, finally, the police coming to arrest the girl's husband.

I was lying in bed, listening to the stillness and the disturbances, when Brian came in, tiptoeing all the way to the room and closing the door softly behind him, taking care not to wake Ma and Dad – he was late.

'Late again,' I said, teasing him. Brian and I were on good terms, considering the fact that we were brothers.

Brian's face was beaming. I could see that he had 'something great' to tell me; Brian often came home like that. I would always listen to him intensely, living in his account of his fortunes and misfortunes.

He sat on his bed and said: 'Phew, that was great. Great!'

'So tell me, if it was so great,' I said, already feeling that painful urge to do some of the things he did.

He sat on my bed and spoke in soft tones. 'I've got something great to tell you. Tonight I did it. I've done it, an hour ago, and it was the greatest thing I've done in my life. Remember I told you I was going to Freddie van der Vyver? Well I went to his house, and we went for a game of pinball, but we were also looking for some chicks to chaff, so first we walked around.

'We were just walking around in the main street, when we saw Penny and Margaret, those blonde twins. I'm telling you, Henry, I thought those two chicks were real lousy, but let me tell you, they're not so bad, not so bad at all.

'Freddie chaffed them how's it, and we started talking to them. After a while Freddie asked them if they wouldn't like to take a walk around with us. I thought Freddie was taking a bit of a chance, but 's true's nuts, they said okay.

'We just walked around a bit, and spoke to the chicks. Freddie only knows how to chaff a chick, I'm telling you, my boy. It was dark already, and Freddie said maybe we should go for a walk in the park.'

Brian stopped speaking for a moment, looked down, and involuntarily I sighed with him.

'I mean, can you handle that? The park, no two ways about it, the park!'

Oh I saw the park all right. Dark, silent, and desolate. Penny and Margaret are bathed in virginal moonlight, and they're both wearing tiny skirts, their legs extending smoothly to their bare feet – their skin is smooth, and shines faintly in the whitish light.

'Then Freddie and Penny walked in front, and once we reached the park I saw he started kissing her. Well, listen, I wasn't going to sit out, so I put my arm around Margaret. We walked a bit, and then she put her arm around me. Freddie and Penny walked off in another direction, and I just stopped. I just stopped and kissed Margaret.'

The embrace – oh, the embrace, I knew it so well. I had seen it many times – in all the movies where at some time the hero and heroine passionately kissed. That fleeting moment of sensual union stuck deep in my brain. Here Brian had brought it into life again, and I saw it over and over. The park is long and black and silent. The grass is thick, but well cut, and dry. The wind is moving slowly, ruffling Margaret's hair. Strands of hair are falling over her face. As she becomes more passionately involved, her long fingers slowly move around Brian's neck, and they tighten their grip on one another, merging into one.

I began to breathe heavily and checked myself. Brian sensed my silence. He looked up at me, and impatiently I said: 'Well, so what happened?'

'Ag man, I had her. I'm telling you, Henry, once you get a chick to a certain stage, it's overs, then she's had it. So, right there, I just told her I wanted to. She said no, but I just told her to come on man and stop playing around. And so we did it.'

Brian's scanty narrative was food for my imagination. I saw the whole act played out over and over, from the moment he kissed her until the moment of that violent, electrifying shock that shook through both of them, and left them breathless, on the grass, in the park.

I knew it, I did know it. I had dreamt it once. The dream was so real I actually *really* felt it.

'Well that was it. And I'm telling you, Henry, it's the best thing in the world. There is nothing in the whole world that can be better. But wait, you want to see proof?' He pushed his jeans down. 'Look at it man, it's blue. There, can't you see? It's blue.'

That was the torture – the grotesque size of it. And that was how Brian left me, with the picture of his manifestation of manhood in my mind, and my hard effort lost inside my one hand.

C. J. Driver

The Cry

During vacations from university I used to have to work to make a little money to help with fees. One of the places I worked in once was a mealie-meal warehouse in the Eastern Transvaal, in a small town about 200 miles from Johannesburg and two miles from my father's farm. I had been offered thirty pounds a month for two months and was to act as foreman of the warehouse. This meant that I had to oversee a gang of about thirty Africans, all of them, with one or two exceptions, much older than me; their job was the unloading of the trains that brought the bags of mealie meal from upcountry, the storing of the bags, and the loading of the lorries which took the meal to the various retail stores in the district.

When I started work, I found that there was already an African foreman who had been doing the job for about six years, who was capable, and who was very popular with the gang of workmen. He was paid about half what I was to get. He was about forty, I suppose, and was called what most slightly educated Africans seem to be called, John. I never found out what his surname was. As soon as I found that I had, in fact, been brought in at double his salary to do a job which he had been doing well, I told him to carry on with the foremanship and that I would just help him when there was a rush order and would otherwise work with the rest of the Africans loading and unloading. I told him that I would not say anything to the white owner of the warehouse. I suppose that it was immoral of me to go on working at a job which I didn't do and in which I was earning more than I should have done. But I needed the sixty pounds badly. Strangely enough, John, the foreman, didn't seem to mind that I was earning double his salary, although I was half his age and without any experience at all. He did resent, as he later told me, having someone put in charge of him when he was doing the work perfectly well. He seemed, however, to accept the fact that since I was a white man, I should be paid

81

more than a black man for less work. I suppose that he had to accept that.

So I became a workman, carrying bags of mealie-meal. It is almost a skilled job – each bag weighs 180 lb. and one often has to carry the bag thirty yards. One does this on one's head. There is a special technique of arching one's back and keeping one's neck absolutely stiff, very much like weightlifting, I suppose. Two men, generally older or inexperienced people, heave the bag by its corners up into the air. One ducks under the bag, back arched, neck stiff and then steadies the bag on one's head with one's arms. Then one runs, or rather does a sort of shuffling short-paced run, to wherever the bag has to be dropped. One has to drop it exactly flat on its side for if one drops a mealie bag on to one of its corners from that height it bursts like a paper bag, even though it is made of strong hessian. One could not, if one was an African workman, afford to drop a bag, since part of one's wages was docked for each burst bag.

It was hot and stinking work. Mealie-meal is so finely ground that it seeps out of the bag, and to carry it on one's head means that the meal is continually dropping down one's face and neck and under one's clothes. It is also very hard work – one can tell how long a man has been a carrier by how bloodshot his eyes are. The strain is enormous and, according to a doctor friend whom I asked about this, most men would not be able to do this sort of work for more than ten years. Yet some of these men had been doing this job for nearly twenty.

The workmen were all incredibly strong – I saw a little African man (who I guess was part Khoi-Khoin – we all called him Bushman), who was about five foot tall and who weighed just over a hundred pounds, carry two of these bags at once on his head, that is, a total of 360 lb. The champion carrier was bigger than this, although he didn't in fact look all that strong. He was a Swazi, called Peter Nkosi Dhlamini, about six foot tall and weighing about 160 lb. He looked relatively slim, although he had a very deep chest. Most of his apparent strength was in fact balance – he was as graceful as an impala, light-footed and agile. Peter could carry three bags of meal on his head for about twenty-five yards and he didn't look unduly under strain, for he could manage even these at his own peculiar dancing jog. He used to say that he could carry four at a time but I didn't ever see him try this. Usually, and sensibly, he stuck to his one bag and with that would do his little dance to wherever it had to be dumped – skip, skip, shuffle, hop and then, usually with a loud whooping cry in Swazi, the bag would be dropped flat on its side at the loading point.

Peter and the African we called Bushman were very great friends, and I, in my turn, made as close friends as I suppose it was possible for a white boy of middle-class stock to make friends with two black workmen in South Africa. Bushman did not, I think, really trust me but because Peter seemed to take a liking to me, Bushman tolerated me – the basis of my friendship with the two was through Peter. He told me that he was the son of a minor headman in Swaziland but was working out of Swaziland to make money. His great ambition was to buy a big American car; the back seat would be big enough to make love in, he explained. He thought that I was mad to want a sports car. His amorous adventures were one of the great talking points among the gang of workmen – every morning he would be asked to describe whom he had had the night before and he would do so in great detail, to the accompaniment of chuckles and cheers from the rest of the workmen. At first I had to ask for a translation into English but when Peter discovered my interest in his sex-life he used to tell the stories in English, using Afrikaans or Swazi only when his English failed him or when he was describing more intimate details of a woman's body.

Probably many of his stories were lies because he enjoyed having an audience too much not to embellish them. Every time I asked him to explain one of the great cries he used when dumping a bag of meal he would come out with a new story. His favourite cry was what sounded like 'Slabba Bjhosjan', which he told me meant, 'Kill the Hippopotamus' – he told me, I think, three different stories about how this cry originated and I remember believing all three. Because he couldn't read or write, I assumed that the stories were either part of the oral literature of the tribes or were his own fictions.

Of all the cries which he used the strangest was one which he could not, or would not, translate for me. I heard him use it only once – when we had had to load all the five-ton delivery trucks used by the warehouse with bags of meal from an open rail truck which had arrived late one day. There was a storm coming and if mealie-meal gets wet it rots. We thought that we had about an hour to get the rail truck clear and the three lorries loaded and it seemed an almost impossible job. We worked very hard to get it done, all the same; the white owner of the warehouse had promised each workman ten shillings extra if the job was done before the storm broke, and ten shillings to a man who is earning less than a fiver a month is more than a tip. We all worked hard, but Peter hardest of all – he was prodigious. We worked in quarter hour shifts, half on, half resting, but he refused to go off shift and while the rest of his shift was panting and sweating in the shade, he kept on. He seemed to do twice as much actual carrying as anyone else too. Although the rest of the men were working at the run, he ran harder than them, seeming to carry two bags to everyone else's one. All of us were covered with mealie-meal – he was white with the stuff except where the sweat ran down, almost in black rivers on his skin. The rest of us took some energy from him – and after a time the extra pay began to seem unimportant. What mattered was that the job should be done before the storm came. But it was Peter who fired us all – duck, grab, stagger, jog, heave, and back to the rail truck for another bag.

We got the job finished in time. The white owner, who was obviously very surprised to see how far we had got, came just in time to see the climax of the loading. All of us had realized what Peter was up to, and, seemingly without consulting each other, left the last three bags for him. He was nearly out by this time but he too realized that we were giving him a chance to finish the job fittingly. The two loaders heaved the three bags, one after the other, on to Peter's head, until they stood almost as tall as him above him, a total weight of 540 lb. I didn't think he would manage the twenty yards to the truck, though I'd seen him carry three bags further than that before. He seemed to sink lower and lower as the weight of the bags pressed down. But he moved off, not at the usual jog, but staggering like an old man. After about fifteen yards it seemed that he would fall. I in fact started to move to help him, but stopped when I realized that the rest of the gang were not moving. Peter stopped, held on to the bags for a moment, and then danced three or four steps – 'danced' is the only word for what he did. Then he stopped, about three yards short of the truck, heaved and the bags went sailing flat on their sides into the truck. As he heaved he let out this great cry, a whooping, animal, incredible cry from some dark place inside the human body – it is impossible to write down what it was, what it sounded like, and, as he told me later, it could not be translated. It may not even have been a word or words at all. Only then did Peter fall, and the other Africans were at his side to help him before I could move. They were wild with excitement, because they knew, as we all knew, that we had seen a man do more than his body should have allowed him to. As they were carrying Peter into the shed next to the rail truck, the storm broke.

Peter recovered within half an hour. I sat with him in the shed, waiting for the time to knock off, and giving him cigarettes. Peter was not a humble man – he knew that he had done something marvellous and he liked being told so. Eventually, when he seemed fully settled and recovered, I asked him what the cry meant.

He told me that it had been used by the warriors of his tribe at the end of battles, to show either that the battle had been irredeemably lost or that the enemy were about to fly. The cry could not be translated, he said, because its meaning had been lost over the generations. He said that, as far as the tribe knew, it had been used for the first time somewhere in the north (and he waved his hand as if to include all Africa as his tribal domain) when his tribe had been fleeing from another and stronger tribe. A band of fifty warriors had been left behind in a valley to hold up the pursuing warriors, while the rest of the tribe, with its women and children, hid in the mountains. The rearguard held off pursuit for two days, until on the afternoon of the third day only three warriors had been left alive. They had sought the protection of rocks on the side of the valley and, using the assegais and arrows of their dead companions, had fought on. At last, only one warrior was still alive. He had walked out from the rocks to face the enemy and, just before he was killed, had thrown his spear, 'right over the heads of the enemy,' said Peter, 'so high that no one could see it, and as he threw he shouted this great cry so loud that the mountains on either side of the valley had fallen, covering both him and his enemy.'

I had no way of knowing whether the basis of the story was true – indeed, it may have been made up entirely for my benefit. But the cry itself, the one Peter had used, had to be believed; it was as real as anything I had ever known. I knew too that the Swazi tribe proper had been a relatively late creation, one of the results of the Zulu conquests – but I did not question Peter, for it did not really matter whether or not the story was true.

After the vacation, when I went back to university, I had no way of keeping in touch with Peter. When I came back for a holiday about a year later, I went round to the warehouse to see my friends there. I saw Bushman and John the foreman, but when I asked after Peter, they told me that he had been sacked. Apparently he had arrived at work one morning very drunk and had 'cheeked' the white owner – there had, as well, been some trouble about another workman's wife. They told me that I would probably find him in the African township, a little way from the village. I drove my father's car out there and asked for Peter and was eventually directed to a *pondokkie* where he was living. He was in and came to the door to greet me. He looked in a bad way – dressed in a dirty singlet, a pair of torn canvas trousers, and no shoes. His eyes had that peculiar glitter that is one of the signs of hunger and he had obviously lost weight.

Since I was a little broke myself and since I knew that my father had no job on the farm for Peter, there was not much that I could do for him. I gave him a pound and told him to meet me in the village next day when I promised to give him some better clothes. I met him as promised and gave him a gaudy shirt which I had been given for Christmas and which I couldn't wear, a dark suit which I had grown out of but which I thought would fit him, a pair of fairly good shoes which must have been a little large for him, several pairs of thick socks and some underpants. He was horribly grateful – and I hated doling out charity to him. What I should have done was to find him a job but I came home so seldom that I didn't know who to approach in the district – and my father had already had to lay off some of his workmen because the citrus crop had been bad that year. I told Peter all this but he said that he had to have better clothes before he could get a job. I saw him again several times that vacation, mainly in the distance; he seemed to be using the new clothes mainly to attract girls and little to help him find work. Once, when I stopped to talk to him, he said that he was hoping to get a job in a hotel but that there was no vacancy yet. He seemed to have some money by then, for he offered to repay me the pound I had given him; but I refused. The next time I saw him, I didn't get a chance to talk to him and soon after that I went back to university.

I didn't come home again for nearly a year and, when I did, I could not find Peter anywhere, even though I went to the township and asked for him. Bushman had left the warehouse and John the foreman didn't know where either Bushman or Peter were. John seemed very constrained but since that was a bad time, just after Sharpeville and Langa, I didn't press him too hard. Indeed, feeling against whites, even sympathetic whites, was such that when I told John I had been into the township, he told me that I was not wise to do so. Just before I left the warehouse, John came up quietly to me and said, 'Look, Master Arthur, I have heard that Peter and Bushman are in Dube in Johannesburg, but please don't tell anyone I told you that.' The *Master* in front of my name was a habit which I had persuaded both Peter and Bushman to drop, but John I could never persuade – and I knew that I would get no more from John than that Peter and Bushman were in Johannesburg. I had no idea why John was so secretive about this information. I didn't think that it could be politics, because I knew that neither Peter nor Bushman had been involved in politics – but I could not ask John, just in case it was politics that had taken them to Johannesburg.

When I went home again, about six months later, I again made inquiries about Peter and Bushman but could not find out anything at all. After a while I gave up trying to find out and it wasn't until near the end of the holidays that I did find out what had happened to Peter.

I had gone over to a friend's farm to play tennis one afternoon and had noticed that one of the farm labourers, working in the orchard next to the farmhouse, was Bushman. As soon as I could get away from my hosts, I and my current girl walked over to the orchard and found Bushman. I greeted him and he seemed very pleased to see me and pleased that I remembered him. I asked how he was, how his family was, whether he enjoyed working as a labourer on a citrus farm, and so on, to all of which he replied comfortably. I then asked him about Peter. He said that he didn't know and for some reason looked very uncomfortable. So I pressed him for a reply, not directly, but by asking specific questions. Was Peter in gaol? Bushman shook his head. Was he still in Johannesburg? No. Was he back in the district? A shake of the head. I offered Bushman a packet of cigarettes which I had but he refused them. There was nothing that he would tell me and eventually I had to go away because my girl insisted that we went back to play tennis.

Later on, in the evening, when we were having drinks on the veranda, the African 'houseboy' came up to me and told me that there was a 'boy' who wanted to see me at the back of the house. The others in the party seemed a little surprised at this but didn't say anything when I got up to go.

I found Bushman waiting for me. He was very embarrassed and a little shifty. I asked him why he wanted to see me and he answered that he wanted to tell me about Peter. He was very nervous and insisted that we walk away from the house a little before he would talk. First, he apologized for having refused to answer me before, in the orchard: 'The girl . . .', he said, implying that he couldn't speak in front of her. Then he told me Peter was dead, that he had been shot by the police in Johannesburg.

What had happened was this. Peter had moved up to Johannesburg to find work there, but because he had no permit to be there he had not been able to find work. So, eventually, he had joined up with a gang in the township; 'robbers', Bushman said, but I knew that the gangs in the townships are worse than robbers; they are usually murderers, rapists and terrorisers of the worst kind. In places like Dube and Alexandra they are, after dark, the law. Their victims are black as often, or more often, than white. Peter had rapidly become one of the trusted men of the gang – and I could imagine that his strength, his womanizing, and his hard drinking would have qualified him for leadership of gangsters. He had sent down to the village for Bushman to come and join him – and Bushman had gone; he told me this so quietly that I could hardly hear what he was saying.

At first, they had done very well but then, as happens when a gang becomes suddenly successful, the police had got after them. One after the other, members of the gang had been picked up, imprisoned and packed off to hard-labour farms, or had been killed. Eventually, Bushman had got out of Johannesburg, back to the village – he had tried to persuade Peter to go too, but Peter had refused to leave. The rest of the story Bushman had heard from people in Johannesburg.

The police had caught up with Peter, eventually, while he was hiding in the house of one of his girls. Two men had gone in to get him; Peter answered the door with a revolver in his hand, and shot the white sergeant and wounded the black constable. The rest of the police sent for reinforcements and surrounded the house. Peter, realizing that he didn't have a chance of escape, told his girl to go out of the front door with her hands above her head. This she did, but she went out too fast, and the police must have thought she was Peter and shot her in the stomach. Peter had run out of the house just after the police shot her and ran to where she had fallen. The police didn't shoot him, but came up towards him where he was with his girl. Then Peter stood up, with the revolver still in his hand, and watched while the police came up. Then he had thrown the revolver high over the heads of the policemen and had shouted out the cry; 'You remember, basie,' said Bushman, 'that one the day we were loading . . .' and then he whispered the cry, very quietly, so that I could hardly hear it. One of the policemen, thinking, when Peter threw his revolver into the air, that he was about to fire, had shot Peter. By the time he had fallen he was dead. Again Bushman whispered the cry, which is impossible to write down and impossible to translate, and which I do not think I could say myself.

When Bushman whispered it it seemed no longer a cry of victory, of triumph at the moment of conquest, but a cry of ultimate defeat. For Bushman it probably was, for without Peter he was no one of importance. But I did not know, nor do I know now, how that cry sounded when Peter cried it out for the last time. I do not know whether it was a cry of triumph or of defeat. I have written all this down because I do not know; if I knew either way, I would not have had to write this.

Ahmed Essop

Gerty's Brother

I first saw Gerty in a shop in Vrededorp. Vrededorp, as everyone knows, is cleft in two by Delarey Street: on the one side it is colonized by us non-whites and on the other side by whites. The whites come over to our side when they want to do their shopping, and return with a spurious bargain or two. I saw her in a shop in the garishly decorated Indian shopping lane called Fourteenth Street. I had gone there with my friend Hussein who wanted to see a shopkeeper friend of his. I think the shop was called Dior Fashions, but of that I am not quite sure because shop follows shop there and this shop didn't strike me as being in any way fashionable. Anyway, that is where I saw her. My friend spoke to the shopkeeper – a fat dark man with a darker moustache – and I just looked around and smoked a cigarette as I didn't see anything interesting.

I sat down on a chair and smoked another cigarette and then I noticed two figures darken the doorway and enter the shop, a girl and a boy. The shopkeeper spoke to the girl and then suddenly laughed. She laughed too, I think. I wouldn't have taken any further notice of the group as I was seated at the back of the shop. But then the shopkeeper switched to Gujarati and spoke to my friend. I heard him say that she was easy and would not give much trouble in removing her undergarments to anyone, but one had to be careful as there was the usual risk involved. Hussein replied that he was keen and that he wouldn't like to waste much time about the matter. I think the shopkeeper introduced him to her at this stage, but I am not quite sure for he went on speaking in Gujarati. He said that he was going to organize a dance at his place on the following Saturday evening, he was in the mood for jollification, and that he was going to invite Gerty and if Hussein was interested he could take her away from his place. All this he said in Gujarati, rather coarsely I thought. I wasn't very interested and thought of smoking another cigarette and going out to buy the afternoon newspaper. Girls were girls and one was as good as another, and if Hussein wanted to sleep with her he could have her and it would make no difference to me.

Later, when Hussein and I had climbed into his Volkswagen and were on our way to Fordsburg, he informed me that to soften her before the party on Saturday he had bought the girl a frock. He asked me how I liked her and I said she was all right as far as I was concerned, though, of course, I had not been near enough to see her properly and size her up. But I said she was all right and he felt very satisfied at having bumped into a white girl. He told me that she lived in Vrededorp, 'on the other side', and that she seemed to be very easy. He said that when he had done with her he would throw her over to me and I could have her as well. I answered with a vague 'Let the time come'. He then said something about 'pillar to post', and laughed as the car tore its way through the traffic into Fordsburg.

Saturday night I was at my landlady's, stripped to the waist because of the heat, reading an old issue of *The New Statesman*. There was a knock on the door and somebody asked for me and entered. It was Hussein all dressed up and titivated with bow tie and cuff-links and shoes that were out of place in my disorderly room.

'Where to, my dandy friend?' I asked admiringly.

'To the dance party. I thought you would be ready. You promised to come with me.'

I said I had forgotten, but that I would be ready in a minute. I dressed quickly, but didn't care to put on a white shirt or a tie. I wasn't very particular about what I wore, and I think it pleased my friend because my appearance was something of a foil to his, and set off to advantage his carefully put-together looks.

We set off in his Volkswagen for Vrededorp and in a few minutes the car braked sharply in Eleventh Street in front of the house of Hussein's shopkeeper friend. There were other cars near the house, but we managed to squeeze our car between two.

We were quite early and there were not many people present. Hussein's friend was happy to see us and he introduced us to those who were there. There were some lovely-looking girls in shimmering coral and amber and amethyst-coloured saris and others in more sober evening dresses and I looked forward to a swinging evening.

Then Hussein wanted to see the shopkeeper privately, and I think they went out to the front veranda of the house. When they returned I saw that Hussein was not too pleased about something or other, but as it was not my business I didn't bother to ask. Other girls arrived, all gaily dressed and very chic and charming and I was beginning to feel at ease. The girls offered me tea and cake and other tasty things to eat and I didn't refuse as my boarding-house wasn't quite a liberal establishment. All this time my friend Hussein was walking in and out of the room, and was on the look-out whenever someone knocked on the door and entered the house. The party got going and we danced, ate the refreshments provided and talked some euphonious nonsense. I was just getting interested in a girl, when my friend interrupted me and said that he wanted to see me urgently. I followed him and we went to the veranda. Someone had switched off the lights and I saw two figures standing there, a girl and a small boy. He introduced her to me as Gerty and he asked me if I remembered her. I thought a bit and then told him. He said that I had a good memory or something of the sort. He then took me aside and asked me if I could drive the two of them to the Johannesburg Lake immediately and leave them in the park for a while, and if I could keep her brother company while he saw to Gerty's needs. As it was a risky business he didn't want the others in the party to know. He would like to get done with it before joining the party.

I said I didn't mind and the four of us got into the car. I drove to the Lake. It was a lovely night in December and we breathed in the luminous wind of the city streets as the car sped along. Hussein and Gerty sat in the back seat. They didn't say much to each other, but I guessed that they were holding hands and fondling. Gerty's brother sat beside me. He must have been seven or eight, but I didn't take much notice of him. He was eating some cakes and chocolates that Hussein had taken from the house.

I dropped the pair in a park near the Lake. Hussein asked me to return again in about an hour's time. The park was a darkness of trees and lawns and flowers, and it occurred to me that it made no difference if one slept with a white or a black girl there.

Gerty told her brother that he mustn't worry and that she was all right and that he should go with me for a while.

Before I drove off Gerty's brother asked me what they were going to do and I said they must be a bit tired and wanted to rest, but that did not sound convincing. Then I said that they had something to discuss in private and the best place was in the park. He agreed with me and I started the car.

I didn't feel like driving aimlessly about for an hour so I drove towards the lake. I asked the boy what his name was and he said Riekie.

I parked the car under some pine trees near a brightly-lit restaurant.

There were people dining on the terrace amid blaring music, others were strolling on the lawns or resting on the benches. I asked Riekie if he would like an ice-cream and took him to the restaurant and bought him one. We went down to the water's edge. The lake is small with an islet in the middle; a fountain spouted water into shifting rays of variegated light. Riekie was fascinated by it all and asked me several questions.

I asked him if he had ever sat in a boat. He said he hadn't. I took him to the boat-house and hired one. The white attendant looked at me for a moment and then at Riekie. I knew what he was thinking about but I said nothing. He went towards the landing-stage and pointed to a boat. I told Riekie to jump in, but he hesitated. So I lifted him and put him into the boat. He was light in weight and I felt the ribs under his arms. A sensation of tenderness for the boy went through me. You must understand that this was the first time I had ever picked up a white child.

I rowed out towards the middle of the lake, and went around the fountain of kaleidoscopic lights. Riekie was gripped by wonder. He trailed his hands in the cool water smelling of rotted weeds, and tried to grab the overhanging branches of the willows along the banks.

It was time to pick up Hussein and Gerty. Riekie looked disappointed, but I said I would bring him there again. At this he seemed satisfied and I rowed towards the landing-stage.

Hussein and Gerty were waiting for us. They got into the car and we returned to the party in Eleventh Street.

The party was now in full swing. There were many girls and I didn't waste much time. My friend stuck to Gerty, and if he was not dancing with her he was talking to her. And by the time the party ended at midnight Riekie had fallen asleep on a sofa and had to be doused with water to wake him.

We dropped Gerty and her brother at a street corner on our way to Fordsburg. Hussein had rooms of his own in Park Road, situated in a small yard at the end of a passage. A tall iron gate barred the entrance to the passage. There were only three rooms in the yard. Hussein occupied two and the other was occupied by a decrepit pensioner who lived in his room like some caged animal, except that no one ever came to see him.

At first Hussein was afraid to tell Gerty where he lived. There was the usual risk involved. But I think eventually he came to the conclusion that in life certain risks had to be taken if one was to live at all. And so Gerty and her brother came to his rooms and she took on the role of mistress and domestic servant and Riekie became the pageboy.

Gerty and Riekie were very fond of each other. The harsh realities of life – they were orphans and lived in poverty with an alcoholic elder brother – had entwined them. Hussein didn't mind Riekie's presence. In fact the boy attached himself to him. My friend was generous, and besides providing Gerty with frocks for summer, he bought the boy clothing and several pairs of shoes. Riekie was obedient and always ready to run to the shops for Hussein, to polish his shoes or wash the car. In time his cheeks began to take on colour and he began to look quite handsome. I noticed that he wasn't interested in boys of his own age; his attachment to his sister seemed to satisfy him.

Riekie would often come to my landlady's in the company of Hussein, or my friend would leave him there when he had some business with Gerty. If I was in the mood to go to the movies I would take him with me.

And then things took a different turn. Hussein came to understand that the police had an eye on him, that somehow they had come to know of Gerty and were waiting for an opportunity to arrest him in incriminating circumstances. Someone had seen a car parked for several nights near his rooms and noticed the movements of suspicious-looking persons. And he was convinced the police were after him when one night, returning home late, he saw a man examining the lock of the gate. As there was no point in carrying on with Gerty – he was not in the mood for a spell in prison – he told her that she should keep away from him for some time, and that he would see her again as soon as things were clear. But I think both of them realized that there wasn't much chance of that.

There wasn't much that one could tell Riekie about the end of the affair. My friend left it to Gerty, and went to Durban to attend to his late father's affairs.

One Sunday morning I was on my way to post some letters and when I turned the corner in Park Road there was Riekie, standing beside the iron gate that led to my friend's rooms. He was clutching two bars with his hands, and shouting for Hussein. I stood and watched as he shouted. His voice was bewildered.

The ugly animal living in the yard lurched out of his room and croaked: 'Goh way boy, goh way white boy. No Hussein here. Goh way.'

Riekie shook the barred gate and called for Hussein over and over again, and his voice was smothered by the croaks of the old man.

I stood at the corner of the street, in my hand the two letters I intended to post, and I felt again the child's body as I lifted him and put him onto the boat many nights ago, a child's body in my arms embraced by the beauty of the night on the lake, and I returned to my landlady's with the hackles of revolt rising within me.

Sheila Fugard

The Angel of Death

Old maps of Africa show the ancient caravan routes. The Sahara. The journey from Fez to Timbuktu, following the trail across the desert along the spice route to the Indian Ocean.

Darfur lies in the centre of the desert, near the region of Savannah, above the Congo, far away from the Ashanti coast.

In Darfur there is a strange structure. Upon a bare hill, against a white African sky, are the ruins of the earliest Christian chapel of Nubia. A thousand years later, Islam conquered.

The Priest had left civilization behind at Fez choosing the 'Forty Day Road' across the Sahara. It was the ancient caravan route.

The Priest had come to the desert out of a longing in his heart.

A river from his boyhood, green shored with all the moisture of summer, pulsed through him. The images of his youth were cast as a negative against the sun.

A pyramid rose from the basin of the desert. He climbed this pyramid of sand. Clouds of dust flew behind him.

Temptation in the form of outrageous beauty appeared as an asteroid moving in the sky like some Centurion and his legions of a modern Caesar.

From the centre of the asteroid came a shower of golden wafers. The Priest knew this to be the celestial host. He was held captive in a tower of glass. The golden wafers came tumbling out of the sky, a volley of golden birds.

He shot them down with the power of his glance. The wafers formed the beads of a rosary.

94

When the Priest tried to pick up the rosary, the wafers had become raindrops soon to be devoured by the desert.

Ghazali, the Arab, was named after the great Persian teacher of Meshed known as Mohammed El-Ghazali. The name El-Ghazali means 'spinner' or 'dyer' which denotes the daughter of Mohammed. It is through this ancient lineage that the Mohammedans trace their ancestry back to the Prophet.

Ghazali, the younger, unfurled his prayer mat. (The prayer mat came from Persia, and legend has it that this same teacher, Mohammed El-Ghazali, had first possessed it. The prayer mat bore only the imprint of male assurance.)

The teacher, Mohammed El-Ghazali, had travelled in Syria, fasting and seeking solitude. He took no books, only allowed his mind, naked as the blade of a knife, to cut through pride.

Ghazali knew no such meditation. He understood only this part of the desert about Darfan. As a child, he had made horses from the stones of dates. He understood horses best – their faces, the Arab dish, and their pacing stride.

In Gao, Ghazali had loved a woman. His manhood had been a dulcimer upon which he played. There was pain in the instrument; it threaded red wheels of blood into a fiery ball, his heart, and spoke to him in clotted sighs.

Mohammed El-Ghazali had written that the nature of a man's mind is of the pig, the dog and the devil.

Ghazali understood his nature.

He left the woman in Gao, and came back to the desert.

The Priest had discarded his cassock. Perhaps burnt it in blasphemy. At Mabruk, he had cajoled an Arab's robe from a merchant. He had feared the robe, a sun-bleached yellow with a black hood. Some said it was a Dervish gown, others that it had once belonged to a Christian Nubian monk.

It was not only the outer aspects of the Priest that had changed. He had always been a tight-lipped Jesuit. Now prayers receded from him like fading hieroglyphics.

At night, the Priest built up a fire. He feared wild animals. Yet neither the tiger nor the lion prowled here. There was only the hyena, lingering beyond his tent, head held high sniffing. The Priest feared that the hyena would snatch his body away, the moment he gave up his life.

A vulture in the sky watched him.

At night, the fire did not keep the hyena nor the vulture away. The ashes, grey as dried vomit, were the visible remains of the Priest's fear.

'Wajd', the rapture, together with 'wujud', existence, summed up Ghazali's experience of the woman.

She had enfeebled his male body. Emasculated him. He felt weak as a garland of flowers, a robe of silk, a skin dripping wine.

There were times when he even desired a boy.

With the woman gone, the desert became a harsh fist that broke his body. His skull dried upon a rock. His decapitated hands grasped the fronds of palms. His thigh bones held up his tent. He was everywhere in pieces, framed in bone and sinew.

The desert became void, and swallowed up Ghazali and the memory of the woman.

Mohammed El-Ghazali, the teacher, had wisely taught that no one can understand his own heart unless he meditates upon God.

Ghazali, the younger, meditated upon the desert.

The Priest made a wager that he would not surrender to the desert. He placed a relic of St Francis, a bone gone brittle with time, upon a rock.

The vulture swooped down, and under the impact of the bird's stare, the relic fell from the rock.

The Priest felt the sun, a battering ram against his ribs, holding him down like a prisoner. He had lost. The desert came in like a sea.

The Priest waded deep into the sand, longing to possess not bodies but eternity. He knew with terrifying lucidity that this was the extinction of his faith; this knowledge of the earth and planets and receptacles of Titanic Gods. These Gods multiplied themselves in a billion forms, and to understand was only to meditate upon a grain of sand.

This was the vision of the desert. Joy vibrated through the Priest.

The teacher, Mohammed El-Ghazali, had understood the properties of Alchemy, and wrote about this in his treatise, the 'Alchemy of Happiness'.

Ghazali, the younger, understood the alchemy of the desert. The desire for women had been transmuted.

The idea of the other man came to him in an overpowering vision. Ghazali first saw the man's skin, then the moisture of his sweat, and finally the torpor of his sleep. The other man's image drenched the rocks with blood, and caused the sky to pulsate.

Ghazali's soul was united with the desert. He knelt down and listened to the ground. He picked up the heartbeat.

Ghazali thrust aside all the teachings of his ancestor – faith, prayers and the giving of alms.

Ghazali rooted out all these hindrances and filled himself only with the nature of the desert, the void.

The Priest wanted to confess. There was no tide of absolution here. Christ did not walk this ocean.

The Priest heard only the whisper of infidels. The scimitar hung in the sky. A gong beat tumult. He refused to listen, and the thousand confessions he had heard came back to him.

The confessions came armed with all their mortal and venial properties; the gossip of idle women; the debaucheries of men; the perversions of artists; the whispers of the profligate; the miserliness of the bourgeois; the niggardliness of the comfortable.

The Priest counted the date stones in his pouch. Each one represented a day left in his life. This was the only alms he received from the desert.

The Priest saw the shadows of the palm trees become poplars. The young cleric he had once been walked again, and the chancel and the cross symbolized only culture and ease.

It was the last confession that he had heard which sent him to Fez, and then out into the desert. The man had knelt before him and said: 'I am innocent.'

The Priest had chastised the man for pride. He then found himself cast down into hell. A fallen judge, he wanted only to prostrate before an empty sky, and the profligate sand.

Ghazali climbed from his horse, and with his scimitar drew a circle in the sand. It was the secret knowledge of the Dervishes of his ancestor, Mohammed El-Ghazali. He would imprison the other man within the circle.

Ghazali spent the night waiting. The next day he squatted in the sand. He turned his mind towards the Prophet.

The poets and holy men passed before him – Abu Bakr, Ibn Riyah, Salman the Persian (all of them first generation), and then Hiran Ibn Haya (one of the teachers of the Four Guides), and at last Malik Ibn Dinar and Sari El-Saqti (those of the Eleven Sheikhly Transmitters).

Within Ghazali, the 'latifa', the centre of reality awakened. He wound a turban of many colours about his head – black, green, yellow and red – all had appeared in his consciousness.

At last the Prophet spoke out of the wind and the darkness.

The Prophet was the manna in the desert, the sudden rose blooming at the Oasis, and the streaming of water.

Ghazali obeyed the command, and whetted his scimitar with his spittle.

The Priest came upon foot as centuries earlier a Hebrew had entered the city of Jerusalem upon a donkey, and been hailed a king, and showered with palm leaves.

The Priest recognised Ghazali as his brother. He drew the body of the Arab close to him, and kissed him as Christ had kissed the traitor, Judas.

Ghazali, the angel of death, led the Priest into the magic circle. First came the vision of the maze of roses, then the host of the sun, and finally the image of God. The colours in the vision were the same as those of the turban of Ghazali.

Ghazali took out his scimitar and slew the Priest within the magic circle of visions.

A hundred white doves flew from the body of the Priest.

Both men had arrived at the region of the desert known as Darfur.

Against the white sky, the tortured structure rises up upon the hill – the Christian Nubian chapel, which in Islamic times had housed part of the Sultan's harem.

Nadine Gordimer

You Name It

She has never questioned who her father was. Why should she? Why should I tell her?

And yet there are times – times when we are getting on each other's nerves as only women and their daughters can – I have such a flash of irritable impulse: You are not . . . I had –

I think I am stopped only by not knowing how to put it most sensationally. How to make her stand in her tracks as she's walking out the door with her boy for a 'drive' (= to make love in the car, that old synonym). To see her face, when she's been keeping it turned away from me half-listening while I talk to her, suddenly wrenched round. Or when I feel it's time to leave the room because I've been monopolizing the conversation among her friends and they are boring, anyway. How to break in: with a name, a statement.

I took a piece of cane waste from the flotsam and wrote on the wet sand:
Arno   Arno Arkanius
The cane was hollow, blackened by fire, and the sharp broken end was a bold quill; it incised letters cleanly.

She couldn't read. There were hundreds of tiny flies feeding on the rotting seaweed among the cane and she sat turning her hands from the wrist in their swarm. She enjoyed the weightless feel of the insects or admired their gratifying response to her presence, I don't know which, she was still too young to speak. While the other children were at kindergarten we walked every morning on that beach which could not be called deserted because there never had been anyone there to be counted absent, except the island women who came to dig for bait. Their black legs in the water and their hunched backsides in old sacks had the profile of wading birds. They did not look up and I never learnt so much as a greeting in their language. We made the staggering progress of a woman with a small child who cannot speak, has no sense of time, and to whom the dirt rim of the sea's bathtub is something to grasp while the blown-glass swells of the Indian Ocean, the porpoises jack-knifing in and out of the water, the spice off the spray, and the cliffs and hollows of Strelitzia palms in flower are outside awareness. Yes – it was a kind of paradise, I suppose, the kind open to people who drill for oil or man air bases or negotiate the world's purchase of sugar or coconut oil. I was born on one and married onto another and met the man who made her with me when transferred to this one. Our names were no guide to our place of habitation. They were the names of different origins all over Europe, cross-pollinated in the sports and games and parties in colonies and islands to which none were native. I don't know exactly what he was; Swedes sometimes have Latin names, but he came from a cotton pasha family that had had to leave Egypt, went to school in Lausanne, and was in the trade section of the consulate of one of the European countries who were losing their colonies but still setting the price for what they bought from them. He stayed two years before he was posted somewhere else – it was the usual tour of duty.

When the baby was born it looked, the first time, exactly like him but it was all right: never again. When I saw it I was filled with love – not for the infant but for him. It was six months since he had made love to me in the stripped bed with his suitcase standing by ready for the airport. Once again I yearned wildly. The emotion brought milk to my breasts. A few warm drops welled from the nipples, like tears. The nurses were pleased. My husband, delighted to have a girl child after two boys, tender and jocular in his happiness: *Now I'm prepared to let her off any more. Duty nobly done, dynasty assured. Unfortunately my daughter's as ugly as her brothers but give her time, we'll marry her yet.*

It was true that she became like her brothers as babies; a baby like all other babies, drooling saliva down the back of my dress when I held her the way she yelled to be held with her face over my shoulder, going slowly red in the face with silent concentration when she sat relieving herself, clutching my skirt when she wanted to pull herself up from the floor, holding her breath to the point of suffocation, in temper; looking so beautiful in her nightly drunken stupor with her bottle slack in her hand that my husband would take guests into the bedroom to gaze at her.

Her father never saw her. We wrote to each other all through the months before she was born; he had tried to persuade an island doctor whom he knew to give me an abortion, but there was his position at the consulate to consider, and my husband's position in the company. We were afraid the story would leak out. Whereas there was nothing exceptionable about my having a third child. He dared not keep a photograph of her in case his wife came upon it. By the time the child was nearly a year old he was on home leave – apparently Europe was selected as home – and we wrote more seldom but I could take advantage of Christmas to send a card showing a colour photograph of the family with the baby girl smiling in the middle. He wrote that she seemed to have a very large mouth? – was that just the photograph? His wife had remarked on it, too. I remember that I walked around the house carrying the letter and stared – nothing but sea, out there, nothing to be got from it but the sound of its endlessly long yawn and the tough glitter of its midday skin, and I went into the bedroom and lay down on the floor in the darkened room with my legs open, spread-eagled on my own cross, waiting for him. I cried to relieve myself, rolled onto my face and let the saliva run out of my open mouth upon the dust and lint of the carpet, like the baby. After a long time I began to hear the sea again, and saw, under the bed in which I slept with my husband, a coin and his lost espadrilles with the backs flattened to the soles by the way he always pushed his feet into them. When the island girl who helped with the children brought them up from the beach I met the baby with resentment for not being prettier, but she did not notice; like everything and everyone around me, she was living a life where this did not matter; and there was no other. There was no other, for me.

I had boasted to him of men who pursued me, including an ambassador, very distinguished and old enough to be my father. But now I wrote that I wanted a tidal wave to engulf the whole stupid life of the island; I did not tell him that I was flirting, and getting drunk at parties, and quarrelling with my husband because he said I neglected the children; to tell the truth these things didn't seem to me to be real – they were what I did to pass the time. Sometimes I wrote and said I was going to get divorced and take the baby and live alone. He replied that he was terrified 'something would happen to me'. We wrote as if these two sets of circumstances – his fearing for me, and my deciding to get divorced – had come about independently of each other, and of us. He instructed me not to write again until he could send a suitable new address – the two years were up once more, he was being reposted once more, and we didn't want my letters lying round the consulate for prying hands to forward. At this time my husband had taken it upon himself to send for his mother to supervise the children and the atmosphere in the house was one of blinding, deafening, obsessive antagonism: the tidal wave that I had wished on myself – I did not even realize that a month had passed without any new address coming. Now I did leave my husband, I went without the baby, without any child. The old reason for leaving was submerged under the fierce rows and recriminations that swept through the house so that the servants went about subdued, eyes lowered, before all that was laid waste while furniture and flower vases stood as usual and the outside man went on skimming the swimming pool with a net scoop. Once my husband had suddenly shouted that I ought to have been taken to a doctor, that's what he should have done – it was only since the last baby was born that I'd behaved like this, I'd changed with the birth of that baby, he wished the bloody baby had never been born!

He, who was so besotted with her that she has been the overindulged darling of the family, all her life. And I, not having the impulse then, at all, to fling back at him a name, a statement to stand out on his face harder than the print of any hand.

It was true that pretty terrible things could happen to me. I took a job as an air hostess on the inter-island service. I had no training for any occupation. The ceiling of the old DC3's flight was in the blanket of humidity and turbulence that rose from lonely mountains covered in tropical forest and lowland plantations of silky green cane. The cabins were not pressurized and I went up and down the aisles collecting paper bags of vomit. He must have heard about it, I'm sure, in his new posting to another set of island paradises, in Malaysia. Because of course, carrying my burdens along the isles, I met the astonished eyes of passengers who knew me as the wife of the such-and-such company's man. The ambassador who had once brought me a box of real lilies-of-the-valley from Europe (orchids were nothing, they grew wild on the island) stared at me from his seat, unsure whether or not to recognize me, although, like most women who have good taste in clothes and who for some reason have to put on a vulgarly provocative outfit, a waitress's dirndl or an air hostess's Courrèges, I know my looks had been made more sexual by the uniform. Another passenger and his wife, to whom I made myself known as a face from the sailing club and diplomatic parties, were on their way to a new posting and she remarked that it was to be Malaysia, this time, where, of course, the ——s were now; it would be good to have someone they already knew, when they got there, and the ——s had always been such fun, the island hadn't been the same since they left, had it? She would give them my best wishes, they would be glad to have news of their friends.

No letter. I did not expect one; I thought of him passionately as someone just as I was, ejected from the mould of myself, unrecognizable even to myself, spending nights in towns that while familiar (all the islands had the same palms, nightclubs, fruit-bats, the same creaking air conditioners and the long yawn of the sea) were not home. Being the distinguished man he was, the ambassador had been particularly friendly and amusing, once I had shown I was to be recognized in my new circumstances, but now that I was, theoretically, available, he did not try to see me again. The pilots were bored with their wives and pestered me. I slept in Curepipe one night with a Canadian businessman who felt it was fated because twice, three months apart, he had come to the islands and found me serving his whisky on the plane. I got what I wanted out of the encounter; a climax of sobbing and self-pity gave me back my yearning for my lover.

Long after, many months later, when I was home and my husband and I were having the house altered and the garden landscaped, there was a letter. *Are you mad? A mixture between a skivvy and a chorus-girl on one of those terrible old crates? What will happen to you?* How he must have struggled with himself, telling himself, as I did every day, there was no use to write. I would see my face in the mirror as if he were looking at it: only twenty-nine, thinner in the jaw since the drudgery and irregular hours of the airlines, longer hair, now, and the haughty look that unhappiness and dissatisfaction give when you are still young. My husband had gone into the shipping business, on his own initiative; the island was about to run up the new flag as an independent state and he had ingratiated himself with the ruling coterie. I still couldn't speak a word of the language but I was one of the first white women to appear at official banquets wearing the long, graceful island dress. My husband became confidential financial adviser to the new president; anyone from the foreign trade consulates who wanted privileges in the regime had to come to him, now.

There were riots down in the native town or the upcountry districts but we really only were aware of them from the newspapers. The regime survived and my husband made a lot of money. His triumph in my return had opened a source of energy in him that nothing could check. Not that we had ever been poor; once you had a house in the bluff district, a swimming pool, and some sort of craft in the yacht club harbour, there wasn't much else money could add to life on the island. Anybody could have the sea, sun, the flowers for the picking and the oysters off the rocks. He wanted to send pictures of the children taken with his super cameras as Christmas cards but I flew out against it and he liked confidently to give in to my whims. He had to travel often to Europe and enjoyed taking me with him. I did a lot of shopping for myself; his greatest pleasure was to buy presents for the children, in particular pretty dresses for the girl. In those days my lady ran about the beach like a little bedraggled princess, wearing hand-tucked Liberty lawn as a bathing wrap – a wild and spoilt child. We used to have to visit his mother who had retired to a hill village in the South of France and on one of these visits I drove into Nice to shop. Sitting in a café open to and noisy as the street I found I had lost the car key; and it was there, in the telephone booth that smelt (I remember it perfectly) of sweaty feet and sour wine, while I was waiting distastefully for my call to the village, that I saw out of the scribblings on the dirty wall, a name.

Arno   Arno   Arno Arkanius

Someone had stood waiting for a connection in that telephone booth in that café and written, again and again, as you might pick up a stick and write on the sand where no one will read, that name. There were many others jotted down, with numbers that belonged along with them; Pierre, Jan, Delphine, Marc, Maria, Horst, Robert. I read them all carefully. They were names common to thousands of men and women, but this name, this combination of first and surname – could it come about to signify another identity? I knew, as if my own hand had held that dark-leaded pencil (it was not a ball-point; a ball-point would never have written so clearly on that greasy wall), that this was he, this statement was about him and no other. Impossible to say who made it, or when; only why. The telephone ring leapt counter to the dulled noise from without pressing upon the glass door and I spoke what I had to say, not taking my eyes off the wall. Arno   Arno   Arno Arkanius. I hung up. I collected from the dirty floor my bag and parcels and went to the bar to pay for the call. So I had forgotten. Somebody else wept and indulged erotic fantasies, somebody else pronounced the name as a devout Jew might secretly speak the forbidden name of Jehovah. While this had been happening I had forgotten, the baby with the big mouth had become my husband's child – it was true, I was deceived and not he, about her identity – because I had forgotten, for days, months on end. I had thought I was permanently unhappy but how could that be? – I had forgotten. There must be many children such as she, happy to be who they are, whose real identity could be resuscitated only if their mother's youth could be brought back to life again.

Stephen Gray

The Largest Dam in the World

In the 60s in Rhodesia it was said that the Kariba dam was the largest in the world. When Mr Richards arrived there for a holiday the valley catchment had been banking up for five years. The lake was not up to the level of the main turbines yet.

As the Zambezi flooded into the dam it slowed and stagnated so that a weed could multiply on the surface. Kariba weed floats round an in-flated sac like a green testicle with roots trailing up nourishment from below. Off the banks of the dam the weed lies compacted over whole square miles. Engineers have tried to poison it or pour oil on it and burn it off. But it continues to choke up more and more of the waterway. Mr Richards read the notices about how to prevent spreading the weed to other stagnant waters of the country by spraying car tyres, disinfecting boots and so on. The posters warned trippers about the unsightly Curse of Kariba.

Mr Richards took a snapshot of the barrage to show his wife and daughters when he returned to Johannesburg – 'You see, Madge, this fantastic wall holds back 175 miles of water, just imagine the pressure. The noise is deafening, I'm telling you, it bursts your head open.'

He was relieved to be on his own for a week but at the same time sorry Madge could not join him because of fetching the kids from school. His Volkswagen was shimmering with heat after two days of solid driving, mile after mile on strip roads, flat-out to get time away from home. For months he had saved up for a luxurious week beside the dam. He had five days left to unwind and enjoy himself. He nosed down to the motel where he had a reservation. He braked, pulled on his suit jacket and stretched his legs. He couldn't stand these long drives – he was so exhausted he'd not have the energy to swim, if it was permitted.

He made for the thatched bungalow: Reception – Mr and Mrs Engelbert

Barnes. The proprietor and his wife greeted him cordially and explained about the only boatel which was for him. 'It's 200 yards behind the rondavels, a bit far from the ablution block.'

'It's *Pieter* Richards.'

'We are very glad to have you. We always welcome people who are interested in the place,' Mr Barnes said blankly.

'Oh, our son's the same name,' said Mrs Barnes. 'He's back to help us through the season.' She had a weatherbeaten resigned English face.

'Would you sign the book, please? It's a necessary formality with so many people coming and going.'

'No, my name is spelled with an "i".'

'Passport number and date of issue, sorry about this,' she said, keeping up the smile.

'There won't really be time to exchange letters, but can I receive mail here?'

'Of course,' Mr Barnes confirmed.

'Nelson, take Mr Richards to the boatel,' Mrs Barnes commanded.

Nelson had caked skin and smelled of sweat. Mr Richards did not normally give people rides. Nelson guided him through the rondavels, under a group of trees and to a parking space beside the inlet. The boatel was a floating hut, rocking gently. It was supported by a number of 44-gallon drums lashed together and the walls were of bamboo and reeds. Mr Richards walked up the gangplank and pulled aside the reed curtain – pleasantly cool as advertised. He selected his bed while Nelson placed his luggage at the foot of it.

'Here,' he said, handing him a tip.

'Thank you, baas,' Nelson hesitated for a moment.

From the opposite side of the inlet, Mr Richards could hear the sounds from the servants' huts. Mr Barnes had to support a whole army of black men to rake the weeds out of the dam.

'What did you say?'

'Dinner at seven o'clock.'

'Okay, Nelson.'

Madge had said she would write to see how he was getting on, but the letter would probably arrive after he left. Typical. The car creaked outside as it cooled off. He felt he was still driving along the strip roads, still in the clatter of the office: 'Mr Richards, the accounts, please!'

He unpacked onto the bed beside his, poured water into the handbasin and swilled it over his face. He lay down, pulling a wet handkerchief over his eyes. He kept hearing the noises of the little girls at home, clamouring in their bath, and the customs officer at the frontier insisting on counting every single cigarette. Soon he could hear only the servants' village, and the pad-pad of the speedboats moored off his boatel . . . she was very kind, the proprietor's wife, in an awkward way . . . the ablution block must be on the other side of the trees . . . easier to empty things over the side . . . Kariba weed must help to buoy up the boatel . . .

He saw an old man drive up towing a home-made caravan. A youth and a younger boy jumped out to wedge bricks under the wheels and erect the tent. The old man was dressed in baggy, well-stained khakis. When he bent he looked like an elephant. The youth was his nephew, overgrown and gangly, and the light-built boy was a grandson. Nelson threw down an armful of wood for them.

'Where we put the blankets, Oupa?' the grandson nagged.

'Anywhere, boy, you don't need them yet.'

The tall nephew climbed on the roof and untied the fishing rods.

'Did you sign the book for us, Oupa?'

'Yes, boy. Careful with the rods, hey.'

'I can't undo this one', the nephew's voice was at once high and low.

'Oupa? Can I go buy some bait?'

'We've got enough for tonight. Wait until it's dark, hey. And don't get so excited now.'

Nelson delivered a second load of fire wood, then jumped from speed-boat to speedboat across the inlet to his village. He stood talking to another man who was pulling on his uniform. One of the village women wandered up to them, handed over two chickens and walked off into the trees.

'When can we have supper, Oupa?'

'When you've finished your bath, I mean –' Mr Richards shook him-self, remembering his daughters were not there. He lay with his face against the reed wall, gazing over the patches of weed. Tell us if the natives make too much noise, Mr Barnes had said.

The noise of the village was about the only thing which fitted in with the landscape. An old man with peppercorn hair sat on the opposite bank, playing on a string held taut between his big toe and his teeth. On the edge, black children flicked hooks over the weed and sat for ever, watching the circles for fish. The burst of the lower turbines in the barrage was almost inaudible.

As the sun set Mr Richards left his boatel. He passed the caravan without greeting the old man, not wanting to get involved with anyone yet. He wore sandals which kicked up a fine, orange dust; his cravat was tied loosely but smartly. He looked among the trees, searching for the ablution block. With natives on one side and campers on the other, he couldn't very well use the lake. Anything he put over the side would float there, like himself. There were cans just sitting and blinking on the weed. He located the block and was relieved to see there were showers. Then he cut past the rondavels, each with lanterns burning and filled with people whose voices stopped dead in the stillness. Nelson advised him to take his seat in the open-air dining room before the first sitting was full.

After a good dinner, he felt considerably rejuvenated, though he had not selected the courses with much relish. He left the dining room for the V-shaped terrace that ran out into the dam like the prow of a ship. He ordered from Nelson a Richelieu brandy as a treat.

'Where do you come from, Nelson?'

'Joburg, baas, Joburg.'

'Good heavens, how did you get to be there?'

'I was working in Johannesburg, baas.'

He left with another tip from Mr Richards.

Madge had given him a book to read, *How to Bring up Children*, but there was not enough light to read by. He pushed it aside to stare across the lake opening out on either side. The surface was partly matted with weed; in other parts the reflection of stars.

The second sitting was under way while he watched a young man – the proprietor's son, he guessed – tying up a dinghy and carrying the guests' catch up to reception. Strange, I know your name, you're Peter and I'm Pieter. He swigged back the Richelieu and went straight to bed.

Next day he wandered round the motel, with all the observational powers of a tourist awakening in him. He lazed on the prow of the concrete ship, watching the motorboats on the lake, and girls waterskiing and plummeting head-long when the weed tripped them. He drove up to the village on the hilltop, saw the church built for the Italian staff and the open-air cinema, and gradually felt he was coming back to life again.

He enjoyed lunch – clear soup, fried Kariba bream, which was delicious if slightly fatty, copious meats and puddings. Then he ambled along to the grocery store beside reception; he glanced at the son behind the counter: I know your name and you don't know mine.

'That was an excellent lunch, I don't know how you produce it all, so far from anywhere.'

'It comes from the railhead,' said the son, his wrists turned out on the wooden counter, his sleeves rolled up on olive skin.

'I would like to buy a cigar, a Dutch one,' said Mr Richards, embarrassed.

The son produced a box and opened it with long, casual fingers.

'Er, could I try, I mean, see these other ones?'

The son rubbed his stomach against the counter and flicked open another box. His eyes were cast down at the cigars, drooping a little, the lids were a fraction puffy.

'Yes, yes, that's exactly what I want. Just one for now please.'

The son fetched a resident's card. He had bare feet and was wearing shorts. He spun the card over the counter and resumed his relaxed attitude.

'Richards, Pieter Richards.' He felt desperate at having to give his name. He wished he had been like this young man in the past. Madge said he always worried, worried. If Madge could see him she'd say: Why can't you be like Mrs Engelbert Barnes's son a bit more?

'Would you sign for it?'

'Of course, thank you.' Mr Richards paused, holding up the cigar and peeling off the cellophane. 'Do you think you could cut off the end? I don't have a pen-knife.'

The son sliced off the tip with one stroke.

Mr Richards left with a sudden feeling of relief. He struck a match and inhaled. It was too hot to stay on the prow, so he returned to his boatel and smoked, taking great care not to set the reeds alight.

'That was nice, hey Oupa?' Mr Richards could hear the campers outside.

'Yes, my boy. I'll come and get you set up in a moment. You'll catch the whole lake.'

Mr Richards walked down his private gangplank and hovered near the area of the caravan. The table under the awning was laid with bottles and tackle. The nephew stood up, slowly rubbing his instep against his other sock, working at untangling a web of fishing line. He was so self-centred Mr Richards did not try talking to him. But the smaller boy was buckled over the rocks of the inlet, washing out more jars and spraying water all over himself. Mr Richards wanted to ask what the jars were for. The child at the water was filled with pride because of the stranger's presence.

'Oupa's got high breaking strain on his tackle. Come, I'll show you what Oupa caught!' The little boy ran zigzag back to the water, imploring Mr

Richards to follow him. He pulled up something repulsive – an inky blue slithering dead fish two feet long. 'A barbel, a barbel, Oupa caught it!' It was colourless on the underside with fins like hairs and a gawping mouth. 'Do you want it? You can have it. There's lots more we gonna catch!'

'I've already eaten, thank you. I don't want it.'

The boy was temporarily disappointed. Mr Richards watched his miniature face, creased with looking into the sunlight.

'We gonna clean them,' he said. He slid his arm down the fish's mouth, wriggled his fingers inside. With a twist he plucked his hand out and held up to Mr Richards the fish's lungs, like a carnation, with the same pattern of red and white. He flung it away and it skidded over the water, remaining above the surface of the weed. Mr Richards made a mental note to submerge it as soon as the boy was not watching.

'Would you like some coffee?'

Mr Richards did not accept or refuse but sat on a stool the old man drew up for him. The nephew stopped picking at the nylon and put on the kettle. The fire of the night before still burned low.

'. . . and my name's Weyden.'

Mr Richards stood up to shake hands with the old man. His hand seemed webbed, for it enclosed Mr Richards' entirely. 'Sit down, sit down. We're just here for a day or two, a short break for the kids. It's always nice to get in some fishing.'

He paused; '. . . no, I'm retired now. I was a boxer once, never professional, but I used to spar with old Roy Welensky before the war. I was a fitter and turner and they wouldn't let me into the war. This caravan is all my own work. Yes, I've lived in it ever since my wife died. And so's the launch. If any of the kids wants to come on holiday with me they must sleep outside!'

Mr Richards stared at the old man. He hadn't shaved recently, and silver hairs crept down his dewlap. The lobes of his ears hung down like those of an elephant, probably because he kept tugging them. The old man talked on. He was one of the first white babies to be born in the first Rhodesian town, Bulawayo. He had once bred a horse which withstood sleeping sickness. He had an endless knowledge of the trees lying in belts across the Rhodesian veld. He had farmed tobacco near the site of the Kariba dam. When construction got underway he lent a hand rescuing wild life from the rising waters. Mr Richards was amazed as he recounted the struggle they had had moving black tribes who would not believe the river could rise permanently over their huts – eventually they had to force the obstinate bastards to higher land. And so on. The dam belonged more to Mr Weyden than to the Barnes family who had no more than built their establishment beside it.

Mr Richards finished his coffee. Although not enthusiastic about catching barbel himself, he promised to watch the boys fishing that night.

Nelson, in a fresh uniform, woke him with afternoon tea. Madge knew how to pour his tea, but this was very smart, an elegant pot, milk jug full and two cups. He filled one and thanked the servant.

Nelson stood in the centre of the bamboo room, streaked with strong sunlight, almost bursting to say something. 'I was working in Johannesburg, baas.'

'How did you know I come from there?'

'By your car.'

'Why were you working there?'

'I come from Joburg, baas.' He broke into the most phenomenal of smiles. Why be so happy about Johannesburg?

He left for the servants' village. Mr Richards felt a hot sensation in his mouth as he saw Nelson and the other waiter curl their pink palms together and return hand in hand, as some of the Rhodesian natives did. He drank down more tea.

With his binoculars he started out for the main building, intending to pick out the different kinds of trees. As he passed the wooded part of the path he noticed another boatel concealed behind the trees, not, he supposed, available to guests (Mrs Barnes had said there was only one). He found a table on the 'prow' terrace and ordered a couple of Richelieus, drank them down and ordered another.

When the dinner bell sounded he went off leaving his binoculars on the table. He ate enormously, anticipating each course and putting it down with the appetite that comes with a touch of alcohol. It was night, the lights went on distantly and he asked for his liqueur to be served him at the same table on the prow.

He felt flooded with heat. His skin was tingling where the sun had reached him and the terrace seemed hypnotically to be breasting out into the water. But there was a hollow inside him which upset his peace, the sort of hollow that brought a salty taste into his mouth. He gulped down the liqueur as though to fill it, but felt worse. He sat alone there, switched off from the haze of voices in the dining room. He could not remember feeling as acutely for years.

Then the dinghy of holiday-makers approached the landing. It edged out of the dark, rowed powerfully by the son, Peter. A young woman in front of the boat squealed as it rubbed against the landing, then pranced about the quay waving her dry bikini.

Mr Richards focused his binoculars on the boat. He watched the young man's shoulders relax as he came out of the last oarstroke. He bent to scoop up the afternoon's catch. Nelson tied up the dinghy as the son stepped off, flexing and swinging the fish, and walked into the floodlights. Mr Richards snapped the binoculars down in case he was seen watching Peter. He jumped up to buy something in the store, hoping to coincide with the son. But he was greeted by Mrs Barnes.

'What can I do for you, Mr Richards?'

He faltered. He could not say he wanted a formal introduction to her son; he wanted her son to acknowledge that, despite the age gap, they were very similar.

'A cigar,' he said.

She scrutinised him closely, almost suspiciously: 'Any particular brand?'

'No, the nearest one will do.' That was a slip. He felt like a criminal.

She handed him one, saying: 'Don't worry, I'll make out the card.'

Mr Richards left, searching aimlessly for the son. He tucked the cigar unopened into his pocket and ended up at his boatel. There he sat staring at the empty bed opposite him.

The moment he closed the screen Nelson tapped and returned him his binoculars. 'Baas can see very well with this,' he said.

He thought he must write to Madge, decided not to watch the fishing, and then resolved not to write at all, as there was nothing to tell her.

'I'm sorry I didn't come last night, but I had rather a headache.'

'That's okay,' said the nephew, 'you must take care of the sun out here, hey, it's not like in Johannesburg, so much dirt in the air there you never see the sun, hey.'

Oupa said: 'I'm going to stand the kids a breakfast; can we join you?'

The four walked off, Oupa saying they should bulldoze the road to make it more practical. The nephew kept quiet, while the boy tagged onto Mr Richards, explaining how Oupa strung the lines with tin cans so that when they got a bite they woke up to the stones in the cans rattling.

Mr Richards glanced through the trees a second, caught sight of something which would worry him. At the dining room the Weydens sat at his table and the three talked while they shovelled down Kellogg's corn flakes. Nelson came and talked too, but Mr Richards did not hear. Instead, he watched the way the son, Peter, bent down in his bathing costume outside the other boatel, always flexing and clasping things, his tanned body almost transparent and shining with light gold hairs like a figure projected on a screen, so perfect.

'Don't you think so, Mr Richards?'

'Oh, yes. Er, if you don't mind I think I'll take a drive. I need to do some shopping and I'll see you later after all.'

He drove fast up the pass to the main highway. Then he curved down to cross the immense dam wall that choked back the entire Zambezi, which meant most of the water that side of the continent, shooting it through the lower turbines which sprayed the workers miles downstream. He drove until he found another inlet, parked with the door open and stared at the trees sinking gradually into the lake. He was choking. He wanted to swim, but he could not bear the thought of breasting his way through the scum of weed.

Finally, he wrote on a greetings postcard featuring the barrage:

Dear Madge, my darling Madge, and Poppet and Tonkie – I really wish you were here. It is so beautiful here, you should just see the trees, how each one is a different colour sinking into the water. Poppet, you could collect the leaves and take them to school for Nature Study. I feel very guilty about you all not being here and that I should have all the fun, but you were quite right because I'm completely forgetting about work, which is just what you suggested. I hope you are all fine, I'm fine. I will post this now before it's too late. I told you our letters would cross. All fondest love to all three of you. Dad.

He arrived back at the motel too late for lunch. Mr Barnes kindly sent Nelson to him with a tray. 'Oh, thank you, Nelson . . . What is it?' The man stood there. 'What is it, hey?'

'Baas, I want to ask, baas . . .' (for goodness sake, don't just stand there) '. . . is baas going back to Johannesburg?'

'Yes.'

Nelson left immediately, and to Mr Richards' annoyance ran to his fellow waiter and talked with great excitement . . . what the hell's he want to go back there for?

He read in the sun all afternoon. Children are not adaptable, the writer said, and the young mind suffers being changed from one environment to another. He flipped the pages . . . I travelled everywhere with my parents and so can't stand one place for long . . . He read how growing girls became fascinated by the difference between male and female, once they discover it, and he remembered Poppet peeping over her sheet at him changing . . . How bloody wonderful, at four, mind you.

He went to the reception office. 'Afternoon, Mrs Barnes, can I go out fishing, I mean with a guide?' He knew there was only Peter. 'I'll pay in advance.'

'Well, my son does take out fishermen. I'm afraid the soonest he can manage is tomorrow afternoon. Not the morning because he promised to take out the people he had last night then.'

The price was exorbitant, but he did not mind.

'It'd work out cheaper if you shared the dinghy with some other guests.'

'No thank you, Mrs Barnes. I like the tranquillity of being alone.' He added: 'I'll settle my account now too. Can I pay by cheque?'

Then the Weyden family arranged an entertainment for him. The boys made the preparations while Mr Richards and Oupa sat over coffee after dinner. Oupa lifted the lid off one of his jars, filled a saucer and gave it to Mr Richards: 'It's my speciality – barbel pickled with onion. Sometimes I do it with peppers, garlic, curry and all boiled up. Try some, it's delicious. Will last for weeks now.'

Mr Richards gaped at the big helping, repulsed by the white cuts of barbel and the spines. He half-filled the teaspoon, slid it into his lips. It tasted off. He was not hungry after the large meal which sat high in his stomach. He pretended to enjoy it, walked over to the boys beside the launch and emptied the saucer when no one was looking. The grandson popped up beside him, explaining the arrangements, as Mr Richards stealthily submerged the barbel meat with his shoe.

'It was delicious, absolutely,' he lied.

'Have some more,' said the old man.

'Not just now, thanks.' The little boy stood in front of him anxiously and Mr Richards wanted to grab his face and ask: Why are you so agitated, what for, is it so important that I listen to you?

'We're ready.' Mr Richards was clamped on the shoulder by the elephantine old man and propelled through the darkness to the launch: 'This will be a special treat for you. You don't see things like this easily in Joburg, I know.'

The old man jerked the starter cord. They chugged past Nelson and his friend, ploughed through an acre of weed and into the open with the launch picking up speed. Mr Richards appreciated their concern for his happiness. He kept commenting on how smooth the water was, how well the launch ran.

'I built it myself,' Weyden said. 'With it I've bruised miles of this weed and seen it wash up dead the next day – it's the only way to get rid of it. That's why I built it flat like this.'

Mr Richards leaned over the side between the two boys. He turned and gazed across the water as they skimmed past the second boatel. The screens were drawn and a lamp was on inside. But still, I'm here and mustn't want to be anywhere else.

The boy tapped his shoulder. 'Hey, look, look!' This was the surprise. Oupa had rigged up spotlights which he switched on. Mr Richards held his breath as the engine cut. He could see right through the surface, through the reflection of his face. Swaying in the light were the branches of trees, black and reaching upwards, graceful and pathetic and beautiful. Mr Weyden rowed in slow strokes over these submerged fantastic trees, each one reaching up, trying to grow but pressurized into fossils. Mr Richards felt shocked trying to stretch across the barrier between himself and them. It was like trying to make contact with someone like Nelson and his millions of relatives, waving gently underwater.

Threading through the branches swam two fish. 'Look! Tigerfish!' They curled upwards with great ripping jaws, then glanced away. 'Put your finger in those teeth and you've had it!' Then a shudder went along from a shoal of bream, winding between the branches. 'Can't see any barbel, they're too camouflaged.' . . . Take those to Miss Faunce for biology, Poppet, put them in your bucket . . . He kept wanting to glance back at the boatel.

'The government stocked all these in here, between parliamentary crises,' said Mr Weyden. 'There were only tiny fish in the Zambezi before.'

'Tigerfish, Oupa?'

'No, tiny, small fish, man!' he cuffed the boy on the neck.

The motor fouled up as they returned, so Mr Weyden rowed them back with more strength than the three others could have mustered together . . . Madge, darling, you should have seen that old man.

They landed and the Weydens set about baiting their lines. Mr Richards thanked them repeatedly, but he left as soon as it was clear that another activity was underway. They would all be listening for the cans to jangle like alarm clocks.

He could not sleep and went out again for a stroll. When he reached the trees he stepped under cover, ducking between bushes and taking care not to make a noise. He was irritated to find that between him and the second boatel there was a strip of water covered with weed. For a few yards he followed the bank, intensely excited, the taste of salt mingled with barbel on his tongue. He sat just opposite the boatel.

From the dressing gown and washstand showing at the bottom of the screen he concluded that he was staring at the back wall. All the walls were streaked with outlets of light. He leaned forward. A foot, bare, jointed to a small ankle, gyrated into view. He almost ran forward, desiring – what? to grab it? Christ, what the hell *was* he hoping for?

He left silently, choking with a sort of energy and desire. He wandered back slowly to his private boatel, composing himself. The Weydens were on the other side of their caravan and did not notice him, or maybe they were watching him enter his expensive resting place. They were watching. He drew back the counterpane – and burst with shock and hopelessness. The boys had placed a half-dead barbel, blue and whiskery, between the sheets. They spluttered and laughed and the old man slammed them on the head.

He wanted to roar out loud, at them, at the whole camp. 'Nelson!' he shouted, 'Nelson, where the hell are you?'

Nelson ran.

'Did you put this in my bed?' Mr Richards whipped the screen open. 'No, no, sorry, of course you wouldn't. I'm very sorry to accuse you. But please would you *throw it out* for me?'

Nelson clutched the offending fish and flung it away. He was extremely apologetic. He took ages to set the bed right again, but by then Mr Richards was falling asleep on the other bed. Nelson drew the screen quietly behind him and left.

Mr Richards watched the motel in a sort of blank which filled up the whole of the morning. He pushed aside his lunch. His anticipation grew as Mr Barnes lethargically explained the details of the fishing tackle: 'For tigerfish you need this hook and line, greater breaking strain.' They were standing under a beam mounted with fish trophies, the mouths with asymmetric teeth gone colourless. Peter was loading the dinghy and beckoned to Mr Richards. Here I go, he thought. As he drew near he tightened up.

'Very good of you to take me. I'm not a brilliant fisherman. In fact, I've never fished before!'

He shrugged, as if he heard that a thousand times a day.

'Where's the best place to catch a tigerfish?'

'I'll take you there, climb in.'

Mr Richards settled himself on the seat in the bows, stripping himself of emotion or excitement. On second thoughts, it would not matter if he appeared enthusiastic, as after all that was what one was supposed to be, going fishing for the first time.

'We'll go that way. When we're out of the weed you can trawl if you like.'

Mr Richards fingered the rod and reel and the canvas bag full of sinkers, and the bait – a pile of minute, flapping fish.

Peter rowed quite suavely, little gouts of lake water spitting off the oars with each stroke. When they were alongside a buoy, he flicked a noose over it and Mr Richards handed him a metal lure hung with four quadruple hooks: 'Vicious thing, that. Do you think it'll catch anything?' He shipped the oars and impaled four fish on the hooks. The skill with which he threaded them on was astonishing. He told Mr Richards what to do, but could not make him understand. He took the rod from the man's hands – a split second of contact – and cast it a distance, whistling over the depths. 'Just let it trawl while I row.' The line tautened as the dinghy rose and fell . . . Well, this is trawling with the man I admire bowing his arms between the oars, his shirt curled up wet over his navel, and me trusting not to catch a fish!

He let down the anchor. 'Do you mind if I take off my shirt? It gets quite sweaty.' Please do, I mean . . . 'By all means,' Mr Richards replied.

'Now sink it, let it sink, that's right. When you feel a jerk on the line, let the fish go on nibbling, then jerk yourself. Then call me.' Call him, with his eyes drooping, smouldering in the sunlight.

A brown current lapped under the stern.

'Hey, I've got something!'

Peter stirred, knowing there hadn't been a bite, and probably would not be the way Mr Richards was dangling the line.

'Sorry, false alarm!'

'Oh shame!' Peter lounged out full, winding his arms about himself, enjoying the aura of sunburn. In the distance the turbines roared. Mr Richards had the impression they were drifting that way. He needed to talk. 'Where did you go to school?'

Peter lounged even more, making himself comfortable in what was, by any standards, an uncomfortable place, the planks on the bottom of a dinghy. 'Oh, I went to school, Mr Richards, in South Africa' – he flicked a wrist down, scratched his leg – 'but I've lost the accent now.'

'Private school?'

'Boys' own private school. Teachers all a lot of old . . . Never mind.' He looked as though he was almost asleep.

He knew he was being watched. Mr Richards was bursting with half-formed questions: dare I ask him? about whether he's sort of eligible or not? what am I thinking about? is this man connected with anything besides the sun, the lake and a glorious afternoon? His only way was to use his prerogative as payer and ask that they move to a better ground for fishing. 'I don't think this part is much use,' he said.

Peter replied obligingly, but formally: 'Where do you want to go then?' And with sarcasm: 'I'll row you there, it'll be a pleasure.'

'I'll hang on here a bit longer, don't worry.' It sounded as though everything he said had another meaning. 'It's very good of you, but don't worry.'

That was it. He could not say or do another thing. In two hours he had not had a bite. The sun was beginning to fall. Peter rowed the dinghy back, tied it up, and they parted in silence.

The following day, his last, Mr Richards was depressed. The account he was given of bilharzia among the Africans depressed him. The cars coming and going, being welcomed and sent off by Mr and Mrs Engelbert Barnes depressed him. There was his feeling that the prices were too high. There was Nelson hovering around him, obliging to the end and hoping for a ride – something quite impossible, so impossible that he did not even broach the subject to Mr Barnes; well, in fact, Nelson had not actually asked for a ride. There was no letter from Madge; he knew exactly what she would say, but that left a gap in the week. Above all there was the fiasco of his fishing trip. It was not that he had expected anything to happen. He did not know what he wanted out of it, just that he wanted to talk to young Peter.

The last straw was the departure of the Weyden circus. He had long forgiven the boys, so when they had come to apologise about the fish in his bed, he laughed it off. But he soured slightly when the old man gave him a jar of his barbel speciality as compensation.

'Goodbye, Mr Weyden, I hope we meet again . . . (sincerely) Goodbye, son, all good luck at school, hey, and for you too,' he said, meaning it all for the grandson. He even had a lump in his throat, the kid was so vital and energetic, and the book about children had said something about the too-trusting being hit hardest.

Nelson tapped coyly on the screen and came in, extremely embarrassed, blushing.

'Please, baas, excuse me. Can I come with – ?'

'Oh, for God's sake!'

'Please, baas –'

Mr Richards was losing his temper. 'Look, Nelson, have you got a passport? Have you got an entry permit? Have you got a job in Joburg? Have you got anything? You can't just leave your wife here, I can't take your wife and your friends. You have no idea how strict they are at the border.'

'Please, baas. My wife in Joburg.'

'What! Oh no, Nelson.' He was deflated. *That* struck at the base of his depression. 'Well, I'm sorry your wife's over there, Nelson, I'm *very* sorry. But no can do.'

He had had his last dinner and could not sleep. It was clammily hot, his pyjamas stuck to him. Moths circled the lamp so he could not read. He kept pinching his stomach as if it were aching, turned and turned, messing up the mosquito net.

Then he slid out of the boatel, hurried barefoot down the path and at last into the shelter of the trees. Skimmed through them. He remembered the curdled weed on the inlet he would have to cross. Blast! he waded straight into the water. Barbels, I'm going to stamp on you, filthy things. Who cares about crocodiles or bilharzia! He lunged forward and caught at the floor of the second boatel. He threw up the screen. His whole body was electrically sensitive, not cooled even by the water. It was late and no lantern alight inside, only the great bloated moon shining down on him and into Peter's bedroom.

There was a sort of yelp. A girl was looking at him, her hair dishevelled – the girl who had gone fishing with Peter.

Peter slung himself out of bed, landing on Mr Richards and punched him in the chest. 'Get him, get him!' the girl hissed. Mr Richards shot out his fists, violently hating what he had to do to defend himself. They tangled on the floor. The girl wanted to scream. Peter had Mr Richards under him, beating him down. Mr Richards sank his teeth into a thigh. Then they fell apart.

Mr Richards looked Peter in the face. 'Forgive me, forgive me, please. It's not what you think.'

The girl teetered across to them, as if it were all a joke. Don't tell anyone about us, she said to Mr Richards, please, and she was sorry about the beating he had got. It was meant for her fiancé if he came snooping.

'Oh, that's all right,' Mr Richards said acidly, 'providing you don't tell anyone it was me that disturbed you.' The girl giggled. She lacked all sense of understanding whatsoever.

Mr Richards got up. They went back with him to the other boatel. Peter helped him pack his case. The girl kept on laughing, disturbing what was now a peace between the two men.

As Mr Richards revved up his Volkswagen, he shook hands with Peter – manfully, like Mr Weyden – and saluted the girl: 'You're the lucky one.'

'Please don't make so much noise,' the girl giggled, 'I don't want –'

But Mr Richards, tired and relieved, let out a whoop: 'Nelson!' The man was standing there with his kitbag, and he piled into the car. Mr Richards waved to the pair, with mad enthusiasm, and hooted as hard as he could to wake the whole motel. He accelerated at top throttle up the pass. As he lit his cigar, he roared through the weed control barrier without stopping at all.

Bessie Head

The Prisoner who Wore Glasses

Scarcely a breath of wind disturbed the stillness of the day and the long rows of cabbages were bright green in the sunlight. Large white clouds drifted slowly across the deep blue sky. Now and then they obscured the sun and caused a chill on the backs of the prisoners who had to work all day long in the cabbage field. This trick the clouds were playing with the sun eventually caused one of the prisoners who wore glasses to stop work, straighten up and peer short-sightedly at them. He was a thin little fellow with a hollowed-out chest and comic knobbly knees. He also had a lot of fanciful ideas because he smiled at the clouds.

'Perhaps they want me to send a message to the children,' he thought, tenderly, noting that the clouds were drifting in the direction of his home some hundred miles away. But before he could frame the message, the warder in charge of his work span shouted: 'Hey, what you tink you're doing, Brille?'

The prisoner swung round, blinking rapidly, yet at the same time sizing up the enemy. He was a new warder, named Jacobus Stephanus Hannetjie. His eyes were the colour of the sky but they were frightening. A simple, primitive, brutal soul gazed out of them. The prisoner bent down quickly and a message was quietly passed down the line: 'We're in for trouble this time, comrades.'

'Why?' rippled back up the line.

'Because he's not human,' the reply rippled down and yet only the crunching of the spades as they turned over the earth disturbed the stillness.

This particular work span was known as Span One. It was composed of ten men and they were all political prisoners. They were grouped together for convenience as it was one of the prison regulations that no black warder should be in charge of a political prisoner lest this prisoner convert

121

him to his views. It never seemed to occur to the authorities that this very reasoning was the strength of Span One and a clue to the strange terror they aroused in the warders. As political prisoners they were unlike the other prisoners in the sense that they felt no guilt nor were they outcasts of society. All guilty men instinctively cower, which was why it was the kind of prison where men got knocked out cold with a blow at the back of the head from an iron bar. Up until the arrival of Warder Hannetjie, no warder had dared beat any member of Span One and no warder had lasted more than a week with them. The battle was entirely psychological. Span One was assertive and it was beyond the scope of white warders to handle assertive black men. Thus, Span One had got out of control. They were the best thieves and liars in the camp. They lived all day on raw cabbages. They chatted and smoked tobacco. And since they moved, thought and acted as one, they had perfected every technique of group concealment.

Trouble began that very day between Span One and Warder Hannetjie. It was because of the shortsightedness of Brille. That was the nickname he was given in prison and is the Afrikaans word for someone who wears glasses. Brille could never judge the approach of the prison gates and on several previous occasions he had munched on cabbages and dropped them almost at the feet of the warder and all previous warders had overlooked this. Not so Warder Hannetjie.

'Who dropped that cabbage?' he thundered.

Brille stepped out of line.

'I did,' he said meekly.

'All right,' said Hannetjie. 'The whole Span goes three meals off.'

'But I told you I did it,' Brille protested.

The blood rushed to Warder Hannetjie's face.

'Look 'ere,' he said. 'I don't take orders from a kaffir. I don't know what kind of kaffir you tink you are. Why don't you say Baas. I'm your Baas. Why don't you say Baas, hey?'

Brille blinked his eyes rapidly but by contrast his voice was strangely calm.

'I'm twenty years older than you,' he said. It was the first thing that came to mind but the comrades seemed to think it a huge joke. A titter swept up the line. The next thing Warder Hannetjie whipped out a knob-kerrie and gave Brille several blows about the head. What surprised his comrades was the speed with which Brille had removed his glasses or else they would have been smashed to pieces on the ground.

That evening in the cell Brille was very apologetic.

'I'm sorry, comrades,' he said. 'I've put you into a hell of a mess.'

'Never mind, brother,' they said. 'What happens to one of us, happens to all.'

'I'll try to make up for it, comrades,' he said. 'I'll steal something so that you don't go hungry.'

Privately, Brille was very philosophical about his head wounds. It was the first time an act of violence had been perpetrated against him but he had long been a witness of extreme, almost unbelievable human brutality. He had twelve children and his mind travelled back that evening through the sixteen years of bedlam in which he had lived. It had all happened in a small drab little three-bedroomed house in a small drab little street in the Eastern Cape and the children kept coming year after year because neither he nor Martha ever managed the contraceptives the right way and a teacher's salary never allowed moving to a bigger house and he was always taking exams to improve his salary only to have it all eaten up by hungry mouths. Everything was pretty horrible, especially the way the children fought. They'd get hold of each other's heads and give them a good bashing against the wall. Martha gave up somewhere along the line so they worked out a thing between them. The bashings, biting and blood were to operate in full swing until he came home. He was to be the bogey-man and when it worked he never failed to have a sense of godhead at the way in which his presence could change savages into fairly reasonable human beings.

Yet somehow it was this chaos and mismanagement at the centre of his life that drove him into politics. It was really an ordered beautiful world with just a few basic slogans to learn along with the rights of mankind. At one stage, before things became very bad, there were conferences to attend, all very far away from home.

'Let's face it,' he thought ruefully. 'I'm only learning right now what it means to be a politician. All this while I've been running away from Martha and the kids.'

And the pain in his head brought a hard lump to his throat. That was what the children did to each other daily and Martha wasn't managing and if Warder Hannetjie had not interrupted him that morning he would have sent the following message: 'Be good comrades, my children. Co-operate, then life will run smoothly.'

The next day Warder Hannetjie caught this old man of twelve children stealing grapes from the farm shed. They were an enormous quantity of grapes in a ten gallon tin and for this misdeed the old man spent a week in the isolation cell. In fact, Span One as a whole was in constant trouble.

Warder Hannetjie seemed to have eyes at the back of his head. He uncovered the trick about the cabbages, how they were split in two with the spade and immediately covered with earth and then unearthed again and eaten with split-second timing. He found out how tobacco smoke was beaten into the ground and he found out how conversations were whispered down the wind.

For about two weeks Span One lived in acute misery. The cabbages, tobacco and conversations had been the pivot of jail life to them. Then one evening they noticed that their good old comrade who wore the glasses was looking rather pleased with himself. He pulled out a four ounce packet of tobacco by way of explanation and the comrades fell upon it with great greed. Brille merely smiled. After all, he was the father of many children. But when the last shred had disappeared, it occurred to the comrades that they ought to be puzzled. Someone said: 'I say, brother. We're watched like hawks these days. Where did you get the tobacco?'

'Hannetjie gave it to me,' said Brille.

There was a long silence. Into it dropped a quiet bombshell.

'I saw Hannetjie in the shed today,' and the failing eyesight blinked rapidly. 'I caught him in the act of stealing five bags of fertilizer and he bribed me to keep my mouth shut.'

There was another long silence.

'Prison is an evil life,' Brille continued, apparently discussing some irrelevant matter. 'It makes a man contemplate all kinds of evil deeds.'

He held out his hand and closed it.

'You know, comrades,' he said. 'I've got Hannetjie. I'll betray him tomorrow.'

Everyone began talking at once.

'Forget it, brother. You'll get shot.'

Brille laughed.

'I won't,' he said. 'That is what I mean about evil. I am a father of children and I saw today that Hannetjie is just a child and stupidly truthful. I'm going to punish him severely because we need a good warder.'

The following day, with Brille as witness, Hannetjie confessed to the theft of the fertilizer and was fined a large sum of money. From then on Span One did very much as they pleased while Warder Hannetjie stood by and said nothing. But it was Brille who carried this to extremes. One day, at the close of work Warder Hannetjie said: 'Brille, pick up my jacket and carry it back to the camp.'

'But nothing in the regulations says I'm your servant, Hannetjie,' Brille replied coolly.

'I've told you not to call me Hannetjie. You must say Baas,' but Warder Hannetjie's voice lacked conviction. In turn, Brille squinted up at him.

'I'll tell you something about this Baas business, Hannetjie,' he said. 'One of these days we are going to run the country. You are going to clean my car. Now, I have a fifteen year old son and I'd die of shame if you had to tell him that I ever called you Baas.'

Warder Hannetjie went red in the face and picked up his coat.

On another occasion Brille was seen to be walking about the prison yard, openly smoking tobacco. On being taken before the prison commander he claimed to have received the tobacco from Warder Hannetjie. All throughout the tirade from his chief, Warder Hannetjie failed to defend himself but his nerve broke completely. He called Brille to one side.

'Brille,' he said. 'This thing between you and me must end. You may not know it but I have a wife and children and you're driving me to suicide.'

'Why don't you like your own medicine, Hannetjie?' Brille asked quietly.

'I can give you anything you want,' Warder Hannetjie said in desperation.

'It's not only me but the whole of Span One,' said Brille, cunningly 'The whole of Span One wants something from you.'

Warder Hannetjie brightened with relief.

'I tink I can manage if it's tobacco you want,' he said.

Brille looked at him, for the first time struck with pity, and guilt.

He wondered if he had carried the whole business too far. The man was really a child.

'It's not tobacco we want, but you,' he said. 'We want you on our side. We want a good warder because without a good warder we won't be able to manage the long stretch ahead.'

Warder Hannetjie interpreted this request in his own fashion and his interpretation of what was good and human often left the prisoners of Span One speechless with surprise. He had a way of slipping off his revolver and picking up a spade and digging alongside Span One. He had a way of producing unheard of luxuries like boiled eggs from his farm nearby and things like cigarettes, and Span One responded nobly and got the reputation of being the best work span in the camp. And it wasn't only take from their side. They were awfully good at stealing certain commodities like fertilizer which were needed on the farm of Warder Hannetjie.

Christopher Hope

The Problem with Staff

Mrs Whitney had a soft, oval body, full, yet light as a balloon. Her plump cheeks were flushed from the hotel kitchen in which she worked unceasingly. Her protuberant eyes suggested an overactive thyroid.

Mr Whitney suffered from a cleft palate. He was seldom seen. Though occasionally, the gentle hrumph, hrumph, of his conversation issued from some distant part of the hotel. He had ambitions which outstripped his capital. Generations of guests heard from Mrs Whitney of his plans to rebuild the hotel extensively. It would reach thirteen storeys and include a swimming pool, hairdressing salon, restaurant and underground parking garage; the Hotel Board would award it five stars. Drinkers in the hotel's cramped little pub overheard Mr Whitney and Mr Stubb, the chemist, endlessly negotiating the inclusion of a select pharmacy. '. . .only sunglasses, suntan oil, the Pill – that sort of thing.'

A feature of the hotel was its waiters: Little David, a mulatto; Big David, a huge, apoplectic Indian; and Patrick, an African. As the hotel was small and rarely accommodated more than four guests at a time, the staff, and particularly the waiters, lived lives very close to those of the guests. In the time it took to breakfast, you could learn a lot. Little David's wife had just had a son. Big David drank a good deal, probably out of boredom, and had a bad heart. His wife had left him. Patrick was a bachelor, and this obviously enhanced his status in the eyes of his colleagues since they discussed his pursuits and conquests in loud voices and with much laughter in the dining room between servings.

So far as anyone knew, the waiters had been with the hotel for years. The respectful attitude of the rest of the staff (an elderly Malay woman, named Anne, and three part-time maids) towards them, testified to their authority. Notwithstanding, Mrs Whitney unceasingly complained that they drank, they were dirty, unpunctual, irresponsible and they smelled.

Breathlessly, she reviewed the problem of staff for anyone who would listen to her and conclude, inevitably, that they would be the end of her.

The Whitneys had a family of two sons who sometimes appeared at breakfast, presumably arriving late at night from the capital where they lived. They never stayed for long. One was training as an anthropologist with the Department of Bantu Affairs; the other was a biologist who specialised in artificial insemination.

On these occasions, Patrick was always assigned to serve the main table, and he did so conscientiously, anticipating every need like a well-trained theatre nurse. Mr Whitney usually joined his sons and would preside at the head of the table. Mrs Whitney spent mealtimes in the kitchen.

'They are funny people,' said Little David's wife, whose name was Maria as they were sitting together at home one evening.

'That is because they are different,' he explained.

Little David's house had one bedroom, a living room and a tiny hallway which they used as a kitchen. The lavatory, a pit latrine, was in the back garden. He had thought once of letting the bedroom to one of the many old men who stumbled about the hotel off-sales and earned their money for wine by doing the odd bit of gardening, dishwashing, poaching and petty thievery, and whose very existence in the area was thus a criminal offence, while his presence there was merely illegal. One of them, not too dirty or drunken, would have made a safe tenant. He'd had several offers, and no good reason to turn any of them down. Maria had been pregnant and they had needed the money. Perhaps working in a hotel with ten rooms, four bathrooms and two lounges, had gone to Little David's head. Maria thought so. It was illegal to sublet council property. But Little David did not think much of this argument. He and his family were officially classified as Coloureds, and the house stood in that area of Steun Bay reserved exclusively for the use of Indian fishermen who worked for the canning factory. Simply living there was against the law. Little David knew that they would be evicted one day. However, Indian labour was hard to come by, and the canning factory had found it necessary to employ Coloured fishermen, and to house them in the Indian township. Until he'd got the job at the Whitneys' hotel, Little David had been a fisherman. He was ambitious. Also, he was reassured by the complexities of the legal situation. When the baby came, he was glad he had kept the room. The Whitneys had given him a rise. Big

David had presented him with half a bottle of brandy. One of the guests, a tall German tourist, who heard about it, shook his hand. Patrick had laughed aloud, clapped him on the back, and asked him if he had got his seed back.

Little David smiled. He was glad of the extra pay. Big David earned twice as much as he did, but then the hotel could not run without Big David. Maria could not get over the resemblance between father and son, in every feature but one; Little David's skin was dusky, the colour of golden syrup, but the baby's skin was almost unnaturally white.

At the hotel, Big David was on duty in the dining room. Although the season was well advanced, there were few guests. Mr Whitney had dined alone. It was eight o'clock and David moved from table to table, replacing serviettes, straightening a spoon, and seeing to it that the clusters of plastic flowers stood firmly in their vases on the centre of each tablecloth, and that the water had not evaporated. His movements were sure and deliberate, but his attitude was abstracted. In the warm evening he perspired freely and he was conscious of the sweat collecting in his eyebrows. Midges darted around the tables, and Big David would occasionally pause to flick a dirty serviette into areas of light where they appeared to congregate too thickly. These sudden movements would cause the sweat to run into his eyes. Big David pushed his fist into his eye and rubbed clumsily until the smarting stopped. He felt tired and his feet hurt. Recently, they had become swollen. The doctor had warned him to expect this. The swelling grew worse at night and so Big David, who seldom took much thought for his comfort, bought himself a pair of expensive black leather slippers and wore them around the hotel from six o'clock onward each evening.

His wife, Jayalakshmi, would have laughed at the slippers. Laughed in the way she did at all his fears and aspirations.

'The new slippers,' she would have said, in much the same tone she had used when he told her of the Whitneys' plans for the new hotel,' '. . . of English leather, no doubt?' A tall woman, in an electric-blue sari, laughing.

When Jayalakshmi left him and went to live with the silk merchant, Naidoo, the Whitneys said nothing, but Big David knew that they were relieved. His wife held positive social and political convictions and liked to express them, often in strong, even strident, terms. Her unexpected outbursts alarmed the guests and infuriated the locals in the public bar.

Although Big David nearly always agreed with his wife's views in these in-flammatory matters, he nevertheless sympathised with the Whitneys, who had their position to maintain. And the more brandy he drank, the more sympathetic he became.

When it was clear that Jayalakshmi would not be returning to him, Mr Whitney drew Big David aside and explained to him his duties in the new hotel.

'You will take charge of the wine stewards in the expanded establish-ment,' he confided in a solemn susurrus. 'There will be fifteen wine stewards and they will wear bottle-green tunics bearing the hotel's crest emblazoned above the breast pocket, with gold chevrons on the sleeve, striped trousers, bow ties and white fezes. They will all be Indians. Na-turally you will be paid more.'

A few days later, the hotel's chambermaid, Anne, met Jayalakshmi in the capital and in the excitement of their meeting, and perhaps in a belated attempt to effect a reconciliation, told her of Big David's future pros-pects.

'The chief wine steward!' Jayalakshmi laughed aloud and several people had stared at them. Anne was embarrassed and had wanted to leave, but Jayalakshmi insisted on driving her to the station. Anne sub-mitted, although the size and opulence of the big, black car scandalised her.

On her return, Anne whispered to Big David the details of her meeting with all the ferocity she could muster. The next day he collapsed at the head of the second flight of stairs while on his way to answer a call from an upstairs room.

Big David sighed. After switching off the dining room light he paused by the door just long enough to view the room by moonlight. It usually soothed him, this sight of crisp white tablecloths each precisely surmoun-ted by a vase of flowers, rigorously squared and stapled into position by shining knives and forks. But the scene was without its usual calming effect of glinting metal so neatly related to gleaming white cloth. The dining room had a savage aspect tonight, showing its tables as if it were baring its teeth, and they were not neat white teeth held back by impeccably positioned braces, but yellowed stumps, rotting in dark places where the moonlight did not reach, haphazardly stopped with stainless steel.

When Patrick arrived at Beauty's room in the backyard of Mr Stubb's chemist shop, he found about half a dozen men and women already assembled waiting for the party to begin. Four gallon-jars of white wine stood on a rickety table beside the door. On the floor beside it were two old paraffin tins filled with home-brewed beer. All the women were sitting on the bed. The men leaned against the wall, smoking. There was no sign of Beauty. Patrick took an enamel mug from the table and scooped a measure of beer out of one of the big tins. The place was growing crowded. Two blackened paraffin lamps swung from the ceiling sending shadows climbing up the rough, whitewashed walls. The smell of tobacco, beer and paraffin mingled with the smell of the skin-bleaching cream the women wore on their faces, and filled the room. He moved over to the gramophone which was on the floor beneath the window. Idly he riffled through the tall pile of records beside it. He decided that Beauty must have gone for more beer.

'Attaboy!' someone called encouragingly.

A woman began to tap her feet. Patrick wound the gramophone and dropped a record on the turntable.

'That's *Mister* Monk,' the same voice approved as the first few piano bars slid into the room.

A woman left the bed and began dancing to the music, alone, twitching her bottom, a buttock at a time, to the rhythm. Patrick caught her eye. She waved invitingly. Patrick glanced about the room. Still no Beauty. Grinning, he rose to his feet and joined the woman.

An hour later, Patrick surveyed the scene again, and told himself that the joint was jumping. Nearly two dozen people had crowded themselves into the small room. The bed had been pushed into a corner to make more space. A couple, hopelessly entwined, lay on it. The dancers were sweating freely and every so often the paraffin lamp lighting on a face made it glimmer briefly. Patrick released his partner, who continued to dance alone, and went in search of more beer. The level in the remaining paraffin tin was low, and Beauty had still not appeared. He opened the top half of the door and leaned into the evening breeze. In the darkness somebody was urinating noisily against a wall. A dog barked in the next-door yard.

The sound of cheering disturbed him and he turned back into the room to see Beauty standing near the window through which she had apparently just entered. She carried a large tin of beer. Patrick grinned. The evening was wonderful. Beauty was wonderful. Smiling happily, he pushed his way towards her.

'Beauty, baby,' he said delightedly.

Beauty stared solemnly up at him.

'Beauty . . . ' he tried again, taking the tin of beer from her and raising it in an expository gesture, 'Mr Booze,' he offered hopefully.

'I have some news for you,' said Beauty grimly.

Mr Whitney was sitting in the hotel's office, beside the desk. He would have sat behind the desk, had he not felt that to do so would have offended his wife, who, since she did the books and paid the accounts, regarded it as her property. In any event, she was going to be badly disturbed by his news. No sense in adding to the confusion, he told himself. Mr Whitney's nose was sleek and sensitive. He rubbed it gently. Then he stood up. He knew what he had to do.

He found his wife in the kitchen, ladle in hand, supervising simmering pots. She eyed her husband cautiously. Mr Whitney came straight to the point.

'I have told Big David that he is to move into the hotel.'

His snuffling voice accorded agreeably with the hissing of the pots. 'For good?' Mrs Whitney asked quietly.

'At least until these attacks of his have stopped. He's had two now, and as you know, the second almost killed him. He can't go on living alone in a miserable room in the native location. He hasn't seen his wife since she ran away with that draper.'

'Why don't you let him go?'

'Be reasonable, Myra!' Mr Whitney decided to be irritable. 'I can't do that. He's a damn good wine steward. How would I replace him? Answer me that. You should know as well as anyone the problems we have finding decent staff for the hotel. Better, in fact. *You're* the one who's always complaining about it. Besides,' his pace slowed, and he articulated more clearly, 'we have a responsibility to our staff. I mean, surely you admit that, hey?'

Mrs Whitney turned her shoulder on this last question, and, taking the lid off one of the pots, peered into it intently. Then abruptly she dropped the lid and faced him, her face pinkened by the steam.

'Sick! You say he's sick. I know his sickness.'

'All right, so he drinks,' Mr Whitney was forcing himself to speak clearly, 'loves his brandy. That's true. The doctor's warned him. Everybody's warned him. In his condition it's tantamount to committing suicide.' Gingerly, he touched his wife's shoulder. 'And that's why I want him here at the hotel. I'll keep an eye on him. I'll put a stop to it.'

Mrs Whitney's eyes bulged a little more than they usually did, but she said nothing.

Encouraged in her silence, he stopped for breath. He had put his foot down and he had won. When he began speaking again he fell into his usual manner, half sibilant, half gurgle, the echo of water in an underground cavern; the sound of a scrubbing brush on bare floorboards.

'He can take one of the rooms in the backyard. That way, he won't actually be in the hotel, but I'll still be able to keep a pretty close watch on him.'

'Let him go,' said Mrs Whitney grimly.

'Then he will die,' Mr Whitney retorted with great force, 'it's not Christian.'

'Let him go.'

'No!'

The pots on the stove reverberated. Mrs Whitney returned her attention to them. Her husband addressed her back: 'There are our plans for the new hotel to consider, Myra.'

Big David found his room behind the hotel very comfortable when Mr Whitney installed him in it the following day. The doctor had prescribed a month's rest after the last attack, and Big David, grateful to Mr Whitney for a place in which to spend the time was even prepared to tolerate, for as long as he could bear it, Mr Whitney's coming between him and his brandy bottle.

Patrick and Little David did not welcome the extra shifts which in Big David's absence devolved on them, but they did not complain. Mr Whitney was pleased with the results of his plan. Mrs Whitney had not spoken to him, or anybody else, since their interview.

Big David had been resting for five days when, quite suddenly, Jayalakshmi returned. To her husband, she seemed not to have altered in the slightest. Her electric-blue sari billowed generously at her ankles as she strode into his room. His heart gave the tiniest flip when he saw who his visitor was. Instinctively his hand went to his chest. Jayalakshmi's face clouded.

'The invalid!' she cried.

It transpired that Jayalakshmi had left Naidoo. It was an affair she regretted deeply, but, she wished him to know, it was behind her now, dead and forgotten, never to be resurrected. She knew that she could rely on him to respect her wishes. His capacity for respecting the wishes of others was his most endearing quality. To think she had been unaware of his serious illness. But he should understand that she had been out of the country at the time of his first attack. Naidoo went overseas regularly on buying missions. He was still there. She had left him in Bombay. On arriving back she had had news of his condition and come to him immediately. He needed her to look after him. She, Jayalakshmi herself, would nurse him.

Big David lay staring up at her solemn face. She made a concession to his bewilderment. He was wondering about Naidoo, she insisted. He was to do no such thing. It was past foolishness. If he liked he could beat her for it, when he was well again. She paused and looked about Big David's quarters in obvious distaste.

'This is a *mean* little room they have put you in. They have a whole big hotel but they stuff you away here. You, the invalid.'

She seemed not to recall their previous accommodation in the native location some ten miles from the hotel and Big David made no attempt to remind her, but smiled gently.

'They are different from us,' he waved a deprecatory hand.

Jayalakshmi's lip curled and she turned and walked furiously out of the room.

Mr Whitney withstood Jayalakshmi's unexpected return as bravely as he could, but his replies to her questions and accusations were hesitant as if the words would not come out of his mouth and hid behind his damaged palate. He agreed that the little room in the backyard would be too small for both her husband and herself. But at the time he had suggested to Big David that he stay there, he had not anticipated her sudden return. Now he would have to look for something roomier, for the two of them. Always providing, of course, that she intended staying on? But his sarcasm was lost on Jayalakshmi who had begun to shout. Trying desperately to mollify her, he explained that, in the changed circumstances, he would make other plans for accommodating her husband and herself. However he could not agree with her suggestion that the room in the backyard had been too cramped in the first place. It was better than the old room in the location. He reminded her that Big David was gravely ill. Here, help was close at hand. He denied her charge of discrimination, and he informed her that he had effected the move as a kindness, yes, a Christian kindness. He did not hate Indians. He implored her not to shout.

In her office, Mrs Whitney covered her ears as Jayalakshmi's voice cut through the hotel. It was clearly audible in the dining room where

Patrick and Little David were laying places for dinner, and they stopped to listen. Little David's admiration for Jayalakshmi swelled inside him.

'Are my husband and I to eat, sleep and excrete in that little pondok,' Jayalakshmi hissed, 'like cattle?'

Grim-faced, Mr Whitney insisted, for the third time, that he realised circumstances had changed and that the room would be too small for both of them. He stressed, however, that until Jayalakshmi's sudden and wholly unexpected return, the arrangements which he had made for her husband's eating and sleeping had satisfied both his doctor and Big David himself. As for the *other* matter which she had seen fit to raise, well, he would point out that separately housed toilet facilities adjoined the room in question. He had no idea where Big David would stay now. He had not thought about it.

'There are plenty of empty rooms on the third floor.'

'But those are guest rooms.' Mr Whitney was shocked.

'And they are always empty,' Jayalakshmi replied placidly.

'For God's sake, woman, I can't let you people stay in the hotel!'

'Why not?'

'It's illegal!'

'It's illegal to have my husband staying in your backyard. I know the law. You have to have a permit from the peri-urban authority if your servants sleep in. I also know; who should know better than I who slept ten years in a filthy, stinking shack in the native location because there was no legal accommodation for my husband within nine miles of his work; I also know that they don't issue living-in permits around here.'

The ground was loosening beneath Mr Whitney's feet. 'I appreciate your concern, and I sympathise, of course. But what can I do about that? You say you know the law. Well then, you will know that Indians must stay in the Indian area. Please see my predicament.'

'The predicament is ours,' Jayalakshmi said coldly.

He stared at her impassive face. From the centre of her forehead her crimson caste-mark glowered angrily at him. Briefly, he wondered how she kept it in place. He sighed.

An hour later, with the help of his colleagues, Big David was settled comfortably in the largest of the guest rooms on the third floor. Below, kennelled in her office, Mrs Whitney listened to the heavy breathing of the waiters as they struggled up the stairs carrying Big David's bed, scrabbling their way along the landing, urged on by Jayalakshmi's sharp, strident directions towards the patient's triumphant installation. The

clang of a chamber pot, a muffled laugh, a series of soft bumps and
scrapes as furniture was rearranged and, finally, the deep creak of bed-
springs. These sounds of Big David's entry into the hotel reached her
clearly, and scratched themselves on her heart. She trembled with anger.

In the bar, Mr Whitney was having a quiet drink with Mr Stubb.

'Perhaps,' said Mr Stubb, 'the new pharmacy might include a massage
parlour. A good hotel needs a massage parlour. And, come to think of
it, the masseuse might double up as a counter assistant. No staff problem
that way.' So excitedly did he lean forward at the thought of this that the
tip of his nose touched Mr Whitney's. 'And such fun, too. Just think of
it, our own little masseuse!'

'And no staff problems,' Mr Whitney agreed, 'important that – staff can
break you in this game.'

He said nothing to Stubb about Big David's move upstairs. But he
was beginning to feel less concerned about it.

He slept well. Mrs Whitney was up and gone before he awoke. She
went to market in the capital on Saturdays. She'd don her one good hat,
a faded wreath, and often returned in a better temper.

Patrick waited on him at breakfast. He wasn't his usual smooth,
efficient self. Beauty's news had unsettled him. But Mr Whitney did not
notice. A fresh problem faced him. Little David had been called home
urgently. He had left shortly before serving breakfast, without an explanation.

He knocked at the door of Big David's room. There was no response
He paused briefly, and then opened the door. Big David was lying propped up in bed with his eyes closed and his hands folded over his fat
stomach. Jayalakshmi sat beside him and did not turn when the door
opened. To his surprise, he saw Little David in an armchair beside the
window. No one acknowledged his presence.

'Well, well, David, I thought that you had been called home?' he
remarked in what he hoped was a voice of cheerful enquiry.

Little David opened his mouth but did not seem capable of speech.

'Early this morning the Coloured Affairs Commissioner served an
eviction order on him and his family. He must be out of the Indian township within twenty-four hours.' Jayalakshmi's manner was brisk.

Mr Whitney had not left the doorway. 'But where is he to go?'

For a long moment it seemed as if his question would go unanswered.
'In the meantime he will stay here.'

He thought his voice was going to desert him. He struggled with it
behind his palate.

'Here,' he managed at last, 'with his family?'

'With his family,' Jayalakshmi answered decisively.

'It's either here or in the Coloured township, nearly twenty miles away,' Big David said softly from his bed, without opening his eyes. 'He's a good waiter. We can't afford to lose him.'

'But not here,' Mr Whitney protested, 'not in the hotel.'

'In the backyard room. The one Big David had,' Little David implored. '*Please*, Mr Whitney. There is just my wife, the baby and myself. There'll be no trouble.'

'Surely you don't object to that, Mr Whitney?' Jayalakshmi asked, turning to face him for the first time since he had entered the room. 'As my husband and I are no longer occupying the room why shouldn't Little David have it?'

Mr Whitney struggled to control his welling emotions, none of which, he discovered with surprise, resembled anything approaching anger.

'But it's . . .'

'Illegal!' Jayalakshmi stamped her foot.

It was hopeless. He found that he could not identify his feelings, control his thoughts or even summon up his convictions. Yet, strangely, this somehow seemed not to matter. Jayalakshmi's icy logic cooled his flushed consciousness. The woman was right. The legality of the move was so far removed from the reality of the situation as to make any discussion of it not merely academic, for matters had gone far beyond that, but absurd.

'Of course, you will have to make your own cooking arrangements,' he said.

It was the strong smell of cooking that drew Mrs Whitney to the room in the backyard. A glance through the window was enough. She wheeled and walked furiously back into the hotel, her eyes huge and shining strangely. She found her husband in the damp little lounge, poring over the blueprints of the new hotel.

'I must talk to you,' she said, walking past him and into her office under the stairs.

Mr Whitney took a deep breath, folded up the plans, and followed her. He would show her what dignity was. She slammed the door closed and turned to face him.

'There are Coloured people in the backyard,' she said. 'Why, yes, there are. I had been going to tell you. Since Little David and his family have been summarily evicted from their home. I reflected on the duty of the hotelier towards his staff, and towards his hotel, and I decided to give them permission . . .'

His wife ignored him. 'There are Indians in the hotel itself, in the bedroom above ours.'

Mr Whitney nodded.

'Are you out of your mind?' she shouted suddenly. 'There are now more of them than us on these premises.'

'I fail, absolutely, to see the cause of your alarm.' His wife was obviously becoming hysterical and he found the sight distasteful.

'After all, they do work here,' he retorted coldly.

'But would you tell me then why they are living here? This is a decent hotel, not a bladdy native location!'

'Myra!' Mr Whitney was shocked.

'What are we going to tell the guests? You must know that it won't be long before they start noticing that we have Indians and Coloureds living next door to them, using the bathrooms. You don't know these people, Theo, I'm telling you, they're not like us. Give them your finger and they'll take your whole hand. And I can't stand to have them living all round me. I'll tell you again, this hotel's getting just like a bladdy shebeen. Take it from me.'

She had never spoken to him like this before. She'd be sullen, or show dumb insolence; but never such language, such shrieks. Her words must have carried to every corner of the hotel. But he'd come into her office determined to take a firm line and now he had no choice but to stick to it.

'It won't be for long,' he said evenly, 'and there won't be any trouble. If you refuse to believe that, and prefer to indulge in this silly, hysterical rage of yours, then I had better leave you to it.' Without waiting for her spluttering reply, he turned and left the office.

A burst of laughter from the third-floor guest room cut short Mrs Whitney's keening soliloquy. She blanched and was silent.

Thus it was more than she could bear when she learnt the following day that Patrick had arranged with Mr Whitney to move into one of the small rooms on the third floor with his new wife, Beauty, who showed early but unmistakable signs of pregnancy. Mr Whitney, now more than ever, was aware of a fitness in things. As Jayalakshmi had explained to him: Beauty had hidden the signs of her condition from her employers for as long as she possibly could. But it would have been only a matter of weeks before they recognised the obvious and, Beauty's sudden marriage to the ever amenable Patrick notwithstanding, sent her packing. As the hostel where Patrick boarded offered accommodation only to single men, the hotel was his last hope.

Two days later, Mrs Whitney fell ill. The doctor was called, but he was unable to diagnose the nature of her complaint, and ordered her to bed. That same night, very suddenly, the air went out of her, and she died in her sleep.

Deeply shocked at the swiftness of her passing, but completely lacking in what he believed to be the natural sense of loss which he had always expected should accompany such a bereavement, indeed, feeling guilty about his inability to grieve, Mr Whitney appeared to take the death of his wife rather well. However, a week later, he suffered a second shocking loss which grieved him bitterly. His elder son, the anthropologist, was tragically killed by a leopard while doing fieldwork among a primitive tribe in Barotseland.

During Mr Whitney's period of double mourning, the hotel continued to run smoothly, although a sudden influx of guests strained its facilities to the limit. If some of the guests thought it strange that none of the waiters ever seemed to go home, they put it down to staff loyalty to Mr Whitney in his time of grief, or found equally noble explanations for the courteous, efficient service they received, day and night: where there should have been chaos, they received five star attention, comparable with the best of the quality hotels in the capital.

Of course, the guests were correct when they gave the staff the credit for the smooth, professional service provided by the hotel over this un-settled period. Big David, although still confined to bed, discovered that he had some talent for figures, and devoted his time to putting the hotel's books in order. Jayalakshmi supervised the kitchen, and, with the help of Anne and the part-time maids, saw to the housekeeping and to the comfort of the guests. Patrick assigned himself to general bar duties, and his reputation for amiability and aptness spread throughout the province. Soon after Mrs Whitney's death, Little David and his family, under Jayalakshmi's direction, moved to a room on the third floor. At once the most reserved and the most ambitious of the trio of waiters, Little David worked closely with Mr Whitney in deciding matters of hotel policy, coming to assume more and more of the responsibility for these decisions. He dreamt of one day taking a hotel management course in Switzerland. His happiness was extended, if that were possible, when Maria discovered that she was pregnant again.

Mr Whitney spent more and more time in the hotel bar. He was often

joined by Mr Stubb, and there, over glasses of brandy and water, replenish-
ed with skilful anticipation by a beaming Patrick, they would discuss, in
whispers, their plans for the new hotel.

Bob Leshoai

Masilo's Adventures

Long, long ago – so long ago that it is really impossible to say exactly when – there lived a very, very poor woman whose name was Mosili. She had only one child, a boy, who was called Masilo. Masilo and his mother lived in a very small but neat hut. Though they were very poor and did not have many belongings they did not let the cares of life worry them. The villagers loved and respected them and brought them food and other necessities of life whenever Mosili and Masilo needed them. Mosili, like all mothers do, wished for the good things for her son. He in turn, like a good child, wished to make life easier and better for his family. Although he worked hard as a herdboy and sometimes as a hunter, like so many other children he spent a great deal of his time day-dreaming. Many of his dreams were caused by the deep desire to see his and his mother's life change for the better one day. It must be said, straightaway, that he never thought of increasing his small earnings by cheating other people. No, he was an honest boy from an honest home!

One day a heavy hail-storm swooped down suddenly on the village like a hawk, lashing and beating men, beasts and crops and finally leaving the whole countryside roaring with destructive lively streams. When it had passed, Masilo went out to see what damage the hail had done to his maize and pumpkin field behind their hut. The black clouds were rapidly drifting away in the strong breeze, and the sun, which had broken through the clouds was shining brightly. For a while he stood at the door of the hut and listened to the many sounds that come after a hail-storm. The half-naked little boys and girls, wearing only their *litseha* and *lithethana*, played in the muddy puddles, shouting and screaming. The cattle and sheep bellowed and bleated with relief. The men and women gathered in loud-voiced groups, viewing and discussing the results of the storm. The birds circled in the sky or sang in the trees. Numerous babbling and chattering streams chased down the hillside into the valley below. He called his mother to join him in enjoying the richness and pleasantness of the air that always refreshes the countryside after a rain. The sky was soon very clear, as they say, 'clear even at the dog's in-laws,' and across the western sky there was a beautiful rainbow which looked like a girl's large necklace.

The gods are always kind to the poor and needy! When Masilo and his mother looked at their small maize and pumpkin garden they were relieved to find that no great damage had been caused by the storm. Like all the other people, they hailed the passers-by and asked questions about what damage it had or had not done to so-and-so's fields.

When the excitement had died down and people had gone back to their daily routines, Masilo sat by his mother and watched her prepare the evening meal. The sun was rapidly sinking in the west. When the food was ready they sat outside on a low mud wall and·talked about the moon and the stars and the night noises. And it was this last conversation that made Masilo ask, 'But tell me, mother, where does the rainbow begin and where does it end?'

'My child, you ask very difficult questions,' she said in good humour. In the dark night her white teeth gleamed from the glow of the red logs.

'But yes, mother, you always say a man must ask questions. Isn't that what you always tell me?' he asked, putting his arm affectionately on her shoulders.

She did not answer him, for her mind had suddenly drifted into the distant, silent past. His eager questions and his tender touch had reminded her of his long-dead father. He had always asked questions when the men met either to work or sing or play or drink, until he was nick-named Ralipotso, 'the one who asks questions'. After a short silence she chuckled and said, 'Yes, Masilo, I'm afraid you are fast following in your father's footsteps.' And then seriously – so seriously that Masilo sat up and listened with pricked ears, 'It was he who told me the answer to your first question.'

'And what did he tell you, mother?' he asked, gently turning her towards him until their noses almost touched. She chuckled lovingly before she taunted him with a tickling finger on his chin as she said, 'The too-curious always get hurt.'

'Oh, please mother, stop your playing please,' he pleaded, getting up from the low wall and kneeling before her with her hands in his and his eyes burning with the desire to know the answer.

She became grave again and said to him, 'Your father once told me that nobody knew where the rainbow started and where it ended. But he did say that it started in a pot of gold and ended also in a pot of gold.'

He almost pulled her off the low wall with excitement as he jumped to his feet and eagerly asked, 'Is this really true mother?'

She answered firmly but tenderly: 'My child, Masilo, we never question the dead, my child. The spirits of the dead are always around to hear us if we abuse them; so be careful my child, be careful.'

These words subdued him and he sank onto the mat at his mother's feet and pleaded, 'Forgiveness, mother, forgiveness.' He saw her nod her head and sit for a moment like a statue with her hands clasped.

'It's time to sleep now, my child,' she said. She picked up the eating things and he picked up the mat while she led the way into the house. He lingered outside for a while, rolling up the mat, and then, wetted his index finger with spittle, flipped it with determination and swore, 'By the gods, the next time I see the rainbow, I shall walk to where it begins or ends!' And, of course, a Mosotho boy never swears vainly in this fashion.

One doesn't have to wait long in Lesotho to see the rainbow. In the summer the rains just come, and it can be dangerous, especially in the mountain regions when there is lightning and thunder. In the afternoons, especially on very hot days, thick black clouds usually roll up like dense smoke over the mountains. Before long the winds howl, carrying dense clouds of blinding and stinging red dust. Soon after, the black clouds rumble with loud thunderous noises and the lightning draws vicious snake-like flashes across the heavens. Sometimes like a flaming pillar, the lightning strikes the mountain-tops, dislodging huge rocks which tumble down and crush anything in their path. It is at such times that witchcraft is always feared, for people or families who are quarrelling are believed to employ evil witches who make the lightning strike across the skies, causing death to innocent people.

So it was then that soon afterwards the rains came again and Masilo saw the beautiful rainbow. He had known it would not be long before the rainbow re-appeared, so he had packed his few clothes days before and had discussed his proposed journey with his mother. Though she feared for his life, she could not refuse him permission to go because she believed what his father had told her. Masilo put on his grass hat and took his stick, to which he had tied his small bundle of clothes, and left his mother watching him with tearful eyes from the door of their hut. She felt proud as he strode manfully away, looking very much like his father. As he disappeared in the distance without having once looked back, she sent after him a silent prayer for his safety from deep down in her heart.

Masilo walked that whole day without meeting any problems; but in the afternoon of the following day, at just about the time the cattle leave the grazing fields, he came to a deep and broad river. Although he was a strong swimmer he knew it was a dangerous thing to cross a river far from a drinking place. Animals are very wise and they never drink where there may be crocodiles. Masilo therefore followed the course of the river, trying to find a drinking place. He found one shortly after sunset and was preparing to cross when he heard a very feeble voice call his name.

He swung round with his stick, ready for action. His heart was beating fast as he looked here and there and over there for the voice that had called him. Something began to move under a nearby bush and called feebly, 'Masilo my child, come near.' It was a very weak and trembling voice. Masilo approached slowly and carefully, stopping frequently to examine what now appeared to be a human being. When he was very near, the thing moved and called again; and with the agility of a leopard he leapt backwards, brandishing his *molamu*-stick threateningly and saying, 'Hey you thing, I'll finish you if you are not careful.' The voice came back, sadder and more pitiful: 'Please, child of my child, help an old and power-less woman, my child.' He approached, for even the cruellest man would have been touched by the sad voice. When he was near enough he bent down on his knees and by the light of the moon saw that it was an old – very old – and wrinkled, but not sickly, woman. She was just very, very old.

His strong young heart melted in the gaze of her dim and watery eyes and he asked, 'And what can I do for you, my grandmother?'

'Carry me across the wide river, Masilo, to the other bank where I have urgent business to do,' was her quick reply.

'But grandmother, how did you know my name? I've never seen you, neither have you seen me.'

'My child, ask no questions, for my business is urgent.'

But Masilo was determined to ask more questions, so he said, 'And what is this urgent business, grandmother?' because he was still very suspicious of the old woman.

Her voice came back feebly but with determination. 'You prattling child, do as I have asked. I'm not in the habit of being questioned like this by suckling boys who still smell of their mother's milk.'

Masilo was moved by both pity and fear, and so he took her gently onto his back and half-waded, half-swam across the wide river, hardly feeling the load on his back. She clung to him like a bush monkey. As he waded through the last few feet of water she spoke feebly but gently. 'Accept my

thanks, child of my elder brother. May the ancestors always be with you.'
He began to climb the sandy banks of the river, and as he landed, with a
last great effort, she sighed with much relief and loosened her grip on his
shoulders. The water dripping from his body, he mopped his wet brow.

She spoke again: 'Now carry me to that bush there near the ant hill and
leave me there.'

His relief was too great for him to ask any questions so he walked to
the bush and gently laid her down on a patch of green grass. 'Accept my
thanks again, child of my brother. Go well, and the ancestors look after
you.'

'I thank you, my grandmother,' he said and vanished into the night.

But he didn't go very far, as the bush was dense and he was afraid of
wild beasts. He climbed up a tall tree and spent the night in its safe branches. Next morning he gathered wild roots and fruits and ate them on
his long journey. He was still quite certain of the direction in which
one of the ends of the rainbow had been, so he walked in that way. Secretly
he hoped that he didn't have to walk for many days. He walked during
the day and slept at night; and soon he began to feel very tired because he
had now reached rough and hilly ground. Because of his fatigue he completely forgot his strange meeting with the old woman. He also began to
have two hearts about whether he should return to his poor mother or
continue the journey. When his bad heart told him to return, he would
remember how he had sworn by the fireside that night. This would, therefore, give him courage to continue. He was also worried now because
there were no roots to eat and no sign of any animals. Only threatening
vultures and eagles circled and glided above and around him and followed
him till sunset each day.

At the end of one rather long, hungry and thirsty day's march he saw
a distant light in the semi-darkness. His heart leapt for joy and his legs
felt stronger and his spirits rose so that he began to hum a low marching
song. As the darkness grew, the light became more distinct and seemed
to come nearer. Many thoughts troubled his mind, but later he thought it
might be herdboys tending their sheep in the meadows. Then he would
hold his chin as he doubted his own thoughts. 'Isn't it true that boys only
go to the meadows in the winter when the grazing lands are empty and
dry?' he asked himself aloud. And his voice and the muffled sound of
his feet echoed into the night around him. He broke into a steady trot, his
mouth watering with anticipation. Slowly he drew nearer and nearer the
light. It was now quite clear it was the light of a home fire, for hadn't he
come home several times at night guided by the friendliness of a home

fire? His fear gave way to more pleasant thoughts of a kindly and welcoming woman, or of laughing and eating with mountain herdboys. 'Yes,' he murmured to himself, 'I can now smell the aroma of meat grilled on the bare coals.' And he sniffed the clean mountain air.

He was soon standing at the gaping mouth of a huge cave through which came the inviting smell of the roasting meat. The fire was made of large logs and crackled loudly, sending the sparks in all directions; but there was no sound or sign of life inside the cave. All that he could hear was the crackling of the fire and his own heavy breathing.

He took a few steps into the cave and coughed. The sound travelled down its length and died in the distance, while he stood and listened for voices or movement. The deathly silence chilled his blood: his curly hair stood upright, his skin tingled and his ears buzzed. He shook his head and spoke emphatically: 'By my mother who bore me, this is a strange place! Travel shows us many things, indeed.' His voice echoed down the empty cave and left him colder than before. He was now resolved to hail the silent inhabitants of the cave so he cupped his hands and called, 'I greet you, young men of the meadows!'

At each shout his voice quivered down the hollow cave and died in its dark and mysterious depths.

'Comrades! Friends! Accept my greetings! I'm no enemy! Do hear you me?'

He stopped and listened, but the only sound was the echo of his voice down the empty cave.

'In truth this is strange,' he sighed softly. 'This must be the home of zombies!' he half-screamed with desperation. Then he tried again.

'I greet you, respectable ones of this cave. Greetings to you inside there, respectable ones!'

Then just as he thought 'Perhaps this is where the rainbow begins or ends and where all the gold is,' he heard the shuffling sound of what seemed to be very big feet. He had such a shock when the owner of the feet did appear that he yelled 'Mother!' and dropped his stick.

It was a tall woman whose body was twice the size of that of ordinary human beings. The severe look in her face rooted him to the ground; and he looked at her with bulging eyes. She approached rapidly and spoke urgently, 'Child, this is Limo's place and I'm his wife. No one who ever enters here goes out. You should never have come.'

He wanted to answer but his tongue was heavy. She saw the fear in his eyes and took pity on him, catching hold of his hand as though to rush him away to a place of safety. Instantly both were frozen like statues by the gruff and ugly laugh of her husband, Limo, who had just come in at the door.

'Wife,' he called out, 'my traps were empty today, but it does appear that the game has brought itself to the hunger.' And so saying, he laughed and his laughter echoed and re-echoed down the dark depths of the cave. Masilo swerved round and fell at Limo's feet, pleading for his life; but Limo merely lifted him up with his two fingers and dropped him into his hunting sack, tied it securely and put it in a special room where he also kept his treasure of gold locked in a huge steel box.

Now Limo was very tired, for he had walked all day in search of game without any success. After his wife had fed him a huge dish of porridge and half a buck he went to sleep, determined to boil Masilo next day in a huge pot. Before long he was snoring loudly and sleeping soundly.

His wife, who was filled with pity for Masilo, crept into Limo's bedroom and took from him the keys to the special room. Then she went into the room and quickly released Masilo, loading him with many pieces of rich gold and sending him on his way with instructions to run all night and never look back. She put a huge stone into the sack, tied it as before, replaced the keys where she had found them and went to sleep. Once Masilo was outside the cave he ran like a hare without once looking back. As he ran he thought of how his and his mother's life would be changed if he got home with all the gold. He had also now completely forgotten about reaching the place where the rainbow ends or begins.

At about day-break he reached the ant hill where he had left the old woman, days ago. His heart sank when he saw again the small bundle under the bush and heard its voice calling him. He was now no longer afraid of the old woman so he went over to her and took her on his back, carrying her across the river to leave her, as she asked, where he had first found her. She thanked him and gave him three tiny pebbles and told him that whenever he was in trouble he should throw one to the ground and wish anything and it would happen. He thanked her for the pebbles and began his long walk with his heavy load, back to his native village where his mother was waiting for him. By the time the cattle went out to their grazing he was very, very far from Limo's cave.

Limo was now up, boiling water in the big pot to cook Masilo. His wife went about her work as though nothing were wrong. The greedy and sourfaced Limo was waiting for the water to boil, and while he waited he sat next to the fire chewing bones to sharpen his teeth. He was a very nasty and untidy monster who kept on spitting chewed bones into his flaming fire. His wife did not like him, for he was cruel to her. He starved her and never allowed her to see the gold he had hoarded in the cave. At times he would eat a whole buck in her presence without even offering her the tripe, which is what women like best. As for his habit of eating human flesh – oh! how she hated the monster!

When the morning dews began to disappear from the grasses the water in the pot boiled and Limo rose from his seat to fetch his 'venison,' as he always referred to humans. He lifted up the sack and found it heavy. He grinned and exclaimed. 'What fat venison! I shall eat till the fat drips off my finger.' His wife heard him and she thought to herself, 'Well, fine venison indeed you shall have today!'

Limo unlaced his hunting sack and had it ready to empty the contents into the steaming water. He stood towering over the boiling pot and shook into it the contents of his sack. There was a great splash followed by a loud crash and the pot split into numerous fragments. The boiling water burnt his face and body and feet and he ran out like a madman.

When he discovered how his wife had cheated him, he threatened her with a big spiked stick but she pleaded for mercy. Limo would have beaten her, but he had no time, as he was determined to recapture Masilo. Limo could run very fast! He quickly took up his sack and followed Masilo, guided by his nostrils, like a dog. He strode over the mountains as though they were small ant hills and soon saw Masilo. He went even faster.

Masilo heard the sound of his running and loud breathing and he thought of the pebbles the old woman had given him. He did not look back, but took out one of the pebbles and threw it to the ground and wished that it turned into a tall tree with a trunk so big that it would block Limo's way. The tree instantly appeared and Masilo climbed high up into its branches. A slippery moss grew on the trunk and made it impossible for Limo to climb; so he ran home to fetch his great axe. This gave Masilo time to climb down and run again.

He could now see the smoke from the fires at his village rise like lazy serpents into the still hot afternoon air. Soon Limo was back with his axe and a few hefty strokes toppled the tree. Masilo heard its loud noise as it fell.

Now Limo raced towards his quarry like a grey-hound after a hare. Again Masilo heard his steps and his loud breathing close behind, so he took out the second pebble and threw it to the ground, wishing it to turn into a high, high mountain. Instantly the mountain was there, with Masilo on the other side. Limo realised he could not cross the mountain so he ran back to his cave and brought back with him a sharp hoe.

Masilo could now see the people of the village moving about like tiny insects, and he regained courage. He began to call his mother's name, hoping that he might be heard by them, but his voice could not reach so far. He heard Limo furiously dig a path through the mountain. His knees felt weak but he ran and never looked back. A few whacks with the hoe opened a wide path and Limo started to chase Masilo again like a wild stallion chasing a mare. His feet sounded like the hooves of a horse. Masilo could feel his hot breath all around his ears, so he threw down another stone and wished that it would turn into a broad, deep and swift river.

Such a river immediately separated Masilo from Limo, whose eyes were now red like burning coals. His nostrils looked like open pits. He was grinding his teeth and shouting insults at Masilo. Masilo did not look back; he just ran and ran. The furious Limo was back at his cave like a flash of lightning. He snatched a huge bucket and before you could count five he was back at the river scooping up buckets full of water. The water flowed as though it had rained, but the river remained full. Limo's whole body was dripping with sweat. When he saw that Masilo was near his village he worked even harder. He leaped into the air, he shook his fists, he danced like a crazy top, but nothing frightened Masilo. He just ran and ran and ran and never looked back. And the river flowed furiously and its waters rose like the waters of the sea when there is a strong wind.

Masilo was now within shouting distance of the village and his shouts attracted the people, as did Limo's mad noises and the sound of the mighty river. When Limo realised that Masilo was on the outskirts of the village he dived into the roaring stream in desperation. But he was already so worn out that he was soon carried away in the strong current and drowned in the deep seas far away.

Masilo's mother and the villagers were happy to see him alive. He built his mother a beautiful house and bought her many cattle and sheep and he was respected and loved by all the people for his courage and sacrifices for his mother's sake. Months later he rode with young men of the village on beautiful horses to bring Limo's wife to live with them in the village. She was happy to live a new and virtuous life and, with her cruel husband's treasure, helped all the people of the village to build beautiful houses and to buy fat cattle and sheep.

As for the old woman, Masilo never found out what happened to her, and what her urgent business was across the river.

And thus ends the story.

James Matthews

11.41 to Simonstown

Near the station, propped up against a wall, was the man who had both his legs amputated above the knee but whose impassive face showed that he had not lost his dignity as a man as he rested on the palms of his hands, in front of him a pile of newspapers. A brief flicker of eyes the only acknowledgement as more than the customary charge for a newspaper was dropped into his cap. The stairs at the top of the subway were guarded by a squad of ticket examiners clad in thick, woollen uniforms.

Except for children, none of the passengers on the crowded platform showed any interest in the trains slithering to a halt at the opposite platform. The train pulled in – the 11.41 to Simonstown. 'Mowbray. Alle stasies Simonstad. Simonstown,' ticket examiners bawled.

It was not the time for the niceties of behaviour. Elbow-gouging was the only way to get a seat or else it meant a long, unsettling stand with fingers curled around a shoulder strap. The carriage was packed and although all the windows were open, the built-in smell of third-class carriage was nostril-prickling, but only those new to third-class travel found the indefinable odours upsetting.

At each stop more passengers forced their way inside, turning the space between the two long benches running the length of the carriage into a market place of parcels, suitcases and squatting children. A puppy gave a yelp of pain as someone trod on its paw.

Conversation was loud and spaced with bellyrumbling laughter. Bottles clinked merrily, signifying the start of the week-end. Those who could not wait until they reached home took out a spare bottle and drank deeply. Bottles were passed from hand to hand.

'Alle kaartjies' . . . 'All tickets' – the voice of authority. The signal for bottles to be hurriedly shoved inside supermarket paper bags only to be pulled out when the ticket examiner had made his exit. An inebriated fellow traveller belched loudly each time the train jerked. Those seated on either side looked alarmingly at each loud protestation. Others in the vicinity wondered how long it would take before an overloaded stomach would weaken.

A series of hip-jolting jerks supplied the answer.

The result was not pleasing to the wearer of the off-white coat seated next to the very much sick-to-the-stomach traveller. The off-white coat was dyed by a torrent of greenish bile.

The wearer of the off-white coat raised a fist in retaliation but quickly withdrew as another torrent cascaded his way.

The 'what must be, must be' from a pipe-thin woman dangling from a shoulder strap was not very consoling to the owner of the soiled garment who glared ineffectively at her and the despoiler of his coat dabbing at his mouth with a sheet of newspaper which he spread on the floor to cover the remains of a liquid lunch.

'Wine is a mocker, and strong drink is raging. Whosoever is deceived thereby is not wise. That my brothers and sisters is found in the Book of Proverbs. And that is God's truth!' The words froze the drinkers and they sat with bottles poised in mid-air, eyes focused on the speaker. 'Yes, my friends. It is written in the Bible that wine will make you as worthless as the swine driven into the sea. The drinkers of wine are like rotten fruit to be ploughed into the earth.'

The voice high-pitched as a boy soprano, face smooth and unlined. Hair shaped into a widow's peak, two lines arrowing down his cheeks to flourish into a neatly-trimmed beard. His eyes sharp and piercing, stabbing at those he addressed, had the haughtiness of a camel. His tall, lean body moved with grace, lending an elegance to the drab olive raincoat he wore.

'Shit!' a drinker ejaculated.

'No, my friend. It is not shit!' the saviour of souls countered, waving his Bible in front of the speaker, his eyes flashing a challenge to further disputants of the veracity of the word of the Lord.

'God so loved the world that He gave His only begotten son to save sinners. Is it too much to ask of you that you should give up wine?'

'But Jesus also made wine,' someone said defensively.

The plea was not worthy of a reply and the speaker was raked contemptuously by the piercing eyes of the preacher.

'It is said here in the Bible, Matthew 6, verse 24: "No man can serve two masters; for either he will hate the one, and love the other." You cannot serve God and wine!'

In the short spell of silence that held sway the adenoidal breathing of a youth with acne-scarred features scraped the air. His short-sleeved sweater proclaimed 'I need Loving' in scarlet letters across the chest.

The preacher stepped back and turned his body aslant, coat twirling, chin raised imperiously and his eyes eloquent with the message delivered. His stance was that of an actor who had delivered a dramatic curtain speech. The histrionics of the occasion were not lost on him as he surveyed his not altogether captive audience, and if there had followed a burst of applause he would have accepted it as his due. A few loud amens showed that he had found recruits to his cause.

The drinkers had not capitulated. Their dissension found voice in a short, fat man, the bags under his eyes testimony to his addiction to the vine.

'Who give you the right to preach?' he challenged. 'Is this your church?'

The preacher strode towards him, Bible held aloft like a banner.

'As the Lord has sent His apostles to preach His word in the highways and the byways, so do I follow in the footsteps of the apostles. The church of God is wher'ver His word is spread.'

'That still don't give you the say-so to tell us what to do. We don't belong to your church.'

The preacher closed his eyes and bowed his head in prayer.

Another voice came to the defence of the drinkers. 'I know where he can shove up that crap he's giving us.'

The preacher twirled around fiercely to face this new attack.

'Mock not the word of God. For those who speak in blasphemous terms, their end will be bitter. Repent before it is too late. Shed yourself of wine and drink of the blood of the Lamb of God. Amen.'

His amen was fervently echoed by his followers.

Retreat Station: some of the adherents from both camps departed. Buildings had thinned and fields flanked the tracks; fields sprouting flowers and vegetables. All it needed to complete the pastoral scene was cattle lowing, or a herd of horses acanter with manes bannering the breeze. Then the smell of ploughed earth changed to the smell of brine; the fields of flowers replaced by a pattern of reeds and boaters exploring the channels cutting through the reeds.

The carriage had turned into two camps. The followers of the preacher were smaller in number but their advocate was more eloquent in speech and adroit in attack. The dissenters, though a larger group, erupted in solitary sorties that were easily routed by the preacher.

The preacher fired another broadside before the drinkers could marshal their firing-power.

Muizenberg pulled in more passengers. Fishermen going through to Fish Hoek; domestic servants staying at Noordhoek. As the train pulled out, one of the girls spotted a companion of hers seated on a bench.

'Hey, Maria. You old jintoe!' she called. Maria, not put out by the slur cast on her character, waved back gaily and responded in a likewise manner; their laughter friendly farewells.

A transistor radio entertained the new passengers. A two-hundred-pound woman got up and went into a shambling dance, flesh shifting in every direction. The younger girls encouraged her with handclaps and shrieks. 'Come'n,' she said, plucking at the sleeves of two fishermen. They could not keep up with her gyrating and retired to their seats to replenish themselves with wine. She hoisted her dress to her thighs, revealing kneecaps the size of chamber pots. She climaxed her dance by grasping the slender pole shooting from floor to ceiling and swung around it like a grotesque queen of the maypole. The fishermen complimented her with ribaldry.

The preacher's eagerness to engage this new group of desecraters of the law of God was emphasized by his words.

'Drunkenness, revellings and such like; of which I forewarn you, that they who practise such things shall not inherit the Kingdom of God.' He flipped open the pages of the Bible to show further proof of the error of their ways. 'There are only two roads in life. The broad and the narrow. The broad road is filled with those partaking of the pleasures of the flesh and the world. The narrow road has but few travellers. For that is the road to eternal happiness.'

A young man, broad of shoulder, moved towards the preacher. Around his neck was draped a silken, tasselled scarf. A copper band glittered at an ear. He planted himself opposite the preacher's band.

'You, preacher. You listen to me,' he said arrogantly. 'I know all the roads. I travel all of them, and all roads the same. They all lead to one place. And that's hell! All of us, we end up there. You too, you and your hymn-singing lot!'

The drinkers were jubilant. 'That's right. Tell him!' they prompted their champion. 'He don't pay for what we drink. It's our own sweat.'

The preacher's followers looked expectantly at the preacher for the words that would vanquish his adversary.

The preacher looked at his attacker, measuring his worth as an opponent.

'You are wrong, my brother.'

'I'm not your brother. My mother didn't lay with every man.'

The preacher shook his head in silent reprimand at the interruption.

'No, my brother. You are wrong. Man has an immortal soul, and by following in the footsteps of the Lord, he shall find his way to heaven on the day of judgement after we have been judged. It is not too late, my brother. Kneel here in prayer with me and your soul will yet find redemption because the Lord is merciful to the lambs that have strayed from His flock.'

The offer of salvation was spurned.

The preacher ordered his congregation to pray for a lost soul. The congregation dutifully bowed their heads.

The commencement of their prayer tapped a flow of vituperation.

The preacher's face reflected his serenity. He had found his Calvary. Each curse was a nail impaling him on his cross. He clasped his hands over his Bible and held it to his breast.

The ticket examiner disturbed the tableau as he reproached the preacher's castigator. 'You're going to have trouble with me if you don't stop your swearing.'

The preacher's coterie smiled their approval.

The examiner's reprimand had wilted the spirit of the boozer's brigade.

Their champion was not cowed by the examiner's censure, and after the examiner's exit he resumed battle.

'I know all your tricks. So don't come up all holy-holy for me. You no better than any of us. You sweet-Jesus us with your mouth and your eyes lead our women to your bed.'

An outraged gasp came from the preacher's followers which the preacher stilled with a flutter of hands. A middle-aged woman with ample bosom, heading three others cast in similar mould, and in whose midst sheltered a tiny, old man, expostulated in shocked tones: 'Have you no shame? You talking to a man of God!'

'Ask him if he know what it is to be converted, a child of God?' one of the bosomy ladies nudged the old man whose wrinkled, skinny neck swivelled from side to side in his wide collar.

The old man, beady eyes flickering at the young man on the opposite seat, drew in his neck like a tortoise, his bobbing adam's apple evidence of his agitation. The ferocity displayed by the young man deterred him.

The presence of the preacher lent strength to the old man and his reedy voice rasped: 'If you had walked the ways of those converted, your tongue, it will not play you false like a serpent.'

The women's section of those who were assured of the salvation of their souls looked with approval on the old man safeguarded by their bulk.

The old man's admonition was too much and the response was another explosion of expletives.

The carriage was hushed, all eyes on the ticket examiner who, at the first curse, had stopped in his task of collecting tickets. Body stiff with fury, he stomped towards the offender.

'I told you I didn't want to hear any more filth from you,' he said as he grabbed hold of the offender's scarf and pulled him to his feet.

The drinkers sat crestfallen as they watched their champion marched to the guard's van.

The preacher spoke quietly, like soft rain, then the words came hard and fast as hail hammering the stubborn earth. 'It is said in Proverbs 23, verse 30 to 32: "They that tarry long at the vine, they that go to seek mixed wine. Look not upon the wine when it is red, when it giveth its colour in the cup, when it goes down smoothly, at the last it biteth like a serpent, and stingeth like an adder." Brothers and sisters, the word of God is law.'

Hallelujahs showered like offerings dropped on an altar.

'Wonderful the ways of the Lord,' one of the women exclaimed. 'He think he can mock the word of God, and see what happen to him!'

The bosomy quartet started singing and the hymn was taken up by the others. The old man's voice was a trembly quaver. Their singing was punctuated by an occasional grumble. The drinker who had first challenged the preacher's prerogative to sound a sermon sat hunched up cradling a bottle from which he took sips in between venom-tipped glances at the preacher who stood unperturbed and triumphant.

The rails were laid flat on the sand; the sea almost within touching distance. Simonstown and naval ships riding at anchor. A white gull traced its route against the blue of the sky. The preacher and his congregation departed singing a paean of praise to their Maker, and a condemnation to those who sought to thwart His work. He led his willing flock across the sand to wash away all signs of visible sin in the waters of the sea of Galilee.

Es'kia Mphahlele

A Ballad of Oyo

Ishola (also called Mama-Jimi because her first son was Jimi) found a tramp on her counter slab at Oyo's central market, where she took her stand ― ... day to sell vegetables and fruit. Furiously she poked the grimy bundle with a broom to tell him a few things he had better hear: there are several other places where he could sleep; she sells food off this counter, not fire-wood – like him; so he thought to lie on a cool slab on a hot night, eh? – why does he not sleep under a running tap? And so on. With a sense of revulsion she washed the counter.

These days, when market day began, it also meant that Ishola was going to have to listen to her elder sister's endless prattling during which she spun words and words about the younger sister's being a fool to keep a useless husband like Balogun in food and clothing. Off and on, for three months, Ishola had tried to fight against the decision to tell Balogun to go look for another wife while she went her own way. Oh, why did her sister have to blabber like this? Did her sister think that she, Ishola, liked being kicked about by her man the way Balogun did? Her sister might well go on like this, but she could not divine the burning questions that churned inside Ishola.

That is right Ishola, her sister, who sold rice next to her, would say. You are everybody's fool, are you not? Lie still like that and let him come and sit and play drums on you and go off and get drunk on palm wine, come back and beat you, scatter the children – children of his palm wine-stained blood, (spitting) like a hawk landing among chicks then you have no one to blame only your stupid head (pushing her other breast forcibly into her baby's mouth for emphasis). How long has he been giving you so much pain like this? How long are you going to try to clean a pig that goes back into the mud? You are going to eat grass very soon you will tell me and do not keep complaining to me about his ways if my advice means nothing to you.

And so goes the story of Ishola, Ishola who was called Mama-Jimi, a mother of three children. Slender, dark-and-smooth-skin with piercing eyes that must have seen through dark nights.

Day and night the women of Oyo walk the black road, the road of tarmac to and from the market. They can be seen walking, riding the dawn, walking into sunrise; figures can be seen, slender as twilight; their feet feel every inch of the tarmac, but their wares press down on the head and the neck takes the strain, while the hip and legs propel the body forward. A woman here, a woman there in the drove has her arm raised in a loop, a loop of endurance, to support the load, while the other arm holds a suckling child in a loop, a loop of love. They must walk fast, almost in a trot, so that they may not feel the pain of the weight so much.

The week before the week before Mama-Jimi started for Oyo Market, her body feeling the seed of another child grow that had not yet begun to give her sweet torment, bitter ecstasy in the stomach. The night before her husband had told her he was going to the north to see his other wiv᷈: He would come back – when? When he was full of them and they of him, Mama-Jimi knew. When he should have made sure that the small trade each was doing went well, he said.

Mama-Jimi looked at his shadow quivering on the wall in the light of the oil lamp as he stooped over her, and loneliness swept over her in a flood. They loved and they remained a promontory rising above the flood. And Mama-Tunji again took her place in the order of things: one of three wives giving all of her to one she loved and taking what was given by her man with a glad heart. Oyo will always be Oyo whatever happens to it, the market will always be there, come rain, come blood, come malaria.

It was the week before only the week before when the rain caught the market women on the tarmac to market. The sky burst and the rain caught the market women on the tarmac to market. The sky burst and the rain came down with power. It rumbled down the road in rivulets. Mama-Jimi felt the load inside become heavy knotting up beneath her navel. Her feet became heavy, the hips failed to twist. But she tried to push on. She could see the others way ahead through the grey of the rain. Mama-Jimi's thoughts were on the market, the market of Oyo: she must reach it. For if she should fall, she thought, or feel sicker, other women were there.

But the woman sagged and fell and dragged herself out of the road. She felt the blood oozing, warm and cold. A life was running out of her, she was sure of it. A life dead just as soon as born and sprouting in her . . .

Two women found her body on the roadside: cold, wet.

Whispers bounced and rebounded at the market that Mama-Jimi was dead, dead, Mama-Jimi was gone, gone in the rain.

Did she know it was there?

Ehe, she did she told me so.

And her man gone to the north, a-ah? So it is said.

Are they going to call him? They must. Only yesterday night we were together and she was glad she was going to give her man a second child.

To die when your people are far far away from you, a-ah!

We are most of us strangers here.

It is true.

This was a week before, and the market at Oyo jingles and buzzes and groans, but it goes on as it has done for many years before when the first Alafin came here.

You know what the market is like every morning, not so? Babbling tongues, angry tongues, silent tongues. Down there a woman was suckling a baby while she sold. Near to Ishola a woman was eating *gari* and *okaran* and gravy out of a coloured enamel bowl. Someone else next to her handled her sales for her. As the heat mounted a lad was pouring water on bunches of lettuce to keep them from wilting and thus refusing to be sold. But the lad seemed to be wilting himself, because as soon as he leaned back against a pole, sleep seized him and his head tilted back helplessly like a man having a shave in a barber's chair.

The mouth opened and the lettuce lost its importance for a while. Mostly *oyingbo* – white people – came to buy lettuce. On and off while he slept, someone sprinkled water on his face. This seldom jolted him out of his stupor. He merely ran his hand over his face, stared at the lettuce and then poured water on it. Some fat women opposite Ishola's counter were shouting and one seldom knew whether they were angry or simply zealous. They also splashed water over the pork they were selling so as to keep away blue flies that insisted on sitting on it. All the would-be buyers who stood at the pork counter fingered the pieces: they lifted them up, turned them round, put them back, picked them up again. There was no exchange of smiles here.

Ten shillings, said the pork woman who herself seemed to have been wallowing in grease.

Four shillings, suggested the customer.

Eight shillings last.

Five (taking it and putting it back as if disgusted).

Seven las' price.

With a long-drawn sound between the teeth to signify disgust, the customer left. The pork woman looked at her fellow-vendor, as if to say, 'Stupid customers!'

Oyingbo women did not buy meat at these markets. They said they were appalled by the number of hands that clutched at it. They bought imported meat in the provision stores at prices fixed seemingly to annoy expatriates. One missionary woman had been known to bring a scale for the vendor to weigh the meat in order to get her money's worth. What! she had exclaimed, you don't weigh meat in this market? Ridiculous! The meat women had looked baffled. The next time the missionary brought her own balance. This time *they* thought something was ridiculous, and they laughed to show it. Even after weighing a piece, she found that she still had to haggle and bargain. Enthusiasm had flagged on her part, and after this she came to the market only to rescue some of the lettuce and parsley from continual drenching and to buy fruit.

So did the other white women. One of them turned round in answer to a shout from a vendor, Custumah, customah! She approached Ishola's counter where there were heaps of carrots and tomatoes. She was smiling, as one is expected to do from behind a counter.

Nice car-*rot*, madam.

How much?

Shilling (picking up a bunch).

Sixpence.

No madam, shilling (smiling).

Sixpence.

Ha-much madam wan' pay? (with no smile).

All right, seven pence.

Ni'pence.

Seven.

No, 'gree madam (smiling).

The customer realized that she had come to the end of the road. She yielded, but not before saying, 'Ninepence is too much for these.'

A-ah madam. If not to say madam she buy for me many times I coul' 'ave took more moni for you.

Towards sunset Ishola packed up. She had made up her mind to go to Baba Dejo, the president of the court of the local authority. She firmly believed that the old man had taken a bribe. Either her father-in-law or Balogun himself, her delinquent husband, could have offered it. This, she believed, must be the reason why the court could not hold a hearing of her case against her husband. Twice Ishola had asked him to hear her case. Each time the old man said something to delay it. The old fox, she thought. This time, she fixed simply on putting five pounds in front of the president. He cannot refuse so much money, Ishola thought. But go back to that animal of a husband, never – no more, he is going to kill me one of these days I do not want to die I do not want to die for nothing I want to work for my children I want to send them to school I do not want them to grow old on the market place and die counting money and finding none. Baba Dejo must take the money he must listen to my case and let the law tell Balogun to leave me alone with the children and go his way I will go mine I know his father has gone and bribed him to keep the matter out of the court and why? – because he does not want to lose his son's children and because – I do not know he is very fond of me he has always stood up for me against his son – yes, he loves me but I am married to his son not to him and his love does not cure his son's self-made madness. Lijadu loves me and I want him let my heart burst into many pieces if he does not take me as his wife I want him because he has such a pure heart.

Ishola was thinking of the day Lijadu came to fetch her in his car and they went to Ijebude for that weekend of love and heartbreaks: heart-breaks because she was someone else's wife someone who did not care for her and even then had gone to Warri without telling her. Now Lijadu was ready to give Balogun the equivalent of the bride price he had paid to Ishola's parents and so release her to become his wife. Balogun and his father had refused Lijadu's money.

Just what irritates me so, Ishola thought. I could burst into a hundred parts so much it fills me with anger. So they want to stop me from leaving their useless son, useless like dry leaves falling from a tree. Just this makes me mad and I feel I want to stand in the middle of the road and shout so as everyone can hear me. That man! – live with him again? He beats me he leaves me no money he grows fat on my money he does not care for the children the children of his own own blood from his very own hanging things . . .

I wonder how much the old man will want? The thought flashed across Ishola's mind, like a streak of lightning that rips across the milling clouds, illuminating the sky's commotion all the more.

If your father-in-law Mushin were not my friend, says the president of the court, Dejo, when Ishola tells him the business of her visit, I should not let you come and speak to me on a matter like this. It is to be spoken in court only.

You do not want me to bring it to court sir.

I would do it if, if –

How much, sir?

Give me what you have, my daughter. He looks disdainful in the face as he says so. It does not please the young woman. He takes five pounds in paper money from her hand.

What is this I hear from your father-in-law, that you want to leave your husband? Ishola feels resentful at the thought that her case must have been chewed dead by these old men. But she presses the lid hard to keep her feelings from bubbling over. I beg that you listen, sir, she says. Balogun beats me he does not work he eats and sleeps he does not care for the children of his own-own blood, sir, he drinks too much palm wine this is too much I have had a long heart to carry him so far but this is the end of everything no no this is all I can carry.

Is he a man in bed?

Not when he is drunk and that is many times sir. She was looking at the floor at this time.

Hm, that is bad that is bad my child, that is bad. What does he say when you talk to him about his ways?

Nothing, sir. He just listens he listens and just listens that is all.

A man has strange ways and strange thoughts.

There is silence.

So he drinks himself stupid. I know there are certain places in Oyo where you can hear the name of Balogun spoken as if he were something that smells very bad. So he drinks himself stupid until he is too flabby to do his work in bed, a-ah! How many children have you by the way?

Three, sir.

The youngest is how old?

Two years, sir.

If a man gets too drunk to hoe a field another man will and he shall regret, he will see. He seems to be talking to himself. But a man who comes home only as a he-goat on heat, the old man continues, and not as a helper and father is useless. I will tell him that I will tell Balogun that myself. Animals look for food for their mates and their brood, why cannot a man?

You have talked to him twice before, sir.

Oh yes oh yes I have my child I know.

Silence.

But your father-in-law Mushin loves you so much so much my child.
I love him too but I am his son's wife not his.
You speak the truth there.
Silence.
It would break his heart all the same. Look at it whichever way you like.
You fill a space left in his heart by the death of his wife and often defiled by
the deeds of a worthless son. Dejo's face is one deep shadow of gravity.
I do not like that boy Balogun not one little moment, he goes on, but
his father will weep because he holds you like his own-own daughter.

Ishola's head is full of noises and echoes of noises, for she had heard
all this a few times before. She has determined her course and she shall
not allow her tender sentiments to take her out of it, she mustn't, no, not
now. Perhaps after, when tender feelings will be pointless. She still bears
a little love for Balogun, but she wants her heart to be like a boulder so
as not to give way.

Let me go and call my wife to talk with you more about this, old Dejo
says as he leaves the room. As he does so, he stretches out his hand to
place a few crumpled notes of money in Ishola's hand, whispering, 'Your
heart is kind, my child, it is enough that you showed the heart to give, so
take it back.'

Ishola feels a warm and cold air sweep over and through her. She
trembles a little and she feels as if something were dangling in space and
must fall soon.

Old Dejo's wife enters, round-bellied: the very presence of life's huge
expectation.

But – such an old man! Ishola thinks . . .

I can see it in her eyes Balogun I can see it in her eyes, Mushin said in his
son's house one morning. Ishola is going to leave us.

She is at the market now, Papa. She loves me too much to do a foolish
thing like that.

When are you going to wake up you useless boy. He gasped, as he had
often done before. What kind of creature was given me for a son! What
does your mother say from the other world to see you like this!

Balogun poured himself palm wine and drank and drank and drank.
I can see the blade of a cutlass coming to slash at my heart, the older man
said, I can feel it coming.

Go and rest father, you are tired.

And Balogun walked out into the blazing shimmering sun, stopped to buy cigarettes at a small stall on the roadside and walked on, the very picture of aimlessness.

When are you going to stop fooling like this with Balogun I ask you? Ishola's sister said rasping out as she sat behind her counter. Her baby who was sucking looked up into her face with slight but mute concern in its eyes.

She does not know she does know this woman she . . . will never know she will know what I am made of . . .

I would never allow a man to come stinking of drink near me in the blankets (spitting). I told you long ago to go to court and each time you allow that old Dejo with his fat wife to talk you out of it. Are you a daughter of my father?

Oh what a tiresome tongue sister has . . . You wait you, you just wait . . .

Just a black drunken swine that is what he is. A swine is even better because it can look for rubbish to eat. Balogun does not know what people are he would not go a long way with me no he would not he does not know people. Eat sleep and lay a pile of dung, eat sleep and lay a pile of dung while men of his age group are working: the woman who gave birth to that man . . .!

Sister! Leave that poor woman to lie quiet in her grave!

I will but not that wine-bloated creature called Balogun.

Lijadu must not forget to send Mushin's money of the bride-price . . .

That piece of pork? a customer asked.

Ten shillings.

Five.

Nine.

Six.

No 'gree.

Six and six.

No 'gree. Eight, las' price.

Seven.

No 'gree.

And the market roar and chatter and laughter and exclamations and smells put together seemed to be a live symphony quite independent of the people milling around.

Black shit! Ishola's sister carried on . . .

Ishola was out of Oyo in the evening, going towards Oshogbo with her three children. Lijadu would follow the next day and join them in a small village thirty miles out so as to make pursuit fruitless. Lijadu joined her at noon the next day, looking pale and blue and shaken.

What is it with you Lijadu? Why are you so pale? Are you sick?

Silence.

Lijadu what is it?

He sat on the ground and said Mushin has passed away. He passed away about midnight. One of the neighbours found him lying cold in the passage. People say they heard him cry the last time: Ishola, my grand-children!

Ishola could not move for a few moments. She seemed frozen cold cold cold.

At break of day each morning you will see the women of Oyo with their baskets on their heads. You can see them on the black tarmac going to the market, their bodies twisting at the hip the strong hip. You can see their feet feel their way on the dark tarmac as they ride the dawn, riding into daylight. The figures are slender as twilight. You can see Ishola, too, because she came back, came back to us. She told us that when she heard of the death of her father-in-law she thought This is not good for my future life with Lijadu I will go back to that cripple.

Mothobi Mutloatse

Don't Lock up our Sweethearts

They had come complaining. Yes they did, and how!
They were complaining, with tears flowing
from their red and tired eyes and flickering hearts.
Theirs was a sincere complaint from the heart;
and this was unexpected from
'so humble and tacit a community'.

And the community of Bogosibatagwa
so small and smart
had thousandfold grievances.
The crowd *was* demanding.
Weren't they justified?
No wonder they were hurling, cursing,
shouting and flinging all sorts of
questions at the Mmuso.
Demanding, rightly or wrongly,
at least an explanation.

In unison they roared: 'Don't lock up our wives,
don't lock up our daughters – please, please.'
And in a harmonious chorus the rabble, yes,
the rabble as far as Mmuso is concerned, thundered:
'We won't condone it. We don't!'
Militant? The work of agitators?

Vigilantly observe there
a fretting father
over the forthcoming bogadi –

now disappointed.
Pity enveloping everyone.
Even that forlorn lover yonder
missing red-lipped kisses.

Imagine yourself from toil
sweating from top to toe
to find your home dimly-lit
and cold because
your sweetheart is 'away',
taken away – by another man!
A reliable rogue of Mmuso . . .
unceremoniously 'raped' by Molao.
And of all God's hours at dawn.

Yes
the people's outbursts were justified.
Justified to an extent, you might add . . .
The community's precious pillars were
cracking under the heavy weight of Mmuso.
It follows too that the whole nation
was apt to crumble.
You see, that refreshing fragrance was gone,
'taken away' . . . by you know who by now.

Simmer down. Don't rush, my soft people, pleaded
roly-poly Ntate Modula-Setulo.
But the crowd was *impatient*.
Unlettered people have no time for dialogue
or diplomacy. Poor man, he was being bombarded
with queries, some noteworthy, some damn silly
and some very thought-provoking.

Don't despair. Never. You shouldn't.
That was the hopeful message.
Yet the townsfolk were seriously
banging their clenched fists on each
other's shoulders,
somewhat order-like:
'Don't lock up our sweethearts!
You hear!'

Hearken, a lean man blurted out:
'Ke basadi ba bo mang?'
The animated audience replied:
'Dus ours. Ke basadi ba rona.'
Some interlarding: 'Ja ja.
Hulle is onse susters; onse ousies,'
carelessly and in inarticulate tongues.

Suddenly a big-bosomed Aunty boomed
from the back of the hall:
'Ke masepa fela.
It is nothing else but bullshit.'
Ntate Modula-Setulo warned:
'This is certainly no bloody shebeen house.'
Courageously a gruff voice replied:
'And definitely *not* a jailhouse',
above the hoarse applause and wild guffaws.

Like a god-sent,
pious balding Ntate Moruti philosophized
compassionately: 'Much harm,'
said he in a musical tone,
'is born out of stupidity.
Therefore, my loving Brothers and Sisters,
I beseech you to give an ear unto what
Ntate Modula-Setulo here has to tell.'

Hush, hush, hush . . .

Those words were like an antiseptic
during the fever of lekkerkrap.
But John Muntu from the bundu
was unconvinced.

'Is it fair? Is it fair, my people,
to be sent to that rodent-infested House?
For a woman to be sent to such a house?
I am speaking from personal experience.
My marital bed is empty, my wife's gone.
Gone to that rodent-infested House –

by force!'
Questioning was like a hobby to that silly,
inquisitive and shrewd John Muntu.
He was unlike the others,
he wasn't a yes-baas muntu.
Just then an energetic Aunty heaved
herself up: 'We are those unloved ones.
We're the victims. Where are our men,
our bold and strong men?
Damn them for condoning these intrusions
by Mmuso. *I am a woman*, I said.'
Yes it is true.
Our men are cool-aids.
Our men are monkeys.
Our men behave like women!
'Shut up!' shouted Ntate Modula-Setulo.
'You sit down. And you. And you too.'

Above all the audience was vehemently emphatic.
No dice, no dice yes.
They said:
'We love our women. We don't want
border permits for them. Our womenfolk
are not chattels. They are priceless pearls –
ours. They are our sweethearts too.'

Behold
that ordinary-looking Muntu had turned
into a dynamo of speech: 'Is it fair,'
he reiterated, 'this attitude of Mhlope's?
He's got no respect; he's got no humility.
Yet we, the so-called heathens and savages
that eat half a loaf of bread,
throw it away and then buy another –
we honour him warmly.
And what in the *hell for?*
Where oh where is Mhlope's reciprocity?'

'For heaven's sake, sit down!' interrupted
Ntate Modula-Setulo.

'For Pete's sake listen,'
squealed John Muntu confidently.
'Let the man speak,' shouted the audience
at Ntate Modula-Setulo.
and *wasn't* he embarrassed?
It was clear:
John Muntu was the people's hero.
John Muntu continued: 'Now, our womenfolk
have been kwela-kwelaed, just because
they couldn't afford to pay R2 fines.
People, are you happy about this situation?'
'No, damn no,' fired back the crowd.
'Don't dare lock up our daughters again!
There'll be hell to pay . . .'

And over there
Ntate Moruti was praying unnoticed:
'Modimo, forgive them, for they know not . . .'
Shame c-c-c-c.

Mbulelo Mzamane

My Cousin and the Law

It had become like a festive season. Mzal'uJola, my cousin, seemed like a man who had struck a fortune. It was a season of reconciliation, too, for we had discovered that Sergeant Mawulawula, the most dreaded policeman in our township and previously an avowed enemy of my father, was a distant relation of ours. I have never been able to understand how he made it up with my father who had always denounced him as an enemy to the bitter end. But then my father is not one to scoff at another's outstretched hand. So Sergeant Mawulawula regularly came to our house after work. Because he addressed us as his nephews we came to regard him as our uncle, although we could never call him anything but 'Sajeni'.

Sergeant Mawulawula immediately developed an affection for Mzal'uJola who felt very awkward at first because he had never been on more than greeting terms with a policeman before. Gradually, however, he warmed up to Sergeant Mawulawula's overtures, and indeed came to value the relationship. Once he had grown used to being on the same side as the law, his tongue loosened. They usually talked of places they had known as children in the Transkei; they came to discuss mutual acquaintances and wondered at the efflux of people from the homeland; they argued at great length about the evils of city life. Their conversation usually wound up with general observations on the various money-making schemes people in the cities were engaged in.

My mother, to the general discomfiture of both, loudly claimed that no good could ever come of mating two dangerous beasts. She had always been hard on Mzal'uJola and hostile towards Mawulawula whom she could never forgive for having twice tried to extort a bribe from my father. Without my father's characteristic ability to mix oil and water my mother would have thrown the two out of the house. Of course, they never gave her the chance because at her entrance they would retire, sometimes on very chilly evenings, to continue their conversation on the lawn.

Mzal'uJola usually left home early in the morning, carrying a small bag which never left his side, to return laden with meat and vegetables in the evening. He would produce his mysterious booty like a conjurer, with such flourish that despite herself my mother could not help laughing at his drunken majesty and dizzy sense of achievement. At first it was impossible to discover where he obtained his goods from. We all knew that he had no regular source of income. My mother used to tell me that he had been described once by a magistrate – whose only fault, according to Mom, was that he had not kept Mzal'uJola in prison but had decided to repatriate him to the Transkei, thus giving him a chance to retire anonymously to our township – as 'a native of no fixed occupation'. Mzal'uJola was so evasive about where the food came from that we were soon reconciled to eating nondescript and perhaps, as Mom never failed to point out, dishonestly procured chunks of meat and vegetables. Only when he brought us bread of the type called 'mbhunyane' did it dawn on us that he brought us food obtained by what-means-we-still-could-not-tell from people employed on the mines where rations of meat, vegetables and 'mbhunyane' are doled out.

Mzal'uJola sometimes returned home wearing the unmistakable air of a small-time tycoon. On such days he would retire to his bedroom with his bag firmly held under his armpits, and lock the door. As this only heightened our curiosity we were always at pains to observe him through the window whose curtains, in his perpetual stupor, he often forgot to draw. On one such occasion I counted no less than thirty-three rand notes and some odd coins. I was convinced that Mzal'uJola was now a wage earner and volunteered the information to my mother who warned everybody, in general, against touching stolen money. Mzal'uJola remained as adamant as ever about divulging anything beyond his triumphant grin. Nor was he willing to part with a penny more than was necessary, consequently none of us received so much as a cent from him. We began to receive less and less supplies of food till the practice virtually ceased.

Mzal'uJola started to sleep out over week-ends and sometimes on weekdays, too. He was now living like a popular man of independent means. Scores of people began to come, singly or in families, to see him at home.

When they found him out they would leave their addresses behind with urgent messages for him to call. One such tense-looking man came to our house twice. On the third occasion he sent his son, all within an hour. My mother was eventually moved to ask the son: 'Does Jola owe your father anything, my son?'

'N-no, aunty. At least, I do not think so,' the boy answered timidly.

'Then why is your whole family after him? I suppose your mother will be here next.'

'No, my mother is still crying over the child.'

'What child?'

'My sick brother.'

'Is that why you have been sent after Jola?'

'Yes, aunty.'

'Are you sure your parents don't want to see my husband, the priest?' my mother asks kindly and suggestively.

'No, aunty,' the boy replies resolutely, 'they asked me to tell Jola to hurry. My father says he's been here twice before.'

'To be sure he has,' my mother puts in absent-mindedly. 'Well, he's not at home,' she pursues, 'but we'll impress upon him the urgency of your father's message when he returns, if he's sufficiently sober, that is, to appreciate the urgency of the matter.'

'Remain well, aunty,' the boy says, rising.

'Go well, my son. There's really no point in waiting for him.'

That was the first hint I received about Mzal'uJola's latest fund-raising schemes. A few days later I was left in no doubt.

Two gentlemen came to our house one morning. Mzal'uJola rose to let them in. They were speaking sufficiently loudly to be heard from my bedroom. The sudden movements from my parents' bedroom convinced me that they were also up and probably listening to the conversation in the kitchen. The strangers seemed to have come to consult Mzal'uJola on some grave matter.

In solemn tones I heard Mzal'uJola explain: 'The best time is always before sunrise.'

'In Durban where my colleague and I worked before coming here we did it with sea water, along the beach, always before sunrise,' one of the gentlemen said in a hoarse voice that made me suspect he was a consumptive.

'Sea water is good, too, but it is simply like salted water in many respects. My mixtures are that and more,' Mzal'uJola announced authoritatively.

'I have never taken them myself', the hoarse voice rejoined, 'but Qwathi here has nothing but praise for your mixtures.'

'Yea, they are excellent for a bad bile. I can vouch for that,' said the gentleman addressed as Qwathi.

'I have the mixtures in the garage. I prepared them last night. They are still warm with potency. We have an ideal spot behind the garage where you can vomit your bile out. Then I can assure you, all headaches and stomachaches and whataches will be a thing of the past . . . This side please, gentlemen.'

The kitchen door was shut with a bang as Mzal'uJola led his patients out. I recalled the many people who often came to consult him, the agitated father and his son, the money he was always carrying, his little bag which had become part of his personality, and felt certain that he was in the herb business. No new game to him this, as I had heard my mother relate once. No doubt, a most resourceful man, my cousin. In every respect a match for his former master, that other daring enterpriser, Jikida, with whom he had had to part. Jikida had accused my cousin of seducing his wife. My cousin had answered back with his fists. There the partnership had ended. Mzal'uJola had certainly rendered himself better service by launching into independent business where he was matching Jikida in all departments. But what a strange man, and so close-fisted too. Can hardly buy himself a khaki shirt or trousers; he still uses my father's. But when it comes to drinking!

The door opened.

I soon heard the rattle of our electric kettle from the kitchen and the noise of cups and saucers.

A hoarse voice hissed: 'My head is feeling quite clear already. I'm sure this will benefit my voice too.'

'The thing is to do this regularly,' put in a professional voice, 'otherwise it turns out like irregular weightlifting. Little benefit it does your body. On the contrary, each indulgence, after each long lay-off, produces painful after-effects on the muscles. But if you exercise regularly you can actually perceive the development of each bicep. It is the same with emitting the superfluous contents of your stomach which can only produce shit or a bad bile. The more frequently emitted, the better for your health. I shall let you have half the contents of that splendid mixture for an additional two . . .'

Somebody was talking in my parents' bedroom. No, they were both up and conversing in low whispers. Probably about Mzal'uJola.

I wish they move out of the house before my mother finds them in the kitchen. Somebody is stirring out of the bedroom. She must be heading for the bathroom, to prepare for work. That should give them a chance to clear out. She must be late for work. No, she is day-off today. Could it be father? He must be getting ready for mass. What a household: a priest, a witchdoctor and a nurse.

I heard my mother's slippers shuffling towards the kitchen and held my breath so as not to miss a single word.

'Good morning,' came my mother's vibrating voice.

Two uncertain 'Morning Ma'am's.

A bold 'Molo, Mama! . . . This side, please, gentlemen.'

Mzal'uJola was most expertly steering clear of the danger zone. I heard the kitchen door bang as they went out.

My sisters who must have been listening to everything, like myself, soon joined my mother. When I walked into the kitchen I was struck by three dirty cups and saucers lying in the sink, a tin of Frisco Coffee, Gold Cross and a bowl of sugar and coffee from the table. However, it was not to be until Mzal'uJola's return, half an hour later.

'Hey, Jola', my mother shouted as soon as she heard him whistling his way back to his bedroom.

'I'm coming, Mama,' he replied and disappeared into the bedroom.

'Hey, can't you hear I'm calling you,' pursued my mother, incensed by his nonchalance.

My cousin reappeared soon after, carrying his small bag.

'Why must you display such impertinence, especially after treating the township to my coffee?'

'I'm not being impertinent, Mama,' Mzal'uJola answered with genuine humility.

'What do you think we buy this coffee with, this sugar, this condensed milk, all of which you spitefully spill on the table?' my mother continued in the same uncompromising tone.

'I'm sorry, Mama, but I didn't entertain the whole —'

'Hey, don't answer back when I talk to you. What do you mean bringing your criminal friends to eat me out of my house? I must inform the police of your illegal presence here. And, please don't bother to return tonight. If you think this is an African eating-house you are mistaken. You can't leave a single penny behind for housekeeping but I'm sure you are the toast of every shebeen queen and husband-seeking widow in the township. Don't think I won't go to the police this time. If Mawulawula won't arrest you I'll have to arrange for your dual arrest. Fancy, keeping a pickpocket with homicidal tendencies in my house. Where's the money you were given for administering poison to those fools?'

'I was given no money.'

'Uyaxoka, Jola! Liar! Give me some of that money,' my mother said, rushing towards my cousin who seemed to have been awaiting one such opportunity for clearing out. As he walked hurriedly through the front door my mother accompanied him a good fifty yards with additional threats and curses.

Mzal'uJola returned home that evening too drunk to allow even my exasperated mother to edge in an insult as he spoke endlessly.

My mother had always instinctively detested the liaison between the two and said the only reason Sergeant Mawulawula didn't arrest Mzal'uJola was because 'dog doesn't eat dog'. The point was brought sharply home to me two days after the quarrel between my cousin and my mother. I happened to listen in, from a strategic but unobtrusive point behind the door, to an argument between Sergeant Mawulawula and Mzal'uJola as they sat smoking in the dining room.

'But, neph,' Sergeant Mawulawula was saying, 'I have given you a whole week's grace to square things.'

'Yes, uncle, but you can't draw blood from a stone,' Mzal'uJola replied.

'But it's a fact, neph, for a whole week I've not had a single penny from you. How would it be if, for a whole week, I omitted to take the police off your tracks?' Sergeant Mawulawula laughed a threatening laugh which, however, seemed to have little effect on Mzal'uJola.

'It seems, uncle, that for the last fortnight you have done nothing but set them after me. You seem determined to cripple the business. Why must you come pass-raiding around my place of work? You know very well what a slight slip on my part as I try to escape may cost us. And the way your chaps keep spilling my herbs so that I have to look for new ones every time. A patient on special treatment may discover that he has been given a different herb from what had been originally prescribed, you know. And, only yesterday my herb-case was almost damaged by *your* kick, uncle . . . No, don't deny it. I saw you before you turned to chase after *me*, uncle. It is almost beyond endurance, dearest uncle.'

'Look here, neph, you know very little about police procedure. We must patrol every little corner of the township. It is our duty to the tax-payer . . .'

'What do you care about the taxpayer's money? Didn't you personally pocket . . .'

'And then,' continued Sergeant Mawulawula, brushing aside Mzal' uJola's remarks, 'it's not as if I let anybody chase after you. I go after you myself so that you can escape. Where is the danger in that? Don't you think I'd contrive a fall myself if you accidentally tripped?'

'Of course, uncle, I appreciate your point of view. But then the necessity of all this has cost us both a great deal. It's probably cost me much in dignity, too. What good do you think it does my professional reputation to be seen leaving my patients in the lurch when I'm supposed to be their protector?'

'Your patients must appreciate your inability to perform miracles.'

'Precisely,' Mzal'uJola put in heatedly. 'I wish they'd learn not to think of me as a witchdoctor. I am a herbalist, in case you also didn't know, uncle. There's as much difference between a herbalist and a witchdoctor as between a white-trained medical practitioner and your apostle of old, in case you didn't know that too. Your apostle could raise Petros from the dead but the doctor claims no such mysterious powers.'

'It's Lazarus who was raised from the dead, neph.'

'Don't be irrelevant, dear uncle. A herbalist, for your information, can no more work miracles than your doctor. Yet my patients will come for love potions and nails to ward off evil spirits. Shebeen queens want come-come to attract customers. And the pity of it is, though that isn't my line, I need the money, uncle.'

'Surely, no harm can come of that, neph.'

'No, indeed, no harm can come of it, save that my rather undignified disappearance must surely tarnish my reputation as a performer of miracles. And that, dear uncle, is not good for our pockets. I have graduated from working for vegetables, stinking meat and stale bread from the mines, you know.'

'There must be some way of capitalizing on the situation,' Sergeant Mawulawula put in ruminatively. 'Supposing, with all the assurance I've given you, you embarked on a campaign, designed to enhance your reputation, and told the people how impossible it is for you to be arrested because of your ability to change into something else, a cat, a mouse, oh! almost anything.'

'No, no, that won't do uncle because these people actually observe me outstripping them, and you in hot pursuit.'

'But, neph, the point is, you only become invisible to the police.'

'Then how come you are able to sit on my back while I tear off like a scooter?'

'Perhaps, because I have supernatural powers, too,' the sergeant put in crisply.

'May that reputation not be more to your advantage than mine? May it not also serve to keep your enemies in check?'

'Precisely,' the sergeant replied warmly. 'The thing is, neph, I'm tired of these upstarts who join the police force for rapid promotion. But then, you and I know that even the best educated of them are superstitious. It is at that weak point we must strike.'

The two men remained silent for a while. I was thinking of the news I'd tell my mother when the sergeant cut through my thoughts.

'Now, my dear neph, we are both men of the world. Both our professions are arts of the expedient. We must live, dear neph. You must admit it's now overdue, I mean my share of the spoils.'

'Uncle, you have the glass and you have the drink. Since drink I must, I'll give you this for a bottle opener.'

My curiosity propelled me into the sitting room in time to see Mzal' uJola pull out a wad of notes, count six, and surrender them to Sergeant Mawulawula. The conversation was momentarily checked by my entrance. I felt as misplaced as a village butcher at an executive meeting of the I.M.F. I made my retreat to listen from my unobtrusive position behind the kitchen door.

'And one more thing, uncle. Rivalry from certain quarters of which you are fully aware is detrimental to our pockets.'

'But of course, neph. I had meant to touch on that point.'

'Oh! I thought you were preparing to leave.'

'As I've said before, knowledge of police procedure is not what you can pride yourself on, neph. Let the law grind its course and our enemies are automatically ground. Now the party in question . . .'

'Must be put out of the way, uncle.'

'The party in question,' Sergeant Mawulawula pursued undeterred, 'is obviously in league with one of my lieutenants and confidants. If I could only, which shouldn't be so long now . . .'

'Of course, uncle, he is. As you never asked me before I thought you knew. I can give you the low-down. I've worked with Jikida before. He is in a better position than me, having been in the police force before where he made invaluable contacts. If he gets his house permit, which expired some years back, renewed, I'll know why. Let me see . . . Moloi, Msibi and Lentsoe, to name but a few, are all in his employ.'

'Which explains it, dear neph. Those three must be the people who tip him for there's no scheme I indulge in without prior consultation with them.'

'I can assure you, uncle, that not only those three but every constable you've ever confided in is in league with Jikida. His contacts have instructions to pass on the names of any new people you take into your confidence so that he may buy them over too.'

'I'll tell you what, neph. We'll pounce without warning. I'll simply collect my squad and strike as quietly as a phantom. Tonight. Did you say the fellow has no permit to be resident in the location?'

'Yes, it expired, let me see . . . Ahem . . .'

'Then how come he is occupying a Municipality house?'

'He has it registered under one of his tenants who has a permit but he is still on the waiting-list for a house. The wife of this same fellow in whose name the house is registered is Jikida's mistress, with the full consent of her husband. The family manages to keep the house bill down that way. I know. I was once one of his tenants.'

'So Jikida has no house permit, no right to be a nuisance,' Sergeant Mawulawula observed musingly.

Both men again fell silent for so long that I began to suspect they had fallen asleep. I was about to re-enter the sitting room when I heard Sergeant Mawulawula begging to be excused.

'By the way, uncle,' Mzal'uJola pursued, 'we don't want the fellow totally broken. That would be callous. Let him lay off our sphere, that is all we ask. A gentlemanly agreement, uncle, if you can reach it. Then we can leave him to earn his living as an illegal landlord. He can go back to his previous racket as a spokesman for those who would have him put their reference books in order, though, I'm afraid, he needs to put his own papers in order first. Why, uncle, you know there's no end to the chap's resourcefulness whereas the herb business is our only outlet. Let him take his monopolistic fingers off the medical profession. That, dear uncle, is all we ask.'

'Anything you say shall be done, neph.' Both men had risen from their seats.

Mzal'uJola proceeded to show Sergeant Mawulawula out as my mother walked in from work.

Alan Paton

The Hero of Currie Road

Mr Thomson was a gentle little man who belonged to the All-Races Party which believed in equal opportunity for all people. Mr Thomson was much liked by many people, but was disliked by many also, some because they thought he was plotting a revolution, some because they thought he would be useless at it anyway.

Mr Thomson's white neighbours definitely thought he was crazy. This was not entirely because he belonged to the All-Races Party. They thought he was crazy before he joined the Party. He always wore an overcoat, summer and winter, and as everyone knows, Durban in summer is no place for an overcoat. His favourite walk was up Currie Road and Grant's Grove to Musgrave Road, down Musgrave Road and Berea Road, and back along Currie Road. He would stop to admire a jacaranda or a flamboyant tree, whether in season for the blossom, or out of season for the shape. To admire the tree he would stand against someone's hedge or wall, so as not to discommode the passersby, and would think nothing of putting his head on one side for several minutes, or of turning his back on the tree, and looking at it over his shoulder.

It must be said that Mr Thomson was well known in the part of Durban where he lived. This was not only because he took his favourite walk at least twice a day, nor because he stopped, sometimes for ten minutes, to admire a jacaranda, but also because he said good morning and good afternoon to all the people whom he passed. Some of them were surprised when he did this, not having seen him before. Others were amused, because they also thought he was crazy. But there were some, especially the old Indian men and women, who would respond warmly to his salutation.

Mrs Thomson never accompanied Mr Thomson on these walks. She had a big birthmark that had plagued her for over sixty years, and she had no intention of letting it plague her any longer. Although she never went out with Mr Thomson, she was a strong supporter of the All-Races Party.

Mr Thomson was also well known in Durban in an anonymous way. He wrote letters under the name of Thos Bilby to the morning paper and Wm Breckenridge to the evening paper. These letters always dealt with civil liberty, the rule of law, and the cruelty and folly of Apartheid. Mr Thomson's great enemies on the left were Cossack in the morning, and Demi-Tass in the afternoon, and these enemies sneered at him for thinking that noble ideals would save South Africa without a revolution. He was also attacked from the right by White South African, Voortrekker Boy, Shaka and Mr J. K. Pillay, for various reasons. It was in the interludes between the battles that he would sally forth, take his walk, admire the trees, greet people right and left, and then return to the fray.

Mr Thomson became famous on September 7th. He and Mrs Thomson were reading in bed when an African scoundrel entered the room with a revolver, and ordered them to put up their hands. Mrs Thomson, a firm believer in the equal rights of the races, refused to do this. The African scoundrel knocked her senseless with his revolver, whereupon Mr Thomson jumped on his back with the firm intention of taking unprecedented steps. Mr Thomson did not use any racial adjective, but merely said, 'you devil'. Mr Thomson was quite unable at his age and weight to sustain any struggle. It was quite impossible for his weak hands to encompass and hold the scoundrel's neck. He was in fact exhausted in a few seconds, and would have fared badly had the revolver not gone off and sent a bullet into the left breast of the scoundrel, who fell down with a groan. When Mrs Thomson came to, neighbours had broken into the house, the scoundrel was bleeding and crying on the floor, and Mr Thomson was being sick into the chamber pot.

'This will be a lesson to you not to stick up for these black murderers,' said one of the nieghbours.

Mr Thomson stopped being sick for a moment.

'I have never stuck up for a murderer in my life,' he said. Then he was sick again.

Mrs Thomson covered up her birthmark with the blanket and shouted at the neighbour, 'I'll thank you to get out of my house.'

Not everyone would have become famous after such an experience. But Mr Thomson did. His heroism was extolled in both the morning and the evening papers. His declaration that his faith in the All-Races Party was unshaken received front-page notice. 'Morally reprehensible but politically irrelevant' was his summing up of the incident. His attitude was applauded by Mr Thos Bilby in the morning paper, and Mr Wm Breckenridge in the evening.

His daily walks became triumphal. White people who had never greeted him before shook his hand. Some of those non-white people who had taken him to be crazy treated him with a new respect. He was photographed by the evening paper talking to an old Indian gentleman, Mr Chetty, in his fruit-shop at the corner of Currie and Berea Roads. Both he and the old Indian gentleman were holding their hats in their hands and addressing each other with old-world courtesy.

All this explains how Mr Thomson came to be invited to address the Annual Meeting of the South African Congress.

It was mainly on the strength of his remark, 'Morally reprehensible but politically irrelevant'. He wore his overcoat as usual, and looked a fragile figure on the platform, flanked by two giant politicians, Mr Andrew Kanyile the Chairman, and Mr George Mapumulo the Secretary, both of whom had been called masterpieces in bronze by visiting journalists. This was the first occasion on which the All-Races Party had been invited to sit on the platform at a meeting of the more militant Congress. It was quite a thing for Mr Thomson to do, because many members of the Congress had been named by the Government as Communists. But Mr Thomson was not likely to be deterred by so small a matter.

He received an ovation on standing up, and delivered a stirring speech to the Congress on the evils of racial discrimination, and the responsibility of social conditions for much crime. However his speech was not received with unanimous approval. Indeed there were very audible murmurs when Mr Thomson asserted that an important cause of crime was unsatisfactory personal relationships in childhood, and that these were unrelated to the type of social organisation.

Being that kind of person, Mr Thomson did not notice these murmurs, but he was a trifle astonished when a party of younger delegates left their seats while he was speaking, not for the purpose of hurrying to some other engagement, but merely for that of lounging around the entrance doors, where they kept up a distracting number of loud conversations. As soon as the address was finished they returned to their places.

Now a strange thing happened. Mr Phumula of Inanda was called upon to thank the speaker for his address. While smiling at Mr Thomson with the greatest affability, he was able to suggest with an adroitness almost amounting to genius, that Mr Thomson's theories of crime were utterly nonsensical, and that the only tenable thing was that crime was caused directly by capitalism, laissez-faire, exploitation of the worker, and the war in Korea. These remarks were greeted with loud applause by the party of young delegates, who had now changed from supercilious loungers into earnest reformers. Mr Phumula went on to enquire whether the Mau-Mau resistance had been caused by dominating fathers, jealous mothers, and gifted elder brothers. These killings of white people were natural acts of zealots who were determined to free their country from capitalism, laissez-faire, exploitation, and the war in Korea. He declared that the hearts of true democrats went out to the Mau-Mau in Kenya.

It must be said that Mr Phumula's remarks created a difficult situation in the meeting. Some of the delegates applauded, but the great majority sat passive and unhappy. If one had been able to observe carefully, one would have noted that Mr Thomson had many admirers, several of whom looked openly disgusted. But there was no time to observe such things; the whole atmosphere of the meeting was tense and unhappy.

Beneath Mr Thomson's gentle overcoat there was boiling up a great passion, much the same as that which had made him launch his frail form onto the powerful back of the scoundrel who had struck down his wife. Being however a democrat, even if not quite the same kind as Mr Phumula, he looked questioningly at the Chairman. Mr Phumula sat down, and the Chairman rose to his feet.

His face was beaming also, and his remarks were conciliatory. He joined Mr Phumula in thanking Mr Thomson for his address. It was wonderful to him how Mr Phumula, who had certain views on crime, could sincerely thank Mr Thomson, who had somewhat differing views. The fact that there were these differing views showed what a complex problem Mr Thomson had chosen for his fine address.

'Thank you, Mr Thomson, thank you.'

'Mr Chairman, I ask permission to say a very few words.'

It was quite clear that the Chairman was embarrassed. He wanted to say no, but could hardly do so. His face beamed but his eyes were not smiling.

'Mr Thomson would like to say goodbye to us,' he told the meeting.

'It is not exactly to say goodbye', said Mr Thomson, 'it is just to say that I, and the Party I have the honour to belong to, utterly condemn murder and violence, whether it be committed by Mau-Mau in Kenya, or the British in . . .'

The rest of Mr Thomson's remarks was lost. Some of the delegates booed loudly, even though the majority, which included Mr Thomson's admirers, kept silent. He looked at the Chairman, and the Chairman looked at him. The Chairman's face was still beaming in spite of the commotion, but in his eyes Mr Thomson could see anger that he had been put into this position.

One thing was clear to Mr Thomson. There was an overwhelming wish that he should leave the meeting immediately. He bowed to the Chairman and, accompanied by the Secretary, came down from the platform. As he passed down the aisle, a few people stood up in their places and bowed to him. Those who had booed him now paid him no attention whatsoever; they had already wiped him out of their lives. It made Mr Thomson feel unhappy.

Outside in the street Mr Mapumulo said, 'We must get a car for you.'

'I should like to walk,' said Mr Thomson, and said goodbye to the Secretary and shook hands with him.

He walked away from the meeting sick at heart. The crowds of people, the Indian shopkeepers and the women in their saris, the African girls walking more gaily and freely than they would have done in the white quarter, the rich smells of the spices from Kajee's warehouse, the windows of goldsmith and silversmith and silk merchant, the white women looking for bargains, the whole surging colourful cosmopolitan scene, the meeting place of three continents, failed for once to excite him. It seemed a monstrous jest of God, this juxtaposition of such different, such utterly different people, people so blind to the vision of harmony and peace, Africans praising Mau-Mau, Indians praising Nehru, Afrikaners praising the Prime Minister, Zulus praising Shaka, the English praising Rhodes. How could he have been so stupid as to suppose that out of all this could come a country of happiness and peace? In an agonising flash of illumination, he saw how overwhelming was the Government's case, that there would never be any peace until the whole country was refashioned and re-ordered, every man to his own place, every people to its own territory, its own jobs, its own shops, its own doctors, its own customs and happiness.

How he had liked taunting the Government under the names of Thos Bilby and Wm Breckenridge! He felt ashamed to think that he at his age could have persisted with such a futility. He had asked the Government whether there would be four, five, six different Parliaments, all separate and equal? Or one Parliament above the other Parliaments? Our just one Parliament, a white-supremacy Parliament? He had then gone on to show that racial domination was unstable. Was it? Would it be any more unstable than a dream state granting equality to Mau-Mau praisers, Verwoerd praisers, Shaka praisers, Rhodes praisers? He felt ashamed of his puerilities. He looked in at a shop window and suddenly saw himself as an ineffectual old man, wearing an overcoat, member of a fragmentary Party, husband of a wife obsessed by a blemish, writer of light-weight letters that no one read, or if they read them forgot them, except other ineffectual cranks like Cossack and Demi-Tass and Voortrekker Boy.

He found his way to the Esplanade and sat down on a bench, one of a dozen benches all marked 'For Whites Only'. It was against his principles to sit there, but his principles, like himself, were tired. He must have sat there for an hour, all through his lunchtime, and he must have at last fallen into a doze, for he was awakened by the small Indian newsboys crying the name of the afternoon paper. He bought one, and his eye fell at once on the headlines:

Currie Road Hero Booed at Congress.

He had no heart to read on. The words, 'Currie Road Hero', so distasteful to him, were exceptionally painful to him in his abject condition. He was aware that elsewhere in the paper there might be a fighting letter from Wm Breckenridge. He was ashamed to think that this might be so. He was ashamed to think that it should be recorded that he had been booed at the Congress he had so often defended. What would Voortrekker Boy and Mr J. K. Pillay have to say about that? He dreaded returning to his home, to the wife to whom he had always talked so boldly. But most of all he was distressed about South Africa, about the new South Africa that he wrote about so confidently, that it was in reality his own private dream, that in reality friend booed friend while enemies mocked at them. How the Government must laugh at them!

He picked himself up wearily, leaving the paper on the bench. He walked to the bus stop, hoping to see nobody he knew. He did not want to meet anyone who would say I'm glad or I'm sad that you were booed at the Congress.

When he got home his wife looked straight at him, which she seldom did because of the blemish. She could see at once that he was tired out and dejected.

'Sit down,' she said, 'have you had any lunch?'

'No,' he said, 'I don't want any.'

'Where did you spend lunchtime?' she asked.

'Excuse me, my dear,' he said, 'I don't want to answer questions.'

She made him sit down and she put on the kettle.

'You mustn't worry about a few hotheads,' she said.

He made no answer. She brought him tea and a plate of small light sandwiches that he liked.

'I don't want to eat,' he said.

He drank his tea, and didn't eat the sandwiches, although he really wanted to. Then he was silent for a very long time.

'You know what you said once,' he asked, 'about going to Australia?'

'I said it,' she said, 'but I didn't mean it.'

'I didn't agree,' he said, 'but I agree now.'

She remembered that he didn't agree. That was a mild way of putting it. He had chastised her with his tongue for about ten minutes.

'It's a few hotheads,' she said.

He was too tired to tell her it wasn't a few hotheads. It was the crowd in the street, and the smells from the spice shop, and the African girls carefree in the Indian quarter, and the white women looking for bargains, and the seats for 'Whites Only' on the Esplanade. It was the whole thing, the whole total impossibility of fighting the Government because white people wanted the Government, the whole crass stupidity of an All-Races Party. He did not tell her this, but the hopelessness of his silence spoke to her. She got up and went into her room, and for the first time in five years dressed herself to go out in the daytime. In spite of his depression he was moved to comment.

'You're going out,' he said.

'I've stayed in long enough,' she said. She looked as though she had more to say, then she didn't say it, then she did.

'It was a silly thing to do,' she said, 'I'm not doing it any more.'

She had not been gone long when there was a knock at the door. It was Mr Chetty with a basket of fruit. Mr Thomson greeted him warmly, not only because it was hospitable, but because it warmed him to see Mr Chetty.

'I brought a little fruit for you,' said Mr Chetty deprecatingly. He was a humble man and always spoke in this manner.

'That's very good of you, Mr Chetty.'

'It's only a little,' said Mr Chetty.

'Sit down, my friend. Would you like a cup of tea?'

Mr Chetty sat down on the edge of the chair to show that he did not presume. He was too old to change. He said, 'I have come to apologise that they booed you at the Congress, Mr Thomson.'

'A few hotheads,' said Mr Thomson.

'We have Indian hotheads too,' said Mr Chetty, 'but God has His time.'

He chatted away politely. He drank his tea, and answered questions about his family, and they ate up Mr Thomson's sandwiches.

'They all know you, Mr Thomson,' he said. 'They know you are a friend of ours.'

'I feel so useless,' said Mr Thomson.

'We are all useless,' said Mr Chetty, 'but God is not useless.'

He rose to go, and asked politely if he might have his basket. Then he went.

When Mrs Thomson opened the front door, she heard the typewriter going. A smile broke out on her face, making the blemish look quite unimportant. She knew what it was; it was Mr Thos Bilby or Mr Wm Breckenridge, knocking the daylights out of Cossack, Demi-Tass, Voortrekker Boy, and the rest of that misguided company.

Richard Rive

Riva

A cold, misty July afternoon about twenty years ago. I first met Riva
Lipschitz under the most unusual circumstances. At that time I was a
first year student majoring in English at university, one of the rare
Coloured students then enrolled at Cape Town. When I first saw her
Riva's age seemed indefinable. Late thirties? Forty perhaps? Certainly
more than twenty years older than I was. The place we met in was as
unusual as her appearance. The rangers' hut at the top of Table Mountain near the Hely Hutchinson Reservoir, three thousand feet above
Cape Town.

George, Leonard and I had been climbing all day. George was talkative,
an extrovert, given to clowning. Leonard was his exact opposite, shy and
introspective. We had gone through High School together but after
matriculating they had gone to work while I had won a scholarship
which enabled me to proceed to university. We had been climbing without rest all afternoon, scrambling over rugged rocks damp with bracken
and heavy with mist. Twice we were lost on the path from India Ravine
through Echo Valley. Now soaking wet and tired we were finally in the
vicinity of the rangers' hut where we knew we would find shelter and
warmth. Some ranger or other would be off duty and keep the fire warm
and going. Someone with a sense of humour had called the hut 'At Last'.
It couldn't be the rangers for they never spoke English. On the way we
passed the hut belonging to the white Mountain Club, and slightly below
that was another but reserved for members of the Coloured Club. I made
some remark about the white Clubhouse and the fact that prejudice had
permeated even to the top of Table Mountain.

'For that matter we would not even be allowed into the Coloured
Mountain Club hut,' George remarked, serious for once.

'And why not?'

'Because, dear brother Paul, to get in you can't only be Coloured, but you must also be not too Coloured. You must have the right complexion, the right sort of hair, the right address and speak the right sort of Walmer Estate English.'

'You mean I might not make it?'

'I mean exactly that.'

I made rapid mental calculations. I was rather dark, had short, curly hair, came from Caledon Street in District Six, but spoke English reasonably well. After all I was majoring in it at a white university. What more could one want?

'I'm sure that at a pinch I could make it,' I teased George. 'I speak English beautifully and am educated well beyond my intelligence.'

'My dear Paul, it won't help. You are far too Coloured, University of Cape Town and all. You are far, far too brown. And in addition you have a lousy address.'

I collapsed in mock horror. 'You can't hold all that against me.'

Leonard grinned. He was not one for saying much.

We trudged on, instinctively skirting both club huts as widely as possible, until we reached At Last, which was ten minutes slogging away, just over the next ridge. A large main room with a very welcome fire going in the cast-iron stove. How the hell did they get that stove up there when our haversacks felt like lead? Running off the main room were two tiny bedrooms belonging to each of the rangers. We removed damp haversacks and sleeping bags then took off damp boots and stockings. Both rangers were off duty and made room for us at the fire. They were small, wiry Plattelanders; a hard breed of men with wide-eyed, yellow faces, short hair and high cheekbones. They spoke a pleasant, soft, guttural Afrikaans with a distinct Malmesbury brogue, and broke into easy laughter especially when they tried to speak English. The smell of warming bodies filled the room and steam rose from our wet shirts and shorts. It became uncomfortably hot and I felt sleepy, so decided to retire to one of the bedrooms, crawl into my bag and read myself to sleep. I lit a lantern and quietly left the group. George was teasing the rangers and insisting that they speak English. I was reading a novel about the massacre in the ravines of Babi Yar, gripping and revolting; a bit out of place in the unnatural calm at the top of a cold, wet mountain. I was beginning to doze off comfortably when the main door of the hut burst open and a blast of cold air swept through the entire place, almost extinguishing the lantern. Before I could shout anything there were loud protests from the main room. The door slammed shut again and then followed what sounded like a muffled apology. A long pause, then I made out George saying something. There was a short snort which was followed by peals of loud, uncontrolled laughter. I felt it was uncanny. The snort, then the rumbling laughter growing in intensity, then stopping abruptly.

By now I was wide awake and curious to know to whom the laugh belonged, though far too self-conscious to join the group immediately. I strained to hear scraps of conversation. Now and then I could make out George's voice and the low, soft Afrikaans of the rangers. There was also another voice which sounded feminine, but nevertheless harsh and screechy. My curiosity was getting the better of me. I climbed out of the sleeping bag and as unobtrusively as possible joined the group around the fire. The newcomer was a gaunt, angular white woman, extremely unattractive, looking incongruous in heavy, ill-fitting mountaineering clothes. She was the centre of the discussion and enjoying it. She was in the middle of making a point when she spotted me. Her finger remained poised in midair.

'And who may I ask is that?' She stared at me. I looked back into her hard, expressionless grey eyes.

'Will someone answer me?'

'Who?' George asked grinning at my obvious discomfort.

'Him. That's who.'

'Oh him?' George laughed. 'He's Paul. He's the greatest literary genius the Coloured people have produced this decade. He's written a poem.'

'How exciting,' she dismissed me. The others laughed. They were obviously under her spell. 'Let me introduce you. This is Professor Paul. First year B.A., University of Cape Town.'

'Cut it out,' I said, very annoyed at him. George ignored my remark. 'And you are? I have already forgotten.'

She made a mock, ludicrous bow. 'Riva Lipschitz. Madame Riva Lipschitz. The greatest Jewish watch-repairer and mountaineer in Cape Town. Display shop, 352 Long Street.'

'All right, you've made your point. Professor Paul – Madame Riva Lipschitz.'

I mumbled a greeting, keeping well in the background. I was determined not to participate in any conversation. I found George's flattering her loathsome. The bantering continued to the amusement of the two rangers. Leonard smiled sympathetically at me. I remained poker-faced, waiting for an opportunity when I could slip away. George made some amusing remark (I was not listening) and Riva snorted and started to laugh. So that was where it came from. She saw the look of surprise on my face and stopped abruptly.

'What's wrong, Professor? Don't you like the way I laugh?'

'I'm sorry, I wasn't even thinking of it.'

'It makes no difference whether you were or not. Nevertheless I hate being ignored. If the others can treat me with the respect due to me, why can't you? I'm like a queen, am I not George?' I wasn't sure whether she was serious or not.

'You certainly are like a queen.'

'Everyone loves me except the Professor. Maybe he thinks too much.'

'Maybe he thinks too much of himself,' George added.

She snorted and started to laugh at his witticism. George glowed with pride. I took in her ridiculous figure and dress. She was wearing a little knitted skull-cap, far too small for her, from which wisps of mouse hair were sticking. A thin face, hard around the mouth and grey eyes, with a large nose I had seen in caricatures of Jews. She seemed flat-chested under her thick jersey which ran down to incredible stick-thin legs stuck into heavy woollen stockings and heavily studded climbing boots.

'Come on, Paul, be nice to Riva,' George encouraged.

'Madame Riva Lipschitz, thank you. Don't you think I look like a queen, Professor?'

I maintained my frigid silence.

'Your Professor obviously does not seem over-friendly. Don't you like whites, Professor? I like everyone. I came over specially to be friendly with you people.'

'Whom are you referring to as *you people?*' I was getting angry. She seemed temporarily thrown off her guard at my reaction, but immediately controlled herself and broke into a snort.

'The Professor is extremely sensitive. You should have warned me. He doesn't like me but we shall remain friends all the same; won't we, Professor?'

She shot out her hand for me to kiss. I ignored it. She turned back to George and for the rest of her stay pretended I was not present. When everyone was busy talking I slipped out quietly and returned to the bedroom.

Although falling asleep, I could pick up scraps of conversation. George seemed to be explaining away my reaction, playing the clown to her queen. Then they forgot all about me. I must have dozed off for I awoke suddenly to find someone shaking my shoulder. It was Leonard.

'Would you like to come with us?'

'Where to?'

'Riva's Mountain Club hut. She's invited us over for coffee, and to meet Simon, whoever he is.'

'No, I don't think I'll go.'

'You mustn't take her too seriously.'

'I don't. Only I don't like her type and the way George is playing up to her. Who the hell does she think she is, after all? What does she want with us?'

'I really don't know. You heard she said she was a watch-repairer somewhere in Long Street. Be reasonable, Paul. She's just trying to be friendly.'

'While playing the bloody queen? Whom does she think she is because she's white.'

'Don't be like that. Come along with us. She's just another person.'

George appeared grinning widely. He attempted an imitation of Riva's snort.

'You coming or not?' he asked, laughing. For that moment I disliked him intensely.

'I'm certainly not.' I rolled over in my bag to sleep.

'All right, if that's how you feel.'

I heard Riva calling for him, then after a time she shouted 'Goodbye, Professor, see you again some time.' Then she snorted and they went laughing out at the door. The rangers were speaking softly and I joined them around the fire then fell asleep there. I dreamt of Riva striding with heavy, impatient boots and thin-stick legs over mountains of dead bodies in the ravines of Babi Yar. She was snorting and laughing while pushing bodies aside, climbing ever upwards over dead arms and legs.

It must have been much later when I awoke to the door's opening and a stream of cold air rushing into the room. The fire had died down and the rangers were sleeping in their rooms. George and Leonard were stomping and beating the cold out of their bodies.

'You awake, Paul?' George shouted. Leonard shook me gently.

'What scared you?' George asked. 'Why didn't you come and have coffee with the queen of Table Mountain?'

'I can't stand her type. I wonder how you can.'

'Come off it, Paul. She's great fun.' George attempted a snort and then collapsed with laughter.

'Shut up, you fool. You'll wake up the rangers. What the hell did she want here?'

George sat up, tears running down his cheeks. He spluttered and it produced more laughter. 'She was just being friendly, dear brother Paul, just being friendly. Fraternal greetings from her Mountain Club.'

'Her white Mountain Club?'

'Well yes, if you put it that way, her white Mountain Club. She could hardly join the Coloured one, now, could she? Wrong hair, wrong address, wrong laugh.'

'I don't care where she goes as long you keep her away from me. I have no need to play up to Jews and whites.'

'Now really, Paul,' George seemed hurt. 'Are you anti-Semitic as well as being anti-white?' My remark must have hit home.

'No, I'm only anti-Riva Lipschitz.'

'Well anyhow, I like the way she laughs.' He attempted another imitation, but when he started to snort he choked and collapsed to the floor coughing and spluttering. I rolled over in my bag to sleep.

Three months later I was in the vicinity of Upper Long Street. George worked as a clerk at a furniture store in Bree Street. I had been busy with an assignment in the Hiddingh Hall library and had finished earlier than expected. I had not seen him since we had last gone mountaineering, so strolled across to the place where he worked. I wanted to ask about himself, what he had been doing since last we met, about Riva. A senior clerk told me that he had not come in that day. I wandered around aimlessly, at a loss what to do next. I peered into second-hand shops without any real interest. It was late afternoon on a dull, overcast day and it was rapidly getting darker with the promise of rain in the air. Upper Long Street and its surrounding lanes seemed more depressing, more beaten up than the rest of the city. Even more so than District Six. Victorian double-storied buildings containing mean shops on the ground floors spilled over into mean side-streets and lanes. To catch a bus home meant walking all the way down to the bottom of Adderley Street. I might as well walk all the way back. Caledon Street, the noise, dirt and squalor. My mood was as depressing as my immediate surroundings. I did not wish to stay where I was and at the same time did not wish to go home immediately. What was the number she had said? 352 or 325? I peered through the windows of second-hand bookshops without any wish to go inside and browse. 352, yes that was it. Or 325? In any case I had no money to buy books even if I had the inclination to do so. Had George been at work he might have been able to shake me out of this mood, raise my spirits.

I was now past the swimming baths. A dirty fly-spotted delicatessen store. There was no number on the door, but the name was boldly displayed. *Madeira Fruiterers*. Must be owned by some homesick Portuguese. Next to it what seemed like a dark and dingy watchmaker's. *Lipschitz – Master Jewellers*. This must be it. I decided to enter. A shabby, squat, balding man adjusted an eye-piece he was wearing and looked up from a work-bench cluttered with assorted, broken watches.

'Excuse me, are you Mr Lipschitz?' I wondered whether I should add 'Master-Jeweller'.

'What exactly do you want?' He had not answered my question. 'What can I do for you?' His accent was guttural and foreign. I thought of Babi Yar. I was about to apologise and say that I had made some mistake when from the far side of the shop came an unmistakable snort.

'My goodness, if it isn't the Professor!' and then the familiar laugh. Riva came from behind a counter. My eyes had become accustomed to the gloomy interior. The squat man was working from the light filtering in through a dirty window. Rickety showcases and counters cluttered with watches and cheap trinkets. A cat-bin, still wet and smelling pungently, stood against the far counter.

'What brings the Professor here? Coming to visit me?' She nodded to the squat man, indicating that all was in order. He had already shoved back his eye-piece and was immersed in his work.

'Come to visit the queen?'

This was absurd. I could not imagine anything less regal, more incongruous. Riva, a queen. As gaunt as she had looked in the rangers' hut. Now wearing an unattractive blouse and old-fashioned skirt. Her face as narrow, strained and unattractive as ever. I had to say something, explain my presence.

'I was just passing.'

'That's what they all say. George said so last time.'

What the hell did that mean? I started to feel uncomfortable. She looked at me almost coyly. Then she turned to the squat man.

'Simon, I think I'll pack up now. I have a visitor.' He showed no sign that he had heard her. She took a shabby coat from a hook.

'Will you be late tonight?' she asked him. Simon grumbled some unintelligible reply. Was this Simon whom George and Leonard had met? Simon the mountaineer? He looked most unlike a mountaineer. Who the hell was he then? Her boss? Husband? Lover? Lipschitz – the Master Jeweller? Or was she Lipschitz, the Master Jeweller? That seemed most unlikely. Riva nodded to me to follow. I did so as there was no alternative. Outside it was dark already.

'I live two blocks down. Come along and have some tea.' She did not wait for a reply but began walking briskly, taking long strides. I followed as best I could, half a pace behind.

'Walk next to me,' she almost commanded. I did so. Why was I going with her? The last thing I wanted was tea.

'Nasty weather,' she said, 'bad for climbing.' Table Mountain was wrapped in a dark mist. It was obviously ridiculous for anyone to climb at five o'clock on a weekday afternoon in heavy weather like this. Nobody would be crazy enough. Except George perhaps.

'George,' she said as if reading my thoughts. 'George. What was the other one's name?'

'Leonard.'

'Oh yes, Leonard, I haven't seen him since the mountain. How is he getting on?' I was panting to keep up with her. 'I don't see much of them except when we go climbing together. Leonard works in Epping and George is in Bree Street.'

'I know about George.' How the hell did she?

'I've come from his work. I wanted to see him but he hasn't come in today.'

'Yes, I knew he wouldn't be in. So you came to see me instead? I somehow knew that one day you would put in an appearance.'

How the hell did she know? Was she in contact with George? I remained quiet, out of breath with the effort of keeping up with her. What on earth made me go into the shop of Lipschitz – Master Jeweller? Who the hell was Lipschitz – Master Jeweller?

The conversation had stopped. She continued the brisk pace, taking her fast, incongruous strides. Like stepping from rock to rock up Blinkwater Ravine, or Babi Yar.

'Here we are.' She stopped abruptly in front of an old triple-storied Victorian building with brown paint peeling off its walls. On the upper floors were wide balconies ringed with wrought-iron gates. The main entrance was cluttered with spilling refuse bins.

'I'm on the first floor.'

We mounted a rickety staircase, then a landing and a long, dark passage lit at intervals by a solitary electric bulb. All the doors, where these could be made out, looked alike. Riva stopped before one and rummaged in her bag for a key. Next to the door was cat litter smelling sharply. The same cat?

'Here we are.' She unlocked the door, entered and switched on a light. I was hesitant about following her inside.

'It's quite safe, I won't rape you,' she snorted. This was a coarse remark. I waited for her to laugh but she did not. I entered, blinking my eyes. Large, high-ceilinged, cavernous bedsitter with a kitchen and toilet running off it. The room was gloomy and dusty. A double-bed, round table, two uncomfortable-looking chairs and a dressing table covered with bric-a-brac. There was a heavy smell of mildew permeating everything. The whole building smelt of mildew. Why a double-bed? For her alone or Simon and herself?

'You live here?' It was a silly question and I knew it. I wanted to ask 'You live here alone or does Simon live here also?' Why should I bother about Simon?

'Yes, I live here. Have a seat. The bed's more comfortable to sit on.' I chose one of the chairs. It creaked as I settled into it. All the furniture must have been bought from second-hand junk shops. Or maybe it came with the room. Nothing was modern. Jewish, Victorian, or what I imagined Jewish Victorian to be. Dickensian in a sort of decaying nineteenth-century way. Riva took off her coat. She was all bustle.

'Let's have some tea. I'll put on the water.' Before I could refuse she disappeared into the kitchen. I must leave now. The surroundings were far too depressing. Riva was far too depressing. I remained as if glued to my seat. She re-appeared. Now to make my apologies. I spoke as delicately as I could, but it came out all wrongly.

'I'm very sorry, but I won't be able to stay for tea. You see, I really can't stay. I must get home. I have lots of work to do. An exam tomorrow. Social Anthropology.'

'The trouble with you, Professor, is that you are far too clever, but not clever enough.' She sounded annoyed. 'Maybe you work too hard, far too hard. Have some tea before you go.' There was a twinkle in her eye again. 'Or are you afraid of me?'

I held my breath, expecting her to laugh but she did not. A long pause.

'No,' I said at last, 'no, I'm not afraid of you. I really do have an exam tomorrow. You must believe me. I was on my way home. I was hoping to see George.'

'Yes, I know, and he wasn't at work. You've said so before.'

'I really must leave now.'

'Without first having tea? That would be anti-social. An intellectual like you should know that.'

'But I don't want any tea, thanks.' The conversation was going around in meaningless circles. Why the hell could I not go if I wished to?

'You really are afraid of me. I can see that.'

'I must go.'

'And not have tea with the queen? Is it because I'm white? Or Jewish? Or because I live in a room like this?'

I wanted to say 'It's because you're you. Why can't you leave me alone?' I got up, determined to leave.

'Why did you come with me in the first place?'

This was an unfair question. I had not asked to come along. There was a hiss from the kitchen where the water was boiling over onto the plate.

'I don't know why I came. Maybe it was because you asked me.'

'You could have refused.'

'I tried to.'

'But not hard enough.'

'Look, I'm going now. I have overstayed my time.'

'Just a second.' She disappeared into the kitchen. I could hear her switching off the stove then the clinking of cups. I stood at the door waiting for her to appear before leaving.

She entered with a tray containing the tea things and a plate with some assorted biscuits.

'No thank you,' I said, determined that nothing would keep me, 'I said I was leaving and I am.'

She put the tray on the table. 'All right then, Professor. If you must then you must. Don't let me keep you any longer.' She looked almost pathetic that moment, staring dejectedly at the tray. This was not the Riva I knew. She was. straining to control herself. I felt dirty, sordid, sorry for her.

'Goodbye,' I said hastily and hurried out into the passage. I bumped into someone. Simon looked up surprised, then mumbled some excuse. He looked at me puzzled and then entered the room.

As I swiftly ran down the stairs I heard her snorting. Short pause and then peals of uncontrolled laughter. I stumbled out into Long Street.

Sheila Roberts

Coming In

Luc, with Maman on his arm, entered the Hotel Woltemade which was, it seemed, all they could afford in this country. Papa came behind, treading in their shadows and carrying the overnight bags. Luc felt tired, his body had loosened uncomfortably, and he no longer cared, as he had when they left the ship, that Maman's make-up was over-emphatic and inexact, especially round the mouth, and that Papa's head had developed a tendency to wobble on its vein-patterned and bristly neck. He really was too tired.

Luc was too mature for seventeen, too adult, and too limply thin, untaut, delicate. So he tired easily. He might not have felt quite so attenuated had they not been forced to stand so long in the sun at the docks, waiting for a taxi, and taunted by a wind that seemed to blow directly from over a desert.

A young Coloured fellow with a serious rosebud mouth and large unavoidable spectacles attended to them at the reception desk, and Luc booked a room containing three beds. Another Coloured youth, wearing a shabbier uniform than the first (for he had only started this portering job and had to use his predecessor's cast-off uniform) led them upstairs to their room. Luc allowed Maman and Papa to go before him up the stairs. Maman's short muscular legs lifted laboriously, her feet clinging to shoes with warped heels that clunked up the uncarpeted stairs, and her bulging buttocks swayed. Papa climbed like some large-footed bird, his body bent, his neck thrust forward. His feet in large shoes, cast-offs from Luc, pointed outwards.

The room they were given overlooked the street.

There was a scratched wardrobe in it and a washbasin. Also a small bedside cupboard containing two very new Bibles and an old chamber pot.

'Don't touch that!' hissed Luc as Maman reached out her hand to investigate. Luc opened the wardrobe and stared morosely at the twisted wire coathangers suspended like felons from the copper rail. The wardrobe smelled of camphor or eucalyptus and old newspapers (or was it socks?). Maman had turned the tap over the basin, but only a subterranean gurgling issued forth. No water. Three uneven beds stretched solemn and thick with secrets under the thin afternoon light. Luc steeled himself to toss, irreverently, the overnight bags onto one of them. He had wrenched them impatiently from Papa's moist grasp, irritated by his father's hoarse breathing.

Later that evening, when they had unpacked a few necessary garments and some toiletries, they became aware of loud voices, mingled in animated conversation, echoing through the floorboards and threadbare mats. They sat on their beds listening. Their faces were washed and their hair brushed. In preparation.

'The bar!' said Maman. 'We are situate on top of the bar!'

'Damn!' said Luc.

They sat in silence. Luc knew Maman was praying.

At seven they ventured timidly downstairs, walking almost on tiptoe. The voices from the bar, clearer now, spoke and shouted in Afrikaans and the laughter seemed threatening, cruel. They hesitated, dreading to offend. They looked into the dining-room. It was small, empty, with a lingering smell of vinegar and old mutton fat. The linen was grey from many old stains and slapdash washings, and the two black waiters talking together in the far corner looked at them but did not stop their conversation. As they stood uncertainly, grouped in the doorway, staring at the dull cutlery and wondering, 'Ag, don't block the blarry road man,' said a woman's voice.

Luc leapt aside and Maman and Papa shuffled.

'Thanks hey.'

A woman, with grizled hair and outlined eyes and lipstick that looked like jam, pushed past them. She wore a shapeless shift dress and had hooked her toes into thong-sandals which flip-smacked across the linoleum.

'Hey, let's have some bladdy service here!' she called to the waiters as she dropped into a chair. Luc stared at the overflow of hips.

'*Putain*,' murmured Maman.

'Shsh . . .' said Luc.

'We come back in a moment, *non?*' suggested Maman.

'Yes,' said Luc.

They walked up and down the street, Maman on Luc's arm and Papa behind, and they looked dully into the shops. There seemed to be a predominance of secondhand clothing shops and pawnbrokers in that street, and they paused silently in front of a window presenting ramshackle turntables, old radios, fingered sheet-music, and cheap guitars. They passed a dark, silent dairy and a dry-cleaners, and then a fish-and-chips shop. At the edge of the next corner, they about-turned.

'I have honger,' said Papa, trying his English.

'I am hungry, *hungry*,' corrected Luc.

'Darling, we cannot eat tonight in that hotel,' said Maman. 'Loose women . . . you never know . . . we wait and see,' she added.

'We . . . perhaps . . . we could be infected?' suggested Luc.

'Well . . . we wait and see,' said Maman with finality.

'Yes . . . the cutlery and the cups . . . where there are whores . . .,' mused Luc.

'Darling, there are whores all over the world. In Blida, in Paris, in . . . in Cape Town . . . in . . .'

'In Youhaneesboorg?' suggested Papa.

'Anyway,' said Luc emphatically, 'listen to me. If you use the lavotory . . . are you listening Papa? If you use it, make sure you first cover the seat with sheets and sheets of paper.'

Papa nodded.

'And we must all wash our hands very carefully.'

'Yes, darling.'

They entered the fish-and-chips shop and pointed to the hot chips and the oily red sausages. Then Luc bought a pint of milk, and they carried it all back to their hotel. Feeling guilty, almost criminal, they crept up the stairs, holding the hot newspaper parcels towards the wall.

That night Luc lay awake in his bed, looking up at the shapes of light and dark on the ceiling in their dim room. The lights from the street and the passing traffic kept the room from being dark, and the voices from the bar maintained a steady hum which rose and fell with its own rhythm until after midnight.

It was foolish to feel that emigrating to a new country was entering the Promised Land. He knew. But still, he had expected . . . something. Something to delight the heart. Some welcome, some presage. Perhaps Johannesburg, the golden . . .

Luc's round dark eyes, blue-smudged, heavy, could not rest under their lids. He watched, thinking. The murky ceiling hanging over him held vermin, perhaps, and the sighing mattresses too. He lay stiff, unmoving, and miserable, his flesh itching, but once he began turning he would not be able to stop and would writhe and toss himself into a frenzy. Better to remain still.

What could they expect? Their money, their property was gone, gone, confiscated. Only the jewels which Maman had hidden. Why should the people here offer them fine hospitality? Why should they? But this was a hotel for white people, and white people he had been told were all wealthy in South Africa, and opportunity was limitless. He hesitated to whisper the word *barbarians* even to himself, but for the moment he was, well, bitter. For instance, where were the showers? Down the corridor there was a bathroom with a chipped bathtub, yellowed round the plug-hole and offering a porous criss-crossed plank *thing* for a bathmat. Did one have to lie in one's own filth? Even the confounded Arabs knew better than that. Unexpectedly, he remembered the little silver dishes Maman used for the gem-like globs of jam they would taste with their chilled water at sundown as they sat on the patio. And the brass dish for the Turkish coffee. On the mild autumn evenings the vines would lie motionless, in subdued passion, under the dying sun, mottling from orange to deep brown. Papa would bring his domino board out and sit waiting for Oncle Henri to come over. He, Luc, had not been strong and could not help on the estate, but he could add figures for Maman and had learnt to keep books. Before all the trouble.

Papa turned on his bed and his tongue sucked against his palate. Maman was sleeping on her back, snoring softly, her hands, clasped across her large stomach, still woven into the beads she had been telling.

When you were old you slept, perhaps because the worst had already happened, Luc thought.

They stood rocking against each other in the corridor of the moving train, waiting for the Coloured railway employee to finish making up their beds. An unending, uninhabited landscape of stubbly plains and angular hillocks flowed along beyond the window. Papa shivered although it was not cold.

'That man, he not fishid?' he begged.

Maman chortled throatily, her sound suddenly delighting Luc. He clutched her plump forearm.

'You stupid,' gargled Maman. 'You big stupid! It is finished not fishid.'

'So this is not my language,' said Papa, but he also smiled.

'Remember not to say pick*less* for *pickles*,' reminded Luc, hoping to make Maman laugh again.

'All right, lady and gentlemens, your bads are right,' said the Coloured man. Luc, immediately hopeful, tipped him two shillings.

'You are also a stupid,' hissed Maman. 'I have two stupid men with me.'

'Never mind, Maman,' said Luc.

They stood in the compartment surveying the three folded blue-blanketed beds.

'Do you believe that *these* are clean, Maman?' asked Luc.

'Yes, yes, these are fumigate, these are fumigate,' answered Papa.

'How do you know?' laughed Maman.

'I know, I know,' said Papa, very seriously.

'Ah . . . well . . .,' said Luc. He looked into the washbasin and pulled and pushed the stopper.

'I think I shall go and look where the toilets are and where the dining-car is,' he said. 'You just wait here. All right?'

Adult and capable, Luc straightened his jacket and re-entered the corridor.

'I want to pass water,' said Maman softly. Papa grunted. 'I am not going to use the lavatory that is for all. Antoine, you stand outside and watch. I am going to sit on this basin.'

'Nora, Luc will be furious, you know.'

'You must not tell him. Go, quickly, outside.'

The old man went again to stand in the corridor, while the old woman pushed a suitcase to make a step so that she could lift herself onto the basin.

Late the next day the train stood tediously long at a Free State platform across which a throng of Africans, mostly wearing coloured blankets and carrying boxes and parcels on their heads, moved noisily. Some were whistling high, monotonously and continuously, others hissed or chanted or laughed. Maman and Papa sat closely together, horrified.

'Darling,' whispered Maman, 'we make a big mistake. We should go with Oncle Henri to Osstraalia.'

Luc drew his eyes reluctantly from two black men who wore their khaki trousers tied under their knees and who were dancing flirtatiously, with high steps, at a group of women sitting fatly amid their bundles and parcels on the station. They sat as if they planned to stay some time, and the men made eyes.

'No, no, Maman. No. This country is better for us. People say there are more jobs and more money. And there are servants. Do you want to polish and scrub floors at your age? And do washing and ironing? So . . . wait . . . don't be prejudiced.'

'*Tous ces noirs*,' murmured Papa.

'I shall have to pray God,' decided Maman.

From Germiston Station onward the train crawled slowly, steadily, across widths of line, parallel and interweaving, and through what looked like closely-built industrial areas. The corridors were packed with passengers, the younger ones hanging out of the windows to spot Joburg first. Luc stood too, but could not bring himself to hang. But his heart seemed to be blocking his breathing and he had clamped his lips, tight and manly. Just behind him, in the open compartment, Maman and Papa sat closer together than they had ever seemed to want to sit in their married life. They waited for their son to tell them they were there.

Then they were under shelters and fluorescent lights, and young, show-off men had doors open, ready to leap and laugh.

A white porter, who seemed determined not to utter a word, helped them with their luggage to a taxi, and Luc, uncertain, again gave two shillings. But this time Maman said nothing.

'We want a hotel . . .' Luc said to the taxi driver.

'What hotel?'

'One for about £2 each a night,' stuttered Luc. 'Do you know of . . .?'

'All right. Get in.'

They drove dangerously up a wide city street closed in with tall buildings and handsome shops, and festooned with bus overhead wires. Luc and Papa watched feverishly, but Maman closed her eyes and prayed to be delivered. Eventually they turned into a narrow street where the shops were predominantly motor vehicle businesses and small factories. Luc wondered if he would be able to bear it . . . this time.

'This place'll charge you about two quid a day each,' said the taxi driver. And it was not for them to protest.

At the reception desk a large elderly woman surveyed them through ornamental, slanting spectacles.

'Yes . . . I think I can let you have a double and a single room. With bath?'

'How much . . .' hesitated Luc.

'£2.5.od each. That's bed and breakfast.'

Luc looked at Maman, who shrugged.

'Yes. We will take these rooms.'

The woman swung the register round towards Luc.

'Fill this in, will you.'

She watched them with serious curiosity.

'You people foreigners?'

'We are from Algérie,' said Maman.

'Where?'

'Algeria,' said Luc. 'We are French.'

'Algeria, hey? But there's Arabs in Algeria, isn't there?'

'Of course. But we are French.'

'French, hey?'

'Yes.'

The woman turned to a numbered board bearing hooks from which some keys hung. She took down two keys attached to small pink planks and, hesitating again, handed them to Luc.

'You are French, hey? You sure?'

'Yes, indeed, we are French,' said Luc and the blood left his face. His eyes, black and ghostly, stared at the woman. She looked away uncomfortably.

'All right . . . hey, Lazarus, come here man. Take these people to numbers 12 and 24.'

A black with a shaved head took all their luggage and led the way.

This time Luc forgot to tip. He stood in the shabby room and heard the unremitting roar of the traffic. Then he started crying noisily, gasping and choking in his own tears.

'*Mon Dieu*,' said Maman.

'Luc, Luc, what is it?' said Papa.

'My head, my head is paining so,' gasped Luc.

'Sit down, darling. Sit down. Maman will go and ask that woman for Aspro. You have done too much. Now you must rest. Maman will see to everything. Even you can lie down.'

Maman waddled out of the room, but Papa stood slackly looking down at his son. He felt frightened and helpless, and dared not sit. Maman approached the reception desk sturdily. The woman behind the counter was asking into the telephone, 'Are Algerians white, Elsie! I mean *French* from Algeria? They look white, but just dark, like Eyeteyes. You think they are? All right then. Anyway, it's not my indaba. That bladdy Cohen is never here to see what's going on in this hotel, and I can't look after everything. You think it's all right. All right, Elsie, bye-bye.'

The woman turned and stared.

'Have you Aspro to sell me?' asked Maman.

'Aspro?'

'Yes.'

'You not feeling too hot?'

'Pardon?'

'You got a headache?'

'No. But my son, yes. His head is . . . hurting him.'

'Well, I haven't any to sell you, madam, but never mind . . . I'll give you two from my bag.'

'*Non, non* . . .'

'Ag yes. You can have them. Here.'

Maman let the woman pour the aspirins into her cupped hand.

'Thank you very much indeed,' she said.

'Ag, that's okay.'

'Listen,' said the woman, softening, 'I hope you like it here . . . in this country.'

'Ah, thank you . . . thank you . . .'

'It's a great country, you know. Finest in the world.'

'Indeed? Yes . . . yes.'

'Anyway, tell your son to take those and lie down a bit, see?'

'Yes. Thank you. Thank you.'

Luc reached the small estate agent's at 8.20 a.m., but the door was still closed. He stood nervously, well out of the way of the hurrying people, and hoping he did not look too inexperienced. Within five minutes, Meiring, the tall man who had interviewed him, arrived and stuck a key into the lock.

'You're here bright and early,' he said.

'Yes . . . I . . .'

'Find the place all right?'

'Yes, thank you.'

Meiring opened the door and entered. Luc followed diffidently, tongue-tied.

'You can sit here,' said Meiring, indicating a desk. 'I'll get you a cushion for that chair and a new blotter.'

'Thank you.'

Luc stood at the desk, uncertain whether to sit or not.

The staff began to arrive. A young fellow in knitted cable-stitch pull-

over and sports jacket introduced himself as Rob Venter, and then introduced Luc to two typists, Marie and Estelle.

'Luc de Chalande?' echoed Estelle. 'What sort of name is that? What
nationality are you?'

'I am French,' said Luc firmly.

Marie merely nodded at him and took her place coolly at the desk next
to his.

'Hmm ... mmm ... a Latin lover,' giggled Estelle.

Luc pretended to be interested in what was in the drawers of his desk.

Until tea-time Luc carefully filled in several forms which Meiring
brought him. From time to time he would glance across at the girl,
Marie, but she ignored him stolidly. Then, as he sat back, relieved, to stir
his tea, he saw her talking heatedly to Meiring. He watched them vaguely,
without much interest, for their voices did not come through Meiring's
glassed-in cubicle. After a while she returned to her seat, and Meiring
motioned to Luc to come through to his office. Luc rose happily, hoping
for work.

'Listen, de Chalande,' said Meiring, 'I'm going to move your desk to
up here ... nearer to my cubicle. It won't make much difference; I hope
you don't mind?'

'No ... no ... not at all ... if that is what ... is wanted.'

'Yes, yes ... just hang on here a minute ... I'll call the tea boy and
the cleaner to move it.'

Meiring came back with the black helpers and the desk was moved up
to a position slightly beyond the 'general office' allocated to the younger
people. Luc took his seat again, puzzled.

At one o'clock he made ready to leave the office, eager to see the lunchtime streets and the shops. Rob Venter joined him on the pavement.

'Don't let it worry you,' he said.

'Worry me?'

'The move.'

'Oh that ... oh no ...'

'Dames are bloody mad, you know?'

'I beg your ...'

'That Marie du Toit. She really behaves like a rock at times.'

'I'm afraid I don't understand.'

'She's helluva narrow-minded and suspicious you know, like a lot of
Afrikaners. She only sticks to her own kind. Just as well. I'm sure none
of us are interested in her. She'll put up with a rooinek ... that's a red
neck, you know, an Englishman, but Jews and Portuguese, never mind

kaffirs and koelies, are out. She once told Estelle that if her father sees her talking to a Portuguese boy or a Jew boy, he'll break her neck.'

'So why are you telling me all this?'

'Didn't you notice?'

'What?'

'That she complained to Mr Meiring about you. Says you are Portuguese and she's not sitting next to you.'

'But I said . . . I am *French*.'

'Well, she's too ignorant to understand the difference. Anyway, don't let it worry you. We all know what she's like.'

'I . . . see . . .'

'So you're French, are you?'

'*Yes.*'

'What made you decide to come here. To this country, I mean?'

'Well, you see . . . we thought . . .'

'It's a good place this. You'll like it. Listen . . . are you interested in stock-car racing?'

'I . . . don't . . .'

'You've probably never seen it. You'll love it. You'll see. One night I'll come and fetch you and take you. All right?'

'Thank you . . . thank you . . .' said Luc.

He walked slower, watching Rob's back as he hurried off, his sports jacket flapping against his grey flannels. He wondered suddenly how Oncle Henri was getting on.

Sipho Sepamla

MaPuleng

For days on end it rained. Listless, interminable rain. People began to wonder. They began to fear. There was something ominous about that rain. Falling as it did after an event which had shaken the whole world, they feared for the world. Might it be coming to an end? And right at their doorstep, they feared for the only big shop within their easy reach. For the level of the dam behind the shop was rising. The banks were hardly visible. If the dam itself looked submerged, then the likelihood of the water streaming over the doorstep of the shop was real. The whole township was in a panic.

It was on one of those rainy days that a child was born to MaMokwena: one of the blessings of the rain. And to celebrate the event, the child, being a girl, was named Puleng. Thereafter MaMokwena became MaPuleng.

Very few people could claim to know the girl's father. One or two possibilities were always mentioned. Even so, many people admired MaPuleng for the courage of trying to face up to life without the permanent anchor of a husband.

Perhaps it was more to lift herself out of loneliness, rather than to seek more hands to make ends meet, that she would take in a man for a spell. And because it was her room, the men's sojourn was dependent upon her very fancy moods. The men never spoke about their ejectment – for manly reasons. Instead MaPuleng would grumble: 'I didn't come to town for charity!'

MaPuleng's finger always pinched a bit of snuff from a little box tucked away somewhere around her hip. The same finger would then be thrust out to point at some house-chores Puleng had to do. Thus the little girl grew up with her nostrils sniffing the air as if looking for something.

To make ends meet at all, MaPuleng took in a lot of washing from

Indian families. The earnings from four of them combined to make up her monthly pay. More money came from her temporary sojourners.

Puleng never got to know her father. By association every adult male became Papa So-and-So. She never asked the big question largely because she had so much to do in the room. Then too there was the washing to carry away on her head. And of course the ten-cent trips to the shop. The very few occasions when mother and child found themselves together got eaten up by MaPuleng grumbling about the inadequacies of her current man.

All in all, Puleng was in a way as useful to her mother as the snuff-box. Also she was kept under the mother's roving finger like the snuff-box. Because she was soft of character and charming, she didn't seem to resent all that.

There was common talk among the neighbours that MaPuleng treated her child like a slave. This always made MaPuleng curse within the four walls. Fuming, she would walk out to the washing-line, peg up a garment or two and then continue to swear at the four winds. The scene always ended up with her thrusting a ten-cent piece into Puleng's hand, saying: 'Take! Bring me a packet of sugar ...! And you must hurry up ...! Rubbish!' It was never clear to whom 'rubbish' referred. For her part Puleng would run the forward journey. On her way back she lingered with friends and the sights on her way. She got home to find her mother swearing. This time the daughter would be the butt of her condemnation. And the neighbours who happened to be within earshot.

One day the prohibition on liquor sales to all people was revoked. From then on everyone was free to buy and guzzle whatever suited his taste. The number of men who got drunk rose rapidly. No one could say where everyone drank because many homes became shebeens. MaPuleng saw the potential. Besides everybody knew she had no husband. And she had begun to complain about the ill-effects of handling too much water.

In her little room she began a liquor business. She would buy K. B. from the municipal depot and resell it at a profit. Soon her market became greater than she could get supplies for. For one thing the depot closed at night, the very time when demand was at its peak. And it wasn't as if her room was next door to the depot. No, as a result of these inconveniences she found she had to augment the supply from the depot. It so happened that her specially flavoured brand of K. B. had the sort of taste and kick which met the requirements of customers. Her room became popular. And its size decreased. What with the number of four-gallon tins growing daily, she couldn't cope.

She changed into the bottled beer business. Profits climbed. She drop-ped the snuff-box and clipped a cigarette between her fingers. Puleng had to float about to meet the demands of the customers and the moment.

Perhaps her neighbours were jealous or she grew airs, it wasn't clear. All the same she fell out with them. Sometimes she complained that the females around her provoked a quarrel with her. Other times they said she belittled them. It all stemmed from the husbands of these females. They drank to be drunk and forgot themselves. Never knew who they were nor where they came from. So as Puleng swept the stubs of cigarettes off the floor, her mother had to usher these men into the street. That way the admiration MaPuleng once enjoyed trickled into the gutter the neighbour-hood used for dirty water and pee.

Mother and daughter looked happy. Puleng was growing rapidly. In time she had adjusted her sights to those of her mother. How much she accepted unbegrudgingly, it could not be said. She went about the room and work confidently. She was able to joke or tease a customer, slapping her own vaselined thigh into the bargain. Her smiles helped to slay a hesitant customer. Under her spell a man would spend more than he had fixed when he first walked into the room. MaPuleng was happy with the efficiency of her daughter, happier to place more cash in her bosom, her favourite hiding place.

Came a day, MaPuleng was bowled over by Bomvana Radebe, one of her customers. He was one of those men who succeeded in giving the im-pression they are unimpeachable bachelors. In fact he had a family in the Transkei. In a sense then he was a free man.

MaPuleng moved into Bomvana's four-roomed house. She was a great acquisition to Bomvana. For deep down there he was a won't-work. All day long he pottered around the house looking for nails to knock into place. Or he could offer to help a customer quaff his drink in company. It was MaPuleng who paid the rent and bought food. It was her daughter who cleaned the floors whilst she, MaPuleng, for the benefit of curious neighbours and passers-by, tended to the needs of the yard.

Something Bomvana enjoyed doing was to kill time with Puleng. Once he told her of his own daughter, Faith. She was somewhere in the Trans-kei. Unlike Puleng, she had been to school and had had an excellent school career. At an early age she had been turned into a lady teacher. He told Puleng he had heard that school children called his daughter 'Mam'. This tickled him. He had never thought his Faith could end up a 'Mam'.

Puleng was left envious, her mind drifting wishfully. She longed for the kind of independence Faith enjoyed. Her problem was how to achieve that. The thing lived in her like an undercurrent.

While Bomvana and Puleng grew to like each other so that she was ready to call herself his daughter, MaPuleng anchored herself in the new neighbourhood. She and Bomvana were soon accepted, at least on the surface, as man and wife.

Presently one of MaPuleng's relatives from the homelands arrived. He was Kgoropedi Manthata, a young man of about twenty-two. His mother and MaPuleng were blood sisters. Knowing nobody around except his aunt, long lost to the homelands, he moved in with her. MaPuleng saw in him more cash flowing into her bosom.

Kgoropedi was made to feel at home by his aunt, his Malume Bomvana and Ntsala Puleng. They were all concerned that he found a job, the reason for coming at all.

But there was a problem in his finding work. He had no pass-book. That meant he was unknown in the area and as such didn't qualify to be a work-seeker in the area. It was left to MaPuleng's resourcefulness to find a solution. Luckily the clerks from the local office were all her customers. Receiving their cheques at the end of a month, they were always at her mercy in the middle of it. Their contribution toward the solution was a fargone thing.

The first step required the Superintendent at the local office to sign some documents. That way Kgoropedi's face would acquire some appearance.

When MaPuleng and Kgoropedi presented themselves before the Super, he showed great interest in the story she recited. Largely it had to do with why he hadn't taken out a pass-book until that late age. She laid it on fine: how he had been born under great odds; how his father (whereabouts unknown) had deserted her and made the child an illegitimate. Neither the Super nor MaPuleng smiled or grinned throughout the narration. As for Kgoropedi, he sat there masked by fear and innocence.

At the end of it all the Super grumbled something about not liking 'this cock and bull story'. Nonetheless he signed the necessary documents. And so paved the way for Kgoropedi to obtain a pass and find work.

The name entered in the pass was Kgoropedi Mokwena. Thanks to the clerks.

Thereafter finding work was no problem. The warmth of his aunt grew greater. Meanwhile the affection between the cousins strengthened. Every time Puleng teased a customer, her cousin would be at hand to share the laughter. Even the iniquities of drunken men they turned into mirth together.

MaPuleng wasn't indifferent to this example of brotherhood, being unenthusiastic about it. Not wanting to upset anyone, she said quietly to her daughter one day: 'Be careful of men.' Puleng passed on the warning to her cousin. It stung him. Coming as it did when he was beginning to flex his muscles with all the money he received on Fridays, it really upset him. For some time he had been feeling an uneasiness in the midst of his aunt and his cousin. The one sucked his manhood's rewards, the other confounded this manhood.

Kgoropedi moved into a hired room of his own. This made MaPuleng to grouse: 'Today's children are very ungrateful!' All the same she offered him the evening meal and the washing of his shirts and so on. Because this would give him the excuse to continue seeing his cousin, he accepted the arrangement.

By this time Kgoropedi and Puleng had come to value the company of each other very much. For her his company was uplifting. She felt a hot happiness. It was for this reason she often slipped away to his room.

It became a matter of time before the neighbours said it loud that the cousins were after all in love. In answer the young ones would reply, albeit as a joke: 'The cows are returning to their kraal.' The expression meant the marriage of cousins was a wise proposition. The cattle for lobola would circulate within the family.

MaPuleng heard the rumour. She was terribly hurt and upset. She was concerned about being the butt of ridicule. For what goes in the homelands is often taboo in town.

She confronted her daughter: 'What are you up to?' she said.

'I don't understand,' Puleng replied, displaying innocence.

'Hey! don't think I'm blind!' her voice had an edge to it.

'What's mother talking about?'

'You and Kgoropedi!' she blurted, arms akimbo.

'There's nothing we have done.'

'Standing in shadows sucking a finger, there's nothing you've done?'

'Mother says strange things!'

'Hey! don't think I don't see you! Every time he's around you are as restless as a hen in a storm!'

Puleng felt a whirlwind build up in her bosom. But she held her tongue. She feared she would shout. That would lose her the game. She had to tell her gently that her happiness could be found only with his company. Her silence was loud.

'Your silence shows up the snake in your heart!' MaPuleng hurled her judgement.

Again Puleng battled to suppress the heaving of her breast. But a thought she must have nurtured in her heart for a time strained at her lips. She flung it out like phlegm. Only her humbleness turned it into a stinging: 'Why do you hate me, mother?'

MaPuleng was thrown into disarray. She never thought her child was growing all ways. More than that she never suspected her mind could harbour such a thought. 'I hate you? Are you mad?' she yelled.

'You hate me.' Puleng shouted in turn. 'You hate me!' she repeated and left the room in a huff.

The days that followed were silent and distant. Mother and daughter went about their share of work without a word to each other. MaPuleng smoked more cigarettes. She exhibited the fact of being mistress of the house more often. Puleng shelled herself within a song. This made MaPuleng furious and she would try to rattle her with jibes such as: 'Better get on with your work. The municipality has built a hall for singers!' A heavy atmosphere would then descend upon the house. If Bomvana noticed anything, he didn't say it loud. He feared to lose the women.

MaPuleng was still simmering when Kgoropedi called on them. And to assert her stand, she turned him out of the house. That day her wrath stood bristling in her eye: 'Out! Out you go!' she said, her forefinger pointing to one end of the world. 'I'm not going to have anyone make a fool of me!'

Caught unawares, Kgoropedi stood at the door hesitating.

MaPuleng continued: 'Blood or no blood, I don't care! I don't want you here anymore, finish and *klaar!*'

Puleng looked away in disgust. Kgoropedi hunched his shoulders and dragged himself away.

Bomvana kept mumbling: 'M'm ya! M'm ya!' until the first customer came to rescue his spirits.

The event marked the final spiritual break between mother and daughter. Many a time Puleng felt tempted to walk out of her home. She wrestled with the idea for days. She couldn't say what made her stick within her ma's place beyond the consideration that it was her home. Perhaps she still hoped for the kind of success she thought was possible as Bomvana's daughter.

As so often happens, the run of events gave answer to her dilemma. Her anger sacrificed her virginity. She found her way to Kgoropedi's room in rapid succession. Entered the physical act with ravenous fury. It was as if each motion was a slapping on her mother's face. Not long after, she became pregnant.

Again it was the neighbours who began to talk about Puleng's condition. MaPuleng seemed blind to it. But when at last she caught up with it she turned grey-black. She gazed at her daughter as if to cry. Then she threw up her hand, palm facing upward, and said bitterly: 'What are you going to get from a thing that hardly has a name? It shows you don't care whether people laugh at me or not . . . ! He doesn't care, after all I'm not his mother!'

At first Puleng managed to hold her tongue. Perhaps the child's motherly condition made her keep silent. But it was this very sharp silence which drove MaPuleng mad. She taunted her daughter: 'What made you feel so excited about that country boy that you spread yourself before him so? . . . *Hayi! mense!* this world is *mos snaaks!*'

With that she left her daughter staring. She glared at her mother until she disappeared into another room for one reason or another.

Next time MaPuleng said to her daughter: 'My mother can bear witness in her grave, I never did funny things under her nose! I was miles away when I got you. I was working in town and she was way back in the homelands . . . And you want to know something, my man had money . . . What has that country boy? M'm, tell me, what has he? Nothing! He hardly knows which direction the door of a bank faces!'

Perhaps Puleng would have borne all these jibes from her mother if only to save her own face in the public eye. But then her mother said: 'I shall never forgive you . . . You have shamed me in the eyes of the devil himself!'

This Puleng couldn't stomach. She despised her mother for being such a liar. She told herself: 'I've grown up enough not to be treated like a baby. Mother has no right to speak to me as if I have sinned. After all, what example is she? How much harder have I grown up without a picture of my father . . . ! I've had to bear the tag of illegitimate child without question. And for all that I am accused like a sinner . . . It is true mother hates me. Silence is pointless.' Aloud she said to her mother: 'I love Kgoropedi!'

'Love him? What cheek! Go to him then!' MaPuleng said this, arm stretched out, forefinger pointing at Kgoropedi's room some two miles away: 'Gwan, go!'

It was meant as a challenge and nothing more. Puleng was her daughter. She would take this as she had taken all beatings from her in the past.

Besides the hour was late for Puleng to take as much as a step outside the gate.

Puleng stiffened for a second or two. She drew in a hugh breath as if she wanted to cheat her mother of all air that still circulated in the house despite the sour smell of beers mingled with the stale stench of cigarettes. Then she stormed into her room. Picked up a blanket, threw it over her shoulder and slammed the outside door behind her. Bomvana's feeble pleas rang in her ears in vain.

'Let her go! Let her go! Who begs her? Not me!' cried MaPuleng.

Bomvana settled his conscience by walking into the bedroom. After the house had acquired a heavy silence, Bomvana came out of the bedroom. He muttered: 'I don't understand town children.'

That evening MaPuleng swore by her dead mother she would fix up Puleng. As if that were not enough, she repeated the oath saying: 'I swear by my grandmother lying in her grave, I'll show Puleng who her mother is! She doesn't know me!'

Not to be considered indifferent, Bomvana said: 'You know, I have never liked children growing up in town. That's why I sent Faith to a country school.'

'School?' sneered MaPuleng, 'what wouldn't she do if I had sent her to school? No doubt she would have said I am not her mother! That's what happens when they begin to speak English through their nostrils. Suddenly they become welfare cases, picked up in forsaken cardboard boxes. Yoo! I'm not mad!'

A few days later mother and daughter stood before the Superintendent. MaPuleng opened the case: 'Morena,' she said, 'I don't want to stand in her way if she wants to get married. All I ask is that she returns home and things be settled properly.'

In answer to which the Super asked for the ages of the two women. Perhaps he was influenced by the pregnancy of the younger one.

MaPuleng suddenly melted into a smile and said: 'I never went to school, Morena.'

Asked to identify an event near her birthday and that of Puleng, she said she was a young girl when the miners were said to have gone mad in Johannesburg. The Super interjected: 'Mad?'

'I don't know, Morena,' she said, shrugging her shoulders. 'That is what I heard.'

'That must be the 1922 Miners' Strike, I suppose.'

'Yes, yes, Morena is right!'

'And the girl?'

'After Hitler's war there was rain, Morena. It fell for days and nights. It fell as if it would never stop. That is when she was born.'

'M'm, I see.'

There was a silence in which the Super seemed to be engaged in thought. When he opened his mouth it was to remind the women about their traditional ways. He said according to custom 'you people' should not be in this sort of meeting taking place then. MaPuleng was about forty-nine and the daughter nineteen. The matter was so domestic they ought to be ashamed to have brought it out in public.

Turning to Puleng, he said in a stern but calm voice: 'Young girl, go back to your mother before . . .'

The man had hardly finished when Puleng, shifting her feet as if to stamp the floor, said: 'She's not my mother!'

The Super was taken aback. MaPuleng was stunned.

'What do you mean she's not your mother?' asked the Super.

'She's not!' repeated Puleng, eyes burning, face tensed. She went on: 'My mother died a long time ago!'

'She lies! She lies! I'm her mother!'

'You are not!'

'I am! Ask –'

'It's not true!'

'Shut up! Shut up!' said the Super, banging his desk as if with a mallet. Things were getting out of hand. '*Kyk hiersô*, you people have forgotten yourselves! This is my office, not a shebeen!' The father of the people thought to assert his authority which had been somewhat battered by the women in conflict. So he said: 'Both of you must keep quiet now. You will open your mouths only when I tell you to do so, do you hear me?'

Only MaPuleng said she understood. Puleng was too furious to care about the meaning of standing before the Super.

At once he gave precedence to MaPuleng: 'Is there something you can show me which will prove this girl is your daughter?'

It was as if MaPuleng had been hit with another blow. For a moment words escaped her.

Then she said in a very emotional voice: 'S-someth-thing t-to show you? H-how do you mean er-M-morena?'

'Birth certificate . . . baptismal certificate, even if it's a duplicate?'

'No, I've neither of them.'

'Nothing! . . . You mean, you mean yours is another of these cases . . .'
The Super threw up his hand to conclude the thought.

'I never went to school!'

'That's got nothing to do with it. These things are not issued by the
Department of Education.'

Again there was a silence. The Super looked at MaPuleng. And then
at Puleng. He saw the fact of her pregnancy once more. It disturbed him
no end.

'Let me see your house permit?' he asked MaPuleng. Then when the
thing lay before him he kept nodding his head, his teeth digging into his
lower lip as if to extract some blood to witness this grave situation.

At last he said to MaPuleng: 'What are you to Bomvana Radebe?'

Again MaPuleng had to search for words. The question was awkward
under the circumstances: 'He's my boyfriend.' She blurted out the words
so that they remained in the air. Then she added: 'I live with him!'

Meanwhile the Super had touched an ear as if the words had hurt. It
was as if that kind of thing was new in his experience. Yet he knew it well
in that world. He turned to Puleng. 'And what are you?'

'He's my father!' she didn't hesitate.

'Puleng Radebe, yes?'

'Yes!'

'And Perfidia Mokwena, you?' addressing MaPuleng.

'Yes!' Then she added: 'But I'm her mother!'

'That's not true!'

The Super eyed Puleng and turned to MaPuleng: 'Where's her father?'

'I don't know!' she said sadly.

'You don't know?'

The Super touched his furrowed brow.

'That is strange.' That is all he could say. Common as the thing was in
his work, he couldn't get used to it, like death.

'He was here with building contractors. I've never heard from him
ever since they left.'

'Shame!' said the Super spontaneously. Then: 'Who is this Kgoropedi
Mokwena?' asked the Super, reading a name from the permit.

The two women hurried to answer that one, speaking almost simultaneously.

'He's my son!' said MaPuleng.

'My boyfriend!' said Puleng.

This time the Superintendent stood up. The oppression of the matter
before him was unbearable. He craved for relief. A pipe or a glass of very

cold beer would have come in handy then. He did the least. He lit a pipe that had been slanting in an ashtray.

'Look here, only Christ could perform miracles. And I'm not Him . . .'
Silence.

He turned to Puleng: 'Who did that to you?'

'Kgoropedi!'

'Your brother?'

'Cousin!'

'But she said just now he is her son.'

'That's not true!'

'Oh! *Here!*' exclaimed the Super, 'you people don't know yourselves!' And in an effort to draw this whole thing to some conclusion, he said: 'Come on, come on, don't waste my time!'

'I'm telling the truth!' said Puleng.

'I'm telling the truth!' said MaPuleng. Just then MaPuleng wiped off something that had been glistening in her eye.

Her heart became heavier when the Super said: 'I wash my hands!' For with that he sat down again. He looked at MaPuleng whose eyes were wet with the pains of childbirth. She was now drying them in readiness to see the regrets which would live in her heart for a long time. He looked at Puleng. It wasn't for long. Her condition dazzled the eye. There was a shame facing the girl, pregnant at that young age, yet brave enough to deny the womb which must have carried the resemblance of their facial features. So the Super said finally: 'You may go! You'll see me when you have made up your minds!'

There was little he could do. MaPuleng lacked the proof. Puleng was of age, and she had gone far already.

Perfidia Mokwena went to the house of Bomvana Radebe, muttering inaudible curses. Puleng Radebe went to the room of Kgoropedi Mokwena, clicking her tongue and wrapping a blanket round her waist now and again.

That day the sun went down as usual for everybody else.

Mongane Serote

Let's Wander Together

There is this young man. Handsome. He has this smile that cuts doubt and restriction like teeth do the peels of fruit. That is how I recall him; those days when I was young and he was too and there was hope.

Now I recall that night when he came and slipped next to me in the blankets. I was angry with him. It was close to two in the morning. He knocked, I opened; he came in smiling that smile of his. Hell. I told him to stop his nocturnal knocks; people want to rest, you know. I remember clearly by people I meant me.

He said nothing. He started to undress; I slipped into the blankets murmuring things intended to hurt him. He seemed indifferent and that angered me. Every time I caught this silly stinking smell of liquor when he coughed. The smell was real dirty. He seemed to be doing something, I don't know what, and his head was next to mine. I was silent with biting anger.

I told him to go to his bed. With his strange positiveness, that always made him have his way even when people he had wronged were on the verge of murdering him, he slipped into the blankets. I felt his cold thighs touch mine. And those thighs were so thin! Good God, I thought, what cheek! He has urinated his thighs wet and he just comes into the blankets like that? I felt his hand move between his and my thigh. I lifted my head to have a clear picture of this beast: I was numb, I could hardly say a word. He looked at me with such sad and painful eyes.

'Brother, I'm in pain,' he said. Strange, I realized this immediately. Immediately I was out of bed. He followed suit, slowly. His nude body turned to the candle light. And there, like a eye, a strangely opened and bleeding wound looked at me. I looked at him questioningly.

'The night watchman stabbed me with his assegai,' he answered. We did things to that wound that night.

The following day, after I had dug out all my persuasive powers, he refused to go to the clinic. And that following day's night he came back drunk again. Weeks passed.

Many things happened. He still came and went. The right time being the night time, to come back. He still knocked at night, I opened; he still slipped next to me, having divorced his bed. We used to talk. Things: 'Sexing' as he used to say, and 'Religion like' and 'them the white people thing'; he used to talk! It is very possible that we saw eye to eye, but he had this 'you inducated too much' idea about me. He would say it, with his index finger shaking warningly at me, he would frown, meaning that spells trouble, 'mmmmmmmm', I'm saying that.

He was born in Benoni Location but lived most of his young days, years, in Alexandra with my father. He persevered through school up to Standard Six. He gave up school to become a caddie. That meant buying anything he wanted. Foodwise, he was good at it; clothes excellent. I loved him. He went, back to Benoni.

When we met again, I was a little man with big thoughts of high school. I think it was at a relative's funeral. He was talking strangely with those wires holding his jaws. He held a small boy's head, jesting about how impossible it was to 'support them, with that girl there'- he pointed at the thin-legged girl who stood staring at the many people.

The next time I saw him, it was the year that includes among its days the night of the wounded thigh. I came home late at night. He was there in my room with my brother.

He was not wearing his clothes; they were hanging from his shoulders and hips. His eyes were blood-shot. His huge hair, beard and the gold earring made him look like he was about to say 'Ha!' You would have really run with fright if he had. He said he wanted a job.

He got a job and lost it. Pass problems. The Benoni Alexandra 'place of abode' thing pointed and picked him out as undesirable to be employed in the 'above-mentioned area'. He got another job and lost it. He refused to say 'baas' and nearly used a hammer in defence of his principle. He went jobless for many, many months. Hot at home, 'you won't work'. Hot outside 'Section 29', as the knowledgeable people say.

He came home late at night, with the dirty smell of his breath and he left in the morning, eyes red.

He stopped talking to me: I had fisted him because he had smoked my cigarettes, a whole packet. I do not think he was ever sorry for that; when there is no hope, things nearest are yours.

I left home. When I came back, maybe prodigally, he had left a day after me. These township boys know what I am talking about here, you want to go but you come back.

Weeks passed and no one knew where this young man was. Months. I met him. It was early morning, about five. He was playing soccer, using a tennis ball, with these grey-bellied kids in the street. He shook my hand vigorously. His smile was there. I loved him. He invited me to tea, 'You don't take hot stuff,' he said. As we walked to this house I realized that he had a piece of plastic bandage above the right eye. What's up? I asked. His hand caressed the bandage; I saw that the whole white of the eye was red – black-red.

'I'm one-eyed, brother,' he said sadly. God!

Something else caught up with my mind. We were on this dusty stoep, he was ahead of me. I could hear people shouting, a man and a woman. He went into the house and welcomed me loudly so his voice could be heard above the shouting. He gave me a chair. I was unsure of sitting down because this man and woman were about to pounce at each other. He seemed not to care, he was telling me how glad he was to see me. And that he was sorry to bring me to a house of people who fight. At that stage the man who had been defending himself for sleeping out came and shook my hand and immediately he answered a new accusation thrown at him by his wife.

I was sipping this real hot and very sweet black tea when this man came and told me we should stay out of the way of unthinking women. We sat on the stoep. He and the young man shared beer and I had tea. I was introduced to this man as 'my beautiful brother', and he shook my hand again and for a very long time. And now and then the shouts slipped out of the door from the woman.

Then we left. No doubt his eye was blind and the wound above the eyes was rotting. I suggested the clinic to him. He refused; I hijacked him there. Established blind eye; more treatments; which he did not go for.

Hymns. People gathered at night. It is a Friday, vigil day in most townships. Venue: home.

I was very angry, perhaps frightened, as I threw soil into that grave. Burying the young man's hopes, and the stab wound, this time, sorry, not a stab wound, but a gash. That killed him. It was so sudden, yet expected.

Barney Simon

Our War

About Us and Our War

Well, this is about our war. Whenever I complained about it, the noise
and the dirt and the stinking and the dying, Mama used to say, 'Listen,
Leiba, be grateful for what you've got. That you're not in London or
Moscow or New York or somewhere. Be grateful you're here where
things always happen easier.' When I got upset about Lily Fine losing her
leg, she said, 'So, but she's still got her head.' And when our house went
up in the second bombardment (which was famous for the first usage
outside of Asia and the Middle East of .22238 Ziggmutt Mortars) and we
built a shelter and it rained all those October days, the way she behaved
you would've thought that it was the Christmas holidays and we were
on holiday at the Imperial Hotel in Muizenberg. But if you think I was a
moaner, you should've heard Rochella. She cried if there were lumps in
the mealie-meal porridge or hair on the soap. She wouldn't wear a dress if
it was dirty and if there was skin on the milk (when there was any) she'd
rather go thirsty. When the mortars got going and there were blasts and
quakes and screams, she complained that she couldn't go to sleep. But,
to be fair, that was toward the beginning.

One Sunday, which turned out to be the day of the eighteen-hour
blast (the fourth time in the whole world an entire ground-to-ground
operation was carried out by the crews of Donizetti rocket units), the
Mizroch family, Zaidah Mizroch, Mrs Mizroch, his daughter-in-law, and
little Mitzi and Mike all went to collect what firewood they could from
Gillooly's Farm, and when they hadn't come back by Friday, we moved
into their house which was a little small for us, but still.

220

About Mama

Mama worked at the Bertha Solomon Social Centre, which was used as a hospital and house for old people since our war began. She did shift work, sometimes at night, sometimes during the day. She cleaned and scrubbed and nursed and sometimes she even helped in the surgery. She didn't like us to come there, but once I did. There were old people all over. On the veranda, on beds, on mattresses, on the floor, all calling her Malka, which is her first name, and asking her to sing. She didn't have a good voice – you know, she never got the tune nicely, but everybody used to ask her to sing because she knew nice songs with nice words. Then they asked her to tell them a joke. It wasn't so good but when she told it she was laughing so much she made us all laugh too.

Old Mr Lapinsky said that she had hands of solid gold. Everybody called for her to turn them over or rub them or massage them where they were sore. Especially Mr Lapinsky whose eyes were all white, and when he died, he left her his watch. At first we thought it was real gold, but when we took it to Maishke, he said it wasn't gold, just golden. She had friends who worked there too, like Mrs Pinchuk, Mrs Maganoff and Bessie Finestein. They weren't friends like she had in the old days like Pearl Reichman, but they were nice all the same.

At home our best times were when she made us potato sweets, and night, when we used to push our mattresses together and lie there in the dark. If you got there first, you lay next to her. First nobody talked and we just breathed. And then she told us about how she was a little girl in a little village in Lithuania and how she was scared of ice-skates, but she used to 'glitzzzz' on her shoes across the ice and how she used to find strawberries in the forests that smelt as sweet as flowers and covered her whole hand and how they used to sleep on the stove (that was always Mendel's favourite) in winter and how when she came here her best friend was the beauty queen and whistler Pearl Reichman and how they used to copy the movie stars' make-up with luscious lips and gypsy eyes, and how when she first came she thought the traffic cop stopped the traffic for her to cross the street and what a nice man she thought he was to do that (that was Rochella's favourite) and how once when somebody asked her to make a bet, she said she could make her own bed thank you (that was mine). Laykella had her own bed-time because she slept in a little hammock and went to bed early. Her favourite story was about the Reb and the Rebbitsen. But that's too long to tell now.

How We Lost Hindella

Three days after we moved into the Mizroch house, we lost Hindella. There was some street fighting, no mortar or artillery, just rifle and a grenade or two. God knows what was happening in Pandora Street. It sounded like hell. Anyway, we were all lying flat on the lounge floor because we were all going out when it started and it didn't sound bad enough for the cellar when Hindella, God knows why, got up, peeped out of the window and plop was down with us again flat on her back with a bright red spot between her eyes.

After that, even before the funeral, Mama couldn't stand the Mizroch house any more, so she sent me out to Auntie Ada in Greenside where we heard it was pretty quiet to ask if we could move in with her and also to tell her about Hindella and her funeral, but when I got there, her house was full of other people who said they didn't know where Auntie Ada was and we couldn't come. So we just stayed on at the Mizroch house and Mama and Rochella spoke and cried in their sleep every night. Mendel and me mind you went on sleeping like logs and Baby Layka of course just went on snoring like an angel.

Hindella's Funeral

We buried Hindella in the cemetery that had been made on the soccer-field in Rhodes Park. On the way there, Rochella asked me to pinch her or something if she started to giggle because she always does. It was a hot day with a very blue sky. Mrs Maganoff, Mrs Katzen and Mrs Pinchuk, who worked with Mama at the Bertha Solomon Social Centre, were there, and Mama and me and Rochella and Tiny Yiddel from Belgravia Shul (he's the one Chesterfield's Circus wanted but he wouldn't take the job and kept his old one opening the shul in the morning and locking it at night and setting out the prayer books) and Rabbi Spitz with his yellow-and-black beard. He was there to say the prayers, but before he did, Yiddel and me dug the grave, and when the service began, we were covered with orange dust. Rabbi Spitz first sang a song and then we put Hindella's coffin into the hole and then we all began to say prayers and old Mrs Pinchuk started crying and Mama lent her her hanky and she started crying too and the wind came up and blew the dust into our faces and when Mama stepped back from Mrs Pinchuk, some ground gave way underneath her and she nearly fell into Hindella's grave. Then Rabbi Spitz took off his torn coat and gave it to Yiddel, and he had on a nice shiny one underneath and Yiddel gave him his prayer-shawl and he put it on and then he took off his black hat and handed it to Yiddel and he had a little yarmulka on the back of his head and then Yiddel handed him his prayer-book and he was ready, with Yiddel holding everything behind him. I tiptoed over to Yiddel and asked him if I could help him, and he said he was fine, but did I hear about the saltenossas he made. When he starts talking about saltenossas it's the end of you, so I tiptoed back to Rochella, and Rabbi Spitz began to talk about the ten plagues of Egypt and how the worst of all was the plague that caused the plagues – the hatred between men, the hatred that rises when we forget about God. Mama was dusting herself off and she asked him to stop talking and just help bury Hindella and Rabbi Spitz said why was he asked to come then and Mama said she never asked him to come, Mrs Pinchuk did, and so Rabbi Spitz took his hat from the top of Yiddel and put it back on his head over the yarmulka, and then he put his prayer-book where the hat had been on Yiddel and he took off his prayer-shawl and began to fold it and Mrs Pinchuk said he should be ashamed to leave the grave of a Jewish child and Mama said, 'Look at us, look where my child is – and he talks about Moses and the ten commandments!'

'The Ten *Plagues!*' Rabbi Spitz shouted.

'What's the difference?' Mama screamed. 'Don't talk to me about God. *This* is the place they should bomb and his churches and his shuls – let *Him* know what it's all about.'

Little Yiddel was standing on the tips of his toes holding onto the prayer-book and the prayer-shawl and helping Rabbi Spitz struggle into his coat. I could feel Rochella shaking next to me, so I pinched her arm. Mama got onto her knees next to the grave and she picked up a pile of sand in her arms and threw it onto the coffin – 'There!' she shouted in Yiddish, 'Nuh!' and she picked up more, and threw and threw shouting, 'Nuh! Nuh! Nuh!' The dust was flying all over, covering her face and her body and all of us. Mrs Pinchuk and Mrs Maganoff and Mrs Katzen also ran to the grave and started throwing sand too, all together, and Rabbi Spitz, still fighting with his coat, started to run away across the field, with little Yiddel following on his little legs, still all orange, carrying the prayer-book and the prayer-shawl.

Mama, Mrs Katzen, Mrs Pinchuk and Mrs Maganoff went on throwing, tearing at the ground when the dug-up sand was finished, until there was a mound on top of Hindella's grave. Everybody was cursing and crying, turning the dust to mud on their faces, and beside me I felt Rochella still shaking.

'Stop laughing!' I shouted, and everybody stopped in the dust and stared at us and Rochella began to cry.

About Pearl Reichman

Pearl Reichman was Mama's best friend from long ago. She used to live down the street when we lived in Troyeville. Sometimes she used to go to the movies with us, to the musicals. She had black hair and a shiny mouth which she always painted red. She was famous as a whistler. People said she should be in Hollywood and when Tyrone Power came to visit South Africa she was one of the girls they took his photograph with at the airport. The publicity men put her third from the left, but when Tyrone Power had to kiss someone on the cheek for a photo, he chose Pearl, and she had to pretend to faint and when she did it was marvellous and then she had to pretend to whistle and she *really* whistled, her speciality, a canary whistling 'Swanee' and Tyrone Power got a real surprise and asked her to do it again so she did a whole performance there in the airport and her picture was in every paper, him kissing her on the cheek and her whistling and everybody thought now she must go to Hollywood because there'd never been a whistling movie star – singers yes, like Jeannette Macdonald, Kathryn Grayson, Jane Powell, Illona Massey, Rise Stevens, Carmen Miranda or organ players like Ethel Smith playing 'Tico Tico' and there were rumours that Pearl was leaving any day so people began to get her to whistle at Bar Mitzvahs and weddings and birthday parties and over the radio once and once when my mother and me were in town with her somebody stopped her in the street and asked her to whistle what she whistled for Tyrone Power so she whistled her speciality, 'Swanee' like a canary, and everyone stood around us and when she finished we all clapped and a woman and a little girl and a boy, all separately asked her for her autograph. Anyway then one summer she went on a tour of all the holiday places like Port Elizabeth, East London, Durban and Mossel Bay and she married a Mr Salzman in Durban who had a shop near the dock which sold everything from a thimble to an elephant (which was his motto, the elephant being a brooch actually) then once when we were in Durban on holiday we saw her at a concert at the Jewish Club and after the concert we went back behind the curtain to see her and everything. But I don't remember much about her there except that her arms were very white and she had a gold filling in her side tooth and a rose in her hair because I had bad sunburn and that was what was really worrying me. Then when the war began and there was a big bombardment of the Natal coast, Mr Saltzman's shop went up and him too and Pearl came back to her family, old Mrs Reichman, the only one left. She called herself Pearl Reichman again and used to walk around in her nightie because she said it was an evening dress. Even Rochella could understand but couldn't explain to her that a nightie isn't an evening dress. Anyhow, the nightie was how we first knew she was going funny and then it just got worse and Pearl got thinner and thinner and then old Mrs Reichman died of natural causes not just our war, and the Reichman house got mortar-blasted and Pearl lived on the veranda swing seat and all the time she went up and down the street looking for food and whistling and sometimes it was beautiful and sometimes it got on your nerves. Then one day we found her in her backyard, dead. It was after the rain and she was lying on her back with her eyes open and her mouth open and her nightie was wet and you could see everything. That's what happened to Pearl Reichman. When Mama came home and I told her how we found Pearl Reichman, she cried and I asked her why. She never cried when Jossel Hurwitz died or Cousin Lily was blown up and lots of other people and she said I didn't know Pearl when she was beautiful and dreaming all the time and Tyrone Power kissed her and she wore her ruby red evening dress at weddings and Bar Mitzvahs. God, Mama said, what dreams she had – sequins and gold handbags and Hollywood and look how she died – dreaming of bread!

The Reb and the Rebbitsen: Laykella's Favourite Story Told by Mama

Every morning Laykella was the first one up. She used to climb out of her hammock and then into my mother's bed and then into mine and each of us had to tell her a story and she would tell us one back.

The Reb and the Rebbitsen

Once upon a time (Mama used to say) there was a Rabbi and his wife, the Rebbitsen. They had lots, l-o-o-o-ts of little children. The biggest one was called Leibella, the next was called Laykella and there were many whose names are too many to tell, but the last one, the very, very last one was called Mottel. He was tiny. Tinier than Yiddel of Belgravia Shul, tinier than Laykella. Maybe he was as tiny as the Englishman Tom Thumb (Laykella always used to say that), maybe he was the tiniest boy in the world. Well, one day the Rabbi put on his yarmulka and his black top hat, and the Rebbitsen put on her shaitel (her wig) and her pink flower-hat and they went to shul where everybody said how nice they looked. But before they went, the Reb and the Rebbitsen said, 'Children we're leaving you alone at home. Whatever you do, don't open the doors for anyone. No matter what they say, what they play, don't open the door.' And the children all said, 'No matter what they say, what they play, we won't open the door!'

Well, there they were, laughing and happy and playing games and singing songs when a big white bear came to the door. 'Kinderlach, konderlach, lost mir arein,' the bear said, 'children, children, let me in – I'll give you honey and sugar.'

'Nein! Nein!' the children called, 'wir haben alein! We have our own!'

'Kinderlach, konderlach,' the bear began again, 'lost mir arein – ich et dir gebben putter mit breit! Butter and bread!'

'Nein, nein, wir haben alein!'

So the bear gave a graiser forts – a big fart – which blew down the door and he ran in and swallowed all the little children. All except little Mottel who hid in a bottle. And when the Reb and the Rebbitsen came home, he in his tall black top hat and she in her pink flower-hat, they found the door broken down and all their children gone. All except Mottel who was banging on his bottle. Well, they helped Mottel out of the bottle and he told them what had happened. How the bear with one graiser forts had broken down the door and then swallowed up all their children. The Rebbitsen was very clever. If you've swallowed so many children what do you do? You take a drink of water and you lie down in a cool place. So she took off her pink flower-hat to disguise herself and she took her scissors and her needle and her cotton and she went down to the river. And there under a big shady tree was the bear with a graiser boich – a big stomach – fast asleep. So she tiptoed up to him and cut open his stomach with her scissors and she took all her children out and then she got some smooth warm stones from the river-bank and she packed them where her children had been and sewed the bear's stomach so neatly together that he never noticed a stitch. And soon the children were all home again, laughing and happy and playing games and singing songs, and when the bear woke up he stretched and yawned and went to look for honey.

How We lost Laykella
One morning, on the 16th of April, we all slept late, mostly because Laykella hadn't woken us. I went in to see Mama at about nine o'clock.

She was sleeping with her arm over her eyes. Laykella was still curled up in her little hammock. I tiptoed up in case she was pretending and I could give her a fright. I swung the hammock up and down but she didn't move inside it. I twanged the strings but she didn't pretend to snore or bark or poop or anything. I tickled where her backside was and waited. Then I slowly pulled the sides apart and peeped inside. Her face was very white, the skin around her mouth was very blue and her eyes were half-open. Her lips were moving. I shouted and Mama jumped up and grabbed Laykella from me and put her on the bed and pumped her legs up and down and kissed her feet and her face. She pulled a dress on and rolled Laykella up in a blanket and picked her up and ran into the street, her feet bare, her hair all over her face. I ran behind. There was a doctor's house on the corner of Phoenix Street and Roberts Avenue. The door was locked and the windows closed. I ran around to the back. It was burnt out. Only one room was left and it was black with soot. There was a dinner-wagon with plates still inside against one wall. I opened the door from the inside and Mama thought it was the doctor and she started to cry when she saw that it was me. We ran ten blocks to the sanatorium shouting for help and for a doctor all the way and Laykella flapping in our arms and people running away when they saw what she looked like.

First we came to the side of the sanatorium. There was a line curled around and around the stairs, the garden and the pavement. Sick people and wounded people were sitting around crying and calling and there was a stink like rotten mangoes. Nobody took any notice of us there. A man in a dirty white coat told us to stand in the line. He wouldn't listen when I told him about Laykella, so we went to the front where nobody was supposed to go and I banged on the doors, then Mama gave me Laykella and she banged even harder and then a woman in a brown overall and a white nurse's hat opened it and said what did we want and Mama showed her Laykella and the nurse said yes, it was typhoid but she couldn't do anything we should try the General Hospital. Behind her I could see people lying on benches in the passage and on the floor and there was the same smell of mangoes. Mama said please to just show Laykella to a doctor and the nurse said what doctor and slammed the door. Then suddenly Mama wrapped up Laykella tight and put her down on the top stair and pulled me up and we ran across the street and as we were about to hide behind a wall, the door opened and the woman came out screaming at us – 'What are you doing?' she shouted, 'leave me alone!' and she burst into tears and slammed the door shut again. We went back to Laykella on the stair and Laykella was dead. We couldn't give her a proper family funeral like

Hindella because she had to be buried in a special typhoid place on the other side of Cyrildene.

Yiddel, Saltenossas and Mama

On Thursday, the 26th of July, I was out in Pandora Street with Rochella looking for wood. Pandora Street had gone down in the big four-day bombardment around about the time Hindella was shot. They used the new A40A bazookas for the first time, but if you looked hard enough among the rubble you could find some floorboards and cellar beams. It was very cold and we were wrapped up with everything we could find, like blankets and sacks and old socks on our hands, so it was hard to even move. Rochella kept complaining, and then she found some marbles and some pieces of a jigsaw puzzle with flowers on it and she started to play with them so I left her, as long as she was quiet.

Anyway, I was climbing all over, pulling and pushing around deep in the cellar, when I heard her calling again. I looked up, and there against the sky was tiny little Yiddel of Belgravia Shul.

'Mrs Pinchuk wants you,' he said.

'What for?' I asked.

'I don't know,' he said, 'but she said you must come now.'

'Okay,' I said, 'I will.'

'No,' he said, 'you must come now.'

'Okay,' I said, 'you go and I'll come.'

'It's all right,' he said, 'I'll walk with you.'

I couldn't think of anything more to say, so that was that. I was stuck with him and his saltenossas, there was no way out. All he talks about is the saltenossas his late mother used to make and how he got those eggs that time when somebody, a stranger, came to the shul and gave him two and he got some flour and milk which isn't as good as cream (which is *really* what you're supposed to bake saltenossas in) but still good enough when *he* does them, and he made his own saltenossa lokshen, and how yellow they were because he used *real* eggs, not like the white lokshen he used to buy. 'Egg lokshen they used to call them,' he said sarcastically, 'but what does that mean? Egg lokshen have to have *eggs* in them, otherwise don't call them egg lokshen!' And then he described how Mrs Pinchuk gave him a little white cheese and how *thin* his lokshen were because he rolled them so hard and he had to use a vinegar bottle because somebody had stolen his late mother's rolling pin (for firewood most probably) and then when he put it all in the oven and he baked them, how the milk bubbled and how beautiful and brown they were on top, and the *smell* – with his eyes closed, he was in his late mother's kitchen, waiting with his plate. Everybody, he said, the whole street, smelt his saltenossas and Mrs Pinchuk, when she smelt them, said to herself (she told him after), 'Es gezunterheit, Yiddel, eat in good health,' and he did! He always laughed at the same point and grepsed on purpose. That's a story you can hear once or twice, but if you hear it too much it can get on your nerves. And then when we were passing the shul he started to look for the key that hung from a pin on his coat but he couldn't find it so we stood there while he pulled his pockets inside out and stuck his fingers through the holes until he saw the door was open and he remembered he had given the rabbi the key. Then while he was pushing his pockets back in, he started to tell me how he only wore tennis shoes on Yom Kippur before our war, but now they were all he had and he showed me how they were glued together with rags and cardboard. Then he asked me if *I* knew where there were some eggs, and if that is what we were *really* looking for up there in Pandora Street. He was sure he heard a chicken when he was coming up the road. I said it must have been Rochella playing with the marbles and he said why should she sound like a chicken when she's playing with marbles and that he noticed feathers among the bricks, and I tried to get him onto the subject of birds in general and how even the sparrows had gone in our war, but he shot back to eggs and saltenossas again, and then just when he got to the part about the milk and how it was bubbling, we got to the Pinchuks' house and old Mrs Pinchuk was waiting outside and Yiddel said, 'Here he is.' And Mrs Pinchuk squeezed me and took me into a room and there was a body on the floor covered with sacks and she bent down and lifted some sack from the head and it was my mother's face. Somebody had just washed it. It was very clean and the hair was wet. Mrs Pinchuk said somebody had started shooting at the corner of Marshall and Browning Streets and my mother got shot. Mrs Pinchuk asked me if I wanted to kiss my mother and I said no. My mother's feet were showing at the other end of the sacks. They were dirty. Mrs Pinchuk asked me if I wanted to bring Rochella and Mendel to see her and I said no, so she walked with me down the street to Headquarters where she said we must see the Captain. She had her hand at the back of my neck and some people were staring at me.

The Captain

The Captain was eating stew. There was a little left. I could see some potato, beans and meat and something red. He stopped when Mrs Pinchuk said who I was and he showed me my mother's papers that they found on her when she was shot and he said she was forty-two.

'That's right,' Mrs Pinchuk said.

'She misses category 627VX/A by seven months and four days,' said the Captain, 'luck of the game. If she'd been born that much later or killed that much earlier, she would've been in. Yesterday there was a case – mother of two – who made it by one single day.'

'I think I know who it was,' said Mrs Pinchuk. 'Is it a Mrs Katzoff by any chance? Two girls – Maisie and Lynette.'

'How many children?' the Captain asked me, but I was watching the stew.

'How many?' he asked Mrs Pinchuk.

'Five,' she said.

He wrote down five.

'Sorry,' she said, 'is it in ink? Two dead.'

'So that's . . .,' he calculated, 'two living . . .' He scratched a two over the five.

'Sorry,' Mrs Pinchuk said, 'I think it's three.'

'Five – two –' the Captain said. 'You're right – three.' He blacked out the five with the two over it and wrote a three beside.

'Names?'

'Leiba – that's him – Rochella and Mendel.'

'Ages?'

'Twelve, seven,' Mrs Pinchuk said, 'and . . . and how old's Mendel?'

'Five,' I said.

The Captain looked at me. 'Do you want some stew?' he asked.

'Yes,' I said. I took the socks off my hands and rolled them together into a ball. Outside, a siren was going, but none of us took any notice. I could hear people running. He gave me his plate and spoon and they watched me finish what was there. I ate fast, staring down at the plate and listening to every chew and swallow in my head and every scrape of the spoon on the plate.

'Your relationship?' he asked Mrs Pinchuk.

'We worked together at the Bertha Solomon Social Centre.'

I licked the plate.

'Did you deal with Mrs Maganoff?' Mrs Pinchuk asked, 'I was with her too. That sniper got her in Flossie Street.'

'. . . C-e-n-t-r-e . . .' the Captain was still writing. I put the plate back on his desk.

'Now,' said the Captain, 'we've got to add a little, multiply a little and divide by three.' He scribbled on a piece of paper. I noticed a streak of gravy still left on the stew plate, so I picked it up and licked it away. The Captain was adding next to a doodle of a girl's face.

'One times one is one and one is two. Twenty-eight pounds thirteen and sixpence. Let me check. Three children. Forty-two years old. Category 627VX/B. Right. You see, if she'd made A, it would've been *thirty*-eight pounds.'

'You can't do anything more?' Mrs Pinchuk asked. 'They're lovely children.'

'How do you want it?' the Captain asked. 'In cash?'

'I suppose so,' Mrs Pinchuk said, 'what do you say, Leiba?'

I didn't say anything.

'Do you want me to keep it for you?' Mrs Pinchuk asked.

'No,' I said.

'So then how do you want it?'

'I don't know.'

'I'll give it to you in notes and silver,' the Captain said. He took money out of a metal box and counted it into a paper-bag. 'Ten – twenty – thirty – a five – one – two – three – in notes – Good – now – two (silver clinked) – four – six – eight – ten – one – two – three – thirteen shillings – and – six – pence! Do you want to check?'

I didn't say anything and Mrs Pinchuk said, 'Don't worry, we trust you.' He gave me the paper-bag.

Mrs Pinchuk was on her way back to the Bertha Solomon Social Centre, and it was on the way home, so I walked with her. She put her hand on the back of my neck again and I was carrying the paper-bag. At the gate to the Bertha Solomon Social Centre she asked me if I wanted to come in with her. I said no. There were some old people on the veranda and I thought I saw Mr Lapinsky among them and I was about to say hello when I remembered that he was dead, but I waved anyway and the other old man waved back. Then Mrs Pinchuk squeezed me and kissed me and told me to look after the money and the children and she went in and I started to walk home.

I walked first to Pandora Street, but Rochella wasn't there anymore, just little Yiddel looking for eggs where we had been. There was nobody at the house either. I didn't want to go inside. I called Rochella's name and Mendel's, walking up and down the street. The all-clear had sounded half an hour before, but nobody in the street had returned. I seemed to be the last person left on earth. I went back to our house, but couldn't stay there. I called their names from the door. Rifle fire began again in the distance. It was an evening sound, like trains shunting or children calling long ago. I went up Highlands Road, now just saying Rochella and Mendel's names. I turned down a side-street, stopping to kick around among the bricks and ashes of a ruined house. Suddenly I heard a bird. Only a bit of a sound, but real and clear. I stood still for a long time, hardly breathing, waiting for it to come again. The rifle fire was getting heavier, somewhere deep in Hillbrow. I moved to where the bird sound had come from and came to a big curly-iron gate still standing between two burnt black pillars. I walked around them into a broken garden, the trees twisted and scattered, the house a pile of rubble glistening with glass. Beyond, I suddenly saw more trees, green and straight, forgotten by our war. I climbed over the house to reach them and when I got there I didn't know properly what to do. I just touched them a bit, the fir needles and the bark. I began to cry and I tried to remember my mother. I tried to remember her living but it was hard. Whenever I concentrated on her I saw her dead, and when I didn't concentrate I saw only the trees. I called again for Rochella and Mendel and then I remembered the bird. I stood still to hear it again, but there was no sound of one.

I went back to the street. It was full of people now and when I got to the house, Rochella and Mendel were waiting for me at the door. When I told them about Mama, Rochella started to cry and Mendel wasn't listening properly. And when I told them about the money, they asked to look into the paper-bag and I let them. Then Rochella said she wanted a cardigan like Leila Scholssburg's and Mendel went outside again to play.

The next day I bought:

5 lbs mealie-meal porridge,
3 lbs sugar,
3 chops (I don't know what kind),
2 loaves of bread,
1 tin Captain Albert's Sardines,
3 marshmallow fishes,
4 carrots,
1 package salt.

Oh yes, and the cardigan for Rochella. A white one. That really got on my nerves. But she wouldn't stop crying for it.

Adam Small

Klaas

Klaas was gazing out over the dry ground. 'Here Mina,' he said. '*Ag Klaas*,' she said, '*moet tog maar nie die. Here Sy Naam ydellik gebruik nie*' ('Oh Klaas, please, everything, but don't use the Name of the Lord in vain'). He said okay. Then he said again '*Here Mina*', and he looked out over the land. The ground.

Ground is what he grew up with, what he was born from, was indeed all he had ever known. It was what he first saw on coming to consciousness, what he had lived with ever since. There were other things – water and fire for instance. But everything else for him always related to the ground, and had no meaning in itself, but only a meaning related to the ground.

And if the elements did not balance, when fire destroyed growth or water life, this meant for him that the ground was stricken. Then he would say '*Dis darem nie reg nie Mina*' ('It isn't right Mina'). And Mina his wife whom he had never married would say '*Jy mag nie die Here hiersovoor blameer nie Klaas*' ('You must not blame the Lord for this Klaas'). It meant for him that the ground was done an injustice. The nature of the ground was Klaas's measure for life.

Klaas was brown like the ground. He had never seen ground another colour than brown, the brown of the skin over his hands and, indeed, over his face. He knew this from the mirror in his and Mina's hovel on the river's edge which they called *huis* (home). They lived on the boundary of the farm, Klaas with his wife, whom he had never wed, and all his children too and it was a matter of deep pride for him that he had never had any *ander meide* (other women) – only Mina. Deep furrows in his face made Klaas look stern, like his morality.

When he was younger he used to *vat 'n dop* (drink), but that was long before he was converted – *voor my bekering*, said Klaas. And after his *bekering,* never again did he put his lips to wine, and he didn't smoke either. Klaas's world was one, and Mina's too, in which the simple criterion of goodness in a man was that you could say of him *Hy rook nie en hy drink nie* (He neither drinks nor smokes). Especially if a man did not drink, he was beyond any question a good man.

All around him there was only the ground endlessly. And the flaming sky, flaming with sunlight, more fire than light, a brilliant painfulness. Long before noon and afternoon, and even to his furrowed face, used as it was to heat, it was unbearable. Everything was breathed over by scorching fire. All around Klaas there was only the scorching drought, endlessly. The days were singing maddeningly with insects hidden under burnt grass and behind tough eucalyptus leaves, a nagging singing on and on and on.

He had not known it like this before, not quite. *Dit is darem nie reg nie.* He had known drought before. You cannot live on this land without knowing drought, without knowing this blatant sun, this repulsive heat and light. But now it was all worse than ever before, and the ground was dancing a wild dance, bobbing up and down, not a joyous dance, and there were pools of water all around, that shone, yet were not pools of water. *Dis duiwelswerk,* they said (It's the devil's work).

Now the sun was springing on one like a tiger. Roaring like a lion in the Bible, like a woman in labour, making one feel miserable. Now the sun, one imagined, was dripping with blood. Klaas knew the Bible. He had 'gone as far as' Standard Four at school, and could read, and he had the Bible which Baas Giel had given him, and the nights were long despite even the fact that he had to be up every morning at just a little past five, for that was when Baas Giel thought his *volk* (labourers) should start moving. And in any case, *'n Man wat bekeer is moet sy Bybel ken* (A man who is converted should know his Bible). He had a sound knowledge of the Word, and the imagery of the Bible for calamities was in his head, and the worst calamity of all for man, of course, was to burn in hell for ever without respite.

'*So sal jy ook brand as jy jou werk nie reg doen nie,*' said Baas Giel and laughed ('You will also burn like that if you don't do your work properly'). And Klaas laughed. And the big white yet not so white hand came down upon his back in a strange, friendly way, and the white voice said, '*Komaan my hotnot*' ('Come now my hottentot') and the tone of voice was not unlike Baas Giel's when he spoke to the horses, the ones that he particularly liked. '*Komaan, Kom nou, Ha-nou, Sója . . .*'

Klaas did not resent this. How could he? He was an animal on the farm

– like one of the animals really – for as long as he could remember. He grew up on this ground first like a little *hansskaap* (motherless lamb), and he grew favoured for his capacity for work, and still later, finding his own level and stature as a worker became for Baas Giel *My hotnot*, Klaas Koega . . . little more than an animal, one of the sheep or one of the horses, but one who was so in a greatly favoured way.

No, Klaas did not resent this. In fact, it was a matter of pride for him so that he relished the jealousy of the other *volk*. He was Baas Giel's favourite *hotnot*. Indeed, things went to Klaas's head.

He felt himself so much one with the ground that he felt – but would, of course, never say so – that Baas Giel who was a *Witman* (White man), because of his colour, which wasn't white but still quite white, did not really identify completely with the ground. For that it was necessary to be brown, like mud, like this island dust, like this rusty earth. *Bruin*. Like the *stofwolk* (dust cloud) that stands on the horizon for days, like *koring-brood* (brown bread). Klaas remembered when Baas Giel was still Klein-baas, and Baas Giel grew up, how he felt pleased to see, as the years went by, that as the sun burned down on everything Baas Giel grew darker and darker, *bruiner en bruiner*, though not quite dark enough. There was a certain pride in Klaas for being at one with the ground in a way Baas Giel was not. And he did not ponder the meaning of the word *Baas* (Boss) beyond this. It had no meaning at all for him beyond this.

Only this ground was what he knew. This ground was his complete experience. Birth on this ground, and growth on this ground and death on this ground. Just up the slope, slanting on the *hoogte* (rise) on the other side of the farm labourers' hovels, was the graveyard. Not the one where ultimately Baas Giel will lie, but the *bruinmense se begraafplaas* (the Coloured people's cemetery). They are born from this great dusty ground, grow up in it like earthworms, die in it, dusty all their lives, *bruinmense*. Then they are buried in this dust, dust unto dust. Klaas was unperturbed, imperturbable.

Still, when one of them was buried, like Tolla a little while ago who was bitten by a snake, and the little congregation of the farm turned out, the women in whatever black they could lay their hands on, the men with tattered hats respectfully carried in their gnarled hands, all of them dumb, even dumber than animals of the farm, and they stood together around the open grave, around the rough-hewn coffin, around the dusty body that was returning to the dust from which it had come and which it had never left to see a horizon apart from this one around the farm, which circled the clump of *bloekoms* (eucalyptus trees) above their *huisies* (little houses) with the brown dust cloud standing on it, not moving, just standing on it, it seemed eternally, then Klaas felt something moving inside him, a kind of resistance to all this that unsettled his breast, something he could not explain not only because he did not have the kind of mind to explain it, but which he could not explain because it was too big a meaning, one that went beyond the horizon, beyond this circle which held his life and Mina's and the lives of all the *bruinmense* on the farm.

Oorkant die water, blinkend en bly, sien ek bemindes, wagtend op my . . . (Beyond the water, shining and glad, there I see loved ones, waiting on me . . .) Every time they sang it, every time in this dust which the men would then shovel over the corpse and coffin of one of their number who had gone to his judgement, every time a lump would come in his throat, which usually was quite unlike his imperturbable self. *Oorkant die water* . . . He was standing at Tolla's grave and they were singing this as the dust rose up.

It wasn't this water, the water of the river, which had no water in it now, of which they were singing, high-pitched, these brown and dusty women, draped in black, these scarecrows who would do better than scarecrows in *Baas Giel se huistuin* (Baas Giel's house-garden), and deep-voiced, these brown and dusty men. It was death they were singing of, and Klaas saw, in imagination, masses of black water, black because it was so deep. Then he looked the way of the real river, out there in the afternoon, beyond *die huisies*, the river whose deep bed the sun was burning, the river without water, and he wondered what lay beyond. He had never been beyond it very far. The horizon here was really only in his eyes and he had no experience of it whatsoever, not ever having been that far.

Klaas only knew the ground.

Pieter-Dirk Uys

God Will See You Now

The television newsreader didn't dare allow his eternal poise to drop when he announced the end of the world. 'Our nuclear missile is on its way to the northern hemisphere, a spokesman for the Department of Defence said a few minutes ago. We have twenty-five minutes left. Massive international retaliation against South Africa has already taken place. Good night.'

His eyes stared out at me for a moment, professional in their glassiness. His purple tie and orange shirt harmonized loudly like an Arab and an Israeli round a braaivleis. But then, unfortunately, his face crumbled and he covered his damaged facade with shaking hands. His image was tactfully faded from the expensive screen.

Good night? the ghost image of the horror hopped around the empty media-arena and played games with my eyes. The moment of terrified screen tension passed and a series of confused and easily recognisable pictures paraded gently across my vision: the SABC-TV logo, an overweight but pretending continuity lady in tears, the dramatic start of a Dogmor advert, labrador in full song, and then, like a cherry on the boil, the pre-recorded Weather Report filled the room with its cheerful news of tomorrow's sunshine and mild afternoon showers. Tomorrow? What tomorrow?

But then, as suddenly, this 'latest rumour' vanished and a running brooklet gurgled across the screen to the tinkles of a Schumann piano piece. Graceful, happy, the alternative to 'Do not adjust your sets.' That too dissolved, this time into a still unreal technicolour picture of Mary Magdalene washing the feet of Jesus, while sombre gravelly religious music whined in solitude, in collaboration, in vain. Why this picture, I thought, still wondering if the newscast hadn't been the end of a recent disaster movie.

Twenty-five minutes? I looked down at my watch. Twenty-two minutes! What had happened to the other precious three?

A scream of pure terror came filtering through the windows from somewhere down the street, followed by a woman sobbing and a car hooter blowing and a baby coughing. It was the first time I'd heard a baby cough. Was it sick? Did it matter? Twenty-two minutes to care and wonder and live.

Twenty-one and a half. But to do what in?

I looked around me and became aware that everything was there for tomorrow and the day after, for a future and a life. Twenty-one minutes.

My friends! My family! I rushed to the phone and started dialling Cape Town desperately to talk to my father. What would I say to him? 'Hello Pa, the world's ending in twenty minutes goodbye . . .'

But then what if he hadn't heard the news? It had all happened so quickly. Yesterday we'd signed the Accord and the United Nations troops had walked around with vygies in their guns and eating kudu-biltong with a smile, and yet now hell was on the way. How can you explain the end of the world calmly and still say: 'Goodbye, I love you' in nineteen minutes?

Eighteen minutes. Suddenly I wanted to cry. I ran out of the little house into the front garden and stared into the street, hoping to find anyone to talk to, to argue with, with whom to die. The darkness hung over me like dirt.

Seventeen minutes. I slammed the door loudly, needing the sound, and walked up and down the small passage of my home, wringing my hands as if I had flu, feeling pain in every joint while staring pointlessly at all the little bits of expendable rubbish that made up my life. Photographs with empty smiles and never-blinking eyes, unaware of the terrible urgency around them. Books filled with enough words to hold together a civilization but no answer to the inevitable demand: why?

Sixteen minutes. I sat at the typewriter and started banging out a necklace of letters that might help, but all that came out in faultless spelling was: O God, if only we had time . . .

There seemed to be no breath left in the room. I took deep gasps of the night air, trying not to imagine what terrors lay in store through death by fire. Roasting, singed, bubbling flesh, popping eyeballs, splintered bones.

The ordinary daily sound of the piercing laughter of a black domestic servant across the road sounded like the final air-raid siren. Laughter at a time like this? Maybe for once we were all in the same boat, both haughty madam and humble maid. Death was not for whites only and heaven only a homeland for those who were good and prayed and fed the poor, and few of 'us' were qualified.

I looked up with repentance and prayer in mind. A jetliner slowly flew across the faces of the angels on its way to safety. Where – Australia maybe? Would the captain greet his passengers like a cheeful door-to-door salesman and point out the silver missiles as they passed and watch the mushroom cloud smudge the horizon fifteen minutes away?

I closed the door to the world as the television changed gear. Mary Magdalene and the mournful Bach vanished and last night's Epilogue tinkled its way into the ending of my life. The good shepherd of a panicked flock smiled and tried to remember his lines. His message to the next fourteen minutes would be 'For God so loved the world . . .' but I switched off in mid-sentence and refused to believe in his canned comfort.

I had put on the kettle somewhere between minutes thirteen and twelve so that I could still have a coffee in my Blue Train Souvenir mug. Out of habit, decaffeinated coffee. Better for the health. No sugar. No cookies. More habit. I had to smile and, with ten minutes left to pick up weight, I stirred in six spoons to make up for all the bitter discipline of the past year. But it was too hot to drink.

There were ants in the cookies. Nine minutes and then the horrible realization that the ants would probably survive the holocaust while I wouldn't crossed my line of thoughts. Over my dead body, I snarled and gleefully murdered billions before I realized I only had eight-times-sixty left.

I became aware of the prettiest fig-tree in the backyard, standing proudly and bandy-legged in the shaft of light. I never remembered ever having seen it before.

The telephone screamed. I picked it up, not knowing whom to expect. A strangely calm voice asked for Mevrou Van Staden. I had to say: sorry, wrong number and then there were only six minutes left.

My last ever phonecall. Five minutes and I thought of a million terribly important things and couldn't remember one. I lay down and closed my eyes, but got up immediately, instinctively not wanting to be caught waiting for the end.

I pulled a record out of the shelf at random and put it on at full volume. It was Judy Garland singing: 'Somewhere over the rainbow . . .' I had to laugh at her optimism.

Two minutes. I silenced Judy and sat listening for the sounds as the angels of death beat their wings on their way to me. But there was nothing that made this evening any different from any other. One minute.

'Oh no,' I shouted at no one in particular, 'it's not fair!' And as I thought 'Who'd feed the kitty?', I did hear the noise and everything went white and very hot.

Christopher van Wyk

Twenty Years' Experience

The ritual at the supper table was always the same. My father opened with the solemn, monotonous:

> Be present at our table, Lord
> Be here and everywhere adored
> These mercies bless and grant
> That we may feast in paradise with thee.

This was followed by a chorus of amens, sometimes in perfect harmony, sometimes terribly discordant, depending on appetite or the quality of food. The last three lines of the prayer I have only just learnt. I could never quite make out what Daddy was asking of God; most of the prayer always drowned in his saliva.

After my father spoke to God my mother spoke to him. She spoke all through supper, all the time. She had even mastered a method whereby she could operate peristalsis and her vocal chords at the same time. And whenever Mum spoke I could've sworn that she had forgotten all about the presence of the Lord at the table. It wasn't that she swore or blasphemed or anything like that. It was just that the way she spoke was not the way one would if you knew He was around.

Terence, my younger brother, and I sat between the parents facing each other. His left ear got the full blast of what Mum said while my right ear did. It was rather harrowing since we were not allowed to talk at the table. Eating was our business there. Sometimes we changed places for the sake of a little variety.

And Mum thought no other topic better than L. H. Sacks Fashion Garments so that I knew that factory like my favourite fork; every prong and cranny of it. Though Terence did not possess a favourite fork, he felt the same way about Sacks.

'I don't know where she comes from,' Mom would introduce a new machine hand to us. 'Mr Sacks put her with us. She's a baster so Mr Sacks just had to put her with us, but is she bitchy!' You see what I mean about forgetting the Lord? 'Now we sit like this at our tables,' Mummy would trace a U-shape which included Terence and I and which never failed to give us a pleasant sense of involvement.

'Okay,' Mum would admit, 'she is good on the machine, bladdy good, and that is the proper place for her to be seeing that she has to pass the jackets to Dora for lining. I think she used to work for S and M Menswear down in Fox Street. You remember where the old Reno bioscope used to be – there.

'I got Elaine in the bus this morning. Elaine works at S and M and she told me that this thing used to work there. Elaine says she works damn good but that she was just so bitchy with the girls there, in fact she got fired because of her shit!

'Now she sits there' (at the base of the U) 'and whenever she sees one of us talking – you know we can't talk too loud – she thinks we're talking about her. Just this morning Lettie was telling me she wants to rush down to the furniture shop lunchtime to pay her account. And won't this bladdy woman jump up and say: "Ja, talking about me again, hey! skindering again!"

'So Lettie told her – you see I told Lettie what Elaine told me in the bus – so Lettie told her she's not at S and M because of her bitchiness and that she won't be at Sacks for long because of that same bitchiness.

'Jesus! you should've seen her face. You see she didn't know we knew where she worked before. And when Lettie told her that, I felt so lekker inside.

'Well what could that thing say? She was caught unawares. Man if I just had a camera, just to take a picture of her face to show you.'

Terence always said he'd like to take a picture of Mum at the suppertable and show it to her.

'Well,' Mum would go on, 'she did afterwards mumble something. She said with her experience on the basting machine she could go anywhere for a job.'

'She's got a complex, this woman,' Dad would explain sagaciously.

'To hell with her complex, man! If she wants to work she must leave her complex at home.'

This always confused poor Terence who was doing his second year in standard two. He always wondered whether a complex was a sickness or whether it could be packed into a bag together with lipstick and a bus coupon.

'And you, eat that bladdy cabbage, mister!' My gaping jaws would be shocked back into obedient mastication. 'Counting my bladdy teeth again!'

That Terence knew he should take seriously.

The story of 'that thing' with her complex and bitchiness went on for another month. Some episodes we had with mince, some we had with soup, some we had with green beans, some we had with cabbage. We had quite a few with cabbage, in fact.

Then one night we heard that 'that thing' had threatened to 'fuck up' the whole bladdy factory. She got fired. That night we ate tripe and mashed potatoes.

And then there was that unforgettable evening of turmoil. My mother sat, posed over a heap of samp and beans, clutching a spoon, her face red, indignant.

'Now how do you bladdy like that! Mr Sacks says it's the new law. From tomorrow onwards it's coming into operation. Every girl is allowed to use the toilet once between each break. And that works out to about four, five times a day.'

'Even that time of the month?'

'Even that time of the month!'

'What time of the month?'

Oh God present at our table please help my stupid brother!

Terence was only ten years old then. He had made very few mistakes in his young life. 'What time of the month?' was one of them.

He got it from both sides. It was as if he was watching a ghastly pinball game. Poor, stupid Terence!

Stupid parents! They went on as if they had suddenly realized that we could actually hear everything they said at the table. In fact they realized that we had heard everything they discussed since Newclare days when we used to eat by candlelight and we didn't have Gavin and Albert and Theresa and Russel and Mark and the radio and the acoustics used to be perfect.

'You seem to have forgotten,' sputtered one parent, 'that children should be seen and not heard.' Together with this attack Terence was further subjected to a hail of mouth to face missiles of parboiled mealies.

Most nights after supper Terence and I would flee to the solitude of our bedroom. There we would chew on the cud of the conversations at the supper table. I am a year older than him so he would ask me the meaning of 'that time of the month.' I didn't know.

Sometimes we advised each other on etiquette. I warned him about his impulsiveness.

'You open your mouth too wide,' he told me. 'One day Mummy'll stop talking and smack you.'

The story of Rachel must have had my mouth at its widest.

Rachel, a cutter at the factory was almost caught selling baby's clothing during working hours. Rachel had wrapped the clothes into an unfinished jacket. This way the jacket would pass through everybody's hands and so all would have a chance to discreetly inspect the goods for sale. This was the procedure whenever anyone had something to sell.

'And while Lena was looking at these things won't Mr Sacks come out of his office and walk towards her. So what do you think she does, she ever so calmly takes the bonnets and bibs, stuffs it under the lining of a jacket she was busy on, and starts sewing it close. Then she gives it to Mr Sacks together with a few other jackets and says ever so casually: "Oh Mr Sacks, won't you give these to Wilfred so that he can do the sleeves, please."

'And Mr Sacks obediently took the jackets to Wilfred. Man he never suspected a thing. When Mr Sacks went back to his office, Wilfred just winked at us, tore open the lining and took out the clothes.'

'So who bought the clothes?' said Dad.

'Wilfred.'

Terence almost applauded but checked himself in time.

I tell you some of those stories were better than the ones we heard at school.

Then one day Mum came home earlier than usual. She brought her scissors, cup, slippers, overall and all the other things she kept in her locker. That always meant only one thing.

'The factory's closed. Mr Sacks says he only got to know about it last night. Ooh! he looked so sad when they came to fetch the machines. He didn't even look like a boss; he was down. When he told us about it he looked at the pieces of lining and cotton and stuff on the floor. He said he was insolvent. He said he knew it would happen but he was scared to tell us about it.'

'What's insolvent?'

'Bankrupt.'

'I knew it. Well he at least gave us two weeks' wages. We didn't want to take it but that only made him feel worse. He actually got quite cross with us. So we took the money, not that I minded.'

Mummy was at home for the next few days. It was bad. There was always extra work around the house we had to do. She also played fahfee heavily – sometimes a whole rand – and we were not supposed to tell Dad about it, especially when she lost. But she told him all about his horrible sons and what they had done today. Terence and I became the new topics at the supper table. We wished hard that she would get a job soon.

One evening while Mummy was busy cooking, Daddy came into the kitchen with the newspaper.

'Hey, listen to this!' He read slowly, about Mr Sacks trying to leave the country with too much money. When Mummy heard 'Mr Sacks' she wiped her hands off on her overall, the same overall that she brought from the factory, and went to stand behind Daddy.

'Mr Sacks said he wasn't doing well in South Africa so he wanted to go back to his own country to start afresh.' The case was proceeding.

Mummy just said, 'Ag' and Daddy said 'the bastard!' and turned to the jobs pages. He read out the jobs to her while she peeled potatoes.

He came across one that said: Woman wanted to start immediately on jumper basting machine. Must be neat, hardworking and have at least four years experience.

'Cut that one out for me. I should get that job if I wake up early tomorrow and go and see them. After all I have got twenty years' experience.'

But I didn't want to hear more because the smell of cabbage was all over the bladdy place. And I can't stand the stuff.

Peter Wilhelm

Lion

Towards the end of summer, everything poised for decay, the final bold shapes tottering under parabolas of hot straining insects, a lion was observed wandering across the rich farmlands to the north-west of Johannesburg: only miles from the city, a golden shape barred by trees fringing mapped-out regions of cultivation and order, crossing the thrusting highways in vast lopes that evaded destruction by the thundering, astonished traffic.

There was no formal record of the lion, so he sprang into the city's awareness fully extant, fused out of the shining air; and the first premonitory twitches of fear manifested themselves in the dreams of the inhabitants of Sandown, Bryanston, Houghton, all the green suburbs with women beside blue swimming pools with drinks at 11 a.m. The pounce, the yellow teeth, the cavernous dark jaws, the feral rush through the flowering shrubbery – it was all there, a night-time code.

Posses of police and farmers – guns out and oiled, trusty – walked through the high grass and weeds, stung by immature maize stalks, looking. They had dogs with them who cringed and whimpered, showing their own calcium-charged fangs, white and somehow delectable like the tips of asparagus. They and the children who ran after them shrieking with terror and breathlessness, black and white tumbled together in the mordant adventure, were all on a hampered search; the skills of tracking were forgotten, they could only go by the obvious. Members of the press went along too, with flushed faces and cameras.

At an early stage it was decided that, given the high price of lions on the international zoo market, the animal would not, when found, be killed: anaesthetic darts would be used to stun it first, then it would be lifted into a cage and transported to a convenient central point for the disposition of lions.

They followed a trail of kills, day after day, puffing and lagging. Here they found a dog contemptuously munched and discarded; there a mournful heifer, brown licked eyes startled by death, a haunch ripped open – purple and blue ravines, Grade A waste spoiled for the abattoir and the hungry steakhouses.

The heavy, overripe rains had given a lush feel to the fields, spreading green paint over growth, and wild flowers and weeds hammered into the air from uncultivated edges. Fruit fell into mud with sodden plops; irrigation ditches and small streams throbbed, the water corded and waxy. It had been a superb year, a harvest of a year, and the granaries and exchequer were loaded. So the lion penetrated a structure of assent and gratitude with a dark trajectory: his streaming mane, a Tarzan image, cast gaunt shadows on the end of the commercial year.

The boots of the hunters stuck in the mud; they were like soldiers going over the top in 1916, sent into barbed wire and indeterminate sludge by drunken generals; they floundered; the brims of their hats filled with rain; their pants soaked through like those of terrified schoolboys. They made no headway.

Inexorably, champing at the livestock, the lion ate his way towards the northern suburbs of the city, past roadhouses and drive-in cinemas showing documentaries on wild-life and the adventures of Captain Caprivi.

The frequency of dreams involving lions and lion-like beings increased significantly among the inhabitants of the green park-like suburbs of the city. The thud of tennis balls against the netting of racquets lost its precision: the shadow was there, in the tennis court, in the cool waves of the swimming pool, in the last bitter juices of the evening cocktail, tasting of aniseed.

The lion came down.

The farmers – who grew plump chickens for the frozen food ranges of the great supermarkets, and poppies for certain anniversaries – were furious at the terroristic incursion. It blighted their reality, shaming them. They woke to fences offensively broken, to minor household animals sardonically slaughtered, not even used for a snack on the road.

The lion behaved precisely like a lion; each animal was decisively killed; there was never any maiming, inadvertent or intentional; his great jaws crunched down on bone and splintered through domesticity.

He took a roving way toward the city: first directly south through well-manured farmlands, then tracing a stream westwards away from the sprawl of concrete and glass – sniffing at it, perhaps, and choosing to skirt.

He seemed to vanish, back into the diminishing lights of early autumn, back into the air, his lithe yellowish body no longer even glimpsed at a distance by the frenzied posses, watched from behind earth walls by large-eyed farmhands, and howled at by dogs with their black testicles in the dust.

The pressure abruptly diminished like that in a garden hose when the tap is turned commandingly to the left.

Something like silence descended, mote-like and uneasy. The lion had gone away; there had never been a lion; the lion had been a hypnagogic hallucination.

Then he killed a man, most savagely tearing out his guts next to a road, and pinpointed on a map the kill showed that the westward drift had been temporary and that the lion had in reality resumed coming back. He had followed a stream away from the city, now he was coming back on the opposite bank: all he had done was seek out a place to cross.

Until the occurrence of the first human death, the press and other communications media had adopted an editorial stance towards the lion in which a certain light-heartedness had been mandatory. There had been jibes at authority's inability to find the beast, or even trace its origins. Now, as telephones began to ring incessantly with queries from troubled householders as to the lion's progress, and a sermon was preached in which the light of Christianity was set favourably against the unplumbed blackness of the wilderness and its denizens, the newspapers realized that public opinion was turning against the lion, and they adopted a harder line: the lion must be shot, or at least swiftly captured, before there were more deaths.

The dead man was reported to be a Bantu male called Samuel Buthelezi, a distant relation of the Zulu royal family.

It emerged that the followers had in fact passed the lion, going west when he was coming east; he had been asleep on a rock, or in a warm bowl of sand, sunning himself invisibly. And so the feeling arose that the search had to be made by professionals; a former professional game hunter was accordingly brought out of retirement to put the affair on a more scientific or knowing footing. However, it was impossible to search by night, which was too preponderantly black to make for ease of vision, silence of movement, of comfort of heart; and so the lion continued to get away. His getting away became the present tense of the searchers and they began to feel it was invincible, that he took devious routes with prior awareness of topography and demography; and when a day or so passed without reports of a kill they indulged in grotesque fantasies – remarking that the lion must be dead in a ditch, or whimpering in a cave with a thorn in his foot. Any of a dozen possibilities, and impossibilities, presented themselves according to the number of searchers involved.

The former professional game hunter was an alcoholic; he drank himself into a stupor and issued contradictory orders.

Small units of the army and air force were summoned to help in the search: it was reasoned that the experience would aid them in tracing terrorists in hostile terrain. Platoons of young men in green and khaki camouflage uniform – bayonets ready at the tips of their rifles – moved lumpily over hills and through lower muddy regions looking for the lion, their boots mired indescribably. In the air fighter and reconnaissance jets flashed from one edge of the horizon to the other, ceaselessly photographing. A helicopter, normally used for the control of traffic and the detection of illegally cultivated marijuana, also chopped its way through the search pattern.

The first white person to be killed by the lion was Dr Margaret Brierwood. A graduate in palaeontology, Dr Brierwood had taken her two children to school and was settling down beside the swimming pool of her and her husband's three-acre holding in a wooded area only ten miles from the city centre. In the course of the preceding night the lion had doubled the distance between him and his pursuers, racing along the fringes of a dual highway connecting the cities of Pretoria and Johannesburg. He had failed to make a kill at dawn and was correspondingly nettled at his own inadequacies – a horse had whinnied to freedom because of a misjudged leap – and driven by hunger.

The Brierwoods' estate was surrounded by a low wooden fence, easily hurdled, and the lion sat for some time within the grounds, panting softly, his tail rapidly frisking dust and grass, before moving. He observed the morning activity narrowly, tempted at one point to carry off a black man who swept the floor of the swimming pool with a long vacuum brush. He was deterred by innumerable activities in his immediate environment: a large fly that bit his haunch and made him snap irritably at the air, two birds that made trilling love in overhead leaves, a subtle alteration in the quality of the morning light which stirred inchoate levels of unease in the beast.

The strangeness of the pool – its non-drinking-place aspects – had a dazzling effect on the mind of the lion. It made him indecisive about striking.

Eventually, however, he made his charge – out of the wooded garden, up a grass slope to the pool's verge, then a leap across a tea table – glass shattering, sugar cubes ascending white in the clear air – and a last controlled embrace with Dr Brierwood, his vast paws over her breasts, the talons holding firm, his jaws clamping down on her neck to draw up spouts of blood.

Dr Brierwood had been mid-way through a paragraph in an article pointing out certain anomalies in a palaeontologist's analysis of recent finds at unexpected levels of the Olduvai Gorge in Kenya. When the intimidating, blood-freezing, total horror of the lion's roar swept over her like a wave of pure death from an opened crypt, she looked up and screamed. The lion dropped down out of the sky to seize her; one finger convulsively jabbed at the place where she had stopped reading; and she felt her bones being crushed with more force than she had ever conceived.

Terrified servants ran for help. Within an hour a cordon of men and weaponry had been set in a ring around the Brierwood estate. For miles in all directions traffic began to slow, to stop, to impact into jarring hooting masses. Thousands of sightseers came from all directions, hampering operations.

At the centre of command was the former professional game hunter, who was half mad from anxiety and gracelessly attempted to defer to anyone in uniform; but orders had been given that he alone was in charge, and as the crisis gained dimension, moving towards a critical moment when something would after all have to be done, he realized that a decision – on something, anything – would have to be taken. He pushed his way through people who shouted into each others' faces and went into a house which instantly transformed into a headquarters. Maps were pinned on walls, markers were moved on boards, grids were established: the military apparatus became dominant, and he realized that a military decision might be inevitable.

To think more clearly the game hunter locked himself in a lavatory and drank.

The lion left the remains of his kill beside the swimming pool and made his way into the woods to sleep. It was a fine autumn morning, holding the last of the summer heat in the bright dappled areas of light under the trees, and soothing and cool in the shade. Drowsiness overcame him and he stretched at his full length to digest Dr Brierwood.

The small, frightened, trigger-happy group which – under the dilatory leadership of the former professional game hunter – finally made its way to the swimming pool and found the dead woman, was incapacitated by the sight. Each registered an atrocity; each felt an impulse to shout, or rescript the terms of the find; inevitably there was a sickly anticipation of retribution and subsequent guilt.

In the judicial inquiry which was later held into the circumstances of the killing, it was considered extraordinary that the grounds of the Brierwood estate were not fully, immediately searched. No search was made; once Mrs Brierwood had been removed the servants were questioned on the movements of the lion, and when two agreed that he had been seen wandering along a stretch of country road north of the estate there was a surge in that direction. The testimony of the servants was instantly accepted: it had a satisfactory emotional content, and the searchers were in any case dazed at the fury that had broken out at the edge of the swimming pool.

On a bed of brown fallen leaves at the outer boundary of the Brierwood estate the lion slept peacefully all day; he moaned softly in his sleep like a dreaming cat, his immense male head on his paws.

By midnight the curious had moved away, and the searchers were bunched together indecisively in a small army camp. A violent electric storm had disrupted communications, and the various groups who were out on the roads and in the fields with torches and guns blundered through wet darkness, seeing nothing, knowing nothing, dead at heart. Damage to an underground telephone cable at 2 a.m. put several thousand receivers out of order in the area; and this contributed to an impression of profound devastation. There was a universal sense of depression, and sleepers were driven down into grey underworlds where faceless statues intoned meaningless arguments.

Shortly after dawn the lion left the woods, through which horizontal light splintered prismatically. He sniffed the wind and plodded south again, through landscaped terraces and sprawling ranch-style homesteads. Down pine-needle matted lanes and across dew-spotted lawns he padded with no more noise than soft rustlings and the snap of small twigs.

Soon the terrain changed, and taking the easiest way he was beguiled towards the exact heart of Johannesburg along the concrete swaths of the M1 motorway. It was a bright, crisp morning, the sky was enormous, blue to violet at the zenith, streaked with high tufts of cirrus, almost invisible. Ahead, the dark autumnal cone of ash and smoke remained to be burned off the city, dense, dirty, but giving a solid emphasis to the tower blocks: an appropriate frame.

He went on through the awakening suburbs, stinging smells of coffee and morning toast, the first cars coughing into life. And then the first cars began to pass him, early motorists staring with incredulity, astonishment, in tumults of weirdness at the apparition. They accelerated around the lion, so that there was an aspect of untampered serenity about his passage.

He walked into Johannesburg, quite alone after a time, since once word had reached the authorities of his route the motorway was closed and for the second time in twenty-four hours traffic choked to a standstill. The lion could hear distant clangour and uproar, meaningless. Soon he began to sniff irritably at acrid fumes and the like, but his entry remained inflexible; he took no off-ramps, and remained on the left of the road within the speed limit.

By mid-morning he was weary, and stopped, and looked around. This was the city; geometrical mountains advanced into themselves, making no horizon, netting together like stone fronds into an impassivity of yellow, grey, gold, black. He had no sense of distance or perspective and could not see into the new environment.

He roared at it.

His roar echoed back.

He stood at the edge of the motorway, where it swept over old buildings and streets and looked down past John Vorster Square to the Magistrates' Courts and the Stock Exchange, and beyond that to the Trust Bank and the Carlton Centre: the shapes impacted up against his sight.

Below him, when he looked again, men and women seethed, their clothing briskly making fresh patterns as they moved around, then settling or resettling into something else.

North and south the motorway spread dully; nothing whatsoever moved; a small wind beat miserably at pieces of brown newspaper gusted over the tar.

He roared at everything. And, tinnily, a kind of echo came back: but buzzing, inconsequential, intermittent. Far above a small black dot came down at him.

The helicopter, the former professional game hunter.

Suddenly the lion was deafened and shaken by fear: a metal thing jabbered at him only yards away, black grit tossed up by mad winds into his nose. Men with strained white faces spilled out into the motorway, pincered him.

And then, of course, the military solution.

Notes on Contributors

Lionel Abrahams (b. 1928, Johannesburg); a volume of poems, *Thresholds of Tolerance* (1975) (Bateleur), and the novel as a sequence of stories, *The Celibacy of Felix Greenspan* (1977), in which *The Messiah* configures.

Jillian Becker (b. 1932, Johannesburg); three novels – *The Keep* (1967), its sequel *The Union* (1971), and *The Virgins* (1976); also new journalism *(Hitler's Children)*. This story not previously published.

Yvonne Burgess (b. 1936, Eastern Province); three novels – *A Life to Live* (1973), *The Strike* (1975) and *Say a Little Mantra for Me* (1979), and several short stories.

Cherry Clayton (b. Cape Town); published short stories in many little magazines; *In Time's Corridor* first appeared in *Contrast* as one of a continuing autobiographical sequence.

Jack Cope (b. 1913, Natal); seven novels – from *The Fair House* (1955) through *The Dawn Comes Twice* (1969), *The Student of Zend* (1972) to *My Son Max* (1977) – and several collections of stories. *Harry's Kid* is uncollected.

Leon de Kock, (b. 1957, Johannesburg); this story first published in *Donga*, of which he was an assistant editor.

C. J. Driver (b. 1939, Cape Town); four novels – *Elegy for a Revolutionary* (1969), *Send War in our Time, O Lord* (1971), *Death of Fathers* (1972) and *A Messiah of the Last Days* (1974) – and *Occasional Light* (1979) in the Mantis Poets series.

Ahmed Essop; his first collection of stories, *The Hajji*, in which *Gerty's Brother* is included, appeared in 1978 and won the Olive Schreiner award.

Sheila Fugard (m. to Athol Fugard, lives outside Port Elizabeth); her first novel – *The Castaways* (1972) – won the CNA award in 1972 and the Olive Schreiner award in 1973. A book of poems – *Threshold* (1975) – followed by a second novel, *Rite of Passage* (1976). This story not previously published.

Nadine Gordimer (b. 1923, Springs); many collections of stories from *Face to Face* (1949) through *Livingstone's Companions* (1972) to *No Place Like: Selected Stories* (1975). Novels from *The Lying Days* (1953) through *A Guest of Honour* (1971), *The Conservationist* (1974) – co-winner of the Booker Prize – and the much-valued *Burger's Daughter* (1979).

Stephen Gray (b. 1941, Cape Town); three novels – *Local Colour* (1975), *Visible People* (1977) and *Caltrop's Desire* (1980) – and poems, *Hottentot Venus* (1979).

Bessie Head (b. 1937, Pietermaritzburg); three novels – *When Rain Clouds Gather* (1969), *Maru* (1971) and *A Question of Power* (1974), and a volume of short stories, *The Collector of Treasures and Other Botswana Village Tales* (1977).

Christopher Hope (b. 1944, Pretoria); a poem in his first volume, *Cape Drives* (1974), won the Pringle prize; many TV-plays, including *Ducktails* (1980).

Bob Leshoai (b. Bloemfontein); selection of plays, *Wrath of the Ancestors* (1972) and a collection of recorded tales, of which *Masilo's Adventures* is the title story.

James Matthews (b. Cape Town); many stories anthologized and a collection, *The Park* (1976). Poems include *Pass Me Another Meatball, Jones* (1979).

Es'kia Mphahlele (b. 1919); three novels – the now classic *Down Second Avenue* (1965), *The Wanderers* (1972) and *Chirundu* and collections of stories including *In Corner B* (1967) from which this story is taken.

Mothobi Mutloatse (b. Johannesburg); editor of Motsisi's *Casey and Company* (1978), and columnist.

Mbulelo Mzamane (b. Johannesburg); *My Cousin and the Law* first published here. A companion story, *My Cousin and his Pick-ups*, is in *More Modern African Stories*.

Alan Paton (b. 1903, Pietermaritzburg); two noted novels – *Cry, the Beloved Country* (1948) and *Too Late the Phalarope* (1953) – and several stories – *Debbie Go Home* (1961) – memoirs and biographies. *The Hero of Currie Road* appears in a collection of general pieces, *Knocking on the Door* (1975).

Richard Rive (b. 1931, Cape Town); a collection of stories – *African Songs* (1963) – and a novel – *Emergency* (1964) – and *Selected Writings* (1977). The story here postdates these.

Sheila Roberts (b. Johannesburg); her debut collection of stories – *Outside Life's Feast* (1975) – won the Olive Schreiner award; one novel – *He's My Brother* (1977). A volume of poems, *Lou's Life* (1977).

Sipho Sepamla (b. 1932, Krugersdorp); three volumes of poems – *Hurry up to It!* (1975), *The Blues is You in Me* (1976) and *The Soweto I Love* (1977), and a novel, *The Root is One* (1979).

Mongane Serote (b. 1944, Sophiatown); four volumes of poems – *Yakhal'inkomo* (1972), *Tsetlo* (1974), the narrative *No Baby Must Weep* (1975) and *Behold Mama, Flowers* (1978).

Barney Simon (b. Johannesburg); collaborated with Dugmore Boetie on the latter's *Familiarity is the Kingdom of the Lost* (1969), a collection of stories – *Joburg, Sis!* (1974) – and, as artistic director of the Market Theatre, Johannesburg, co-scripted *Cincinatti: Scenes from City Life* (1979).

Adam Small (b. 1936, Wellington); his first of many books of poems was *Verse van Liefde* (1957), and there is *Black Bronze Beautiful* (1975). His plays include *Kanna Hy Kô Huistoe* (1965) and *The Orange Earth* (1980).

Pieter-Dirk Uys (b. 1945, Cape Town); dramatist, whose plays include *Paradise is Closing Down* (1978), *Die Van Aardes van Grootoor* (1979) and *God's Forgotten* (1980).

Christopher van Wyk (b. 1957, Johannesburg); his first slim volume of poems appeared in 1979 as *It is Time to Go Home*.

Peter Wilhelm (b. 1943); his first collection, *LM and Other Stories* (1975), was followed by a novel, *The Dark Wood* (1977). A volume of poems: *White Flowers* (1977) (Bateleur).